The Runaway's SALVATION

HELEN BRIGHT

VINCI
BOOKS

By Helen Bright

The Runaway Series

The Runaway & The Russian
The Runaway in Love
The Runaway's Ruin
The Runaway's Salvation

Vinci Books

vinci-books.com

Published by Vinci Books Ltd in 2025

1

The publisher and the author have made every effort to obtain permissions for any third party material used in this book and to comply with copyright law. Any queries in this respect should be brought to the attention of the publisher and any omissions will be corrected in future editions.

A CIP catalogue record for this book is available from the British Library.

Paperback ISBN: 9781036707743

The EU GPSR authorised representative is Logos Europe, 9 rue Nicolas Poussion, 17000 La Rochelle, France

contact@logoseurope.eu

Chapter One

TESS

The nightmares began the night after Roman left us. At first, I blamed the stress from everything we'd gone through, combined with a lack of sleep from Roman's clandestine after-midnight visit. But sadly, they'd carried on throughout the next few weeks—my yelling and screaming sending waves of terror throughout the entire household.

The first night had been awful Lily had been grumpy all day due to Roman waking her up extra early so he could see her before he left. He'd told her he had to make a special trip to Sicily to collect a part for Santa's sleigh and would deliver it to the North Pole, so he thought he'd visit her along the way. I could tell that Lily didn't believe him, but she was too tired to argue. Still, the extra-early morning left her tired and grouchy with everyone, and she threw a tantrum of epic proportions when a badly hungover James refused to go in the pool with her. I tried to get her to take a nap with me, but she just wouldn't give in to it. So, by the time we went to bed that night, we were both about ready to collapse.

I must have only been asleep a couple of hours when I awoke to find Ivan, James, and Lainey in the room with me and Lily. James had Lily in his arms, trying to stop her crying, while Ivan had my arms pinned to the bed. He'd been yelling my name, trying to wake me, and even through the haze of troubled sleep, I could clearly see the worry in his and Lainey's eyes.

It took twenty minutes of reassuring Lily that I was okay and that I'd only had a bad dream before she finally went back to sleep. Knowing that I'd frightened her made me feel terrible, even more so than the dream did, although that was bad enough.

Lainey had stayed in my room with Lily while I went downstairs with Ivan and James. Danny was already in the kitchen making me a hot chocolate, and Franco came in on his crutches a few minutes later. He'd been discharged from the hospital in the afternoon and should have been resting, but apparently my screams had been loud enough to wake him, even though he was staying downstairs in the annexe. Carl and Tanner were working security and had to convince our new Italian guards that everything was okay.

Danny made me tell everyone about my nightmare, even though I didn't want to. He said that talking about it might help prevent it from happening again. I wish he'd been right.

I'm not quite sure how the first nightmare began, but I recall being at sea in the dark of night. I could feel the sway of the yacht under my bare feet as I padded across the deck, and a slight breeze flipped my ponytail around as we sailed towards a cove lit by moonlight. Kolya was behind me; he stood so close I could smell his cologne and feel his breath on my neck. I smiled and reached out behind me to grab his hand, but when I did so, he laughed. Only...the laugh wasn't Kolya's. It belonged to Yannis. I let go of his hand and ran across the deck, leaping out onto rocks, where I could see bodies lying facedown in a shallow pool. The rocks hurt my bare feet as I made my way over to the macabre scene, but I didn't let the pain stop me. Needing to check it was definitely Yannis, I grabbed his hair and lifted his head, but those lifeless eyes and the deathly pale face belonged to Kolya. It was at this point in my nightmare that I woke up screaming.

Everyone around me on the night of that first nightmare offered me a valid reason for the terrifying event. Ivan blamed Roman for telling us so casually how his men had staged Yannis and his guards' bodies, which made sense given the direction of the dream. James blamed it on the fact that Yannis had been an evil bastard who'd caused his father's death, a sentiment that everyone else around the table was on board with. Franco said it was because I'd been expecting a phone call from the police in Greece about Yannis's sudden demise, but that hadn't happened.

The news had broken in Greece by early afternoon, and I'd been stressing over what I'd say to the police if they contacted me. After all, I'd been staying with him the day before they found him dead. James and I had discussed it and decided I should say that Yannis had asked me to loan him three million euros, and he'd been angry with me when I refused him, so I'd arranged for James to come and collect us and left without Yannis knowing what we were doing.

So again, what Franco said had an element of truth to it. I had been worrying about the police phoning and about what I would say to them, despite going over everything with James.

The only one who didn't bother with reasons or excuses that night was Danny. He told me outright he thought it likely I had PTSD. James asked if he meant it was from shooting Yannis. Danny shrugged his shoulders and said, "Take your pick. Could be from that, or it might be from finding out that Yannis had orchestrated it all. Or it could be from the attack on her home when she had to hide Lily away and shoot an armed man who'd just killed my dog in front of her. Could also be from losing her husband and guards to a terrorist who sent a video showing his men kicking the hell out of their lifeless bodies. It could be any number of things that have happened to Tess over her lifetime or a culmination of all of them. All I'm saying is we shouldn't ignore this because no good could ever come of that."

Franco and Ivan agreed, suggesting I speak to George or Devina about some counselling, sooner rather than later. I promised I would do that as soon as the police had contacted me about Yannis—if the nightmares persisted. Everyone seemed surprised by the fact that I'd be willing to talk to someone. Kolya and Franco had tried to get me to speak to one of the counsellors after I'd been shot, but I'd always refused.

I'd never been comfortable talking about my feelings before. I thought it would make me vulnerable, but I knew I couldn't continue the way I had been. If the grief wasn't crippling enough, with everything else that had happened, I could feel myself...unravelling, if that makes sense.

And that feeling still remained.

With every new day, more threads came loose. My grief would tug them hard, and then a turbulent mix of anxiety, fear, and despair had them twisting around and around. Pretty soon, I knew the threads that made up the tapestry of my life would be scattered around in unmanageable, messy piles. I wondered just how long it would take until I unravelled completely, and there was nothing left of the old me.

Mark spent three days in the hospital before he was allowed to come back to the villa. He still looked pale and weak but was in good spirits, telling us how he'd been looked after by the most beautiful nurse he'd ever seen. He opted to stay in Sicily to recuperate, though I think that had as much to do with his devotion to Fia, his nurse, as his loyalty to us. I must admit, the healthcare provided by the hospital was second to none, and Franco's daily physio-therapy sessions meant he only needed to use his crutches and leg brace occasionally.

Kevin and Andy flew over from England the week before Christmas and brought our pre-lit Christmas tree and all our decorations. Having our other guards here calmed something inside me. They were my family, and I missed them so much. If they could have brought Dave, Nan, Jack, and Jean, that would have made it even better, but sadly, that wasn't going to happen.

Dave and Nan were still recuperating back home, and though I spoke to them regularly via video chat, it wasn't the same as being with them in person.

The distance creeping between Nan and me seemed greater than the miles that separated us. I couldn't put my finger on what had first created it, and despite our regular video calls, I felt it more keenly with each passing day. I asked Ivan if he thought it was because I'd killed Yannis. He said it wasn't that at all.

It horrified Nan and Jack to learn that Yannis was behind Kolya's death and the attack on our home, and they were glad that he was no longer a threat. But you know when you just know something? Well, I knew that Nan and Jack were disappointed in me somehow, and I wished more than anything that someone else had pulled the trigger on Yannis Markos.

Kevin decided to stay with us over Christmas, which Nate was thrilled about. They'd been apart so much because of their different duties, and I could tell it was taking a toll on their relationship.

Tanner and Carl had to share a room to accommodate Andy and Mark, then Yuri arrived, so we had a full house over the holiday period. With so much hustle and bustle, you'd have thought my mind would have been far too occupied for all the dark thoughts and nightmares, but that couldn't have been further from the truth.

With every smile or happy thought, I felt a sharp stab of guilt pierce my heart. Yet I knew I had to try, not just for Lily, but for everyone else in the villa who was putting on their own fake smile. It was all a show. Our own fictional version of a happy Christmas without Kolya, Jonesy, and Lucas. Charles Dickens, eat your heart out!

On my phone's playlist, I had "Someone You Love"—a song by Lewis Capaldi—playing on repeat. The words resonated deeply with me. It was as if he'd written them about my own personal feelings. I'd been tough and kept an emotional distance from everyone other than Jean and Sarah—until I met Kolya. Then I let my guard down, but his death pulled the rug on all the comfort and happiness I'd enjoyed since we'd come together. I'd got used to being someone Kolya loved. But now his love was lost to me forever, and I almost wish I'd never let down my guard at all, so I wouldn't feel the crippling pain of loss. But then I wouldn't have Lily or Ivan, Franco, and James, and everyone else who'd brought meaning to my life over the past six years.

I became slightly obsessed with looking through all the

photos I ever took of Kolya, right from when we first met until the last ones I had of him. It made me feel sick to my stomach to see those of him and Yannis together before the Graysons' Halloween party, so I went through all my photos and deleted every single one I had of Yannis Markos, and carefully cropped him out of the ones that contained Kolya. I'd arranged for the make-up artists to have Kolya and Yannis made up exactly the same, and apart from their eye colour and height, they'd looked uncannily alike. My soul demons. Maybe that's why my nightmares changed?

I'd been having the same one nightly—the one where it was Kolya, not Yannis, who was lying dead in the shallow pool of water. Sometimes I'd wake up yelling *no*, or I'd shout out something incoherent. But a few days before Christmas, the nightmares took on a more horrifying edge.

The new nightmares began with us at the airport in Kefalonia. Mark had been shot, and Ivan was carrying me up the steps of the aircraft. I could see Franco and James on the ground, and I knew that Yannis and his men would end up killing them if we didn't intervene. Just as I did on that fateful day, as soon as I was able, I took the shot. But instead of the bullet hitting Yannis in the throat, it hit him right in the centre of his chest, and suddenly everything about Yannis's appearance changed. Blood spread rapidly across his white shirt, obscuring the word SOUL as it did so. He looked up at me, his face now painted in the Halloween soul-demon skull design, yet his eyes were my husband's mesmerising ice blue. It might only have been a bad dream, but watching Kolya die right in front of me, knowing I'd fired the shot that ended his life, made every-thing in my world seem so much darker. Since Kolya's death, we'd all felt like we'd been living in the shadows, but now everywhere I turned felt as dark and cold as a mid-winter night.

I think I frightened everyone on the first night of that particular nightmare. My reaction to it lasted longer than everyone in the villa considered normal. I'd screamed bloody murder, threw up twice, and couldn't stop shaking for over an hour. I was so upset that I wouldn't go back to sleep that night. Franco volunteered to stay up on the sofa with me, and Ivan slept with Lily, so she wasn't on her own.

James blabbed to Roman about my nightmare episodes, and he, in turn, spoke to Signor Russo, who organised for a doctor to come and visit. I wasn't too happy about it, but I was polite with the doctor and must admit he was kind and listened without judgement to all my woes, though I couldn't tell him everything, of course. I just told him that my husband and his guards had been killed by terrorists and our family had also been under attack since, so obviously, this caused me to feel anxious and low, and the nightmares were a new and unwelcome symptom. Doctor Bianchi offered to prescribe me medication to lift my mood, but first, he wanted to run a few blood tests. He noticed how pale I was, which I must admit was more so than usual, and I had lost weight recently—though that was understandable since my appetite had diminished over the past few weeks. He gave me a form, and Nate, Carl, and Franco took me to the hospital to get the blood test done later that day.

Doctor Bianchi came back two days later with my test results. I was anaemic, so he gave me a prescription and said I might want to wait a couple of weeks to see if my low mood and anxiety improved when my iron levels built back up. He said my sleep pattern should improve, too, so I took him at his word and decided to ride it out. He prescribed me three nights' worth of sleeping pills, and though they helped me sleep, they also left me feeling like the walking dead the next day, and I had to leave Lily with Lainey and Danny while I took a nap mid-afternoon.

I woke up from that nap screaming and crying after having the dream where I'd shot Kolya again, so I wasn't too keen on taking any more of the sleeping pills.

When Franco wasn't doing his physical therapy, he was by my side, helping to keep Lily occupied and making sure I could cope with whatever life in Sicily threw at me. Franco's ability to speak Italian was an enormous help, especially with the extra guards that Signor Russo provided whenever we went anywhere.

Kolya's brother Yuri arrived five days before Christmas. Lily was thrilled to have him with us, especially since he brought a ridiculous amount of presents, all neatly wrapped and ready to place under our tree that we'd only just finished decorating. He and Ivan were as thick as thieves, and more than once I'd almost stumbled upon them discussing something they obviously didn't want me or anyone else to overhear. I don't know what they were talking about specifically, but I heard them mention Aleksei and the name Simeon quite a few times.

Ivan and Yuri stayed up drinking on his first night in Sicily, so they were still awake when I had my nightmare. Yuri had known about them, but he was shocked by how long it took for me to shake off the terrifying dream. The panic and fear gripped me hard and wouldn't let go, no matter where I was or who was holding me in their strong arms and telling me I was safe. It all felt so real to me, and I couldn't seem to make anyone understand that—apart from Danny, that is. Ivan looked helpless; James seemed angry about it, and Yuri... I didn't have a clue what Yuri thought because he was slightly drunk and whispering something in

9

Russian as he held me in his arms and rocked me like a baby. Franco glared daggers at Yuri and seemed kind of disappointed in me, which set me off crying and made everything ten times worse.

After that terrifying episode, Yuri decided someone should sleep beside me every night until the nightmares passed. So that's just what we did. Lily slept on her own in one bed, while Lainey, Ivan, and Yuri took turns at sleeping beside me, although in the end, it was mostly Yuri who stayed with me.

James had little patience with me since we'd arrived in Sicily, but to be honest, I wasn't the only one he'd been snapping at. He was glued to his laptop and phone all day —working on various KOLCAT UK and US contracts— but he was drinking heavily every night, and we were all worried about him.

Chapter Two

TESS

Christmas Day was never going to be easy for any of us, but as adults we owed it to Lily to make it as magical as we could. She had the same idea about us, too, because although she smiled and tried to show excitement, it was clear to see she was missing her father more than anything. Kevin filmed Lily opening her presents so we could send the video to Roman. It was normally Kolya's job, so seeing someone else do it highlighted the fact that he wasn't here anymore.

James kept trying to get Lily to play with her new toys and have fun, but you could tell that her heart wasn't in it. She was also feeling quite tired, having woken up in the early hours with me screaming for her father—not something she could easily forget.

James had had his first drink at 10 a.m., and by the time we sat down to eat later that afternoon, he was becoming a little unsteady on his feet.

Lily and I sat between Yuri and Ivan, with Franco, Lainey, and Danny beside him, then Nate, Kevin, Tanner,

Carl, and James, followed by Mark and Andy. Yuri's regular guards from Moscow—who were staying in a cottage behind the tennis courts—were guarding the property until early evening, when Andy, Nate, Carl, and Tanner would take the next shift. I'd hoped that having everyone together like this would help Lily and I get through the day, but sadly, things didn't quite go according to plan.

With it being Christmas, Lainey had insisted we say a prayer before we ate, thanking God for the plentiful food and asking him to bless the ones we loved, both here and in heaven. Before she could finish, Lily folded her arms across her chest and said, "I'm not talking to God. I've fallen out with him because he takes daddies to heaven and doesn't bring them back at Christmas, even when you've been behaving and doing everything Mummy says."

"Good on you, kiddo," James slurred. "You shouldn't have to pray to someone so cruel. He takes mothers, too, you know. He took mine and Ivan's. And Daddy and Uncle Yuri's. So make the most of your mummy while you can, Lily, 'cause no doubt he'll take her, too. He won't allow our family to be happy. We're all fucking cursed."

James knocked back the last dregs of whisky from the bottom of his glass, ignoring the angry yelling from everyone around the table. Lily's eyes filled with tears, and her bottom lip wobbled as I gathered her in my arms, assuring her I wasn't going anywhere, and that James was only saying mean things and swearing because he was drunk. But Lily knew that James's mum had died when he was a child, and that Kolya's mother had passed away when he was sixteen, so she knew there was some truth to the hurtful things her brother had said.

Yuri rose from his spot at the head of the table and walked around to where James sat. Without saying a word, he fisted his hands in the front of James's shirt and hauled him up out of the chair.

"Nephew or not, if you weren't so drunk, I'd make you pay in blood and bruises for the hurt you caused your sister and her mother just now. Do you hear me?"

"Loud and fucking clear," James said as he tried to shake off Yuri's grip. "Now let me go so I can eat my Christmas dinner. I wouldn't want to miss the only decent thing about today."

"You won't be eating in here, James, unless you want to eat off the floor like a dog," Yuri replied.

He glanced back at Ivan, who had his arms around me and Lily. "Take his plate into the sitting room, along with a glass of water. I won't let him continue to upset Lily and Tess, nor anyone else around this table."

I shook my head. "No, we should all be together. He didn't mean it, Yuri. He's had too much to drink, and today has been a tough one for all of us." I couldn't keep the hurt and anger out of my voice, despite my placatory words.

James's bloodshot eyes fixed on mine, and I thought he might carry on throwing hurtful words our way. Then his expression changed to one of *"What the fuck just happened here?"* and he staggered back, away from the table and Yuri.

"I'm sorry, Lily, Tess. I don't know what…I'm just so sorry. I can't do this. Not today. I can't… I have to go."

James turned to leave but stumbled into the doorframe. Yuri was there to catch him, and he was joined by Nate a few seconds later. Both men hooked his arms over their shoulders and escorted James out of the kitchen.

I half expected Tanner and Carl to follow, but when I looked their way as if to question them, Carl shook his head and said, "He won't listen to us, Tess. We've tried talking to him about his drinking, and the reasons why he feels the need to do it, but he just won't listen. He even threatened to fire Tanner yesterday when he suggested he speak to George about it."

"I don't care what he has going on in his head; it doesn't excuse what he just said to Lily." Franco slammed his cutlery down and got up from his chair steadily. He seemed to struggle with his leg a little, but he was trying not to use his crutches. After allowing himself a few seconds to rest, he made his way over to me and Lily.

Ivan let his arms fall away from us and sighed heavily. "I agree that what James did is unforgivable, but he's hurting, Franco. It's not just from grief and loss; he's harbouring a lot of guilt, too. Every time he sees you struggle to get around, the guilt tears through him. He knows you only got that wound through protecting him. And you, Tess"—Ivan cupped my cheek and tilted my face until his eyes held mine —"what you had to do that day and the consequences you are troubled by because of it—the nightmares especially— he cannot bear to see you suffer so."

"He shouldn't feel bad for me," I insisted. "I'll be okay. I just need a little time, that's all. I think everyone does, including James. I'll talk to him later when he's sobered up. In the meantime, we have all this lovely food waiting for us. Let's not waste it."

Though everyone ate their food on what was normally such a special day, there was little to celebrate around the table. The meal was just as tasty as it always was, yet there were few who cleared their plates, and no one had seconds of anything, not even Ivan—a sharp contrast to all our previous Christmas dinners, where everyone ate Nan's festive feast until they could barely move.

Ivan was quite a heavy sleeper, especially after drinking vodka with Yuri.

And he snored.

Loudly!

I didn't have a nightmare the first night he stayed with me because he snored so loud that I couldn't even sleep. It wouldn't have been so bad if he wasn't a snuggler. He pulled me into his side so we lay like spoons, then he flopped over onto his back with his arm still underneath me and snored out a weird sort of sawing sound. Whenever I tried moving away from him, he pulled me back and carried on snoring. Ivan wasn't too bad if he only had a couple of drinks, but any more than that, and it was pointless trying to sleep beside him at all. Lily woke up twice and asked if someone was landing the helicopter when Ivan slept in our room.

Lainey slept beside me for a night, but I didn't want to keep her away from Danny's bed over the Christmas holidays. I felt bad enough that she'd cancelled her trip back home to see her family. Franco also volunteered to sleep beside me, but getting up and down the stairs wasn't easy for him, and I worried that I'd accidentally knock his wound if I was tossing and turning during the night.

So Yuri spent the rest of his time in Sicily sleeping beside me, and true to his word, he woke me the first moment he thought I was having what he called a night terror.

Yuri used to wake up earlier than Lily and me, but on the morning after our dreadful Christmas Day, I beat him to it. For just a few sleepy, blissful moments, I thought the man beside me was my husband. The resemblance was so striking in the early morning light that it took my breath away.

The Barinov men looked so alike. All were extremely handsome, with strong cheekbones and masculine jawlines and the same brown hair, although Yuri's was greyer at the sides than Kolya's and Aleksei's had been. And they'd all inherited Roman's piercing, ice-blue eyes. As had James and Lily.

Yuri opened his eyes and caught me looking at him. Perhaps I should have looked away and apologised for staring, but right at that moment, I didn't have it in me. It was as if speaking the words would break the spell, and for just a few minutes longer, I wanted to hang on to the pretence that this was the Barinov who'd told me he loved me every single day since we'd first made love.

Yuri must have realised what was going through my mind because he reached over to my side of the bed and pulled me up against him, so we lay chest to chest. Then he wrapped his arms around me and held me close, stroking his hand down my back and placing soft kisses on my forehead. He was about the same height and build as Kolya, and it felt good to cuddle up to him like that. Yuri always slept shirtless, with long flannel or jersey pyjama bottoms, and the warmth from his bare chest felt comforting. We only stayed that way for a matter of minutes, but for the first time in what seemed like forever, my mind knew a little peace.

Too bad that couldn't last.

Chapter Three

TESS

While Yuri was in the shower, Lily brought me my make-up bag and asked if I'd make her look pretty. I laughed and told her she didn't need makeup to make her pretty, but she insisted she wanted to wear some. She said it would be nice if we could be what she called *"matchy-matchy,"* so I applied a pop of pink cream blush on the apples of our cheeks and pretended to brush translucent powder over our noses, making her giggle. When she went to do the same to Anna, I applied a little concealer under my eyes to disguise the ever-increasing dark circles, and for the first time in weeks, I actually looked healthy. I even applied mascara—waterproof, of course. With how much I cry nowadays, I couldn't take the risk with the regular kind. Rather than attempting a high ponytail on my and Lily's hair, I left our hair down, our coppery curls hanging loose around our shoulders.

By the time Yuri and I came downstairs with Lily, everyone else was already awake, and it didn't take a genius to work out that something had happened during the early hours. I could hear raised voices in the kitchen and lounge, and Carl and Tanner carried suitcases towards the door. Before I could ask where they were going, Lainey stepped in front of us. After plucking Lily out of my arms, she said, "Someone tried hacking into KOLCAT UK at four a.m., and there was also a physical security breach at one of the UK sites. Northampton, I believe, but they were unable to gain access inside any of the buildings. You'd better go straight in there if you want to catch James and Kevin before they leave. I'll send Danny in with tea and coffee for you while I get my favourite little girl her breakfast."

I thanked Lainey, then glanced up at Yuri nervously once she and Lily were out of earshot.

"What does this mean for us here, Yuri? Are we ever going to be safe? Because I have to tell you, I'm considering packing our bags and coming to live with you and your dad in Moscow."

Yuri pulled me into his arms and held me tightly. "No, Tess. As much as it would please me to see you and my darling niece every day, I cannot allow you to move to Moscow. Believe me, whatever this is, you are much safer away from the Barinov Bratva life. I would not subject my own flesh and blood to it, so I cannot allow my brother's family to be surrounded by it."

"But I'm scared, Yuri," I admitted. "I don't know if I have it in me to keep on fighting an unseen enemy."

"Do not worry, my darling. If Ivan and I think for even one minute that we cannot keep you and Lily safe, we will whisk you away so fast and without anyone knowing, you will barely have time to think. And I guarantee, where we send you, you will both be well taken care of."

"I don't want to be away from my family, Yuri. Nan, Jean, and all our guards mean the world to me."

Yuri cupped my cheeks and placed a gentle kiss on my forehead before rubbing his nose against mine. "Ah, but you and Lily *will* be with family, Tess. I can say no more right now, but you can trust me on that, okay?"

Yuri's words reminded me of something Ivan had said the night Roman arrived at the villa, but I couldn't allow myself to dwell on it while everything was so up in the air. So I gazed into those familiar ice-blue eyes and nodded.

Yuri rewarded me with a beaming smile and then took my hand in his. "Come, my beautiful Tess, let us find out more about the security breach."

When I turned around I saw Franco leaning against the doorjamb with his arms folded. He was glaring at Yuri with such anger, and I thought for a moment he was about to yell at him.

"Franco?" I questioned.

He spared me a fleeting glance and then shook his head. "Their flight leaves in an hour. Better be quick if you want to speak to them before they go."

Though I wanted to find out what was up with Franco, I was more concerned with finding out what had happened to KOLCAT overnight and what that meant for us going forward, so I let Yuri tug me into the lounge behind him.

James was pacing the floor while on the phone with Gustav. He looked a little worse for wear and… No. He looked like absolute shit! His mid-brown hair was stuck up at all angles, no doubt from him pulling on it like he was doing now. He had dark circles under his eyes, and his pallor had taken on a sickly hue. He was dressed in stonewash jeans and a grey T-shirt, but there was a suit carrier draped over the sofa where his laptop sat open.

Danny came into the lounge with tea for me and coffee for Yuri, which we gratefully accepted. Kevin sat on one of the other sofas with Nate, who looked so glum. Yet who could blame him? Kevin was meant to be staying with us until after the New Year, but as he oversaw KOLCAT's technical security—as well as the technical side of our personal security—it was pretty obvious he wouldn't be back for a while.

"Why don't you go back with him?" I suggested. "Andy can stay here with us."

Nate looked up at me and smiled. "He won't let me leave you here, Tess. Besides, you know what my man's like. He's gonna be stuck in front of keyboards and monitors until he's found a culprit and dealt them some serious cyber karma. Ain't that right, Kev?"

Kevin smiled, though it didn't reach his eyes. "You know it, babe."

"How bad is it? Did the hackers do any serious damage?" Yuri asked. He was staring hard at Nate's hand, which he'd placed above Kevin's knee. It took a moment for me to realise why it would bother Yuri so much. It wasn't that he was against same-sex public displays of affection; he just wasn't used to seeing it—or seeing people so comfortable around it.

My heart hurt for Yuri at that moment. How different would his life be if he were able to share his love with another man so openly? How lonely must he be, day in, day out, knowing that the relationship he craves will never be accepted by his father or his Bratva brethren?

"I have alerts in place that let me know of any web-based suspicious activity for all the KOLCAT sites, as well as the umbrella network server. Each country where KOLCAT has a base or build site has its own specific hacker alert." Kevin squinted down at the screen of his laptop before pinching the bridge of his nose and closing his eyes.

He took a deep breath and then opened his eyes and fixed them on Yuri. "Whoever this was tried to hack a dedicated server at the Northampton base, as well as the main KOLCAT server. This tells me they were looking for information from that specific UK base. Now it can't be a coincidence that the majority of the stolen missile launcher was designed and built there. We know there've been previous hacking attempts on Kolya's KOLCAT email address as well as his private email account. We anticipated those and ensured they'd be met with nothing but a big ol' cyber *fuck you*. But this, along with the attempted break-in at the Northampton base, leads me to believe that Riass hasn't given up on finding the guidance system and codes."

Everyone in the room nodded in agreement.

"We can also assume he was unable to extract important information from Kolya. If he had, then Riass would have known that the guidance system was built and shipped from Berlin, with only part of the original prototype coming from the Northampton base."

I winced when Kevin said the word *extract*. It was much better than saying that Riass hadn't tortured the information out of Kolya before he'd killed him, but it still hit home that Kolya and Jonesy most likely suffered before their deaths. It was something that James had struggled with, though I tried my best not to think about it.

Previously, Riass had filmed the torturing and executions of his higher-profile captives. It's one of the reasons why Roman had been willing to believe that Kolya and Jonesy might still be alive when we'd received the video, though he'd recently admitted that was highly unlikely after all this time.

"I assume you have the culprits who attempted the break-in," Yuri surmised.

Nate nodded. "He also has a lead on the hacker."

"It's not a direct lead, but it looks promising," Kevin confirmed. "I've got Steve on it back home. I also had a couple of…let's call them *associates* working on it within forty minutes of the attempted hack. Trust me, these two might not come cheap, but they're the best in the business at what they do. The boss was aware of them and had previously okayed their…*assistance.*"

Kevin shrugged his shoulders. "Basically, if you want to find a hacker, hire another hacker. I know them well, and while my skill set was almost on par with them a few years ago, I'll admit that my day job means I'm lagging behind right now for going deeper and darker into web-based challenges and resources. Something I plan on rectifying as soon as we get Tess and Lily safe in the UK again."

"Are we at risk here, Kevin? Is that why you want Nate to stay with us?" I asked with more calm in my voice than I was feeling.

He shook his head. "No more than you were before this happened. But now that Carl and Tanner are leaving with James, there's only Ivan, Andy, Danny, and Lainey here who aren't compromised through injury. So it makes sense that Nate stays behind until we can get you back to the UK safely. And there's something else, Tess. Until I can be sure they each have a secure line, I don't want you contacting anyone outside of this villa apart from your father-in-law and Signor Russo. So, no contact with Nan, Jean, Karen, or Amina. Not only could it put you at risk, but it could compromise them, too. And it won't be for long; I'll sort something out as soon as I get back to Oxford."

I crouched down in front of Kevin, who had to close his laptop to see me.

"Be honest with me, Kevin. How soon can you make Glengarran safe? Give me a date to aim for, please. I want to come back to England to see everyone. I need realness and hugs more than a beautiful hideaway that isn't mine. Lily needs to see the people she loves, too, and she needs to be at school around kids her age. We can't heal here, Kevin." I looked around the room and added, "None of us can."

Kevin leaned forward with a determined look on his handsome face. "Think about it, Tess. If this attempted hack *has* come from Riass, we could get enough leads from it to trace him, or at least his UK terrorist cells. I know what's going on right now is nothing but a headache for KOLCAT as a company, but for you, James, and Lily as a family, and even you and your father, Yuri," he said with a nod towards my brother-in-law, "this could be the lead we've all been hoping and praying for."

Yuri nodded. "I will speak to my father. He will want to hear this."

"You're too late, cousin. Your nephew beat you to it," Ivan said as he approached us. "How were you last night, Tess? I did not hear you cry out, so I assume you slept well."

Ivan held out his hand and pulled me up to stand in front of him. As per usual, he looked me over from head to toe. I wasn't sure what he expected to find, but he nodded in approval. "You look much better today. More like the old Tess. It warms my heart, *milaya moya*," he remarked as he patted his chest on the left side.

"The car's here," Carl yelled from out in the hallway. I made my way towards James and waited for him to end his call. He glanced my way but quickly averted his eyes and turned away slightly like he was avoiding even looking at me. I couldn't have that. Phone call or not, we had to speak before he left.

As soon as he ended the call, I grabbed his arm. "James, I'm sorry all this has happened and you have to go. We'll miss you, and I hope you'll come back to spend New Year's Eve with us."

James shook his head, but he still wouldn't look at me. "I'm going to be tied up with work in the UK where the main breach was, then back at KOLCAT US. Just because they hit us this morning and failed doesn't mean they won't try again."

I couldn't believe he wouldn't be here for our first New Year's Eve without Kolya, but he seemed resolute and not at all sorry about it.

"You weren't going to be here anyway, were you? You'd already made plans to leave," I stated. I don't know how I knew this, but the truth of it seemed so glaringly obvious.

James pocketed his phone and then closed his laptop before answering, "It's for the best."

"Best for whom?" I argued, stepping in his path as he picked up his suit carrier and laptop and tried to leave.

"Best for me, okay," he yelled. "I need to get away from here, Tess. Away from you."

I backed away from him and shook my head. "Away from me? Why? What have I done?"

"What have you done? Are you fucking kidding me? You shot him, Tess. You had to shoot him because I couldn't hold my fucking anger and rage in long enough to lie to Yannis about why I was at the airport. And my stupidity on that day got Franco shot and made you do something that's fucked with your head so bad it takes you hours to shake off

24

a nightmare." James sucked in a breath and carried on, though his voice had quietened a little.

"I should have had my shit together, Tess. Should have been more like my dad. It ought to have been *me* who took Yannis out and kept *you* safe, not the other way around. Every time I replay each incident in my mind, it makes me feel so ashamed. You had to keep Lily safe that day at the house when they came to kill me. And at the airport, you saved the day again while I lay under Franco being protected like a child. Being around you reminds me of all that, and of how inferior I am. My grandfather says you were made for this life, and he's right. You're more a Barinov than I'll ever be. You are family, and I love you, Tess, but for all the reasons I've just mentioned, I can't be around you right now. Not until I've come to terms with everything. You're not the only one who's fucked in the head over this."

"James, I... I'm sorry," I mumbled, not knowing what else I could say.

"No! Dammit, Tess, don't you dare apologise," James commanded as he tossed his laptop and suit carrier back onto the sofa and pulled me into his arms. "And don't you dare cry, either," he whispered when he heard me sniffle. "This is all on me. Staying away until I get my head together is me owning my shit. Well, that's how Tanner put it. I'm not a good person for you or Lily to be around right now. What I said yesterday, Christmas Day of all days, was so fucking wrong. I hope you can both forgive me."

"You're already forgiven, James," I sobbed. I wanted so desperately to ask him to stay, but he was already pulling away from me. When I opened my mouth to try a last-ditch attempt at getting him to return for New Year's Eve, Ivan stepped between us and shook his head.

"You heard him, Tess. James needs to take a few weeks away to process everything that has happened. He needs to heal; in here and in here," he said, pointing to his head and his heart. "You want that for him, don't you?"

"Yes, of course I do. But we're his family, Ivan. We all need to stick together and be there for one another," I reasoned, though my words had no effect on James, who grabbed his belongings and made his way out into the hallway, closely followed by Kevin, Nate, and Yuri.

"Don't go after him." Ivan grabbed my arm when I made a move to leave.

"What about Lily? Is he going to leave without saying goodbye to her?" I'd be damned if I'd let that happen.

"I'm sure he's saying goodbye right now. If not, I can take Lily out to the car and force his hand," Ivan added with a raised eyebrow.

With a grateful smile, I replied, "Thank you, Ivan. She'd be so upset if he left without saying goodbye. He'll be yet another person in a growing list of people who've disappeared from our day-to-day lives."

He guided me to the sofa and set me down.

"I will not leave you, Tess, other than for the odd holiday here or there, and I'm sure you will welcome the break," Ivan said with a low, throaty chuckle.

I tried to laugh along with him, but the tears rolling down my cheeks spoiled the cheerful look I was aiming for.

"Where is my Lily?" Ivan yelled as he made his way to the kitchen. I knew James hadn't left yet because I could hear Carl and Tanner in the hallway. Only seconds after Ivan left, they came into the room.

"Couldn't leave without catching an early New Year's kiss from my second-favourite redhead," Tanner said before dropping onto the sofa beside me and planting a quick kiss on my lips. I was a little taken aback because he'd never done that before. He'd kissed me on the cheek or forehead, but Kolya wouldn't allow anyone to kiss me on the lips for any occasion, and they wouldn't have risked angering him. But then again, Kolya wasn't here anymore. Even so, I knew that Tanner wouldn't normally be so bold. So what was he up to?

"Are you trying to distract me?" I asked.

"That depends. Is it working?" he replied as a curious smile spread across his dark, handsome features.

"It might have if you'd said favourite redhead instead of second favourite," I teased.

Carl crouched down in front of me, also dropping a quick peck on my lips. "You know you're *my favourite*, Tess," he said. "Especially after that other little red-haired hellion stole all the chocolate out of the last week of my advent calendar, then closed all the windows to hide the god-awful crime. I mean, seriously, have you actually searched under your daughter's hair to see if she has triple six hidden away there?"

Remembering the look on Carl's face when he realised his chocolate was missing from the advent calendar Nan sent him made me giggle.

"She was getting you back for stealing from Ivan," I reminded him.

"One chocolate, that's all I took."

I raised my eyebrow.

"Okay, two. I took days sixteen and seventeen, but that's it!"

"Time to go, guys," Danny called from the door.

Tanner and Carl each grabbed one of my hands, but it was Tanner who spoke. "Listen, Tess. If you need us, just call, okay? Day or night, it doesn't matter. We know we're

27

assigned to James, but you are our friend, honey. We care about you and Lily, and your safety and well-being are important to us."

"Yeah, what he said," Carl added gruffly.

"I love you, both of you. Make sure you keep safe for me. And keep James on the straight and narrow, too," I told them tearily.

"Don't cry, honey. This is hard enough as it is," Tanner whispered as he pulled me in for a hug. I couldn't help it, though. I'd miss them so much. They'd protected us at the house when we were attacked, and Carl saved our lives at the airport when he took out Yannis's men. But they were more than just my protectors; they were part of my family. I didn't need to share DNA with anyone I awarded that name, only my heart. And there was a place in what was left of the broken remnants of mine that was reserved for these two men.

"Promise you'll come and stay with us for a while when we move to Glengarran?" I insisted before letting Tanner go.

"Only if you don't make us wear kilts," Carl replied.

"Yeah, 'cause we all know he ain't got the legs for it," Tanner declared as he pulled away from me.

"Says the guy with legs like tree trunks," Carl responded with a goading smirk.

"It's called muscle, Carl. Something you don't have a lot—"

"Guys, come on; we're waiting to go," Kevin said as he made his way towards us. He tugged me up off the sofa and hugged me tightly.

"I miss you already, love. Don't worry; I'll make sure I put a rush on all the security at Glengarran once we've got this hacking shit sorted. And I'll phone you every day and message you every night, just like before," he promised.

"Check in on Nan and Jean for me," I prompted.

"I will. You'll also need to speak to George at some point, Tess. I can get him to call you from the tech room back in Oxford. That way, you'll know you have a secure connection, so you don't have to hold anything back. Just remember not to call anyone other than the people who've been here at the villa with you, okay? It should only take me forty-eight hours to supply Nan and Jack, Jean, Karen, and Amina with burner phones and secure numbers."

"I hate that we have to do all this, Kevin," I mumbled when he pulled away from me.

"I know, love, but it's better than the alternative of blocking them altogether. I doubt Nan would settle for that, and I *know* Karen and Amina wouldn't. You Yorkshire women are like a dog with a bone when it comes to getting what you need. Bloody ruthless, the lot of you," he said with a smile. "But I wouldn't have you any other way, Tess. Never change. Not for anyone."

But I had changed. I don't know how Kevin couldn't see it. That true Yorkshire grit he was talking about, that courage, determination, passion, and perseverance that exists in so many northern women—and indeed most women from poorer backgrounds—had begun its rapid erosion the day my husband died. I felt even more of it crumble away as I watched Kevin leave the room, knowing I couldn't follow and wave goodbye because James didn't want to see me.

What kind of defence can you offer when your presence alone causes offence?

I played over what he'd said in my mind, yet I couldn't make sense of it. I felt hurt by the things he'd mentioned and also quite annoyed. I'd been the bigger person that day at the airport, and apart from a quick burst of fearful anger when James first told me how Yannis had found out about him being there to collect Lily and me, I'd let it go and supported James when he needed me. Was I wrong to do that? And what was all that about me being more of a Barinov than him?

The whole thing was just so confusing. James said I wasn't at fault and that his head was as fucked as mine was, which no one disputed. So, yeah, everyone else thinks I'm cracking up, which is something that worries me. What if they think I can't take care of Lily?

James mentioned my nightmares, and I knew I'd scared everyone with those, including Lily. Stopping them would make me seem less *"fucked in the head,"* as James put it. The trouble was, I didn't know how to go about it, other than pills or counselling sessions with George or Devina, or maybe a combination of both. But they weren't likely to be a quick fix. It's not how those things worked.

I didn't want to talk to anyone here about it. They were too close to the situation and couldn't really grasp where I was coming from when I tried to relay how I felt about shooting Yannis. Or maybe it was me who couldn't express it correctly? I don't know. But there *was* someone who'd spoken to me about having nightmares after a traumatic experience, and just as I wondered whether I should call him, Ivan strode into the room with Lily under his arm and announced, "They've just left. Lily made James promise to go buy her a puppy or a dragon when she gets back to England. Oh, and Signor Russo is here to see if we need further security due to the KOLCAT hack and breach."

"Err, what's all this about a puppy or a dragon, Lily?" I questioned as I stood to greet Signor Russo, who was chuckling at my daughter. Lily wriggled out of Ivan's arms and came to stand beside our visitor.

"I couldn't decide. A puppy would be nice because I miss Bess, but a dragon would be great because it could fly and light fires with its fire breath if we were cold." Lily gasped, then added, "What if James could buy me a Loch Nest monster for the loch at Glengarran? If it was a girl, it could be my best friend, and John could feed her when we aren't there, and she could grow really big because the loch is really big and—"

"And I think a puppy sounds like a great idea, Lily," I interrupted her wild, imaginative suggestions. "But only once we've settled back in England or at Glengarran again. And perhaps when the weather's a bit warmer because puppies need to be taught to go outside to wee. They don't want to do that if it's cold."

Lily looked like she was about to complain, so Ivan said, "Listen to your mother, Lily, or you will have to clean up after your new puppy if it pees or poops in your new home."

Lily pulled a face, making her feelings clear about cleaning up after her new pet.

"I think I would like to see this Glengarran. It sounds like a magical place if it has a loch big enough to hide its own loch monster," Signor Russo declared as he crouched down beside her.

"Glengarran *is* magic," Lily agreed. "It has lots of magic secret doorways that look like bits of the wall or a shelf, and when you pull or slide something, a door will open to a magic secret passage or stairs. John says they were used hundreds of years ago when the Scots were at war with the English, but our housekeeper, she's called Mrs Braeburn," Lily added before taking a deep breath, "she said the servants used them when they wanted to move from one floor to another without being seen by the laird and his family or any visiting royalty. Because Glengarran is a castle, though it doesn't have any kings or queens, or even any princesses living in it." Lily shrugged her shoulders and raised her hands palm up in a gesture that said, *"I've no idea why it's still called a castle if it doesn't belong to the royal family."* She carried on, "But anyway, John is *so* clever, and he knows all about history and legends and magic. He tells much better stories than Mrs Braeburn, especially about the Loch Nest monster. And he plays the bagpipes, too."

"I think you can tell she's a fan of the old gamekeeper," I remarked.

Signor Russo smiled. "It appears so."

"His son, who is also called John, has the position now, but old John is still at Glengarran helping out most days. He lost his wife a few years ago, so being at Glengarran gives him something to do and helps keep the loneliness at bay," I told him.

Signor Russo nodded in understanding. "Some of us don't do so well with a leisurely retirement. We need something to keep our minds and bodies occupied, so it's likely that even if his wife hadn't passed away, he'd still be compelled to work. I, too, am like your magical John," he said, with a nod towards Lily. He turned back to look at me. "So is your father-in-law. Could you imagine either of us having nothing more exciting planned than a light lunch followed by a round of golf? I might say I'm retired or semi-retired, but I'm still a decision-maker and oversee a number of business dealings, though obviously not as many as in my younger years. It is who I am, and it is who Roman is. The day I give that up is the day I meet my maker and offer him penance for all my sins."

Looking puzzled, Lily asked, "Didn't your mummy make you in her belly? Because my mummy grew me in her belly until I was ready to be born, but my daddy had to plant a seed in her belly first. Only, I'm not sure how he did that because me and my daddy planted lots of baby trees near our home, and we had to use spades to dig big holes to put the baby trees in, so—"

"And we won't be having that talk today, Lily," I interjected. Signor Russo did his best to cover his laughter, but Ivan didn't even try. I elbowed him in the ribs in an attempt to shut him up, which made him laugh even harder.

"The look on your face," he spluttered through each loud guffaw.

Then Lily laughed, along with Signor Russo, and it was just the tonic I needed after the shock of James's ill-timed departure to spread some much-needed warmth through my heart and soul.

"What have I missed?" Yuri asked as he strolled back into the room. He was accompanied by Nate, who looked like he carried the weight of the world on his shoulders, followed by a scowling Franco.

"Lily was just telling us—"

I cut off Ivan's words with, "Signor Russo is here to find out if we need further security. I'll leave you gentlemen to sort it out while I go and have breakfast, but before you leave," I said, placing my hand on Signor Russo's arm, "I wonder if you'd mind taking a short stroll with me around the grounds? There's something I'd like to discuss with you. Something personal," I added quietly.

He placed his hand over mine and smiled. "Come and find me when you are ready, Tess. And bring a basket so we can pick some fruit from the trees."

The whole room had gone silent as everyone tried to

listen in on our conversation, obviously wondering what the "*something personal*" was I wanted to discuss with him. Nosey sods.

"I will, thank you," I replied, holding my arms out to my daughter. I didn't want her in the room while they discussed the steps they were taking to keep us safe.

Chapter Four

TESS

Lainey bought Danny a set of remote-controlled boats for Christmas, which Lily was fascinated with. They'd spotted them while out shopping in the local town. Danny had admired the expertly crafted wooden vessels, so Lainey had sneaked back out later with Franco and bought them for him. Lily jumped at the chance to try them out in the pool with Danny and Ivan. From the excited voices and laughter going on out there, I could imagine more of our guards heading down to the little artisan shop when it reopened after the holidays. From where I sat at the long kitchen table, I could see Lily and Danny on the left side of the pool, with Yuri trying to supervise from one of the sun loungers. I hoped my sneaky little daughter wouldn't persuade him to let her get in.

As I finished off the last of my tea and toast, I felt the presence of someone else nearby. I glanced around the room and noticed a tanned muscular arm bearing Franco's familiar tribal tattoos as he made a silent retreat.

"Are you avoiding me?" I asked, my voice slightly raised.

His hand gripped the fancy architrave on the doorframe for a moment before letting go, and then all six feet plus of brooding Italian American manliness appeared before me with his arms folded across his chest. He wore a tight black T-shirt and jeans, the colour suiting his dark mood perfectly.

Why, oh, why did Franco have to look so bloody sexy when he was angry? When I'm angry, my cheeks go a mottled red, and I'm pretty sure I look plain freaky rather than *drop-dead freaking gorgeous*.

"Pretty hard to avoid you if I'm meant to keep you safe," he replied.

"You say that begrudgingly. Have I done something to upset you?" I asked. "If I have, you're going to have to enlighten me because I can't think what it could be."

"Oh really?" he sneered as he placed his hands on the table in front of me, blocking my view of Lily, Danny, and Yuri.

"Yes, really, Franco. I came down this morning to all this shit going on, and it was obvious you were already angry with me by then. So tell me, did the way I walked downstairs piss you off? I mean, we were fine last night, weren't we?"

"Tess, don't try me. Not today," he spat. He pushed up from the table and took a step towards the doorway, but I ran around the table and stopped him before he could get there.

"It's the jeans, isn't it? You don't think indigo is the right colour denim for me. You'd rather they be stonewashed, right?"

"Your jeans are just fine," he answered, trying to push me out of his way.

"Then is it the lemon-coloured blouse? Of course it is!

Or maybe I should have gone for short sleeve than rather long sleev—"

"Maybe it's because someone else had his hands and lips on you," Franco fumed. "Maybe it's the flush I could see in your cheeks and the fact you seemed so rested. I gotta say, sleeping with Russians really suits you, Tess. So you tell me, marks out of ten. Which of the brothers is a better fuck?"

My right hand came up almost automatically, slapping Franco hard across his left cheek. Of all the reactions I expected from him, not one was the satisfied grin he sported.

"If I'd known that's all it would take to get you to touch me, I'd have pissed you off sooner," he grunted.

"You've not pissed me off, Franco; you've hurt me. That flush in my cheeks and my rested look?" I grabbed a napkin off the table and dribbled a bit of saliva on it. "Spit wash, that's what my mum used to call this," I told him as I wiped the blush from my cheeks and the rest of the concealer from under my eyes that hadn't come off in my earlier crying bout. "And as for Yuri holding me and kissing me, ON MY FOREHEAD! He's my brother-in-law, Franco. He was comforting me after I told him I was scared. Scared that I couldn't protect my daughter against this enemy that none of us saw coming."

Franco took hold of my arms and held them up between us. He appeared contrite, a hint of sadness in those dark brown eyes. But I wasn't having any of it.

"And how dare you insinuate that sleeping beside Yuri has been anything more than the word suggests? For God's sake, Franco, my daughter sleeps in the same room, and it's barely eight weeks since my husband died. Do you think so little of me?"

I felt a momentary pang of guilt when I uttered those

words. I'd let Yuri pull me into his arms earlier, imagining for just a moment that it was Kolya. But I hadn't wanted him in a sexual way, and I certainly wasn't Yuri's preferred gender. So that unnecessary pang of guilt was short-lived.

Franco shook his head and then pulled me into his arms. "No, Tess, fuck no. I'm so fucking sorry. Please, you gotta believe me. I just…I saw him hold you, then he kissed you like you were close, you know, and I saw red. It's jealousy, pure and simple. I flipped my lid and took it all out on you because I'm so fucking jealous—of Yuri, of Kolya—of any man that's lucky enough to get to touch you and have you smile back at them like they mean the world to you.

"I've waited for so long," he admitted. "I tried not to love you. God only knows how fucking hard I tried."

Letting out a low, throaty laugh, Franco added, "No matter how good a soldier I used to be, that was a battle I was never gonna win. I know that now, 'cause that feeling inside my chest, right about here," he said, placing my hand against his heart. Keeping it there despite my struggles. "It just wouldn't fucking go.

"I was gonna leave, 'cause watching you with him was torture. In my head, I knew you belonged to someone else, but my damn heart kept insisting you were meant to be mine, and in the end, I had to settle for all I could get. I wasn't allowed to have you, but at least I could keep you safe. Then everything went to hell, and you were on your own again, and I thought, is this it? Is this the reason why I couldn't let you go?"

"I don't want to hear this, Franco," I told him. "I can't deal with anything else right now."

"I'll let you go if you tell me you accept my apology." He nuzzled my earlobe and then whispered, "I won't ever do or say anything to hurt you again, Tess. You have my word. You know that means something where I come from. 'Cause you and me, we're cut from the same cloth. We do whatever we can to protect the ones we love."

"I accept your apology," I mumbled, and I felt him smile against my cheek. I wasn't sure whether he'd try to kiss me, so I held my breath, my body tense. My head was reeling from all Franco had just admitted, and I wasn't exactly sure what he was apologising for. Being jealous? Upsetting me? Loving me?

At that moment, all I wanted to do was get as far away as possible from Anthony Franconni.

After a few more seconds, Franco finally let me pull away from him, and as I did so, I heard Signor Russo clear his throat and say, "There you are, Mrs Barinov. I can come back later for our walk if you're busy."

He stood there with a knowing, smug smile on his handsome face, and I so desperately wanted a hole to appear on the kitchen floor so I could fall into it and disappear.

I apologised for keeping Signor Russo waiting and collected the basket I'd left on the countertop. Instead of accompanying me immediately, he hung back for a moment to speak to Franco—though I have no idea what they spoke about, having made my escape onto the pool terrace where I sat beside Yuri.

The day was unusually warm, though not especially bright, and Yuri remarked that he thought it might rain. From the look of the thick grey cloud gathering to the west of the villa, I was in full agreement. I thought about backing out of my walk with Signor Russo, but after what he'd just observed in the kitchen, I knew he'd have something to say. I also wanted to speak to him about dealing with my nightmares. He'd admitted having experienced them, and I thought he'd answer me honestly.

Gianni Russo seemed like the sort of guy who wouldn't bullshit me, and I needed that right now. I needed someone to tell me how to live with the terrifying clips of distorted reality invading my dreams.

As the man in question descended the steps to join us by the pool, I turned to Yuri and asked, "Will you keep an eye on Lily while I take a walk with Signor Russo?"

"Of course." He hesitated a moment before nodding towards Signor Russo and asking, "What is it you want to speak to him about?"

I decided to be honest with Yuri because I knew he'd tell Ivan and the others they had nothing to be concerned about, so they'd leave me alone when I came back.

"On the night your dad visited, Signor Russo mentioned he'd had nightmares about a traumatic event. I wanted to ask how he'd learned to cope with them and if he could recommend anything that would help."

Yuri stood to greet him when he approached, then he held out his hand and pulled me up from the sun lounger.

Signor Russo wore a charcoal-grey cashmere jumper over a sky-blue shirt that suited his silver hair and tanned skin. Charcoal-grey trousers and black leather loafers completed his outfit. He wasn't exactly dressed for picking fruit, but as I'd never seen him wearing jeans, this was probably as casual as he went.

Before he let me go, Yuri kissed me on the cheek and squeezed my shoulder. It meant nothing really, just innocent gestures of affection between family. But my eyes scanned the poolside perimeter for Franco as a wave of guilt swept over my conscience.

While I knew I didn't have to justify any of my or Yuri's behaviour to Franco, I didn't want to hurt him either. Perhaps if he knew about Yuri's sexuality, he'd feel less threatened? Whatever the case, it wouldn't be me who told him. My brother-in-law doesn't share that information openly. In his world, it isn't so readily accepted.

"Tess, are you feeling all right? I asked if you were ready to go, but you seemed miles away already." Signor Russo looped an arm through mine and looked at me with concern.

"Yes, I'm fine; it's just that I'm not sleeping very well and … that's what I wanted to talk to you about." I grabbed the basket from the table beside the lounger and allowed Signor Russo to guide me away from the pool where Lily, Ivan, and Danny were yelling encouragement to a boat that couldn't hear them. Over the next couple of minutes, we made our way to the relative peacefulness of the abundant orchards, with Nate and one of Signor Russo's guards following close behind.

The air was alive with the most exquisite floral yet citrusy fragrance, and even though it was becoming cloudy, the odd sunbeam creeping through lit up the colourful fruit trees, painting a picture full of lush greenery and striking orange.

"The night Roman came, you told us about what happened to Franco's father. You said you'd had nightmares about it, in which you relive it and hear and feel it all." I'd stopped walking for a moment and looked at him when I said this.

Signor Russo closed his eyes as he took a deep breath and nodded.

"Go on," he encouraged.

"I'm having them, too. About when I shot Yannis Markos at the airport to stop him from shooting at James and Franco. And I see it all so clearly before it changes to where... I don't know how much you know about how Yannis was found, but I somehow see that scene too, but that's not all. The nightmares begin to change, and instead of the bullet finding Yannis, it's my husband who is dying. I shoot my husband in my dreams, Signor Russo, and though I know what's coming, I can't seem to wake myself up to prevent it. So I need you to tell me how to stop the nightmares because I can no longer sleep on my own. I'm scaring everyone, including Lily. Yuri has been sleeping beside me so he can wake me up as soon as I begin to toss and turn, hopefully before I scream the whole villa down. James left because I make him feel guilty that he wasn't the one to save us from Yannis. He thinks that shooting him is making me go crazy, and that the nightmares are evidence of that. Maybe he's right?"

Signor Russo cupped my cheek and ran his thumb under my eye, wiping away the tear I hadn't realised had fallen.

"You aren't crazy, *mia cara*. You are grieving and processing so much right now, that's all. James was wrong to send his guilt your way. If he were still here, I would have had a thing or two to say to him about that, believe me."

"In his defence, he's grieving too. Not just over his father, but for the Yannis he thought he knew, as well as coming to terms with the backstabbing bastard he really was. He tried to have James killed, you know?"

Signor Russo shook his head. "Doesn't matter how

42

James feels. You and your daughter should be protected at all costs, and I don't just mean physically. You are a woman, and you are family. So, rule number one: whatever and wherever the bad shit is, keep it away from you. If you were in my family"—he raised his arms and spread both hands out, gesturing at the landscape—"or in any Sicilian family, you would be kept out of all this business. But here you are, right in the thick of it."

"It wasn't my or anyone else's choice," I protested. "Yannis began this chain of events. My husband was killed, and people attacked our home; we went to stay with Yannis, then found out he'd betrayed us; he attacked us, I shot him, and then we ended up here. I couldn't keep out of that if I tried."

"Who taught you to shoot? And why?" he asked.

"Kolya, Franco, and Jonesy, because Kolya wanted me to be able to defend myself in case someone attacked us. And he was right to do so, as it turns out," I answered.

"Was he? Could he not have just increased your safety and protection detail? Been more careful in his business dealings?" Signor Russo held his hands up in front of me in a placating manner when I began to protest.

"I'm not trying to disrespect your husband. He is the beloved son of a good friend, and I know he was extremely successful in business. But I question his need to have his wife become so familiar with guns. It was enough to know what he did for a living; you didn't have to see it and live it. There should have been steps in place for…unfortunate situations."

"You mean when terrorists kill your husband and then invade your home? If so, then yes, there were. I took out my hidden Ruger and put fifteen bullets in the mercenary who came into my daughter's room. And for the other unfortunate situation, I used my friend's gun to off that one. So I had two Italian saviours that day: a handy Beretta and you, Signor Russo." I tried to look nonchalant, but inside I was screaming.

"Stop it, Tess. You are not fooling me. You are justifying your actions, and yes, you are right; your skill with guns saved you, your daughter, and others. But I still say you should never have been in that situation in the first place. Call me old-fashioned, if you will, but I believe women should be treasured, and as protected from the harshness of this life as possible. If you had been, you wouldn't be having the nightmares, and you wouldn't know the nagging sickness that invades your mind after you've taken a life."

"Well, we can argue the finer points on why I have them, but that won't help me stop them, will it?" I said crossly. Steering the conversation around to where I needed it to be, I asked, "What did you find helped with yours?"

Signor Russo sighed. "I'm afraid there is no quick fix to the nightmares, *bella*. Some nights I had them worse than others, and I'd wake up in a cold sweat, crying out for Tony to get off me, to save himself and to get in the car. On other nights I'd sit bolt-upright in bed, gasping for breath. I could still hear everything happening in my nightmare, but I was wide awake, seeing my bedroom, the furniture, and the walls. That was almost worse than the crying out. I truly thought I was going crazy when I had those. I felt exhausted and physically sick—like I was coming down with something. Someone suggested pills, but I couldn't risk it. I didn't know who set us up, so I had to stay sharp and on my A-game, and the Feds kept pulling me in to interview me."

He laughed for a moment, then added, "The only time I didn't get them was when they had me locked up for a couple of nights in the cells on my own. Maybe they thought sleep deprivation would make me talk. Who the hell knows? They'd let me sleep for forty or fifty minutes or so, then wake me up by banging on the cell door. They'd interview me every four hours, thinking I'd give something away, but truthfully, during the second night, I felt better than I had in weeks. I hadn't had one nightmare because they'd not let me get to that place in my sleep where my nightmares began. So the Feds did me a favour, in a way."

"What happened when they let you out?"

"I still had nightmares, but they didn't happen until I'd been asleep for about three hours, and I was able to bring myself out of them quicker. I cried like a bambino for feeling good about that, though, because, in a way, I felt like I should be suffering for Tony's death. I went to my church a lot and had a few one-on-one visits with our priest. Father John knew who and what I was, yet he sat and listened to what little I felt I could tell him about what happened that night without passing judgement. I asked him how he could allow me and my men in his church every Sunday, knowing what we were part of. He said it wasn't his place to judge, only God could do that. So I said, *what if I asked for penance?* Father John said penance for me had to be more than a few prayers and a good deed here or there. Penance would mean I was repentant and ready to leave the Mafia life for good. But once you're in, you don't get to leave unless it's in a casket, and that's if you're lucky. So I said to Father John, *You'd better pray for my soul because I doubt God will be as easy to bribe as the judges in New York.*"

Signor Russo paused for a moment, then let out a humourless laugh. "I think, deep down, Father John knew I wouldn't be able to leave *The Family*, but what was he supposed to say? I'd already accepted I'd be going to hell, but I gave him the hundred dollars I had in my pocket and asked if he'd hold a mass for Tony on his birthday. I wanted to give my faithful capo every chance I could to get into heaven. I just hoped that God could forgive him the sin of saving someone as corrupt as me."

His breath hitched a little when he finished speaking, and it was clear to see how much the death of his friend still pained him, so I ran my hand up and down his forearm to offer him comfort. He tapped the back of my hand and then held it against his arm as we continued walking further into the orchard. His cashmere jumper felt warm and soft against my skin, and as the cool breeze rustled through the trees, I wished I'd also had the foresight to wear something a little more climate appropriate.

"His son is so much like him, you know," Signor Russo noted. "About the same height and build, same features, though I can see his mother in his eyes. But young Anthony is a lot like his father in his mannerisms."

I waited for Signor Russo to mention interrupting us in the kitchen, but it seemed he was waiting for me to make the first move.

"I don't know how much you saw or heard back at the villa, but—"

"I heard enough to know that my first guess was right: Tony's boy is in love with you. But from what I saw, you don't seem to feel the same way about him," he said in a voice so low it was almost a whisper. He stopped and turned slightly so I could see his face, then he tilted his head to the side with a nod towards Nate and his guard.

I nodded in return, indicating that I knew he wanted us to keep this quiet.

"It's okay," I reassured him. "Nate is a good friend of Franco's. They served in the army together before working for Kolya. I consider him a good friend, too."

"Even good friends can be bought or switch sides when they have something to lose, *bella*. Never forget that."

"Not all friends," I argued. "Some are loyal and will stay that way to the last."

"True, but what you have to ask yourself is: who are they most loyal to? And the answer to that is often more complicated than friendship."

"Are you warning me against trusting the guards who've been with my husband for years, Signor Russo?" Before he could answer, I added, "Of course you are. I mean, why not toss a little paranoia into my growing mix of crazy."

He shook his head and, in a low voice, advised, "I warned Tony's boy, and now I'm warning you, Tess. And if you value your life, I suggest you listen. You and him? It can never happen. Not while Roman is alive and still head of the family. You belong to them, *cara*, and he will not let you go so easily. Yuri is unmarried and, as far as I am aware, unattached. I imagine that once Roman comes to terms with the fact that he won't find your husband alive, he will eventually push for you and Yuri to wed. You have a young child who bears the name Barinov. Your father-in-law will not allow her to be raised by someone outside the family."

I pulled away from him and accidentally dropped the basket. "No, you're wrong. Roman wouldn't do that; he—"

"Listen to me, Tess. I have known the man for many years. Roman is all about family and bloodlines, even more so than us Sicilians. You are the mother of his granddaughter; he both adores and admires you. You carry his name, so you are family. At the moment, you can do no wrong in his eyes. But if there is one thing that Roman Barinov cannot abide, it is infidelity."

"But—"

"I know what you are going to say. You are not doing

anything wrong. You did not ask for Franco's attention, and you no longer have a husband to be unfaithful to. But I doubt that Roman will see it that way. That's why I stayed back at the villa to warn Anthony, and now I'm warning you. The one thing he asked me to do was to keep you safe, and I intend to do that. Even if it's his love I have to protect you from. It will probably make him hate me even more than he does now, but if it keeps you and him alive, so be it."

"Is everything okay, Tess?" Nate questioned as he closed the distance between us.

I glanced up at him and knew immediately that the look on my face had given away the torrent of emotions I was currently feeling.

"Come on, I'm taking you back to the villa," he declared as he placed his hand on my shoulder.

"No! I mean, not yet I... We haven't picked any fruit and—"

"We'll come back and get some later when you're not so upset," Nate assured me as he glared at Signor Russo.

"I'm not upset, Nate. Well, maybe a bit. You see, Signor Russo kindly offered to talk to me about my nightmares. He told me he has experience with them, yet discussing how they affect me is making me feel quite emotional. But as long as he's willing, I'd still like to pick some fruit for later?" I delivered this more as a question, with a smile on my face and in my voice, in the hope that Nate would stand down and accept my part truth.

"Tess tells me how loyal you are. She's lucky to have you by her side at such a troubling time. Franco, too," Signor Russo acknowledged. "I hear you served together. That must forge an even greater loyalty."

"Yes, sir. We were in the same unit. Afghanistan was

hard going, and I was grateful that Franco and the rest of my unit had my back. He knows I'll always have his, and for more than just our friendship and shared service history. Franco also saved the life of Kevin, my partner, when he was attacked. He's a good man, and I love him like a brother."

Signor Russo tapped Nate on the shoulder and then glanced my way, one eyebrow raised. "I thank you for your service, and I understand why Tess speaks so highly of you. I'm sure we can put aside the tastiest fruit for you today. What do you say, *mia cara*?"

"Definitely."

I knew Signor Russo was trying to communicate something, but I wasn't sure what. When Nate fell back a few paces, apparently satisfied I was no longer upset, it allowed me to ask my companion what he meant without being overheard.

"So, what was the raised eyebrow all about?" I asked as we stopped by a tree that was heavily laden with clementines.

He grasped a clementine, twisting it until the stem detached from the tree, then placed it in the basket.

"I believe we have an answer to where your guard's loyalty will lie if shit ever hits the fan with Franco," he said with a nod towards Nate.

"As I've said, that's never going to happen. I love my husband. It doesn't matter to me that he's no longer here to share that love. He's the only man I've ever wanted in that way—apart from silly, childish, movie-star crushes when I was younger. I can't imagine loving anyone else."

"It doesn't have to be about love. It can be about loneliness, wanting to feel close to someone, even for a moment. A physical connection to someone—sex or otherwise. In the coming months or years, you'll find yourself wanting that, Tess, and though for most people that wouldn't pose a problem, you aren't most people. Your surname and your daughter mean your relationships will be under direct scrutiny by one of the most dangerous and powerful men in the world. That man happens to be my friend, and I wouldn't want to go up against him. But I owe Tony's boy a debt. He asked that I keep you and your daughter safe, and I intend to do that—even if it means I fuck up my friendship with Roman for good."

As he placed more fruit in the basket, he said, "So here's what's going to happen. Tomorrow, I will send you a gift. A burner phone and charger with a pre-programmed number on there. If you ever need protection for whatever reason, you call that number, and you say, *'Tell Gianni I need him,'* then I will call you back and get you and your daughter to safety. Have you got that, Tess? Do you understand what I'm saying here? If you are ever in a situation where the people"—he waved his hand in a kind of circle—"guards, friends, and family who currently keep you safe seem like they are about to turn on you, you call that number and say those words."

"Tell Gianni I need him," I repeated.

"Good girl. You make sure you keep that phone charged and with you at all times. If you can't get to it, you have my number anyway, but it will be more difficult to get you away if they are keeping tabs on your number and tracing or listening in on your calls."

I captured his hand as he dropped more clementines into the basket.

"Thank you. For offering me and Lily help. It means a lot," I told him.

"Thank your Franco. He's the one I owe the debt to. I

just wish you could get him to see sense and use his head. But the heart wants what it wants, and you'd have a better chance at stopping waves rolling to shore as telling a man with Italian blood in his veins that he cannot have the woman he loves."

Chapter Five

My conversation with Signor Russo left me reeling. Would Roman really try to control my personal life by pushing for Yuri and I to marry? The idea that he could do that appalled me, and I'm certain Yuri would object, being as he'd rather have a husband than a wife. I also didn't know how to take the implication that my life could be at risk if I began a relationship with Franco. I'm sure my father-in-law wouldn't stoop so low as to have me killed, for Lily's sake, if nothing else.

I did, however, take on board what Signor Russo had said regarding the reduced sleep pattern stopping his night-mares. Hearing him talk about the trauma of his past so openly made me feel that I could trust him. True to his word, the day after we spoke, I was approached by one of his guards, whom he'd sent over with fresh baked bread and pastries. He waited until I was on my own, then handed me a box that included a simple Nokia handset and charger.

I went straight upstairs and switched the handset on.

There was only one number in the contacts list, and I wondered if I'd be able to memorise it, as I'd done with Kolya's and my own.

It's hard to remember mobile numbers because we rarely dial them. It's normally a case of opening your contacts and swiping to the person you want to call before you hit the green button. Simple. Our minds don't have to store the numbers because they're always available to us.

I remember Jean's number, and oddly enough, I still remember the number for the liaison officer at the support group Mum used to attend every time she tried to convince everyone she was coming off drugs. Maybe it's because I enjoyed it there? It was warm and friendly, and they always had fresh fruit and biscuits. When Mum went to one of her group sessions, I and a few other kids used to go into a small room with books, Lego and various board games. Mum's liaison officer was called Jane, and I memorised her number from a card she gave out, which is a good thing because Mum never could keep anything safe, and the drugs she wasn't supposed to be taking left her too spaced out to remember anything.

I hid the fully charged phone inside a pair of leather ankle boots I'd bought on a Christmas shopping trip in Catania, then I put them at the back of the wardrobe. I didn't want the questions I'd receive if anyone found it.

Signor Russo took Lily and me to meet his family, and Lily played with his granddaughter, Sofia, who is the same age as her. We'd also attended mass a few times with Signor Russo and his family, and whilst the words were in Italian, I kind of enjoyed it more. Nate, Ivan, and Franco always came with us, and Franco admitted to feeling torn. Despite him being polite and respectful to Signor Russo, he felt he was betraying his mother if he came to like the man himself. But I could tell that the more time we spent with the Russo family, the harder it was for him to mirror his mother's loathing of Gianni.

Franco seemed a lot happier since Yuri left. He'd stayed with us until New Year's Day and had insisted on sleeping beside me every night, even though the changes I'd made to my sleeping pattern meant I'd been able to keep the nightmares at bay. I think he suspected I wasn't telling the whole truth about listening to guided meditation on my phone to lull me into a calming, restful sleep, or the need to keep my smartwatch on to check my resting pulse and heart rate.

Okay, I know it wasn't exactly the healthiest way to go about it, but I decided to utilise the information that Signor Russo had given me. He said that the Feds would wake him every forty or fifty minutes, thinking sleep deprivation would make him spill his secrets, when in fact, it stopped him from getting to that place in his sleep where the nightmares began. So I set my alarm on my phone for fifty minutes and put my wireless earphones in, while I pretended to listen to a meditation guru talking me to sleep using quiet, calming tones. I even picked a few sessions out to play clips to everyone to see what they thought about it. Of course, they'd all been supportive and agreed that it was worth a try, and after my third night without a nightmare, they were all thrilled I'd found something that was working for me. I set my alarm for every fifty minutes until five a.m., then I let myself sleep without disturbance, knowing that Lily would be awake within a couple of hours.

Yuri questioned the need for me to hold on to my phone

all night, but I explained it away as if it was sort of a safety blanket for me. So if I felt anxious and woke up during a nightmare, I could press play on some guided meditation techniques. He didn't say I was lying, but I could see the accusation in his eyes. That was on New Year's Eve.

It was a day and night I'd been dreading. We'd normally be away on holiday, usually on the yacht, spending the day together as a family. When Lily went to bed, we'd celebrate the New Year with all the adults. Lots of food, drink, and music. But as soon as the clock struck twelve, Kolya would take me in his arms and whisper, "Happy New Year, Mrs Barinov," before placing a soft, sensual kiss on my lips. It was a promise of things to come. Despite the alcohol flowing freely, he made sure we let the New Year in with a better bang than any firework could create.

I declined Signor Russo's offer of spending New Year's Eve at a party he was hosting. I also couldn't face staying up and celebrating the New Year with everyone at the villa. Not that there was much celebrating going on. The place still had to be guarded, and let's face it…what did we have to celebrate about the coming year? A year without the man I thought would be mine forever.

So, Lily and I went to bed at 9 p.m. after video chatting with Nan and Jack, Jean and her nurse, and Mrs Braeburn and the rest of the staff at Glengarran. James didn't call, but he did send me a text. He said he didn't feel like celebrating or marking the occasion, and I could totally understand that. He said he hoped for good health for Lily and me for the New Year, and I wished him the same. I don't think either of us wanted to tempt fate by texting each other *Happy New Year*.

Ivan and Yuri got blind drunk. I could hear them talking with Lainey and Danny about how much they were missing

Kolya. They were obviously distraught, and I'm sure both of them were crying at some point. They also spoke about Aleksei, although they didn't seem so upset about him. They spoke about him more like someone you know who you'd not seen for years, but then, it had been almost twenty months since Aleksei and Talia's plane went down, so they'd had time to come to terms with their grief. I didn't know if I could ever do that.

Kolya and I were two halves of a whole. Without him it felt as though I could only live half a life. So tell me, how could anyone learn to come to terms with that?

Ivan and Yuri also raised a glass in celebration of Simeon, and from what I gathered from their drunken, loud whispering outside my bedroom when Yuri came to bed, Ivan was supposed to visit him over the New Year. I thought at first that maybe he was an old friend of theirs, but Ivan kept saying *malysh*, a Russian word for a baby or child.

Despite living in a household with two men whose mother tongue was Russian, I hadn't learned much of the language. I didn't need to. Kolya only ever spoke Russian at home when he was arguing with Ivan, and though Ivan used to struggle with some of the English language, even he could pass as being completely fluent now.

The loud whispers outside my bedroom door about the mysterious Simeon had piqued my interest, and I resolved to ask Ivan about them when I had the chance. When I did so, he stared at me for a moment, like he was contemplating what he could say. He bit down on his bottom lip, as though he was trying to stop himself from speaking, then he shook his head and told me that one day soon he would show me a photograph that would explain many things, but right now, it wasn't his story to tell. I could see he was torn. Ivan and I were as close as best friends could be. More like brother and sister but without sharing DNA. I knew he wouldn't keep secrets from me if he had a choice, but he did make me promise never to mention Simeon's name in front of Roman, which made me worry.

What the bloody hell were Yuri and Ivan hiding from him?

Chapter Six

TESS

Four weeks later and the new sleep regime I'd implemented —the one that had made me feel more empowered and in control—had begun to take its toll.

In the first weeks of setting the fifty-minute alarms, I'd coped well with the tiredness. I think the utter elation of finding something that prevented the nightmares was worth more to me than a restful sleep at that point. I began eating more, my body craving extra fuel to keep it going when all it wanted to do was slow down or stop. Ivan has a sweet tooth, but he had nothing on me in those first couple of weeks. I ate chocolate, pastries, cakes—anything that would give me enough of a sugar rush to get me motivated.

During the last week or so things began to change. I'd gone from just being tired to thoroughly exhausted. Instead of craving food, my appetite had waned. Everything seemed to make me angry and frustrated. I'd snapped at everyone, including Lily, and I didn't know how to stop myself from doing it. You know when sometimes you can hear yourself saying something, and inside your head you're screaming at yourself to stop? That seemed to be happening a lot, especially around Franco and Ivan. They knew something was wrong and kept trying to get me to admit to what I was doing. But I never did.

I had to figure out a better sleep pattern—one that didn't destroy my health while freeing my dreams.

Lainey, Danny, Nate, and Ivan were by the heated pool with Lily, but I couldn't face it. I'd been sitting in the kitchen since breakfast. The glare of the sun through the floor-to-ceiling doors in the lounge was just too much for me. The last two days had been unnaturally warm for late January in Sicily, hence the short-sleeved T-shirt dress I wore instead of my usual jeans.

Over in England, Nan said they'd had heavy rain for days, and up in the Scottish Highlands, Mrs Braeburn said they'd had five inches of snow overnight.

I could understand the need to be outside, enjoying the rare heat at this time of year, and I bet that Nan and Mrs Braeburn would have swapped with me in a heartbeat. But some days your mood or needs call for the complete opposite of what you have. This was one of those days for me.

It was quieter in the kitchen…until I put the kettle on for a strong cup of tea, which I sorely needed. I also poured a mug of coffee for Mark, who was manning the security room off the hallway, and put four chocolate chip cookies on a plate for him. He was healing well and would be back to full fitness in a week or so. He and Franco seemed to be in a friendly competition over who could get back to full strength before the other. Franco still had a slight limp, but only when he'd overdone it. Both men were strong, healthy, and determined, and I had the utmost admiration for them.

"Thanks, Tess," Mark said as I placed his mug and cookies beside him.

Including the laptop he had open, he had four monitors to view. I could see two of Signor Russo's men behind the gates of the villa on the first monitor. The second showed the pool area. Ivan and Lainey were in the pool with Lily while Nate and Danny kept watch. The next two screens showed part of the orchards and tennis court. Mark picked up a cookie and pointed it at the screen showing the pool.

"Why aren't you out there today, Tess? Are you all right?"

"I felt like having some time to myself today, that's all," I told him.

Mark nodded in understanding, then dunked his cookie in his coffee.

As I turned to leave, I bumped into Franco in the doorway, his face was like thunder. His dark brown eyes fixed me in place when he asked, "Are you feeling okay?"

"Yeah, I'm fine. Why does everyone keep asking if I'm okay?" I huffed out an exaggerated breath and rolled my eyes, but despite my dismissive words and actions, Franco's dark, intense gaze was making me feel nervous.

"You sure you aren't feeling tired?" he questioned as he reached out and tucked my hair behind my ears. I'd left my curls loose after my shower, though my hair had long since dried. But even putting my hair up in a scrunchie seemed like way too much effort.

"No, I'm not tired," I lied. "What's this? Twenty questions?"

Franco stared at me a few seconds longer, then grabbed my hand and said, "Come with me."

"Where are we going?" I asked as he led me through the villa, down the corridor off the hallway and into the annexe. The door to his bedroom was ajar, and I could see his laptop open on his bed.

"There's something I want you to watch. Something I found very interesting when I played them back over the last two mornings," he said as he ushered me inside and closed, then locked the door.

Franco pocketed the key and gestured towards the bed, "Why don't you get comfortable, and I'll set up the recordings?"

Sitting back against the headboard on his king-sized bed, I asked, "The recordings? Has Kevin found more intel about the hack?"

Franco shook his head, kicked off his running shoes and came to sit beside me. He wore a white T-shirt and dark blue workout shorts. The scar on his calf had healed well, but he'd caught a little sun on it when he was by the pool with Lily yesterday. I made a mental note to remind him to cover up or wear sunscreen later.

He picked up his laptop, typed in his password and pulled up a recording with the day before yesterday's date. Before he hit play, he said, "I'm gonna ask you again, and I want you to give me a truthful answer this time. Are you feeling tired? And if so, is there a reason for that? I want you to be honest with me, baby, 'cause there's never been any bullshit between us, and I don't see why we should start that now."

I glanced up from the laptop to find him watching me intently. My eyes flicked back to the recording, a feeling of utter dread rolling through my gut at what was behind the pause button. With a certainty I could bet money on, I already knew what would be on that video.

After a few moments of silence, it became apparent to Franco that I wasn't about to reply, so he hit play on the recording, and just as I thought would happen, an image of me in bed appeared on the screen in night-vision mode.

"This is just before the first alarm goes off at twenty-three fifty, though you were still awake and ready for it to happen. I didn't know what you were doing at first, but it became apparent after the next two fifty-minute alarms what the pattern would be. I wanted to give you the benefit of the doubt, hoping I'd gotten it wrong, so I set the camera up to record again last night, and whaddya know?" he said, closing that recording and bringing up another. "Little Miss 'I'm Not Tired' is setting her alarm on her damn phone to wake her up every fifty minutes until five a.m."

Watching the black-and-white image of myself on the screen of his laptop felt surreal at first. It was as if I was watching someone else. Spying on the pitiful, crazy woman who was rubbing her eyes and fumbling with her phone at 3 a.m. so she could try and convince everyone she was fine.

I wanted to deny it, to tell him he'd got it all wrong, but what would be the point? It was there in black and white. Literally!

Franco closed the laptop and placed it on the bed beside him. I waited for him to say something: to chastise me or call me a liar. But he did neither. Instead, he wrapped his arms around me and asked, "Why, Tess? Why did you do it?"

For a flicker of a second I almost crumbled. I'd had tears of sorrow brewing behind my eyes as soon as I realised what the recording was, knowing my secret was out and I wouldn't be allowed to control my nightmares anymore. But the sorrow turned to frustration, then anger at having my privacy invaded.

I pushed at Franco's chest so hard he fell back onto the mattress, and then I leapt off the bed and began pacing the room.

"Who sanctioned the camera in my room? It had better not still be there! I bet you all had a little talk between yourselves, deciding you knew what was best for me—filming me in the privacy of my own fucking bedroom? Where my daughter and I sleep!" I raged.

Unperturbed, Franco sat up and folded his arms across his chest. "I set the camera up. No one knew about it but me, and I removed it twenty minutes ago. I knew something wasn't right, and I wasn't falling for that meditation bullshit. You were making yourself sick; that's not acceptable to me. And technically, you don't actually sleep, so—"

I held my hand up in front of me, closed my eyes and shook my head, willing myself to calm down so that I didn't cross the room and punch him in the face.

"You're shaking, Tess. You're so fucking angry right now and you're trying to control it. Why, baby? You gotta learn to let this stuff go, 'cause bottling everything up inside is what's got you where you are now. A shadow of the woman you were. One who can't eat, won't sleep, and who lies to those who love and care for her. You need to allow yourself to feel, Tess, even if those feelings hurt," he insisted. But I didn't want to listen.

"You don't get to tell me what to do. No one does. What you did was wrong, Franco, no matter what justification you think you have. I could fire you for it."

He shrugged his shoulders. "Go ahead. Then we can show everyone the recordings. I'll even let you know where the best bits are—you know, where you set the alarm so you can try to get another precious fifty minutes of sleep."

"I've had enough of this," I told him as I walked

towards the door. "Destroy those recordings, Franco, or you can find yourself another job."

"You can't get out," he said with a grin. "I locked the door when we came in."

"You think this is funny?" I yelled. "You know what, Franco, I'd actually thought it was me that was losing it with all the nightmares and stuff, but I haven't got a patch on you. You're absolutely crazy, I swear."

"You want the key, come and get it. Fight me for it. Let off some of that steam by throwing a few punches. Here." He picked up the laptop and placed it on the dresser, then went back to the bed. "We can pull off the mattress and place it on the floor so I won't hurt you as much when I drop-kick your ass."

Was he for real? After a heavy sigh, I stepped up beside him and held out my hand, demanding, "Give me the key and let me leave, Franco."

Before I knew what was happening, he'd grabbed hold of my arm, throwing me over his shoulder onto the bed. Too stunned and winded to move, I wasn't quick enough to prevent him from pinning me bodily to the mattress.

"Come on, Tess, throw me off. Show me some of those moves you were so good at."

I tried to push back at him, to buck my lower body and use my legs as leverage, but I didn't have the strength anymore. I used to be so good at self-defence. Franco and Jonesy taught me well. But over the last couple of years, I'd been so busy with Lily and Sarah's Legacy that I'd let that part of my fitness regime lapse. And now I was too bloody tired to execute even the most basic moves.

A thought occurred to me then—a memory from almost six years before when Franco had goaded me into a similar situation. It was the day before my foster sister's funeral, and as well as being upset, I was also feeling nervous about speaking out in front of everyone who'd be attending. There were some important things I needed to say, for Sarah's sake and for others like her, but I'd been so anxious I almost hadn't done it. Franco had challenged me, just like he was doing now. He made me fight back, and he even gave me a coping strategy to use on the day, which involved pinching myself to the point of pain. He also did it the day Kolya was killed to help prepare me for a meeting in the tech room. Despite how sick it might sound, it got me through it.

Franco helped me find my strength that day, just like he was trying to do now in his own messed-up way.

I stopped struggling, my body becoming lax underneath his. Then I reached up and touched his cheek.

"I know what you're trying to do, Franco, but it won't work this time. It's not a case of just getting me through the next day. I've got years of this hurt ahead of me."

He raised his upper body from my chest and rested on his forearms. Gazing down at me, he replied, "The same applies, Tess. You find something that helps get you through from one day to the next. But it has to be something that allows you to feel, not bottle everything up inside. Keeping your hurt and your demons locked away keeps you static. You can't move into a new day if you're broken. And before you say you don't want to move on, you have to, Tess. You're a mom. Lily needs to see you fit and well and living your life so she can follow in your footsteps. I know what's happened is eating you up inside, but you need to find a better way to deal with it, baby, 'cause what you're doing to yourself...it just ain't healthy."

"I don't know how, though, Franco. I can't change what's already happened. Kolya's dead, I've killed two men, and just when I thought we could go back to the UK, there's a security breach and I'm told it's not safe. I can't talk to my friends about any of it, obviously. Jean's out of the question; Nan avoids talking about the attack on the house and Yannis's death at all costs. Kevin was supposed to be setting up a video call between George and me from the tech room in Oxford, but as you know, George's mother had a stroke. She passed away last week, so I've sent flowers and told him to take as much time as he needs to grieve. And as Devina's no longer working with him, that's my counselling option out of the window. So tell me, Franco, what do I do?"

"Use me," he said in all seriousness. "Let's start training again. Get your fitness levels back up to scratch. Self-defence, hand-to-hand combat, weapons training. You name it, we do it. Every day. We get you focused and so fucking exhausted and aching that you can't wait to fall into your bed at night. You know I won't go easy on you, Tess. I never did."

"No, and neither did Jonesy," I said with a whisper. Blinking back a tear, I admitted, "I miss him so much. I wish he were here with us."

"So do I, baby," he said as he lowered his head and kissed away my tear. He nuzzled my cheek and rubbed his slight scruff of facial hair against my jaw.

I reached up and ran my fingers through his glossy black hair. It had grown so quickly since we'd been here. I think it suited him, but as it was longer on top and kept falling into his eyes, Nate and Mark had begun calling him *Boy Band*.

"Don't you start with that boy band crap," he warned.

"I wouldn't dream of it," I lied. Trying not to laugh, I added, "I mean, I've heard you sing, and you certainly don't have the moves, so there's no chance you'd end up in a boy band. Besides, you're way too old for it."

Franco frowned. "I can sing; I just prefer not to. And who are you calling old? I'm still in my thirties, so this here is prime Italian meat," he said with a roll of his hips. He reached back, lifting up my right leg and wrapping it around his thigh before repositioning himself slightly and rolling his hips once again. My dress had ridden up, and my eyes grew wide at the feel of Franco's hard length against my core. Even through the thin cotton of my underwear, the friction his cock provided against my clit had my cheeks flushing and my heart racing.

Franco wrapped his arms around me. Running his nose over my ear, he whispered, "Still think I don't have the moves, baby?" before kissing his way up and down my neck, over my jaw, and finally, my lips.

My eyes remained open at first, but it was as though I was having an out-of-body experience. Yes, I knew it was happening, and I knew in my head that it was a bad idea and I should stop it, but for the life of me, I couldn't bring myself to do so. Because, for the first time in months, I was actually feeling something other than sorrow and despair. Warmth spread through my whole body, not just from my core, but from what seemed like everywhere. My belly, my legs, my chest, my arms, and lastly, my head, it felt... I felt... *alive*.

I kissed him back, wrapping my arms around him and holding him tightly. Revelling in the feel of his hard muscular chest and abs and the warmth from his body. He carried on moving his hips, his pelvis rocking into mine, his length rubbing against me in the most delicious way, causing me to whimper and moan with need.

I wrapped my other leg around his thigh and placed my hands over his buttocks, grinding my lower half against his. My body was chasing the rush of a climax I knew I'd no right to experience, and in a brief moment of clarity, I almost put a stop to the heady rush of sensations coursing through my body.

Almost.

But the sheer unadulterated pleasure was too intoxicating—too addictive to resist. So, instead of putting an end to this moment of sensual madness, I let the long-dormant sexual need win and gave myself over to the passion that blazed between us.

Franco must have instinctively known I'd finally decided to capitulate and enjoy what was happening. He let out a groan and then sighed against my throat before his lips found mine again. The kiss was so full of passion that it was almost frantic. The pressure from his lips was near brutal, his tongue tangling with mine as if in a fight for dominance. When we finally broke apart, both of us gasped for much-needed air, yet seconds later, we were kissing again while clawing at each other's clothes.

I tugged Franco's T-shirt up his back and he stopped kissing me for a moment while he pulled it over his head and threw it on the floor. Instead of pulling my dress off, he shoved it up over my breasts, then pulled the lace cups of my bra down until my nipples peeped out over the top. Then he was on them with his hands and mouth, one after the other, not gentle or reverent in any way. He sucked and twisted and bit, and it was glorious in its intensity. Though he wasn't even touching me there, my clit began to throb, and I could feel how damp my underwear was becoming. I needed him inside me. I needed it with a passion and ferocity I never thought I'd experience again, and I needed it right now before I had a chance to think about it further and lose the precious feeling of being alive.

I brought my legs up higher and, using my feet, pushed his workout shorts down his hips.

Franco stilled; his body taut. "Tess?"

"Franco, please... I need you," I half whispered, half moaned.

"Then I'm all yours, baby," he declared with a sexy-assin smile. He ran his tongue over my bottom lip before kissing me softly, slipping his hand down the front of my knickers as he did so. I was so sensitive from him rocking against me earlier that as soon as he ran his finger down through my folds, my back bowed and I cried out in pleasure.

"Fuck, Tess, you're soaked." Franco sounded and looked surprised, but he carried on stroking me, taking me nearer towards that longed-for climax. But I didn't want it to happen like this. I knew if it did, it wouldn't be as fulfilling.

"Please, Franco."

His hand stilled, and then he sat back on his heels and tugged my knickers down and off before pulling his shorts and boxers down to his lower thighs.

"You are a fucking queen, Tess. You should never have to beg for this. Ever. If you want something from me, I'll give it to you. Whatever you need. You got that, baby?"

Franco groaned as he ran his cock through the wetness at my core before burying himself inside me in one hard thrust.

There are times when you have sex that you have to put the effort in to get to that special place where your climax is so beautiful you almost hear angels sing. But there are occasions when you're so ready for it and fit together so perfectly that it takes no effort at all to have you barrelling towards an orgasm. This moment with Franco was definitely the latter. Every time his cock slammed home, it lifted me to a higher plane of ecstasy. The way he moved, pressing into my pubic bone, hitting my clit just right. His drugging kisses, the feel of his hard warm body on mine. Everything about it was pure bliss. He let out a guttural groan as his hands slid under my buttocks, pressing me harder against him, and that's all I needed to send me soaring—coming so hard I saw flashes of light behind my eyes—the orgasm lasting longer than I remember they used to. And that's what finally brought me back down to earth. Remembering.

Remembering I made a vow to be faithful to a man who'd only been dead for three and a half months, and I wondered if Kolya would somehow know what I had done and would think I didn't love him anymore.

As if a switch had been flipped, my post-orgasmic panting became hard, heavy sobbing.

"Tess, what's wrong? Speak to me, baby. Did I hurt you?"

I pushed at Franco's chest and winced as I felt his rapidly softening cock leave a trail of wetness down my thigh. We'd not even used protection. How could I have been so stupid?

"I need to go. I shouldn't have done this. I don't... I'm so sorry, Franco."

He rolled away from me and pulled his shorts and underwear up as I adjusted my bra and dress. Without looking me in the eyes, he handed me my knickers and unlocked the door. Before I could walk through it, he said, "I'm not sorry this happened, but I am sorry you're upset. You shouldn't be, but I get why you are. I'll go and make you a drink if you want to stay here and gather your thoughts for a while. I'll give you some space if that's what you need."

I shook my head and wiped the tears from my eyes.

"Thank you for offering, Franco, but I need to go to my room now."

He reached out to tuck my hair behind my ear.

"Like I said, I'll give you whatever you need, Tess. Always."

And with that, he opened the door and watched me walk away.

Chapter Seven

TESS

No amount of showering could wash away the guilt I felt over what had happened between me and Franco. I cried the whole time I was in there and had the water as hot as I could stand it, leaving my skin feeling so tender that even the soft Egyptian cotton of the towel hurt. Once dry, I put on a nightshirt and climbed into bed. I didn't want to see anyone. I couldn't face their condemnation, even though I knew I deserved it.

I couldn't blame Franco for what had happened—even though I was still a little angry at him for filming me. He'd been worried about me, and he knew me too well to accept my lies about the guided meditation methods.

No. I was to blame for all of it.

I could have owned up to what I'd done and sat and talked to him about my reasons, letting him help me move forward in an acceptable way—the way a platonic friend would. Instead, I tried pulling down his shorts and pleaded with him to have sex with me.

Despite the suffocating guilt and the crushing regret

invading my mind, my body felt surprisingly good. Gone was the tenseness in my neck and shoulders; the muscles in my body feeling more relaxed than they had in weeks. My nipples felt a little sore, and I was slightly tender inside. It had been so long since that last night with Kolya, and Franco hadn't been gentle. If he had, I'd have felt so much worse about it. What we did was unplanned, and it certainly wasn't making love. It was raw, primal sex, and it felt amazing. But it could never happen again. Signor Russo's warning wasn't delivered lightly. I had to think about not just myself but Franco, too. Roman wouldn't be happy to learn about our indiscretion, and it's never a good idea to make Roman Barinov, the most feared pakhan in the Russian Mafia, unhappy. Besides, I didn't love Franco the way he wanted me to. How could I, while Kolya still owned every piece of my shattered heart and blackened soul?

"Tess. Hey, I didn't want to wake you, but we're about to eat, and I thought you might be getting hungry."

"Hmm...?" It took a moment for Ivan's words to register and my eyes to focus through the sleep-filled haze.

"Are you okay? You're not ill, are you?" He switched on the bedside lamp and placed his hand against my forehead. "You don't feel hot."

"No, I feel fine; I... Ivan, what time is it?" I'd closed the curtains before I climbed into bed, but it still hadn't been dark in the room.

"Nearly seven p.m. I know it's late for Lily to be eating, but you were sleeping so soundly when Lainey came in to get her a change of clothes, and she didn't want to wake you. Nate's fired up the barbecue, and Danny and Franco

73

have set out the patio heaters. You'll need to wear a jumper and jeans because it feels chilly out there tonight, even with the heaters."

At the mention of Franco's name, I felt the blush rise in my cheeks, but as well as my embarrassment, something else began to register. It was nearly 7 p.m., and I'd climbed into bed just before noon. I'd slept nearly seven hours without a single nightmare. I shook my head in disbelief. There'd been no setting of alarms, no denying myself more than fifty minutes' rest. All that sleep had been achieved naturally, and if truth be told, if Ivan hadn't woken me up, I'd still be sound asleep.

My belly grumbled loudly, reminding me I'd not eaten anything for hours. I hadn't had much of an appetite for a couple of weeks. Yet all it had taken to cure me of my terrifying nightmares and loss of appetite was hot sex and a toe-curling orgasm.

I made a strange sound that was somewhere between a laugh and a cry before grabbing my hair with both hands.

What a mess! How was I going to face Franco after what we'd done without everyone knowing? I was blushing just thinking about it.

"Tess!" Ivan pried my hands from my hair. "You are beginning to worry me. Tell me what is wrong. I cannot help if I don't know what it is."

I looked him in the eyes and shook my head. "I can't tell you, Ivan. If I do, you'll hate me, and out of everyone on this earth other than Lily, if you hated me, I'd—"

"Do not waste another word, Tess, for they would all be useless," Ivan declared. "I could never hate you. You and Lily are my family. My world. I'll love you beyond my last breath and long into the hereafter. Nothing you say will change that, *milaya moya.*"

He pulled me up into a sitting position and held me against him, kissing the top of my head and stroking my hair.

"Get it off your chest, Tess. You should not keep everything bottled up. It is not good for you," Ivan murmured.

"Yeah, that's what he said. It's what started it, and it just went on from there."

"Who said? And started what?" Ivan questioned.

I pulled back from him and looked him in the eyes. "If I tell you something, promise me you won't get mad."

"I already said that," he replied impatiently.

"No, Ivan, you said you wouldn't hate me. This is different, and you really might be mad at me because I did something stupid that could have made me ill," I told him.

Ivan frowned. "Did this have something to do with that sleep thing on your phone? The one where the man had the voice of a serial killer?"

"Yes, I mean, no I... What the hell do you mean by serial killer? It was supposed to sound calming," I argued.

Ivan raised both hands palm up and shrugged. "We watched *Silence of the Lambs* together, yet you could not pick out the voice of *Hannibal Lecter* from the creepy, boring meditation thing. You were obviously not yourself, so I did not make an issue out of it, but I knew it was him."

I closed my eyes and pinched the bridge of my nose before taking a calming breath.

"It wouldn't have mattered who was speaking because I wasn't listening to it. I was setting the alarm on my phone every fifty minutes so I didn't get the chance to fall into a deep enough sleep to have a nightmare. I did it because I knew you were all worried about me. James had left because he thought I was going crazy, and he felt guilty about it. I didn't want anyone else questioning my sanity."

Ivan stared at me, open-mouthed. When he finally found the words to speak, he asked, "How long were you doing this for?"

"Just over a month. I know you suspected that something wasn't right. Franco too. What I hadn't expected him to do was set up night-vision cameras in my bedroom."

"He what?" Ivan got up from beside me and began to pace. It was obvious he was angry, but whether he was more pissed off with me than Franco, I had no idea.

"I was angry with him at first, but I know why he did it. The thing is, I wouldn't have stopped what I was doing, even though I knew it wasn't healthy. Franco tried to goad me into an argument. He says I'm bottling things up and I should let my emotions out. He tried to get me to fight with him like he did the day before Sarah's funeral. He wanted to prove to me that I was still strong. He thinks if I get rid of some of the pent-up hurt and anger and start self-defence and combat training with him again, I might be able to sleep without nightmares."

Ivan walked over to the window and opened the curtains. He folded his arms across his chest and stared down at the scene outside. He still looked angry, and I assumed he had his eyes on Franco.

Pushing back the covers, I climbed out of bed and went over to stand beside him.

"Don't be angry with him," I mumbled as I leaned into his side.

Ivan glanced down at me with one eyebrow raised, then shook his head.

"I'm angrier with myself than Franco. I should have done what he did. As you say, I suspected you were not telling us the truth about your nightmares stopping so suddenly. You know I love you, Tess, and, of course, you will always be beautiful to me. But, forgive me, *milaya moya*, these last few weeks you've looked like shit."

I laughed a little at that, but I had to agree. There were dark circles under my eyes, and my skin looked sallow and dry. Even my hair appeared to have lost some of its vibrancy, and I seemed to be shedding more with each wash.

Ivan put an arm around me and pulled me in for a hug. "I know I snore when I drink, but I already told you, I wouldn't touch a drop if you needed me to sleep beside you. Promise me you won't do anything like that again. Lily needs you to be well, Tess, but I need you, too." Tapping his finger against the window pane, he said, "And everyone else down there cares about you so very much."

I turned my head and placed a kiss against his bicep. "Love you, Ivan."

"That's understandable; I'm a very loveable person," he acknowledged before turning me towards my wardrobe. "Now, put on some clothes and let us go and eat. Those steaks should be ready now."

"Ivan, I can't. Franco's down there."

"So? You didn't actually fight with him, did you? If you did, don't worry. I've seen him, and he doesn't look bruised," Ivan said cheerily.

"That's because we didn't fight after all. In fact, you could say that what we did was the complete opposite of fighting," I admitted. Turning to face him, I asked, "Do you want to revise your opinion on whether you could hate me? Because I hate myself for what I allowed to happen earlier."

I saw the moment Ivan realised what I'd been trying to tell him. His eyes grew wide, and his brows almost disappeared into his hairline, but then he frowned and stepped towards me.

"Did he force you, Tess? You said you allowed it to happen, but you sounded like you had no control over it. Tell me he did not—"

"No, I didn't mean like that. Franco would never..." I shook my head and sighed. "It was me who lost control. I don't know what else to say. It just happened. One minute we were arguing, then we...well, then we weren't, and I knew I should have stopped it. I love Kolya. It doesn't matter that he's gone; I love him with everything I am, and that's not going to change. But what I did with Franco made me feel alive. I don't know how to explain it. It probably won't make sense to anyone else, but in some ways, I've felt as if I died alongside Kolya that day. I haven't been able to feel much joy in anything, not even Lily, and I'm ashamed to admit that, Ivan."

He grabbed my shoulders and held me firmly. "Do you not listen to me, Tess? I told you that nothing could make me hate you. Nothing at all. As long as you are happy, you can have anyone you want. Just make sure that Roman doesn't find out. He will seek to interfere in your life if he does, and you know that wouldn't be good for Franco. With regards to how you've been feeling, as soon as George is working again, you will have as many grief counselling sessions as it takes to make you realise that you still have a long, full life to live. One that, with enough time and the right goals, will bring you and Lily so much happiness." He tapped my cheek, then winked, adding, "As long as I am still with you both, of course. I mean, obviously, you'll be happy if I am around."

"Obviously," I repeated with a smile. I wanted to ask Ivan more about Roman, but his stomach made a loud growling sound, and as everyone can attest, a hungry Ivan isn't a patient man.

"Turn around; I'll be quick," I told him as I grabbed my clothes.

As soon as I was dressed, we ventured downstairs. The mouth-watering scents of chargrilled chicken, beef, and pork hit me as soon as I stepped outside.

"Mummy," Lily shouted before taking a bite out of something covered in ketchup. It spread around her mouth, making her look like a clown.

"Hey, you two," Franco greeted as we approached. "I hope you're hungry. Nate's gone overboard with the meat, and Danny's prepared a pasta salad."

I thought our first encounter after what happened might be awkward, but Franco didn't make it that way. He smiled at me warmly and pulled up an extra patio chair beside Lily for me. The warmth from the patio heaters and pretty pool-side lighting gave the gathering a pleasant, relaxing feel.

"Sit down, Tess. I'll fill you a plate and bring you a drink. What would you like?" he asked.

"Anything," I replied, returning his smile.

"As long as it's not fava beans and a nice Chianti," Ivan quipped, then he ducked before I could clip him around the ear.

Chapter Eight

TESS

Franco was a harsh taskmaster. For a man supposedly in love with me and worried about my health and safety, he certainly didn't go easy when it came to my self-defence and combat training. I hadn't had this many bruises in forever. I can honestly say I felt the aches and pains more now than when Lily was still a baby. Franco, Jonesy, and I used to train for hours back then, and apart from being a little tired from having a young baby waking me up at night, I was always ready to take what they threw at me in the combat ring. To say I was lacking that same speed and agility would be an understatement. I might only be in my twenties, yet I felt decades older. I looked so much different now, too.

I knew I'd been putting on weight before Kolya was killed. I'd grown softer around the middle, and my hips and bum were a lot bigger. Kolya never complained and was as horny as ever when we were together. I just wish he'd been at home more in that last year. I used to miss him so much whenever he was away, and if I'd known what little time we'd had left, I would have pulled Lily from school and followed him wherever he went. But I didn't know. No one ever knows, and for that reason I felt like screaming out to couples that they should make every effort to be together, to live each day as if it's their last. I wish Kolya and I had done that. Perhaps if we had, I wouldn't feel as empty inside.

I gingerly turned over in bed, wincing at the ache in my shoulder from today's workout, along with the nagging ache that told me my period was due. After doing four sets of ten pull-ups from a tree branch, Franco had hung up a punch bag. He had me beat the hell out of it for a full ten minutes before pitching it lower so we could go ten minutes kicking at it. Due to Franco still receiving physiotherapy for the gunshot wound on his calf, we'd mainly stuck to upper-body workouts in the week since beginning my training sessions, so he'd devised other ways to build up my lower-body strength and resistance.

Neither of us had mentioned what happened between us, and to my relief, he hadn't tried to initiate anything else. Although, if I was being truthful, I'd often thought about having that level of intimacy again. Not because I'm in love with him or anything; I just miss the feeling of being held by someone in that way. Being with him that day reignited the need to feel wanted and loved by someone intimately. Though the person I wanted to share that with wasn't here anymore, it didn't mean I couldn't still have those feelings. Signor Russo had mentioned it on our walk that day, and he was right about so many of the things he'd said.

Of course, Signor Russo had also mentioned he thought I shouldn't have been exposed to guns and weapons training with my guards. I had to disagree with him for the simple reason that by having had that experience, I was able to save Lily, James, and Franco. But on the flip side of it, I would hate for Lily to be where I am now. That's why she needed to have a life away from KOLCAT.

Signor Russo had called by three times since I began training. On the first two visits, he'd voiced his displeasure at seeing Franco spar with me so roughly, but when he came by today, I actually made him smile. It was after our warm-up when Franco and I had gloved up and gone against each other in the makeshift ring. After feigning a dive, I caught him off guard and accidentally clipped the side of his jaw harder than planned. Franco went sailing backwards onto the yoga mats and Signor Russo and his guards fell about laughing like it was the funniest thing they'd ever seen. Of course, Franco got up and praised me immediately, but I think their continued laughter dented his pride a little, so maybe that's why the rest of today's workout was so gruelling.

I picked up my phone to check the time. It was just turned midnight, so I'd been in bed for an hour without sleep, which was nothing new. Despite me being so utterly exhausted after my workouts and looking after Lily, I was still struggling to get to sleep, although the nightmares were becoming less frequent. When they did happen, they didn't leave me with the same terrifying aftereffects—no panic attacks, screaming the villa down, or throwing up. I'd only had four since starting my new fitness regime, but Ivan had agreed to sleep beside me, just to be on the safe side.

I caught sight of him in the light from my phone. He was in Lily's bed, and his big, tattooed arms were wrapped around my daughter, a cuddly koala bear, and her doll. Ivan had promised not to have his usual vodka nightcap, so we hadn't had to put up with his snoring all week, which was a huge bonus. He'd been as good as gold with Lily, as per usual. He never once complained about having to move her back down the bed when she ended up lying across the pillows with either her bottom, feet, or hair in his face while she slept.

Ivan will make a great dad one day. Whichever lucky lady manages to land Ivan as her husband will have the most loyal, loving man with the world's biggest heart. They just have to get past that tough-guy persona and approach him when he's not hungry to find out what a catch he is.

Though I ached much less than I did during the night, the nightmare I'd had around 4 a.m. had left me feeling out of sorts. It wasn't like the rest of my nightmares—in that it didn't replay or twist things that had already happened. No, this was a strange yet disturbing one where Lily was calling for me and I just couldn't find her. It had shaken me so much that I had to climb into bed with her and Ivan so I could touch her, reassuring myself that she was here.

The fear of being apart from Lily just wouldn't leave, so when Franco told me to get ready for my training session, I point-blank refused. When he began to call me out on it, Ivan stepped in on my behalf and told him I'd be spending the day shopping with him and Lily. Franco had stood with his arms folded, feet apart, glaring at Ivan as if he were about to protest, but then his eyes widened a little when something seemed to pass between the two men. I don't know how Ivan communicated my anxiety to Franco, as I was sat behind him and couldn't see his face, but whatever he'd expressed, Franco immediately dropped the stern trainer act and volunteered to come with us.

In the end, everyone but Nate and Mark joined us in Catania, and we had a fantastic day sightseeing, shopping, eating one of the most delicious meals I have ever tasted, and taking lots of photographs.

The buildings in Catania are a fabulous mix of baroque and rococo, with pretty patterns on the pillars and ornate mouldings. Lily particularly loved it in the square due to the black lava elephant statue with the obelisk on its back, and we had to visit it every time we came here. It's in the middle of a fountain in front of the Cathedral of St Agatha, which is one of my favourite places on the island. Not only is the architecture and the artwork gracing the walls spectacular, but when I allow myself a few moments to sit there in silent prayer, I feel an overwhelming sense of peace. I know it shouldn't matter where you pray—it should be the depth of your faith that makes the difference—but there's something about the cathedral that calls to me. In fact, there's something about Sicily in general that really appeals to me. I feel safe at the villa. The winter weather is so much milder than at home, and the island itself is beautiful. I wouldn't want to stay year-round, but I could see myself coming back to Sicily time and time again, and when I said as much to everyone over dinner, they wholeheartedly agreed.

Before heading back to the villa, we stopped for gelato at Lily and Ivan's request. Of course, because Ivan ordered two cones for himself, Lily automatically wanted the same, so being Ivan, he gave in and bought her what she wanted, knowing full well he'd get to eat her second one anyway. Being premenstrual, the double chocolate chip with chocolate syrup was kind of a no-brainer for me; the chocolate-flavoured cone was an extra indulgence.

It was just as we were taking the first lick of our gelato that we felt the ground begin to move under our feet, along with a loud rumbling that seemed to come from everywhere all at once.

I dropped my gelato as I bent to grab Lily and ended up with hers on my jumper when I picked her up and held her close. Ivan's arms surrounded us while he used his bulk to shelter Lily and me from danger, but the minor earthquake was over within ten seconds or so.

A few moments after the rumbling stopped, Ivan let go of us and took a step back, cursing as he trod in one of the gelatos that he or I had dropped. Out of everyone walking through the square in Catania, only our party of six plus a few tourists looked panicked. Franco's eyes scanned the area around us, darting here, there, everywhere, looking for any visible threats from falling masonry before trying to herd us forward.

"We need to get back to the villa," Lainey declared. Her dark skin had become quite ashen, and although she was taking charge of the situation, she was visibly shaken by what had occurred. I hated seeing my friend so scared.

Danny tugged Lainey to his side and threw his arm around her. "Take a minute, Lainey," he commanded. "Do you see the locals? They don't seem worried by what just happened. This could be a regular occurrence to them, so if they aren't panicking, I suggest we don't, either."

Danny looked calm and collected; only the slight quiver in his voice gave away his unease at nature's show of force.

The man who'd served our gelatos came out of his shop and looked up above the buildings across from us. Franco conversed with him in Italian, following the man's gaze as he answered. He gestured towards me and said something else to Franco.

"What did he say?" I asked, thinking it couldn't have been all bad because he'd chuckled before ambling back into his little shop.

"He said it was probably Mamma Etna making her

presence felt. Whatever it was, I don't like it, and I agree with Lainey: we should head back to the villa ASAP. But Giuseppe here wants to replace your gelatos."

We all looked up above the buildings and saw that the volcano's smoky ash plume had become even denser than before, and wasn't that...? Bloody hell! Every now and then I spotted a fiery orange glow leaping up through the thick grey cloud that appeared so menacing against the darkening sky. Impressive though it was to behold, it was also quite worrying, and I couldn't wait to get Lily out of there.

***

Along with Nate and Mark, Signor Russo called us on our way back to the villa, reassuring us that, geographically, due to where the villa was built, we had nothing to fear from either earthquakes or *Mamma Etna*. He went on to tell me about the last time the volcano had erupted, which sent some of his earlier reassurances right out of the window, although realistically, I knew we'd have plenty of warnings if it ever did have a major eruption.

My normally so brave daughter wasn't so fearless when it came to discussing the earthquake with Nan via video call later that evening. I thought the anxiety she'd felt might have passed by then, but it hadn't.

Lily seemed fine with it at first, laughing over the fact I was covered in gelato. She thanked Giuseppe—the kind shop owner—for replacing the one I wore, and she even took a few licks of the fresh one as we made our way back to the vehicles. But when I picked her up to put her into her car seat, she refused to let go of me and threw the rest of her gelato on the ground.

It took around five minutes to get her to stop crying and

finally agree to sit in her seat. All the way home, Lily held my hand like she was afraid to let go, and it hurt to see her so distressed.

As soon as we arrived back, I told her I needed to take a shower, which Lily normally hates. But as she didn't want to leave me, she took off her clothes and followed me inside. Once I was finished, we ran the bath for her and talked about what happened. I told her she didn't need to be scared and tried to explain that we weren't in any danger. I truly thought she believed me at the time, but as she sat sobbing in front of Nan on the laptop, I saw how wrong I'd been. It didn't help that Nan began crying too, closely followed by Lainey—who hardly ever cries. I normally wouldn't have stood a chance of escaping without shedding a tear or two, but strangely enough, I was able to avoid crying.

It was only when Franco came in with a book he'd downloaded on his iPad that Lily began to calm down. It was a children's story all about Mount Etna and what it meant for the people of Sicily to live in its vicinity. The book was in Italian, so he offered to read it to her. What he hadn't expected was an audience of seven, as everyone in the villa other than Nate gathered on the surrounding sofas to listen in, learning how the volcano made the soil extra fertile so that more crops could grow, which made the farmers happy. After that first book, he downloaded and read another, then another, pointing out a few easy words in Italian for her to recognise. Franco wasn't normally so talkative, but he had all the time in the world for Lily—answering all her questions in a strange mix of his usual no-bullshit style with a side of child friendly. Had he been any different, I don't think she'd have let go of that fear. By being more like his usual self, she trusted he wasn't just trying to trick her into believing it was safe to be here.

By the end of the third story, Lily was fast asleep, so I took her up to bed and lay beside her. Ivan joined us a couple of hours later. He'd eaten his way through most of the food in the kitchen, which is his usual MO whenever he feels anxious.

"We'll need to go shopping tomorrow," was all he said before climbing into bed beside Lily.

After I spent a couple of hours tossing and turning, Ivan turned my way and mumbled sleepily, "Do you want me to make you a hot chocolate?"

"It's okay, I'll do it. I might stay up and read for a while," I whispered. I placed a gentle kiss on Lily's cheek, then leaned over and did the same with Ivan before slipping my robe on over my pyjamas and heading downstairs.

The tiles were cold underfoot, reminding me I'd forgotten to put on slippers again, so I grabbed my flip-flops from the bench in the hallway before checking to see if whoever was on duty in the tech room needed a drink. Nate sat at the desk, flicking from one screen to another, adjusting the focus of the camera around the front gates.

"Is everything okay?" I asked. Nate had been so focused on his task that I made him jump.

With his hand on his chest, he muttered, "Geez, Tess, warn a guy next time you decide to creep around after midnight?"

I placed my arms around his shoulders and hugged him from behind. "Sorry, I couldn't sleep, so I came down for a drink. Do you want anything?"

"No, I'm fine, honey. Are you okay? Did the earthquake shake you up? I gotta say it broke my damn heart to see Lily so upset."

"It shook me up at the time it was happening, but my main concern was for Lily. Knowing the earthquake was likely caused by Mount Etna feels kind of odd. Part of me is curious and finds it thrilling, but the part of me that's all mum wants to get Lily away from here as soon as possible," I admitted.

"I can understand that. When you're dealing with forces of nature, you're dealing with the unknown. No matter how much scientific evidence you're presented with, you can never be sure exactly what will happen. Me and Franco went to visit Sam, a buddy of ours who lived in Anchorage, after we left the army. We'd served together in Afghanistan, and his mom had recently passed from cancer, so he was hurting. Anyway, on our second night there, we were at a bar—a real fisherman's joint with rods and reels and fish decorating the walls. Although it was still early, we were already pretty wasted, and at first, I thought that was why the floor and walls seemed to move. I remember they had a giant swordfish hooked onto a wooden board that hung on the wall above the bar, and within a few seconds, the board went from tapping against the plaster to banging the hell out of it until the damn fish fell off and landed right there on the bar in front of us."

"What did you do?" I asked, imagining the scene he'd just described. "Were you scared?"

"It lasted fifteen or twenty seconds, that's all, and I think it took me at least five or six of those to realise it wasn't the alcohol causing everything to move. When it was over, the old bartender walked up to the swordfish, picked it up and said, '*Well, shit, Sherman, you're gonna give yourself a damn injury if you keep flippin' off your perch.*'"

I laughed out loud at his accent and the face he pulled as he did it. I'd not seen Nate smile so much lately.

"Anyway," he continued, "everyone in the bar went back to drinking; the guys at the back had to restart their game of pool 'cause the balls had obviously moved. The bartender and waitress picked up the rest of the stuff that had fallen off the walls, and that was it. When we'd arrived at the bar, I can't say I took much notice of how the drinks and glasses were placed, but I realised later they had a pretty neat setup with wire and rubber matting, making sure that all the alcohol and glasses were safe in the event of an earthquake. They were used to it, you see, so they adapted their lives around it. And it sure as hell wasn't gonna stop them drinking."

"I should think not," I said with a smile. I saw Nate glance down at his phone and then look up towards the monitor showing the entrance to the property. The high stone walls and tall gates were punctuated by a persistent fluttering moth, which looked so eerie when in night-vision mode.

"What's up, Nate? Are you expecting someone?" I asked with a nod towards the monitor.

"What? No, of course not. I just... I haven't heard from Kevin since this afternoon, that's all. He's been quiet all day, and I know he's been busy, but... I have a feeling there's something he's not telling me, Tess. And because I'm pissed with him, I'm doubling down my focus here to take my mind off it," he said, gesturing towards the monitors.

"You should have gone home with him, Nate. It's not good to be apart from the one you love. I missed so much time with Kolya with him being away on business, and I really wish I'd have put my foot down and demanded he stay at home."

"Do you think he would have?" he asked.

I shrugged my shoulders. "I like to think so, but I couldn't say for sure whether he would have put me and Lily before KOLCAT."

Nate didn't assure me that Kolya would have done as I'd asked if I'd given him an ultimatum. All he said as he tapped my arm was, "Kolya loved you, Tess. Never doubt that."

"Yeah, he did, but that didn't keep me warm at night every time he went away. And he did that so often last year. All those long, lonely nights I could have had Kolya with me, if only he'd made the decision to stay home and let someone else go in his place. So whenever you have the chance to be with Kevin, take it, Nate, because you never know what tomorrow will bring."

I left Nate to think about what I'd said and went to make a hot chocolate. The brand Signor Russo suggested was deliciously decadent and had become a firm favourite of everyone at the villa. I'd shipped some over to Nan, Jean, Karen, and Amina, and the latter had declared she was in love as soon as she'd tasted it. I could see it being a regular international order when we moved back to the UK. Mrs Braeburn at Glengarran is a big fan, too, and she sent me a photo of her and John enjoying a cup last week.

As I stirred my hot chocolate, I thought about how different our lives would be once we moved back home. I'd get to see Jean, Nan, and Jack in person, as well as my friends Karen and Amina, along with the rest of the staff at Sarah's Legacy. I'd been speaking to Dave, Kevin, and Andy via video calls, like everyone else, but I missed seeing them in person, especially as I'd been used to being in the company of these men almost every day before... before my world was ripped right down the middle and I lost the other half of my soul.

I missed Jonesy and Lucas, too. Lucas was quiet but caring and was a good listener. Jonesy was someone I and everyone else adored. He had that knack of making you feel better, even in the shittiest of situations. His jokes were hilarious, and he could sing better than anyone I'd ever met. He was tough when he needed to be, but like Ivan, he had a soft heart and loved fiercely. He was Kolya's chief guard for a reason, and not just because of his close protection abilities. Because, out of all of his guards, Kolya thought of Jonesy as a genuine friend.

Why did Kolya have to take Jonesy and Lucas with him? Why did he have to leave me and Lily just to open another build site? Weren't we and the life he already had enough for him? That last question, one I'd asked myself so many times since his death, seemed to pierce my armour this time.

A sudden wave of grief hit me from out of nowhere, almost dragging me down to the cold kitchen floor. I held on to the back of a chair for support, gasping for breath as hurt, loneliness, fear, and anger compressed my lungs so much that taking in oxygen just wasn't possible. I heard a smash and felt a few scalding splashes through my pyjama bottoms, but I couldn't cry out; my throat had closed off to air and sound. Luckily, Nate had heard the smash and came running into the kitchen.

I couldn't hear what he said at first as he lifted me in his arms and then sat on a chair with me on his lap; it was as though I was underwater, hearing him speaking to me from up above. I was vaguely aware of him taking out his phone, though I didn't know who he'd called until a bare-chested

Franco—wearing nothing but workout shorts—approached us. His hair was all mussed as if he'd been asleep, but his eyes were alert and focused on me.

"Come on, Tess, just breathe with me. I've got you, honey. You're safe with me," Nate murmured against my cheek as he rocked me back and forth. He placed his hand on my breastbone and commanded, "Deep breaths in and out now. Enough to see my hand rise and fall as your chest expands. That's it, honey, you're doing real good."

Franco crouched in front of us and placed his hands on my knees. When I glanced down at him, he shook his head. "No, baby, I want you to focus on Nate for a little longer. Just keep regulating your breathing in time with his, and while you do that, I'm gonna take a look at your legs, 'cause I'm assuming that's hot chocolate and not milkshake on those pyjama pants."

I nodded slowly and then burst into tears, taking in deep, gulping breaths with every sob.

Nate lifted me slightly so that Franco could pull my pyjama bottoms down my legs, adjusting my knee-length robe to cover my modesty. He tossed my pyjama bottoms on the floor beside my flip-flops, then examined the areas the hot chocolate had scalded.

"Just a few spots of redness here and there, Tess, but none look bad enough to blister. I'm gonna soak a dish towel in ice-cold water to cool them down, then we'll take another look, okay?" Franco said in a soothing voice. He used the table to haul himself up steadily, and I realised that crouching before me must have aggravated his injury.

Franco squeezed my hand gently before taking a step towards the sink, but as he released me, I grabbed his arm and didn't let go.

"Tess?" Franco raised his brows, glancing down at my

hand clutching his arm before meeting my eyes once again. Whatever he saw in them made him change his mind.

"Nate, can you carry her to my room? I'll make sure she's okay once we're there, then you can get back to your security detail."

Nate shook his head. "It's okay. I called Mark after I called you, so I can stay with Tess."

Franco kept his gaze fixed on mine before replying, "We got this, Nate, don't we, baby?"

"Franco, I don't think this is a good idea," Nate interrupted.

Franco held up his hand, then carried on speaking.

"We have a history of battling through tough times. Our girl here, she'll be fine once she lets a few of those fears go. I'll make that happen; I always do. You know that, don't you, Tess? You trust me to keep you safe, that we'll all keep you safe."

"I do," I sobbed. "I need to clean up this mess in the kitchen first—"

"Don't worry about that, honey. I'll take care of it." Nate pushed up from the chair with me in his arms, then followed Franco through to the annexe and into his bedroom. "I have some cream in my kit if you think the burns need it," he said as he placed me on top of Franco's unmade bed. The low light from the bedside lamp cast a soft glow over the polished wood furniture and crimson duvet.

"This one?" Franco asked as he opened up his toiletry bag and showed Nate a tube I couldn't see the name of.

Nate laughed and slapped Franco on the shoulder. "Dude, I guess it's true what they say. You *can take the man outta the military, but you can't take the military outta the man.* We all pack for every eventuality."

"And yet you moan at me for what I carry around in my bags," I remarked as I wiped my eyes and blew my nose on a tissue I found in the pocket of my robe.

Nate's eyes flashed to mine and he let out a bark of laughter.

"Honey, you don't need a purse or bag. You need a large cart with wheels for the amount you put in them. I mean, carrying the one you use for work is a health risk. You're gonna end up a hunchback."

Franco got me to raise my leg on the bed as he pressed what looked like a wet T-shirt against the small red burns. "Remember when she was looking for that bookmark Lily made, and she tipped her workbag out," he said. "I took one look at all the crap piled up on her desk as she rifled through it, and my first thought was, *'no fuckin' way did all that shit just come out of there,'* and then I watched in absolute fascination while she not only put everything back in, but she also added a book, a folder full of paperwork, and the gift Karen brought her from her vacation. Yep, that's when I knew our Tess here had a touch of witch about her," he said with a wink. Then he added, "But I should have known that already, 'cause she had me spellbound right from the start."

"That's a cheesy line, Franco. Does it normally work for you?" I asked with a groan, though I couldn't help smiling.

"It's not a line, Tess. You know that, and Nate knows it, too. I couldn't hide it from my best buddy here."

Franco smiled in reassurance, but I recalled what Signor Russo had said about loyalty and began to feel uncomfortable.

Nate must have noticed my discomfort because, as Franco went into the bathroom to wet the T-shirt again, he bent low to whisper in my ear.

"Tess, I think you should come with me or go back to

bed. You're obviously pretty shaken up from the earthquake, which could cause you to make decisions you might regret later."

Nate was right, and I swear I was about to leave with him, but when Franco came back in from the bathroom and handed me a cold, wet face cloth, telling me to place it over my eyes to take away the puffiness, I hesitated, just for a few seconds.

"Come on, Tess, do as you're told. It's late, and I'm too fucking tired for us to throw it down tonight, but I could pinch you if that helps?" Franco sighed, though he had a glint of humour in his dark-brown eyes.

"You're nuts, Franco, you know that?" I said as I pressed the cloth against my eyes and, decision already made, lay back on the bed.

"Yeah, and I love you too, baby," Franco replied before his lips brushed mine.

From the other side of the room, Nate said in a voice barely loud enough for me to hear, "Think about what you're doing, brother."

"Don't worry about it, Nate. It's all good," Franco reassured him. I heard the door close with a click, but the turning of the key in the lock seemed louder.

Chapter Nine

TESS

The room was silent for what seemed like an eternity after Nate left, and I thought Franco had left with him, but then I felt the bed dip slightly when he sat beside me.

"How are you feeling now, Tess?"

I blew out a breath, grateful for the cloth covering my eyes. "Honestly, Franco, I'm confused. I really don't know what set all that off. I was fine, I swear. I was talking to Nate in the tech room. He was telling me about when you two experienced an earthquake in Anchorage."

"Oh, yeah, that was weird as fuck. Did he tell you about the swordfish landing on the bar? Herman or Sherman, or whatever they called it. No one seemed to give a shit. It was like we were in the twilight zone; everyone went back to drinking and playing pool. Unfuckin' real."

"Were you scared?"

"Hell yes! If I hadn't been drunk, I'd have probably shit my pants. But I couldn't be sure at first if it was the drink causing the bar to sway. I'd had to hold the wall while taking a piss before it all happened, so I just thought, *I guess they make stronger beer in Anchorage,*' cause I sure as hell never saw the floor and room shake whenever I'd been drunk before."

I smiled at the tone of Franco's voice. It was normally quite gruff, and he could often seem dispassionate, but tonight he sounded relaxed and kind of playful. Wanting to see the facial expression that accompanied this different-sounding Franco, I lifted the face cloth from my eyes. Once again, my breath caught in my throat, but not from panic this time. Franco's full lips were pulled into one of the sexiest smiles I'd ever seen. A smile so genuine it caused creases at the corners of his eyes. Eyes that were heavy-lidded and framed by long black lashes that I, and probably every woman he met, was insanely jealous of. With his strong bone structure, tall height, and muscular physique, he looked like the kind of man the Romans would have commissioned a statue of. And he was here, with me, alone on a bed. The door was locked and we wouldn't be disturbed. If I just reached out and touched him…

"What do you want, Tess?" Franco asked. It took a moment for me to realise I'd been tracing my fingers across his chest.

"I think I want…" I shook my head. No, I didn't *think* I wanted him. I *did* want him. Wanted him to give me what he did last week. Needed him to grant me the intimacy I craved; to make me feel not only alive, but also at peace. Oddly enough, it was how I'd felt in St Agatha's Cathedral, and that was way too bizarre to think about right now. So I took a deep breath and admitted, "I want you, Franco."

For a moment, he said nothing. His facial expression went from playful to neutral, and I wondered if I'd just made a huge mistake. Then his eyes bored into mine as he asked, "Be sure this is what you want, Tess, because it's not gonna be like last time. You know that, right?"

"Yes, I do." I licked my lips, anticipation making my heart beat faster and my mouth water.

"But first, I'm gonna put some cream on your leg. I don't think it's that bad because your PJs were loose, so they protected you from the worst of it, but it won't hurt to be cautious."

What the hell? I thought Franco would waste no time at all before stripping me naked and doing the deed. What I hadn't expected was for him to delay having sex to take care of me. Not when he'd made it clear on so many occasions how much he wanted me.

Franco reached over to his toiletry bag and again pulled out the cream that he and Nate had talked about. Squeezing out a tiny amount, he gently smoothed it over the small, scattered burns.

"They don't hurt that much," I admitted, my eyes glued to his face the whole time. "It's just a slight sting, if that."

"That's real good, Tess. But you gotta tell me if you're hurting. You can't hold that back from me, baby. Whether the pain is here *or* up here," he said, tapping my leg, then my forehead, before placing the cream on his bedside table. "Promise me you'll tell me if we need to stop."

"I promise," I whispered.

Franco lifted my left leg and kissed the top of my foot before placing it flat on the bed, pushing my leg until my knee was fully bent. He did the same with the other leg, kissing my right foot and placing it flat on the bed, only this time, he pushed both knees apart. My knee-length towelling robe fell open, almost exposing my bare sex. All I had on underneath it was my Tatty Teddy pyjama top, hardly sexy by any means, and I felt a little self-conscious.

"Hey, where'd you go?" he questioned as he leaned over me and placed his hands on either side of my head.

"I was just thinking, I'm not exactly dressed for seduction, am I?" I bet I looked a mess, too, with my eyes all red and puffy from crying. Again!

Franco smirked. "I'd prefer it if you weren't dressed at all."

He lowered his head and began kissing from my left knee up my inner thigh but stopped just a few inches from where my robe covered the most intimate part of me; then he did the same with my other leg, again stopping short of where I thought he'd been headed. Though I felt an almost desperate need to have him take those kisses higher, I knew I'd regret it later.

It might seem odd to some people, but oral sex has always felt more intimate to me than intercourse itself, and I wasn't prepared to share that with anyone else yet, so when Franco moved my robe out of the way and kissed higher up my thigh, I put my hand over myself and said, "No, not that."

"Why not, Tess? I can make it good for you," he said with a seductive smile. Shaking my head, I moved to sit up, but he placed his hand on my belly, keeping me still.

"I can't give up everything, Franco, not yet. I'm not ready for it. I don't know if I'll ever be."

Franco moved from between my legs to lie beside me. Turning me to face him, he asked, "Then what do you want, Tess? If this is too much right now, I can wait. Believe me, I'm just happy to have you with me. I know you still have feelings for him; you'd have been a shitty wife if you didn't. I also know you feel a lot of guilt over what we did, and what we are about to do, but you shouldn't. You're not doing this because you're in love with me; you're using it and me as therapy. And I'm okay with that, baby, 'cause I know that won't always be the case. I told you before, I'll always give you what you need, and right now, you need me and what my body can give you."

Whatever resistance I had melted away at Franco's heartfelt words, and to prove it, I looped my arms around his neck and kissed him in a way that showed him just how much those words had meant to me. But before we went any further, there was something we needed to discuss that we had left to chance the last time.

Pulling away from him slightly, I took a steadying breath and asked, "Franco, do you have any condoms? Only, I'm not on any contraception, so…"

"Yeah, I—" Whatever Franco was about to say was lost when the realisation of the risk we had taken last week finally hit. His mouth opened as if he was about to say something, then closed again quickly before he uttered a word.

"Kolya and I were going to try for another baby, so I cancelled my Depo appointment," I told him. "The protection the injection gave will have run out months ago. I'm sorry, I should have mentioned it before."

Franco shook his head. "No, Tess, that was all on me. I should have thought to ask, but just so you know, I'm clean. What happened that day, getting so carried away that I didn't use a condom? I swear I've never done that before, not even when I was a horny teenager," he said with his hand over his heart for emphasis.

His gaze roamed down my body, coming to rest on my lower belly. "Is there a chance we could have made a baby? 'Cause you have to know, I'd be all in, Tess. We could get married, raise our family wherever you want, and give Lily a little brother or sister."

I closed my eyes before any tears could escape. It's what I'd wanted and planned with Kolya. Adding to our family, giving Lily a little brother or sister or both. Franco was offering me the life I'd so desperately wanted with my husband. It would almost be like living a dream, a good one this time. But if Signor Russo was to be believed, Roman Barinov would cut either Franco's or my own life short if we pursued it.

"I think I'm about to get my period any day now if the pains I've had are anything to go by, so I'd say we're safe. All the same, if we're going to do this, I'd be more comfortable if we use protection," I admitted, although I didn't share all my reasons.

For a moment, he looked disappointed. Whether it was because I didn't think I was pregnant or that he had to use protection, I couldn't really tell. Franco's sexy smile was back in place when he climbed over me to reach into his toiletry bag. He pulled out a condom and tossed it on the bed beside us.

"That's all I got, but don't worry; I'll get some more tomorrow."

Tomorrow? Franco thought this was going to be a regular thing, but I still wasn't sure what I wanted, and I knew it certainly wasn't safe to let too many people know, so we'd need to have a conversation about that. But now wasn't the time to discuss those things, not when Franco had untied the belt on my robe and was slipping it off my shoulders. After kissing my lips, jawline, and neck, he pulled my pyjama top over my head and tossed it on the floor.

"You're so beautiful, Tess. I love all your freckles and your perfect pale skin. You don't know how many times over the years I've wanted to kiss each freckle across your chest and shoulders."

Franco did exactly what he'd talked about, kissing and occasionally running his tongue across my chest, collarbone, and shoulders. I couldn't understand his fascination. I hated them, but Kolya used to say and do the same thing.

Thinking about my husband caused a sharp stab of guilt to slice right through me. I closed my eyes and remembered the last time he'd seduced me this way. We'd been for a late-night swim, and he'd stripped away the top of my bathing suit while kissing, licking, and sucking at my chest and shoulders. There's probably a place in hell reserved for people who think about another man when they're about to have sex with someone, but as I was probably headed there anyway, I let myself indulge in those thoughts for a while. Him rolling me onto my back and kissing me, touching my breasts, his tongue tracing circles around my nipples again and again before working his way down my belly. The slight scruff of his short, trimmed beard providing a rasping contrast against the sensitive skin below my pelvic bones, just like Kolya's used to before he shaved it off. It was that thought that brought me back to the here and now with Franco.

Grabbing a fistful of his hair, I tugged a little, so he'd look up at me.

"Don't worry, baby, I wasn't gonna go any further, but I gotta say, I'd love to make you come with my tongue, *over* and *over* again," he said as he circled a patch on my lower belly with his tongue before flicking it rapidly and sucking it between his lips.

Franco may as well have been doing what he'd just said from the reaction he caused. I gasped loudly as my clit pulsed and wetness coated my sex.

"Oh, fuck yeah, that's what I like to hear. You keep gasping and panting and letting me know how you're feeling," he said as he rolled to his side and slid his workout shorts off. Franco had been wearing nothing underneath, and his long thick cock sprang up towards his belly button now that it was finally free.

I couldn't help but compare the size of Franco and Kolya's manhood. But to be perfectly honest, they looked about the same. Same length, same girth. Kolya's was slightly paler, but Franco had a darker skin tone, so...

"Hey, Tess," Franco interrupted. "If you find my dick that fascinating, you can always touch it."

He wrapped his hand around it and gave it a few tugs, something I'd always found incredibly hot whenever Kolya did it.

I shook my head. I had to stop doing this. Thinking about Kolya while I was with Franco was so bloody unfair to him.

"No, put the condom on, Franco, or aren't you as ready for me as I'm ready for you?" I teased.

Franco smiled and tore open the wrapper. "Oh, I'm ready for you," he said as he slid the pink-coloured latex down his length. "In fact, I think it's about time you found out just how long I have been ready."

Instead of lying beside me, Franco remained where he was: kneeling on the bed and looking down at me with an almost feral look in his eyes. It made me slightly nervous, yet I also couldn't deny being highly aroused. He traced his fingertips over my breasts slowly, making his way down towards my pelvis with the gentlest of touches before grabbing me roughly and spinning me over so I was on my knees with him behind me. Instead of doing as I'd expected and taking me from behind, he pulled me upright, my back against his hard, muscular chest, my bottom resting on the front of his thighs.

"What the—"

"Shhh, it's okay. I got you, Tess. Just like I had you so

many times down at the range when I was teaching you to shoot; 'cept now we're both naked, and I get to touch you how I imagined doing then. So be a good trainee for me and hold those arms out steady as if you're holding a pistol," Franco commanded. Taking both my hands, he made them make the shape of a gun, then raised my arms out in front of me and demanded I keep them there.

"That's it, baby, you keep that position no matter what I do, 'cause that's the test you gotta pass tonight," he whispered in my ear while trailing his fingers up and down my sides. I flinched when he hit a ticklish spot near my waist.

"Oh, no, Tess. You gotta have more control than that when you're training. I learned that the hard way." He emphasised the hard by poking my bum cheek with his latex-covered length.

Franco moved my hair to one side, giving him access to my neck. "I had to control myself so many times when I was teaching you to shoot. We got so close while you learned to get your centre and steady your aim. Can you remember? I used to press my hand against your belly, just like this, so you could feel that centre and regulate your breathing," he said in between placing soft kisses on my neck.

"Sometimes I'd hear you hitch in a breath, and your pupils would dilate, and I'd wonder and hope, but I couldn't say anything. It took everything I had to keep control when all I wanted to do was run my hand down into your under-wear to see if your pussy was as hot and wet as I imagined it to be.

Franco's hands and fingers matched his words, and I let out a soft moan when he ran his fingers through my folds before circling my entrance, slipping a finger inside me.

"Just as I thought," he whispered before licking around the shell of my ear. "Hot, wet, and so fucking perfect."

My arms fell to my sides, and I whimpered my objection when he removed his finger, but I closed my eyes and tilted my head back against his shoulder when he ran it up the seam of my sex to find my clit. Franco didn't tease the little nub with gentle strokes or featherlight touches; he used a firm, consistent rhythm that had me bucking against his hand, begging him to make me come. And he did, letting me ride out my orgasm the way I needed, easing the pressure of his fingers slightly, yet not stopping the pleasurable rhythm, making it easy for him to send me soaring once again.

Before I could come down from my orgasm-induced high, Franco had me on my hands and knees with only the head of his cock inside me. I tried pushing back against him, wanting nothing more than to be filled by his thick, hard length, but he grasped my hips and held me still.

"No, baby, this is all about control, remember? I know you want more right now, just like I did when we were doing self-defence training on the mats and I'd pin you down. You'd buck your sexy ass up against my crotch, and it took every ounce of inner strength I possessed not to tear down those little shorts you used to wear and fuck you into oblivion, especially when you ignored what I told you and gave me sass. I wasn't sure whether to spank your ass or fuck it. And from the way your pussy just squeezed the head of my dick, I can tell that neither would have been a punishment for you. You'd have fucking loved it, wouldn't you, baby, getting down and dirty on the mats with me?"

Franco slammed home before I could answer, making me cry out in sheer bliss at finally getting what I needed. The sex was punishingly rough, yet desperately hot. I couldn't get enough, but then he slowed it down, reaching around to stroke my sex in time with each thrust, and my arms began to shake.

He pushed my shoulders flat to the bed, then grabbed a fistful of my hair and tilted my head to one side. The feel of his chest hair against my bare back when he draped himself over me sent tingles down my spine, but his lips on my neck directed those tingles straight to my sex.

"I couldn't do any of the things I wanted to do to you because you weren't mine, but I was already in love with you, Tess, and too fucking obsessed to walk away. And keeping you healthy and safe has always been more important than how I feel. Always has been, and always will be, no matter what happens between us. So I kept your training my number one priority in case someday you'd need it. And you excelled in it, baby. You always did good, even when I pushed you hard. You made me so proud, and you still do. Every. Damn. Day."

With his cock buried so deliciously deep inside me, his fingers massaging my clit and my body cocooned by his, I came harder than I had before, almost screaming my pleasure into the mattress. His words had an effect, too. They made me feel worshipped, almost, but definitely loved.

After the fog of ecstasy cleared, I realised Franco was muttering something under his breath in Italian.

"Franco, are you okay?" I asked while trying to pull away from him.

"Jesus, Tess, you gotta stay still for a minute, or this will all be over real quick," he said through gritted teeth. After a few seconds, he took a deep breath and then eased out of me, saying, "Your pussy gripped me so tight that when you came, you almost took me with you."

With a giggle in my voice, I mimicked, "It's all about control, baby."

Franco slapped both my arse cheeks and then rolled onto his back.

"Climb aboard, Tess; it's time to show me your moves," he declared as he helped me straddle him. Bedcovers scraped against the minor burns on my leg when I moved, but the slight sting of pain didn't bother me as much as what I was doing.

Something about this position caused an ache in my chest. I went through the motions required—holding the base of his cock so I could sink down onto him, adjusting my position so I could move freely—without once looking at his face. Because although the man underneath me loved me, he wasn't the one my heart still pined for. So I kept my eyes closed as I moved, trying hard to keep the tears at bay.

"Hey, look at me, Tess," Franco murmured.

I opened my eyes to find him gazing up at me lovingly, and I felt like such a bitch.

"If you don't feel comfortable doing this, you just gotta say, and we'll stop. No questions, no pressure. We just stop, okay?"

I couldn't do this to him, not when he'd just given me so much pleasure. I had to be as honest as I could without hurting him.

"I don't know how many women you've had sex with, Franco, and I'm not going to ask. It's none of my business. But you're only the second man I've had, and I never thought I'd be here, doing this with someone else. Part of me still feels this is so wrong."

"Then why do it?" he asked.

"Because last week, when you and I were having sex, it's the first time in months I've not felt dead inside. You made me feel alive, Franco. And just for a while, it gave me peace."

Franco sat upright and wrapped his arms around me, whispering how much he loved me and how I never have to feel like that again. Then he kissed me, softly at first, but when I kissed him back and lapped my tongue against his, the kiss changed to one so full of passion, I'm surprised we didn't combust.

I began to move, though he had me in such a tight grip that I could do little but grind down against him, yet it hit me in exactly the right place. "Oh, Franco, right there, just, ahh."

"Yeah, just like that. You're taking every fucking inch of me," he groaned.

Franco thrust his hips up into every grind, and that's what had me moaning out loud, saying, "Franco, I can't, I can't, I can't," before spiralling into a climax that he refused to let me deny myself.

Franco lifted, then lowered me, slamming me down onto his cock over and over until he erupted inside me. Despite the condom, I felt every pulse and each splash of heat as he came.

"You're amazing. My own Mamma Etna," he mumbled against my throat.

Still breathing heavily, I pulled away from him slightly. "Did you just compare me to a volcano?"

Franco lay back on the bed and, smiling cheekily, held up his hands. "Hey, I wasn't the first to say it. Giuseppe at the gelato shop mentioned it earlier. He said the earthquake was from Mamma Etna, and if I looked, I'd see she looked like you: fierce and topped with fire."

"So he compared my hair with molten lava? Well, that's a first. I've had carrot top and ginger nut, but never lava.

And he definitely got fierce wrong, especially after the panic attack I had earlier."

"Give yourself a break, Tess. You are dealing with more than just your first earthquake. And anyway, I think you're fierce. You dove straight for Lily and made sure she was safe. You didn't wait for us to do anything; you went straight into mamma mode and didn't give a fuck about your own safety. I think you're just like Etna, Tess: fierce and hot as hell! And right here and now, you're all mine. So lie with me, just for a few minutes, before you have to go back and be a mamma again."

Chapter Ten

TESS

As soon as I awoke, I could feel that something wasn't right, even though I'd managed to sleep for over five hours without waking up from a nightmare. I'd climbed back into my own bed after leaving Franco and must have fallen asleep as soon as my head touched the pillow.

Lily was still fast asleep, but I could hear Ivan speaking Russian in hushed tones from behind the en-suite bathroom door. I climbed out of bed and hurried towards it, knocking as quietly as I could before whispering, "Ivan, is everything okay?"

He opened the door and beckoned me inside before closing it behind me.

Switching to English for my benefit, he said, *"I will call you as soon as he gets in touch again, but you know I cannot leave Tess and Lily, especially after what you've just told me,"* to whoever was on the line. He paused for a moment, then whispered, *"Paka, Yuri. Keep me updated, and I will do the same for you regarding Simeon."*

"What's going on, Ivan? Has something happened to

Simeon?" I asked as I stepped towards him. He reached out and pulled me into his chest, holding me tightly against him.

"I received a call from Al…my friend. He told me his little boy had a fit last night after suffering a fever, and he's been taken to hospital. They are doing tests at the moment to see what is wrong. I called Yuri because I knew he'd be concerned. He wanted me to go to him, but I can't leave you and Lily."

"Of course you can go," I told him. "I have enough people here, and I'm sure that Signor Russo will send a guard."

Ivan squeezed me a little tighter before taking a step away. Wiping a shaking hand across his face, his chest heaved with a troubled sigh. His *Star Wars* sleep shorts were the only piece of clothing on his tattooed muscular body, and combined with the slight overgrowth on his normally neat beard and his dark brown hair sticking up on one side, our big Russian behemoth seemed so vulnerable.

"Oh, Ivan. I know how worried you must be, but try to keep positive. He has doctors and nurses with him now, and I'm sure they'll have him right as rain in no time. Febrile convulsions aren't uncommon in babies and young children, and as long as they manage to lower his temperature, he might not have another. The most important thing is that they find out what's causing the fevers, and now that he's in hospital, they should be able to do that."

"Yes, you are right. I know this," Ivan replied. "It's just that…he's still a baby, Tess. And he only has his mother and father with him. No other family can be there other than me, even though he has so many who would love him." Ivan shook his head as if clearing away his thoughts. "It has to be that way, you see. We have to keep everyone safe at all costs. Even if it's at the price of a child's happiness."

"No other family?" I queried. I tried to replay in my mind everything that Ivan had said to me about Simeon, and a thought suddenly occurred to me. "Ivan, is Yuri Simeon's father?"

Ivan raised his sad blue eyes to meet mine. "Define what makes a father, Tess? Is a man worthy of that name simply by means of biology, or is the name earned through caring for the child through sleepless nights, endless toilet training, fevers, picky eating, and bedtime stories? We can all throw the word love around, though I think few people understand the true meaning. What I can tell you is that Simeon has two men who love him unconditionally, yet he will only ever call one of them father. Maybe one day I will be able to say more, but right now, it is not my story to tell."

I nodded slowly and squeezed his arm in reassurance. I knew that he was right. The Barinovs' secrets were often dangerous, and if Roman ever found out that Yuri had fathered a child with someone, he would want that child to be brought up in their world. Yuri was poised to take over from Roman when the unthinkable happened, so the fact that Yuri had a son gave him another heir. But I'd always thought Yuri was gay, not bisexual. I would never have imagined him being in a relationship with a woman. Maybe it had been a one-night stand…

"There's something else you need to know," Ivan said as he sat on the edge of the bath. "Yuri says they've found Riass. They received intelligence saying that he was hiding in Azerbaijan near an area that borders Turkey, and after forty-eight hours of reconnaissance, they confirmed it. Roman's team, along with Rashid, Greg, and eight men supplied by Gustav, are about to storm a village he's taken over. Their orders are to take Riass's men by deadly force while searching for captives, of which, as we guessed by now, there has been no sign. Riass is to be kept alive, if possible, so they can question him further, but you and I both know he will not talk."

My stomach sank, and my vision blurred. I wanted to sit beside Ivan, but my feet felt like lead weights, and I couldn't seem to move.

Could it really be true? Had they finally found him?

I looked him in the eyes and asked, "When?"

"They're going in now, Tess. I assume that's why there are people up and around downstairs. We have to be prepared for retaliation, and to do that, we need to get you and Lily back to Oxford."

Ivan held up his hand when I went to protest.

"You don't have to stay in the extension. Kevin has made the guards' quarters in the old manor just as safe as the main property. You and Lily can sleep in my room with me until the threat level is low enough for us to find a more permanent home." Shrugging his shoulders, he added, "Or if things go well today, we can always come back here."

I closed my eyes and took in a deep breath. "I don't know if I'm ready for this, Ivan, and I don't mean the upheaval and the journey back to Oxford."

Ivan pulled me into his chest and wrapped his arms around me. "I know what you mean. It won't be easy to find out exactly what Riass did with the bodies after he killed everyone, but they are owed a decent funeral where their families and friends get to say goodbye to the person they loved and lost. It is a right that no one should be denied. And it will help with the grieving process, too. You will also need to decide where you would like to bury him. James will probably want his grave to be in the UK, possibly near his mother, but Roman will insist he's laid to rest in the Barinov family plot next to Kolya's mother. I know this is probably not a great time to bring it up, but I didn't want you to be blindsided by demands from either of them, if or when they get information from Riass."

"Thank you," I said, and then I hugged Ivan as tight as I could before finally letting go. Whatever happened, I knew he'd have my back.

"I'm going to grab a quick shower before Lily wakes up," I told him as I took a clean towel from the rack. "I'll pack enough essentials for the next few days and leave the rest here. I'll have to buy new clothes for Lily anyway because we're hardly equipped for wintery UK weather, and she's grown so much in the last few weeks."

"I'll go downstairs and see what the plan is before I go back to my room, then after I've showered, I'll call Yuri for an update. No doubt Kevin will be taking orders and intel from Gustav, but Yuri will give me information from Roman's side. I feel it will be good to have it from both perspectives, do you agree, Tess?"

"It depends on what the information is," I replied before closing the door behind him.

I stared at myself in the mirror before getting undressed. I should have been more prepared for this, but they'd been trying to find Riass for months without success. Unlike James, I chose not to think about what they'd done with Kolya and his men. Seeing their bodies being beaten and piled on top of each other like rubbish on a heap—the blood on their shirts and the fatal bullet wound in Lucas's head—all those images would stay with me forever. I tried to think of the last time I saw each man full of life and vitality, rather than those macabre scenes. Most of the time, that worked for me, but my nightmares were another matter. James couldn't get past his father's suffering and how they'd attacked his body after death, and Roman would never be able to rest until he brought Kolya's body home. Though I worried about the outcome of today's raid, I hoped it would ease some of their sufferings and bring closure for James and Roman.

The water always took a minute or two to heat up, so I switched on the shower and then went to the loo while I waited. Seeing the blood on the toilet paper when I wiped was such a relief. While I'd had period pain and the usual monthly symptoms, I'd still had that nagging doubt that they were all in my head, as if they were only there by wishful thinking. If the news I'd just woken up to had taught me anything, it's that what Franco and I did was definitely a mistake, and though he probably didn't want to hear it, pregnancy would be a dangerous complication while my surname was still Barinov.

The repercussions of finding Riass and his hideout would likely take weeks or even months to settle— depending on whether we involved other, more *legitimate* agencies. Knowing Roman, he'd want to extract information by any means necessary from Riass and his men before finding and eliminating any existing cells or hideouts in his own lethal way. Of course, Gustav would insist we play by the rules, but if it were up to me, I'd back Roman and his methods. Although Riass and his followers no longer claimed to be ISIS, they were all still terrorists, and terrorists deserve no mercy.

I'd just fastened my bra when Ivan strolled back into the bedroom with two cups of tea. Luckily, I'd already got my knickers on, but I doubt he would have batted an eye even if I was naked.

"Have you looked outside yet?" he asked as he put the cups down on top of the chest of drawers.

"If you haven't already noticed, I'm still getting dressed," I replied, pulling on my jeans. They went on so much easier now. I wasn't sure how much weight I'd lost, but I'd had to start wearing a belt in the first couple of weeks of being here. Lily wasn't the only one who needed new clothes once she got back to England.

Ivan completely ignored me and pulled back the curtains.

"Look, Tess, you have to see this before they get rid of it. Nate said it started falling around 5 a.m. and only stopped an hour ago. Signor Russo's men are sweeping it away, but he'll have to get someone in to clear the pool."

Picking my green sweater up off the bed, I made my way over to the window.

"What the hell is that?" I asked a bit too loudly, causing Lily to stir in the bed behind us. But my sudden outburst could certainly be excused after first laying eyes on the scene below.

"It's ash and tiny bits of rock from Etna. It's everywhere, Tess. Apparently, this is nothing compared to how bad it is in Catania. Russo's men are sweeping it into piles; they've already done the driveway. The ash cloud has cleared now, but Catania Airport will be closed for another five hours, at least. Yuri could send us a plane to Palermo Airport, but it means travelling across the countryside for two and a half hours to get there, which Franco said would cause a fuck ton of problems with security. So I think we'd better stay put until later."

"I agree; it leaves us open and vulnerable along a much longer, unfamiliar route. Any other day it wouldn't have been a problem, but knowing what's going down…"

"Exactly," Ivan affirmed. Neither of us had taken our eyes away from the strange scene below, and I had to admit, I found it oddly fascinating. But I knew Lily wouldn't see it that way.

"We have to find a way to spin this to Lily so she's not scared." I pulled on my sweater and lifted my hair out from under the neckline. "Any ideas?"

Ivan scratched his head. "In the first story Franco read, it said Mamma Etna gave farmers the gift of fertile soil to make the crops grow, so we could say that the black ash and rocks mean Mamma Etna has decided it's gift-giving day. We'll let Lily choose something she wants and say it has come from Mamma Etna." He passed me a cup of tea, then took one for himself.

"Good thinking," I told him. After taking a sip of my tea, I asked, "Did you go outside?" although I already knew the answer. Ivan was curious like me and would have had to see for himself the consistency of it.

He grinned. "Of course I did. I had to know what it felt like. Some of it comes apart in your fingers, like soot, but a lot of it is like gravel. I'm taking some back with me for Nan and Jack so they can put it in their plant pots."

"Are we going to see Nan and Jack?" Lily piped up from behind us. She stretched out her arms and yawned loudly before climbing out of bed.

After taking another drink of my tea, I said, "We're flying to England today, Lilypot, so we'll see them soon."

"What are you looking at?" Lily asked as she came to stand beside us.

Ivan put down his tea and lifted her up to show her. "Mamma Etna decided to give everyone a gift to make the plants and trees grow. Can you see it?"

Lily gasped, then put her hand over her mouth as she

took in the black debris covering the pool, patio and orchards. "But it's everywhere, Ivan, even the pool. Plants and trees shouldn't grow in swimming pools, should they, mummy? I think Mamma Etna must have made a mistake."

"It wasn't in the pool at first," I fibbed, "but the wind blew it around where it wasn't supposed to go. Silly wind. But never mind, we can always sweep it up and take it where it needs to go, and because Mamma Etna has made it a special day for giving, you are allowed to choose a gift before we go back to England and see Nan and Jack."

Lily's eyes lit up, and a huge smile spread across her face. "Are we going to see them today?"

"I'm not sure. We have to wait a while until the plane arrives, so you have plenty of time to choose your gift from Mamma Etna."

Lily waved her hand dismissively. "Oh, don't worry, I already know what she can send me."

"What's that, Lilypot?" Ivan asked.

"My daddy."

I didn't say anything because what more *could* I say about Kolya not coming home that hadn't already been said?

Glancing over Lily's shoulder, Ivan stared at me for a moment, silently asking what we should do. I shook my head, hoping she'd forget about it. At least she wasn't frightened by the black ash and rocks covering our beautiful Sicilian hideaway.

Chapter Eleven

TESS

After hours of waiting around for news of when our journey home could be arranged, we were finally told that Roman had a plane en route to us and could expect a flight back to Heathrow departing at 8 p.m. Sicilian time. As Sicily was an hour ahead of the UK, it meant we would land at Heathrow at 10 p.m. Adding in the extra time it would take us to get back to Oxford meant Lily would be exhausted when we arrived at the manor. I tried to get her to have a nap during the day, but she was having none of it. To be honest, I think she was feeding off the pent-up emotions coming from everyone around her. We'd been on tenterhooks all day, eagerly awaiting more information since learning about their successful capture of not only Riass but also one of his main men, Najaf Bashir—also known as the executioner—the terrifying man who'd beheaded Riass's captives on camera for all the world to see.

As far as we were aware, Roman's men had Riass and Bashir, and the rest of the terrorists were dead. But other than our flight information, we'd heard nothing more from anyone, despite our constant calls and messages. What concerned us most was not knowing whether we had suffered any losses or injuries during Riass's capture, and the only reassurance Kevin could give us was that our men were coming back to England. Dave couldn't seem to get us off the phone quick enough, and the last time we called James he wouldn't even answer.

Nate had slept most of the day, after having been up throughout the night, and seemed both angry and disappointed with Kevin, accusing him of keeping him in the dark, but Kevin either couldn't or wouldn't give us any further information.

Franco and Danny manned the tech room all day, and though both men had tried frequently to get updates through the secure system, neither gained any intel.

It just didn't add up. I had a feeling there was something major they weren't telling us, and I worried that perhaps the threat against us here was bigger than we thought, especially when Signor Russo came to the villa to escort us to the airport with seven armed men.

He'd been with us earlier that morning while we'd waited for information and had promised to keep the villa free for us to return to, although we'd packed up all our belongings, just in case.

Signor Russo hadn't seemed as on edge earlier. He'd told us stories about Mount Etna and said the amount of ash and debris we'd woken up to wasn't anything new. He admitted it had taken his family quite a while to get used to after all those years spent living in the States, but he made light of it for Lily's sake.

Russo and his brother had been born near the villa where he now lived, but the family moved to New Jersey when he was four, so he remembered very little from his childhood on the island. That gave me hope for Lily. Would she still remember everything that had happened with the gunmen back in Oxford when she was an adult? While I hoped she wouldn't, I knew deep down it was likely to be a memory that would never fade.

Before we left, Signor Russo spoke to Franco alone for five minutes, then came to find me. When pressed, he said he'd heard no more than we had about the capture of Riass, but due to the circumstances, he'd ensure his men protected us until we were safely in the air. He also took a little time to ask me about the burner phone he'd given me. He reiterated what I should do if I needed him, but I assured him I'd be as safe as possible once we were back in Oxford, even though the mere thought of being near my former home made my anxiety level spike.

Rather than take all our luggage with us, we opted to leave some behind in case we came back. Our host kindly offered to send it down to the yacht if we stayed in England.

After Roman had told us they'd flown Yannis's and his guards' bodies back to the Princess Annis before staging their deaths elsewhere later that night, I couldn't bear to even think about the vessel. The yacht had featured in so many of my nightmares that, apart from wishing all the crew a Merry Christmas and instructing our accountant to send each of them a huge seasonal bonus in their wage packet, I'd put it to the back of my mind.

Leaving the villa felt wrong, which made no sense at all since I'd been pestering Kevin to let me know when it was safe for us to go to Glengarran. No matter what was going on with Riass or with any other threat, I'd made a connection with Sicily in the past few weeks that would stay with me forever, and I'd felt safe on the stunning Mediterranean island. Even the active volcano didn't bother me as much as going back to a place where armed men had taken us by surprise and turned me into a killer.

At least Etna gave people prior warning when things were about to get dangerous.

Saying goodbye to Signor Russo at the airport brought tears to my eyes. He'd become a good friend and confidant during our stay, and I vowed to keep in touch, no matter the miles between us. What finally made those tears fall was seeing Franco returning Signor Russo's warm embrace before we boarded our plane. I couldn't hear any of the words spoken, but both men smiled, and I'm sure I spotted tears in the older man's eyes.

Franco sat beside me on the plane, with Lily and Ivan sitting opposite. She fell asleep almost as soon as we'd taken off, so the three of us chatted quietly about security going forward. Apart from asking if the tiny burns on my leg were okay, Franco hadn't mentioned what happened between us last night. To be honest, we'd hardly had any time alone to discuss it, and at the moment, that suited me fine.

Lainey, Danny, Mark, and Nate took the seats behind us, playing poker for most of the flight, though Nate kept getting up and moving around the cabin. He was restless, growing angrier with Kevin by the minute for not answering his calls. Ivan also had a similar lack of response from Yuri, though he'd answered some of his earlier messages—albeit with vague one-word answers.

Ivan and I stopped calling James after leaving what must have been our tenth voicemail. Dave rang Ivan just before we stepped on the plane, telling him he'd be waiting for us at Heathrow and that Ivan would have to fly us back, as Andy was busy with James in London. I wondered if he was meeting with someone from the security services about intel that Riass might have unwillingly given, but when pressed, Dave wouldn't or couldn't say.

Roman had made it clear that, other than arranging our safe transportation from Sicily, he would be busy extracting information from Riass and Bashir. Of course, Roman was still in Moscow, and as far as we were aware, Riass and Bashir were being held somewhere near Turkey, but when I'd pointed that out to my father-in-law, all he said was, *"Moya doch, it is surprising what you can do online these days,"* so I supposed Roman was overseeing Riass and Bashir's torture remotely.

I thought I'd been prepared to face England's cold February weather, but stepping off the plane at Heathrow proved a bit of a shock. It was so frosty that even the surface of the runway was slippery.

I'd woken Lily up so she could go to the toilet before we disembarked. She was absolutely exhausted, so she wasn't at all happy about it. Lily remained in a grouchy mood right until we were seated in the helicopter, where she'd promptly fallen asleep again, thank goodness. Not even the promise of seeing Nan and Jack tomorrow had stopped the strop she'd thrown when we'd passed through security. Luckily, Dave had been there to greet us, so we'd not had to wait long in the airport's VIP heli-lounge before Ivan got us a take-off slot, enabling him to fly us back to Oxford within the hour.

The anxiety and dread I felt on our approach to what had been my home for almost six years were so bad it almost made me throw up. I wanted to tell Ivan to turn around and take us back to the airport or Glengarran, anywhere but here, and I might have done just that if not for Franco taking my hand in his and whispering, "Breathe, baby, just breathe. We're all here with you. You're not doing this on your own. If you don't feel right being here, we'll fly back to Sicily tomorrow."

I gripped his hand tightly until we landed, taking deep breaths in and out as slowly as I could to prevent another panic attack, and before I knew it, we were ready to disembark.

Franco unbuckled Lily and lifted her up carefully so he didn't wake her. Then the door opened and Greg greeted us. I'd assumed he was still in Turkey.

He hurried us into the newly refurbished kitchen where the kettle was boiling and two plates of sandwiches sat waiting for us on the table. Kevin appeared a few seconds later, and after greeting us, pulled Nate into his arms.

"God, am I glad to have you home," I heard him murmur against Nate's neck.

Nate seemed reluctant to hug Kevin back at first, but then his shoulders sagged and he returned his loving embrace.

"Why all the secrecy, Kev? What was I supposed to think when you were avoiding my calls?" he asked.

"I'm sorry. I know I owe all of you an apology about that, but Roman said he made you a promise, and he wanted to be the one to tell you what you need to hear," Kevin said. "Please understand, Tess, I wasn't on board with doing it this way, but then someone else gave the same order, so I had to obey. We all did."

"What are you talking about, Kevin? Roman said he was busy with Riass and Bashir; he hasn't spoken to us in hours," I told him.

"I'm sorry, Tess, I can't—" Kevin stopped speaking and

glanced down at his buzzing smartwatch before taking his phone out of his pocket.

"How long?" Greg questioned.

"ETA three minutes," Kevin replied. He stared at me, and I could see he desperately wanted to say something.

Everyone in the kitchen had stopped moving, and all eyes were on Kevin.

From just inside the doorway, Ivan asked, "Is James on his way?"

Kevin ignored Ivan and glanced down at his phone again before typing something on the screen.

"Who the fuck is coming here, Kevin?" Franco asked in a menacing tone. Lily stirred in his arms but didn't wake.

A thought occurred to me. "It's Roman, isn't it? Shit, Kevin, you should have put him off. It was risky enough in Sicily, but coming here is madness."

Kevin's phone rang just as I heard a helicopter overhead.

"It's for you," he said as he put it on speakerphone and passed it to me. He signalled to Greg, who promptly went outside.

A quick glance at the screen told me it was my father-in-law.

"Roman, what's going on?" I asked as I made my way over to the window. I could see the lights from the helicopter as it descended.

"Tess, I made you a promise the night the mercenaries attacked your home. Can you remember what that was?"

Though he obviously couldn't see me, I shook my head as I watched the helicopter touch down.

"You were so distressed whenever I spoke about finding Kolya alive, knowing that all the intel we'd received so far had come to nothing. So I promised I wouldn't speak about finding my son again until I could bring him home to you."

Greg opened the door to the helicopter and Tanner stepped out, closely followed by James.

Roman carried on speaking as I watched James help someone else out of the helicopter. "*Moya doch*, tonight I can fulfil the promise I made to you."

When the man turned his face towards the lights, my breath caught in my throat, and my knees buckled.

Lainey, Danny, and Nate rushed towards me, checking that I was okay, but I couldn't find the words to answer. Nate offered to help me up from the floor just as James and his father came into the kitchen.

Ivan cried out Kolya's name, but it sounded like it had come from afar. Franco yelled, "Tess," and I heard Nate say, "We've got her," before he pulled me upright, though my legs were like jelly.

"Is this a dream?" I asked as my vision blurred with tears.

Someone wrapped their arms around me, and a voice I never thought I'd hear again answered, "No, my darling, I am here with you. Where I belong."

Chapter Twelve

TESS

I threw my arms around Kolya and held on tightly, never wanting to let go ever again. He collapsed to his knees, taking me with him as tears streamed down my face. He pressed his lips against mine, but our convulsive gasps of heavy sobs kept breaking the kiss. I leaned back a little, running my fingers down his face, tracing every feature of the handsome man I loved so much.

He'd lost an extreme amount of weight. His eyes appeared sunken, and his cheekbones were as sharp as blades. He wore a plain grey sweatshirt and matching joggers, which made him appear bigger than he seemed, but with my arms around him, I could feel how prominent his ribs were. When he looked at me and smiled, I noticed he had an upper tooth missing.

"Oh, Kolya, what have they done to you?" I sobbed.

"Shhh, not tonight, my darling. We can talk about it tomorrow, but for tonight, I want to hold you and forget. Can we do that?" he asked in a croaky, tear-filled voice.

"We can," I whispered, and pulled him into an even tighter hug, breathing him in.

"What about Jonesy?" Ivan asked as he wiped the tears from his eyes.

"He's still in hospital," James replied. "Both he and my dad received fluids and whatever emergency medical treatment they had available at the scene and on the flight back to the UK, and I took them straight to the hospital when they landed. Jonesy's nose, left arm, and wrist were broken during his captivity, so he's having surgery to realign and reset the breaks. Other than that, he seems as well as can be expected. Dad has to go back tomorrow for a few more checks, but he wanted to be home with his family tonight."

Kolya turned his head towards Franco. "Can you bring her over, Franco?"

I pulled away from Kolya and wiped my eyes, watching Franco walk towards us. He crouched down and placed Lily in Kolya's arms.

"I'm glad you're okay, boss," he said, then his eyes met mine. The utter devastation I saw in them made my heart sink.

"She's grown so much," Kolya whispered while running the back of his fingers against her cheek. Lily sighed in her sleep, and Kolya smiled as he placed a gentle kiss on her forehead. "Though I don't want to take my eyes off either of you, I'm too exhausted to do anything other than sleep."

James came and knelt beside us on the kitchen floor. "Come on, Dad, let's get you something to eat and then to bed. The doctor said you need plenty of rest. Do you want to take the sleeping pills he gave you?"

Kolya closed his eyes and sighed. "I don't want to take them, but I think I might need to. Not to fall asleep, you understand. It's to keep me that way. They used to wake us regularly. I don't know how many hours they let us have before doing so, but it didn't feel like long. I want to be in our bed tonight with Lily sleeping beside us, and I don't want to keep waking her up if I can't rest."

"I understand," I told him, which wasn't a lie, but he needed to know I couldn't sleep here.

"Would it be okay if we slept next door in the manor? After what happened the last time we were here, I really don't feel comfortable staying the night."

Kolya shook his head. "James told me a little about it, and I can't tell you how angry I am that you and Lily were under threat." Glancing around the room, he said, "Thank you, everyone, for keeping my family safe that day."

"If it wasn't for Tess, things might have turned out very different on more than one occasion," Franco remarked.

Kolya seemed confused. He glanced at James, who patted him on the shoulder. "We can talk about all that tomorrow, Dad. Let's all get some rest tonight. God knows we need it."

James looked around at everyone and shook his head, placing a finger against his lips to let us know not to say any more about it. While I understood his reasons for not telling Kolya the truth about what happened here, he wasn't the one struggling to keep the memories of the attack at bay.

Ivan took Lily from Kolya, and James helped him stand. He looked so weak and vulnerable that I decided to go along with whatever he wanted, despite my reservations. I knew I wouldn't be able to sleep, but that didn't matter. I'd probably spend the entire night watching over my husband to reassure myself he was truly here.

After taking off Lily's coat and shoes and tucking her in my and Kolya's king-size bed, Ivan and I made our way back to the kitchen, where Kolya sat at the table with Kevin and Nate drinking tea. He had a half-eaten sandwich on the plate in front of him but looked in no hurry to finish it. James had been on the phone with Roman, who informed him they'd been able to extract valuable information from Najaf Bashir, although Riass hadn't been as accommodating.

"Are they still breathing?" Kolya asked with a menacing tone in his weary voice.

"For now," James replied. "But you shouldn't dwell on that tonight. Just leave it all to me and my grandfather. Are you sure you don't want me to make you anything else to eat?"

Kolya shook his head. "The doctor said I should try to eat little and often or my stomach will rebel. We sometimes went several days without food."

Ivan swore under his breath. "Kolya, I am so sorry for all you went through. I can't tell you how happy I am to know you are safe. We all thought you were dead after seeing the video."

Kolya looked at me. "I honestly thought I was going to die the morning of the ambush. Darius said he was feeling sick, so I asked Lucas to pull over. When we did, he opened the door and ran. That's when we realised it was a setup. Lucas tried to get us out of there, but Darius had left the front passenger door open, so he had no protection from their bullets. Darius had removed all our weapons from inside the car while we were in the meeting, so we couldn't even return fire. They eventually pulled us out of the vehicle and had Jonesy and I kneel. I felt the barrel of a gun at my back and thought I'd breathed my last, but they hit us with a sedative instead of killing us. We woke up later that night in a cellar of some sort before being moved again. Riass already had the missile, so he thought he only needed me for the codes. Obviously, Darius wasn't aware that we transport every guidance system separately. Riass thought he could still get his hands on it, so he kept us alive, believing he could use me and Jonesy later."

"I'm sorry about Lucas," I whispered as I bent to kiss his cheek.

"He was a good man, and he didn't deserve to die that way," Kolya declared. "I wish I could get my hands on Darius."

Everyone in the room voiced their agreement.

Ivan sat at the table beside Kolya. "I will raise a glass or two for Lucas tonight, and a few more to celebrate the safe return of you and Jonesy," he declared. Then he added, "While it may not seem like a good time to leave you, I have to go away for a couple of weeks. My friend's son is ill in hospital, and I promised I would visit when I could. You have Andy and Mark available to fly you anywhere you need to go, but I assume you will take a couple of weeks to reconnect with your family."

Kolya nodded and took my hand in his. "I never want to be away from them again," he said before pulling me onto his bony lap.

Chapter Thirteen

TESS

I lay beside my husband in our bed, my hand on his arm, listening to him breathe. The extra security lighting Kevin had installed shone through the gap above the curtain rail, casting an eerie light around the bedroom.

Being in our home made me anxious. Even the slightest noise from outside our room had my guts churning. If we were attacked right now, Kolya wouldn't be able to protect us. He was out for the count even before his sleeping pills kicked in.

I still couldn't believe he was here beside me, living, breathing, loving, and guilt rained heavily on my soul for all that had happened with Franco.

Kolya would be devastated when he found out, and though I didn't want to break his heart, I knew I couldn't keep it from him. But where would that leave us? Would he still want me as his wife? Would he find it in his heart to forgive me?

If I'd thought for one minute that Kolya was still alive, I would never have slept with Franco, and I hated myself for what I had done, not just to Kolya and our marriage, but to Franco, too. He wanted something I'd never be able to give him, especially now that the man I loved had returned.

Lily whimpered in her sleep and turned over. After a few seconds, she turned back towards me and yawned before telling me in a sleepy voice, "Mummy, I need a wee."

I carried her out of bed into the en-suite bathroom and closed the door quietly before switching on the light. After pulling down Lily's leggings and underwear, I set her on the toilet while she did her business, her eyes blinking rapidly as she got used to the light.

"Mummy, are we at home?" she asked as she glanced around the bathroom.

"Yes, love, we're at home, and you've been asleep in Mummy and Daddy's bed. Now let's wash our hands and go back to sleep." I carried her over to the sink and switched on the cold tap.

"I don't want to sleep here, Mummy," she said as we washed our hands.

"It's only for tonight, Lilypot; then we can sleep next door in the guards' house," I assured her. "Besides, you have the best surprise in the world waiting for you out there."

Lily screwed up her face and began to cry. "I don't want a surprise. I don't like it here. Please, Mummy, let's go and stay with Ivan."

I pulled her to my chest and rubbed her back. "Shhh, Lily, you'll wake everyone up. It's really late, and everyone's fast asleep."

She pushed away from me and cried even louder. "They shouldn't be asleep. If the bad men come back, they won't hear them, and then the bad men will make them dead, like Daddy and Jonesy and Lucas and Darius. I don't want to die, Mummy. Please don't let the bad men make us die."

I swallowed past a lump in my throat and held her close. Stroking the back of her head, I told her what I'd wanted to keep quiet until morning.

"Daddy's not dead, Lilypot. He's here, in bed. They found him yesterday, and your brother brought him home. But he's very tired right now, so he needs to sleep. If you stop crying, I can take you to him."

"No," she screamed. "I don't want Daddy; I want Ivan. The bad men won't come if we stay with Ivan."

"Shhh, Lily, please. If you just quieten down, I'll take you to Ivan." I didn't want to leave Kolya ever again, but I also didn't want him hearing Lily say she'd rather be with Ivan. Not after everything he'd been through. I knew it wasn't true. She was just scared, tired, and emotional. It was the first time she'd been back home since the mercenaries came, so of course she'd feel frightened.

As soon as Lily quietened down, I left the bathroom and hurried towards the bedroom door, and after one last look at Kolya, I reluctantly made my way down the hallway and into the kitchen, where Andy sat nursing a hot drink.

"Is everything okay, Tess?" he asked. "The kettle's only just boiled if you'd like me to make you a drink."

"No, thanks, Andy. We're off to stay with Ivan. She's scared to be here after what happened, and I don't want her to wake Kolya with all this crying."

"You can come with us, Andy," Lily sobbed. "You shouldn't be here in case the bad men with guns come back."

Andy came over to us and put his hand on her shoulder. "The bad men won't be coming back here, Lily. Your mummy and the rest of us scared them off. We all know how scary your mummy can be when she shouts. But I'll stay awake tonight and keep an eye out for anyone, just in case, so you can go straight back to sleep as soon as you get in Ivan's big bed, okay?"

Lily nodded and sniffled loudly. Andy passed me a tissue to wipe her snotty nose, and while doing so, I heard raised voices coming from the hallway that led to Nate and Kevin's room.

"They've been at it since you went to bed," Andy remarked. "I can understand why Nate's angry, but he must also understand that Kevin's hands were tied. Your father-in-law and James made him swear not to say anything. James said it would be better for you if you were at home when you found out. He mentioned you still had nightmares, and he thought you were struggling with PTSD, so you might not handle it well."

"Oh, really? How considerate of him," I said, my words dripping with bitterness and condescension.

Nate and Kevin's voices grew louder, and I didn't want to hang around and overhear any more arguing.

"Right, we're off to see Ivan. Will you let Kolya know where we are if he wakes up before we're back?"

"Yeah, I will, don't worry. But let me walk you across, Tess. There's no heating in the new passageway to the manor, so here, put my jacket over Lily to keep her warm," he said.

Kevin sent photos of all the building refinements, but we had a lot going on after our arrival to take much notice of them in person, and I wasn't that interested right now, either. I hoped Kolya would take us away somewhere else, for Lily's sake, if not for my own.

Andy draped his coat over Lily, and I wrapped my arm around it, glad that we'd all gone to bed without getting undressed; at least we wouldn't feel too cold.

Andy left us by the staircase in the manor and headed

back to the kitchen. I'd felt Lily relax in my arms as soon as we left the extension, and I could have kicked myself for not considering how bad her reaction would be to being back.

We could hear Ivan's loud snoring even before we reached his door. I guessed he'd been telling the truth when he said he'd raise a glass to everyone. By the sound of it, he must have raised quite a few. He only snored that loudly when he was drunk.

I knocked on his door, but the noise didn't disturb him, so I tried turning the handle, hoping he hadn't locked it. No such luck.

"Knock again, Mummy," Lily commanded. So I banged on the door twice and shouted his name, which made no difference. Ivan couldn't be roused.

Lily began crying again, so I shuffled her in my arms, intending to grab a few blankets out of the linen cupboard so we could sleep on the large sofa downstairs, but I heard a tired voice ask, "Tess, Lily, what's wrong? Are you okay?"

I turned around and saw Franco leaning against the doorjamb outside his room, which was across the hall from Ivan's.

"Franco, I want to sleep here," Lily cried, holding out her arms for him to take her.

"She woke up and was scared," I told him as he took her from me. "Because of what happened the last time we were here."

"I can understand that," he said. "Well, ladies, you'll not wake Ivan, so how about you sleep in my bed tonight? I wasn't planning on sleeping, anyway."

I followed him and Lily into his room and was surprised to see an open suitcase and two duffle bags full of his belongings. I knew he'd not brought this much back from Sicily, so he must have been planning another trip.

"Are you going somewhere?" I asked as he pulled back the covers and laid Lily on his bed.

After tucking her in, Franco placed a kiss on Lily's forehead and said, "I'm gonna miss you, honey. You be good for your mommy, you hear?"

Lily nodded and turned over onto her side.

I glanced around the room at his luggage again, then back at Franco. "This isn't for a holiday, is it?"

It was more of a statement than a question, and he didn't deny it.

"As soon as Lily falls asleep, we'll talk," he said, getting up from the bed and walking past me without so much as a look.

Five minutes later, my daughter was fast asleep again, so I got up from the bed as gently as I could and made my way over to Franco, who sat on the floor folding T-shirts before packing them in his suitcase.

I sat beside him and leaned back against a chest of drawers. "When are you leaving?"

Franco paused his folding for a moment and sighed. "In the morning. My flight to Newark leaves at eleven. I'll be travelling to the airport with Ivan—if he wakes up on time. I won't be returning, Tess, but I think you already guessed that, didn't you?"

I nodded slowly and blinked back tears.

Franco put his arm around me and pulled me into his side. "Don't cry, baby. You know I have to do this. If there was any chance of you leaving him, I'd stay, but we both know that will never happen. You've always been his, Tess. Even in death."

Franco was right, though I wouldn't tell him that. I couldn't speak past the tears and the lump in my throat.

"What we did, how close we were back in Sicily, your

husband can't ever find out about that. But if I stay, he'll know. He'd see it in the way I look at you; he already knows how I feel about you. He used to taunt me by kissing or touching you, and just before he went missing, he made sure I saw him finger-fuck you at that Halloween party you went to."

I wiped away my tears and looked up at him, wanting to see the lie in his eyes. Franco held my gaze, and the truth was plain to see.

"But why?" I croaked. "Why would he do that?" I felt both angry and ashamed, and I wondered if anyone else had seen what we'd done.

"Your husband is a cruel man, just like his father."

"No, he's not cruel," I protested. "Kolya's a good man with a big heart. Look at what he did for me when we first met."

"Yeah, let's look at that, shall we? Let's remind ourselves how many men he killed in your name. Farid Ali was the first; we did that at the hotel. Your big-hearted husband beat him to a pulp and ordered me to break his neck. Then there was Hassan Akbar—he caved his skull in with a planter and left him to rot in the marsh. I've seen men killed in combat, and it hits you hard, but Akbar's body was a fucking gruesome sight. I wasn't there when he killed Tariq Akbar because that was in Pakistan, and I was guarding you at the time, but I assume he made him suffer like he did the other two."

I knew Kolya had killed Farid and Hassan, but as far as I was aware, Tariq was hiding in Pakistan and was untraceable. Kolya hadn't even mentioned him.

I had to look away from Franco's soulful eyes. He was expecting me to say something, either in Kolya's defence or in disgust. But I didn't know what to say.

Franco grabbed my chin and forced me to look at him.

"You made a choice to be with him, but you don't have to stay. You have an out, Tess. Your husband demands a lot from his employees, but he pays well. I have enough money put away that could buy us a nice home somewhere. We could go back to Sicily. Russo offered me a job, so I'll have work."

"Please, Franco, don't do this," I begged. "You know I won't leave him. I love him, and I can't imagine ever not loving him."

Franco smiled sadly, his thumb brushing away a tear from my cheek before he let me go.

"Just so you know, I'd have loved you my whole life through, Tess. You *and* Lily. I might not be as rich and entitled as he is, but I'd have given you a good life, one without the dangers that life with him entails."

I could have argued the fact that life with Franco would be dangerous for both of us, because I knew Signor Russo wasn't lying when he said that Roman wouldn't allow it, and that's before we knew Kolya was alive. But there was no point arguing. Franco couldn't stay, not after what had happened between us.

I watched Franco put the last few pieces of clothing in his suitcase, marvelling at how quickly and neatly he'd packed.

"You didn't waste time packing up your stuff. Were you planning on saying goodbye before you left?"

"I was gonna call you from the airport."

"So after all these years, that's all you thought I was due? A quick call before you board your plane. Wow! Thanks for that, Franco." I tried to sound cross, but I couldn't hide the crippling pain of losing one of the people I trusted the most. I loved Franco dearly, just not in the way he wanted, and it hurt to know he was going to disappear from my life without warning.

"You don't get to make me feel guilty, Tess. You aren't the only one who's hurting here. But if it were a competition, my wound is deeper than yours."

Franco was right. It was wrong of me to make him feel bad, and I didn't want the last few hours we spent together taken up by petty arguments, no matter how keenly I'd feel his loss.

I grabbed his hand and laced his fingers through mine. "I'll never forget you, Franco, and I hope we can still be friends. My life won't be the same without you in it. You always *'call me out on my shit,'*" I said in my best Franco impression.

He laughed, although sadly, and bumped his shoulder into mine. "Yeah, you needed it sometimes. But you were young and trying to find your place in the world, and you had a lot of crap going on in your life. I gotta say, I admired your guts and loyalty. Still do, even though that loyalty is breaking my heart."

He squeezed my fingers and said, "Promise me you'll get some help to overcome the anxiety and nightmares. I hate seeing you so down, Tess. You are so much more than what this life has made you. Find a way to bring back the woman you used to be before all this shit happened, 'cause she was a force to be reckoned with and could accomplish anything."

"I'll try," I promised, then covered my mouth as I yawned.

"That's my girl," Franco said. He patted my knee, then added, "Climb into bed beside Lily while I take a shower. I'll wake you if you have a nightmare."

Pushing myself up from the floor took more effort than

I'd imagined. Physical and emotional exhaustion swept over me, and even the few steps to the bed seemed like such a monumental task. Before I pulled back the covers, I yawned again and asked, "Will you wake me up before you leave?"

Franco gave me another sad smile before replying, "Yeah, baby, whatever you need."

Chapter Fourteen

KOLYA

Waking up had been a frightening experience since that fateful day in Estonia. I'd often awoken to pain or humiliation, whether that be because of the regular beatings, sleeping on a cold, damp floor, or being pissed on by Riass's men—amongst other unspeakable things. But one thing I'd never done was wake up alone.

Although Riass had separated us in the early days of our capture, Jonesy and I were locked up together at the end of each interrogation and torture session. Jonesy's presence and my determination to see my wife and children again helped me withstand the harsh treatment we received. So waking up alone in my bed had been a shock to my system. No doubt Tess had taken Lily for breakfast so I could sleep a little longer.

The effects of the sleeping pills were still present in my system, and along with the warmth and comfort of my mattress and bedding, made me feel as though I was in a dream. I'd had plenty of those since my capture, but I knew this wasn't a dream because my wife wasn't beside me or under me.

Sitting up was a monumental undertaking; my body and mind protesting in tandem with one another, agreeing that the effort needed to get out of bed and head to the bathroom was a burden I shouldn't have to endure. But I wasn't about to piss myself, despite having done so during my imprisonment. Sometimes the physical pain had been too much to bear, and I couldn't move from where I'd been thrown after they were done with me. Getting up from the floor and going to a corner to urinate was a luxury my aching body and throbbing head could ill afford, especially after going days without food.

Jonesy had fared no better than I in that respect. He'd suffered so much more at the hands of those fucking terrorists, yet my loyal guard had taken it all to spare me the worst of it. I owed him my life and most certainly my sanity, and I couldn't say which unnerved me more: the absence of Tess and my daughter or that of Jonesy.

After stumbling to the bathroom, I lowered the joggers and boxers that James picked up for me yesterday and sat down to pee. The relief I experienced at making it here in time was quickly overtaken by the humiliation I felt at being reduced to a weaker, demoralised version of the man I'd been before.

After a couple of minutes sitting on the toilet, I finally felt well enough to stand without falling, yet pulling up my clothing had me grabbing the sink for support. A few deep breaths in and out helped, though I still had an ache in my ribs from the beating I'd endured at the hands of Najaf Bashir a few days ago. An X-ray at the hospital had confirmed that nothing was broken, though it certainly felt like it.

Almost all of my body was covered in bruises of various colours from yellow to black, depending on how long I'd had them. Along with the numerous cuts and scrapes, they blended to form a macabre work of art across my chest, back, rib cage and limbs, but at least I'd not been subjected to any broken bones. Jonesy hadn't been as lucky.

Washing my hands and face at the sink helped lift the brain fog left behind from the sleeping pills, and a quick scrub under my arms with a soapy sponge, followed by a few squirts of deodorant, meant I was fresh enough to face the day without having to shower. James and Dima, one of my father's guards, had helped bathe me at the hospital when I was too weak to stand. It had taken two long, hot showers to rinse off most of the grime, yet I was still unconvinced I was clean. So James had filled a bath with something herbal scented that the hospital provided, letting me lie in it until they came to give me another round of IV fluids.

Benedict Grayson had been in full-on doctor/surgeon mode along with his colleagues, ordering test after test on Jonesy and me, making sure my guard was fit enough for the surgery he needed to fix the breaks in his nose, arm, and wrist. The staff on the wing at the private hospital where we were being treated had accepted the guards stationed outside the rooms and exits, just as they had with Tess when she was recovering there. But this time, there were more of them, and the majority were Russian, which seemed to make everyone a little warier. Not that my father's guards posed any more threat to them than the usual close protection they'd see whenever they treated an A-list celebrity or royalty, but I felt their wariness shouldn't be discouraged. After what Jonesy and I had been through, anything that said *"don't fuck with us"* was worth its weight in gold.

Brushing my teeth reminded me of the fact that I was missing a tooth. Bashir had extracted it during the last few weeks, although I couldn't precisely say when. It was after they'd moved us to Azerbaijan; I know that much. The days and nights blurred together into one continuous nightmare when we arrived at that hellhole.

After brushing my teeth, I glanced in the mirror and almost didn't recognise myself. I looked gaunt, my skin sallow, with dark circles around my sunken eyes. Even the ice-blue Barinov eye colour seemed duller. My hair had grown almost two inches, despite the malnutrition, and the amount of grey around the sides seemed to have multiplied. In short, I looked like an old man, and I felt it, too.

I wondered how Tess felt about my appearance. Last night she was so shocked and relieved to see me she probably hadn't thought about it. It was obvious to anyone who looked at me that I'd suffered, and that had hurt her immensely. But in the cold light of day, or rather, in our bed alone at night, would she still want me? Could she look past the old, beaten-down façade and find the man who used to turn her on?

Call it vanity or pride or whatever you will, but I had to do something about my appearance. Grayson said he could recommend an excellent cosmetic dentist, so I could get my missing tooth taken care of. Jonesy would also need to see them when he was fit enough. An appointment with my tailor and a personal shopper was also on our list. Both of us had lost a lot of weight, and despite our best efforts during the first few weeks of our capture, we'd lost muscle mass, too. A well-fitting, perfectly tailored suit gives you confidence, and we'd need that for what will surely come.

Gustav alerted the authorities in Europe and the US

about our successful extraction before I left the hospital. As far as those in power are aware, a group of mercenaries took the forty million reward my father offered for our safe return and told him that Riass, Bashir, and several of their soldiers had been killed while carrying out the covert mission.

Although exhausted, James had flown back to the States in the early hours so he could hold a press conference at KOLCAT US and speak face-to-face with his contact from the security services, who'd been blowing up his phone with calls and messages once he'd heard the news. As had the Home Secretary here in the UK. No doubt I'd receive a visit from him or someone from SIS. Although I wasn't ready for their questions, I doubt I'd be able to put them off. MI6 are persistent fuckers, for obvious reasons.

I would have to attend a press conference at some point, hence the need for a confident appearance. Despite having suffered so brutally at the hands of Riass and Bashir, I am still a Barinov. We are conquerors, not victims. I will wear my perfectly tailored, ridiculously expensive business suit as armour, so that the shots from all the cameras, along with the rapid-fire interrogating from journalists, do not find me as weak as I feel under the defensive fabric.

Gustav had already circulated photographs taken just after we'd been rescued. They showed the squalor of the pit where they'd kept us and how poor a condition we'd both been in when found. Seeing us emerge from that state to present ourselves to the world as men who will overcome any adversity will be *"good press for KOLCAT as a whole,"* according to Greta, my PA.

I thought it best to book a session with George before I faced questions from the press. According to James, Tess would need time with him, too. She'd been suffering from panic attacks and nightmares since my abduction and supposed death, as well as the attack on our home and the shoot-out she'd witnessed when Yannis was killed. James told me that Franco had saved his life that day. I was so grateful to each of my guards for keeping my family safe.

James said Tess's nightmares had been so bad that my brother had to sleep beside her when he visited them over Christmas. From how James had explained it when we spoke on my flight back to the UK, it sounded as though my wife had PTSD.

It was for that reason only that I hadn't insisted they call her immediately. Who knew what the shock of finding out I was still alive could bring on in someone who was in such a fragile state? My father concurred with James about keeping Tess in the dark about my rescue, though he seemed to have very different reasons for doing so, and he'd painted a much braver picture of my wife than my son had.

When quizzed about it in the hospital, James had gone into detail about how they'd found out that Yannis had betrayed me. Hearing how the man I loved like a brother had planned not only my demise but also that of my son, hurt me more than any torture I'd received at the hands of those terrorists.

Thinking about the lengths Yannis had gone to while trying to bring me and my family down made me feel physically sick. Although my reaction was understandable, I couldn't afford to let it affect me in such a way. I was skating a fine line with my health after so long in captivity, and I needed to deal with what happened and move on from it. After everything I'd been through, that would be easier said than done.

I took a moment to collect myself before selecting a

warm woollen jumper from the wardrobe. It was much too big for me, of course, but at least it would keep me warm. After running a comb through my hair, wincing as it caught in the longer lengths at the back and sides, I deemed myself presentable enough to face my wife and daughter without causing them to worry. So I willed away my exhaustion and made my way to the kitchen.

"Good morning, boss—I can't tell you how good it feels to say that again. Can I get you some breakfast?" Mark asked.

I'd expected to see Tess and Lily eating breakfast, but apart from Mark and Greg, the kitchen was empty.

"Where are my wife and daughter?" I enquired while gratefully accepting the hot mug of tea he handed over.

"Lily woke up during the early hours and became upset when she realised where she was, which is not surprising, considering what happened the last time she was here. Tess decided they should stay with Ivan rather than disturb you."

Greg frowned. "She's not with Ivan. I've just taken him some painkillers and Tess wasn't there. He's in a bad way, which isn't surprising after the amount he drank."

"She probably took Lucas's or Jonesy's old rooms," Mark suggested.

Greg shook his head. "Dima and Pavel have taken those. Kevin gutted the room Darius used when he found out he was involved in what went down. There's no furniture in there, and he's only just had the floorboards put back. He was convinced he'd find some sort of clue as to what they could have been planning, but Darius was thorough in that respect. I'm just glad he didn't know about the hidden weapons stash; we wouldn't have taken his hired men out so easily if he had."

I picked up a slice of buttered toast and took a bite. "I'll go and find Tess and Lily. No doubt they'll be with Danny and Lainey," I commented as I made my way to the kitchen door.

"They're not with them, either. I passed them both on the stairs before they went for a run," Greg replied.

I stiffened in response to his words, knowing right then exactly where I would find my wife and daughter.

They'd be with him. The guard who'd coveted my wife since the day he met her.

A man nine years younger than me; a good-looking bastard in the prime of his life.

Franco!

I ignored the rest of what Greg was telling me and made my way through the new covered walkway into the old manor, ignoring the voices in the kitchen while moving as quickly as my lethargic limbs would allow. By the time I reached the top of the long staircase, I had to pause for a minute to get my breath—an unwelcome necessity that fanned the flames of my fury to even greater heights.

Franco sat on the old chaise outside his bedroom door, a suitcase and two duffle bags beside him. I carried on walking until I was standing right in front of him.

"They're still asleep," he said, tilting his head towards his bedroom door.

I clenched my fists and willed myself to remain calm, knowing I wasn't in a fit state to come out victorious if we fought, and I cursed the fact I'd not come armed. Franco would have looked much better with a bullet between his eyes.

I stared at him for a moment, trying to assess his demeanour, but although he looked tired, his expression remained blank. I wondered how long he'd be able to keep it up.

"So, are you leaving for good?"

"I've emailed you my letter of resignation. Unfortunately, I won't be able to honour the contracted four weeks' notice period."

"Tell me something, Franco. How many times have you had my wife in your bed? Once, twice, three times? Or has it been such a regular occurrence that you've simply lost count?"

Franco held my gaze and shook his head. "Expecting her to give her love to someone so soon after you'd gone shows just how little you think of your wife."

I huffed out a laugh. "I didn't mention love. I'm talking about fucking. How many times did you fuck her, Franco? How long did it take for you to be inside my wife? I bet it feels good to know she'd leave our bed and seek you out rather than sleep beside me."

Franco scowled. "Is that what's brought you over here with your accusations? The fact that you woke up alone and found out she was with me? Fuck you, asshole. If you had any idea what your wife and daughter went through the last time they were here, you'd know why they couldn't stay. But it looks like your son decided to keep you in the dark about a few things and told everyone else to do the same. I can understand that to an extent. You've obviously suffered while you were gone, but you're not the only one to do so. Tess and Lily went through their own hell the day those mercenaries attacked your home."

"James told me about that and—"

"Did he?" Franco interrupted. "Did he tell you that Tess and Lily were in Lily's room with no way to escape to safety?"

"Yes, he did," I replied. "He also told me it didn't take long to eliminate the threat."

Franco smirked. "And I suppose he told you he was involved in taking them down. It wouldn't surprise me if he did. He'd want to look like a tough guy, someone who could protect his family. I know if he hadn't been down in the gun range with me, Nate, and Ivan when they attacked, he'd have grabbed a gun and given them hell right from the start. But we came out when it was almost over—after Carl, Tanner, Dave, and Kevin killed all but the one who made it into Lily's room."

I took an involuntary step back; the information he'd just given me hitting me hard enough to stumble. Neither James nor my father had told me that the gunmen had been anywhere near my wife and daughter, and none of the guards had volunteered the information.

Franco carried on speaking. "Kevin couldn't activate the shutters because whoever had access to your phone had overridden his command. Luckily, Tess had seen the armed men getting out of the helicopter and had the foresight to hide Lily in a drawer. She covered her with a Kevlar vest and told her to stay quiet and hidden. Then the woman you're accusing of betraying you took out a rifle and got ready to kill whoever had come to hurt them. The gunman shot little Bess when she tried to defend Tess, so Tess hit him with fifteen bullets before he could fire again, and she didn't fucking move or give away Lily's whereabouts until she knew the threat had gone."

I shook my head, not wanting to believe or imagine what he was telling me.

"Maybe now that you know all that, you'll understand why they didn't want to stay there last night. Lily, in particular. Tess tried to say something, but James cut her off, which didn't surprise me. He hasn't given much of a fuck about either of them lately," Franco spat. "No wonder Tess turned to others for support."

My eyes flashed to his angrily. How dare he speak about my son that way?

"Is that what you've been giving her? Support? Did you play with the grieving young widow's emotions before she let you play with her body?"

Franco pushed up from the chaise and ate up the space between us in two quick strides. While I braced myself for a punch, I warned, "Careful, Franco, I might not be at full strength, but I'm still the boss. Raise a hand to me and I'll take your life, whether I owe you for saving my son or not."

"Saving his life? Is that what he said? Yes, I'll admit to covering him so he wouldn't be hit by the shots fired by that betraying bastard you called a friend, but I won't take credit for saving his life. Your wife did that by shooting Yannis in the throat. She should have been on the plane with Lily, but she knew that James and I were fucked. I'd already been shot, and Yannis and his men clearly had the upper hand. But Tess wouldn't leave her family and those she cares about vulnerable. She took him out with a single shot while Ivan carried her to safety."

What the...? I knew there'd been a shoot-out at the airport, and as far as I was aware, Yannis and his men had been taken out by Carl and Franco.

Could Tess really have killed Yannis? They'd had a few arguments in the past, but Tess got on so well with him. He wasn't just my friend, he was hers, too, and I knew she cared about him.

I stumbled back again, hitting the wall and then sliding down until I sat on the floor with my hands resting on my knees. I closed my eyes, banging my head against the old oak panelling, trying to take it all in.

My wife had killed Yannis! A bullet fired by the woman I love killed the man who had plotted my demise so thoroughly. The woman I'd survived those long, torturous days and nights for. The poetic justice in that made me laugh out loud, though the response wasn't a true representation of my overall feelings on the matter.

Tess shouldn't have been the one to pull the trigger. I hired ex-military to protect us for a reason. Though I'd made sure she was fully trained in the use of firearms, I never expected she'd be put in a position where she'd have to use them to kill someone she knew. An action like that could tear you apart. No wonder she was struggling with PTSD. She'd taken the lives of two men, one of them a friend. James and my father were right to hold back on telling her I was alive, though I was angry with them for keeping me in the dark about what had happened. If I'd have known, I would have swapped rooms with Ivan last night.

Franco held out his hand. "Come on, if you need to sit, use that," he said with a nod towards the chaise. "You don't want her to wake up and see you down on the floor. She's gonna need you to be strong to help her overcome some of the shit she's had going on in her head. Tess has been having trouble sleeping, and her appetite has suffered. I made her resume fitness and self-defence training, which has helped, but she's gonna have to open up to a professional if she ever has a chance to move on from all this."

I reluctantly accepted Franco's hand and he hauled me upright. Before letting go, he said, "Never threaten my life again, 'cause if you come after me or mine, I swear I'll take you down hard."

"Oh yeah? And how will you manage that on your lonesome, Franco?" I taunted.

"One word, boss. Evidence! See, I've had front-row seats to you beating one man almost to death and killing another. You busted your knuckles on Farid Ali and bashed Hassan Akbar's head in with a planter. You left me to dispose of Farid's body and said pot. Sure, Jack and I burned the body, but I kept the handkerchief you wiped your hands on. That and the planter are hidden away somewhere with instructions to release their whereabouts—along with a written statement to the police—if you ever come after me or my family."

My eyes grew wide and my stomach lurched from the betrayal of someone else I'd trusted.

"Why? Why would you do such a thing? I trusted you, Franco. I've been a good employer and always treated you well. Why would you want to betray me that way?"

"Treated me well?" Franco echoed. "You knew how I felt about Tess and you taunted me time and time again. Touching her intimately, getting her to say how much she loved you whenever I was around. Yet you kept me on to protect her because you knew I'd willingly give my life for hers in a heartbeat if she were ever under threat. You knew it would go beyond what I could offer as a bodyguard, and you used me to ensure the person you loved the most was safe."

"I'll admit to that now. But I didn't do it in the beginning when we killed Farid and Hassan," I argued, wishing more than anything that I had the strength to take him down.

Franco held up his hands. "You're right. In the beginning, my reasons were different. I knew how much you wanted Tess. Hell, even a blind man could see that. You were obsessed, watching her constantly. It was fucking unhealthy. Tess was still a teenager and didn't fully understand the life she'd have to live with you—the wife of an arms dealer and daughter-in-law to Russia's biggest Mafia don. So I saved the evidence as a way out for her. You'd never have let her go without a fight, but knowing you risked a murder conviction might have prompted you to set her free."

"So you could pick up with her where I left off?" I pushed at his chest, although he didn't move an inch. "I wasn't the only one obsessed, Franco, but *I was* the only one she fell in love with. You should have accepted that and moved on. The fact that you didn't proves just how fucked up *you are*," I yelled.

A door beside us opened, and Ivan said, "Hey, keep the noise down. Some of us are dying over here!"

My cousin came out of his room with his hair wet, looking dishevelled and less than healthy.

"You ready to go?" Franco asked.

"As ready as I'll ever be. But I have to warn you, the room is still spinning, so I might throw up along the way," Ivan replied, rubbing his stomach and grimacing. "I swear I'm getting old. Vodka didn't use to affect me so much."

"No? Well, maybe it was the absinth you drank after you finished the vodka," Franco suggested as he slung his duffles over his shoulders and grabbed his suitcase.

Ivan groaned and wiped a hand across his face. "Yeah, that's probably it."

While pulling his suitcase out of his room, he asked, "Are Tess and Lily awake?"

"Why don't you ask him," I said, gesturing at Franco. The man in question sighed.

"Tess brought Lily to your room last night, but they couldn't wake you up to let them in. Lily had awoken during the night and didn't want to stay over there. She was sobbing her little heart out, saying she was afraid that the bad men would come back, so I let them have my bed while I packed my shit. I slept out here on that fucking uncomfortable half sofa," he replied, pointing at the chaise. "I checked on them after I brought you the coffee. They're still asleep."

"I shouldn't have had a fucking drink," Ivan mumbled. "I knew she didn't want to come back home, so I should have stayed sober."

"You were celebrating, buddy. You saw your cousin again after months of thinking he was dead, and finding out that Jonesy's alive and well was another thing to celebrate. Trust me, I'll be doing the same when I get back to Jersey." Franco glanced down at his phone and added, "The Uber's here. We'd better get going."

Before I could say anything else to Franco, Ivan pulled me in for a back-slapping manly hug that I felt in every aching muscle and bone in my upper body.

"I'll see you in a week to ten days. Call me if you need me, and tell Tess and Lily I'm sorry I didn't get to see them before I left. Take care of yourself, Kolya, and for God's sake, fuck the Estonia project off and spend more time with your family."

After one more hug, Ivan picked up his suitcase and followed Franco to the stairs. I watched them descend, mulling over my conversation with Franco, feeling more nauseous than Ivan probably did.

I felt so many things at once, and all were lying heavily on my mind. Confusion, betrayal, hurt, and anger. Way too much anger. Combined with the fucked-up memories from my time in captivity, it was a recipe for disaster, and I knew I had to escape and clear my mind before I lashed out in a thunderous rage.

Before I could step away, a tired voice asked, "Kolya, is everything okay?"

And then it was too late. Too late to escape to a calm environment so I could work everything out and gain some peace and clarity. Too late to stop myself from doing something I might regret.

Chapter Fifteen

KOLYA

I allowed myself a moment to truly look at my wife before I answered. My beautiful Tess. The innocent little virgin I'd claimed as mine had given herself to another in my absence, of that I was sure. Although Franco hadn't admitted to sleeping with her, he'd not denied it, either, conveniently skirting around my questions with information that my father and son had held back from me. I would deal with them later, but for now, I had a wife to contend with.

"Kolya, why are you looking at me that way?" Tess asked as she tentatively stepped towards me.

"In what way would that be, my darling?" I answered, my voice devoid of emotion.

"Like you hate me."

"What reason would I have to hate you, Tess?"

"No reason at all," she replied nervously, her eyes darting over to the window.

"If you're looking for your lover, he just left with Ivan," I informed her. Her eyes widened and her breath hitched.

"Kolya, it's not what you think, I promise."

And there it was, an admittance of my greatest fear. Tess had slept with Franco.

"You promise? Why should I pay heed to anything you promise? After all, you promised to be faithful to me on our wedding day, and it didn't take you long to break that one, did it?"

She shook her head and blinked back tears. "Kolya, please, listen to me when I tell you that——"

"That what, Tess? That it didn't mean anything? Because I can assure you, it means something to me," I spat.

"It wasn't anything either of us planned, and despite what you might think, it really did mean nothing to me. I was hurting and——"

I held up my hands, interrupting her pathetic excuses. "Spare me the details, please. It's bad enough knowing that you fucked someone else. I don't need to hear about your sordid encounters."

"I'm sorry. If I'd have only known that——"

"That what? That I was trying desperately to survive that torturous hell so I could get back home to the woman I love? The woman who was missing sex that much she decided to fuck her bodyguard?"

"No, that wasn't what happened, Kolya. We were arguing and then it——"

"Don't bother telling me it just happened. Franco has wanted you since he saw you recovering from a gunshot wound in that hospital bed. You must have known that, if not at first, then at some point during the past few years. You can't have been oblivious to his feelings."

"I was, but *you* obviously knew. So why did you keep him around, Kolya? Why would you employ a man knowing he was in love with me? I wouldn't have kept a female member of staff who wanted a relationship with you."

"Because I never thought for one moment that you'd choose him over me. Over what we had together," I yelled, trying to keep the wretched, overpowering hurt out of my voice. "I trusted you, and I believed you when you said you'd love me always."

"I do love you. I never stopped loving you, even when I believed you were dead. But I can see you're in no mood to listen to me right now, so why don't we talk about this when you've had a chance to calm down and think rationally?"

I laughed cynically. "You're right; I'm in no mood to listen to you or your feeble excuses. In fact, I'd rather not hear your voice ever again. I'd been so desperate to see you and touch you, but now all I want is for you to disappear from my life as if you never even existed. You are dead to me, Tess."

Although my words were so far from the truth it was unimaginable, Tess must have believed them. She retreated back towards the bedroom door and covered her mouth, as if in shock.

"You can't be surprised I'd feel that way. How did you think I'd react to your betrayal?"

She swallowed hard and then shook her head. "I don't know, but not this. He tried to warn me, but I didn't listen. I never thought that you'd be the threat."

So, Franco tried to warn her about my reaction. Did he tell her to lie about their affair? If he did, it proves that he never really knew her at all. My wife never lies, though, in this instance, I almost wish she had.

"Threat? Oh, Tess, I'll do so much more than threaten you." I covered the last few feet between us as quickly as my aching limbs would allow and fisted my hands in her thick woollen jumper, pulling her up against me so we were face-to-face.

"You should have thought twice about cheating on a Barinov. We aren't known to forgive and forget."

I let her go and retreated a few steps before turning away. I couldn't let her see that the effort it took to appear threatening had left me weaker than a kitten.

"I never thought you'd turn out to be as cruel as your father," she said fearfully.

"And I never thought you'd be a whore, like your mother. I guess it's been a day of revelations for both of us," I replied.

I turned back around to find Tess with her hands cupped over her face, her shoulders jumping as she cried silent tears. My instinct was to take her in my arms and comfort her, but a part of me enjoyed seeing her cry. She *should* cry over what she'd done to our marriage.

The door behind her opened, and my darling daughter walked out into the hallway, rubbing her eyes. When she looked up and saw me, her face lit up like the glow from a thousand stars. She raced towards me, squealing, "Daddy!"

I dropped to my aching knees and took her in my arms, raining kisses down on her chubby cheeks while telling her how much I loved and missed her.

"I knew you'd come back from heaven," she told me in all seriousness. "It was gift day, and I asked Mamma Etna to send you to me. Santa didn't bring you, but Mamma Etna spits fire and lava up into the sky, so I bet heaven didn't want her to get angry and send fire there."

My father had mentioned that a friend of his had offered a safe place for my family in Sicily, and at the time, I hadn't even thought about the fact it had an active volcano. I would *never* have allowed them to stay there under any circumstances.

"Weren't you scared of Mamma Etna?" I asked.

She shook her head, her copper curls bouncing as she did so.

"I was a bit scared when she rumbled loud and made everything shake. It made me drop my ice cream and I cried. But Franco told me some stories about her and how kind she was to the farmers. She sends ash out all over the land, and it makes the crops grow so that all the people have enough to eat. Signor Russo has lots of trees with fruit on them, and he let us pick some. I don't think he's a farmer, though." My beautiful chatty daughter pondered for a moment before turning to her mother and asking, "Is he a farmer, Mummy?"

Tess surreptitiously wiped her eyes and cleared her throat before answering, "No, he's not a farmer, but he does have lots of trees."

Lily struggled to free herself from my arms so she could get to Tess, but I wouldn't let her go. It took a lot of effort to hold on to her, and my frail body protested.

"Why are you crying, Mummy? Daddy's back from heaven, so you don't have to be sad anymore." Turning back to me, Lily added, "Mummy cried for you all the time, and she even cried when she was asleep. Sometimes she'd scream and wake me up, and that's when Uncle Yuri came and slept with us. Then when he went home, Ivan slept with us, but sometimes he snores, so Mummy made him promise not to get drunk because that's when he snores really loud." Lily groaned, rolling her eyes for extra effect.

I knew I wouldn't be able to carry her back to our kitchen, so I set her down in front of me and tried to push myself upright with as much dignity as I could muster.

After I got my breath back, I took my daughter's hand in mine and said, "Come on, Lily, let's go to the kitchen and have some breakfast. I bet you're hungry after all that travelling yesterday."

Lily gripped my hand tightly. "You mean this kitchen in here, Daddy?"

"No, Lilypot. I mean our kitchen, where we live. It's nice and warm in there, and I'm sure we have all your favourite cereal."

She let go of me and ran over to her mother, throwing her arms around her legs. "I don't want to go to our old kitchen, Mummy. Can't we have breakfast here, instead?"

"Yes, love, we can have breakfast here," Tess agreed. She picked Lily up and rubbed her back, soothingly.

It both worried and upset me that Lily had run away from me. Had she forgotten that I used to make her breakfast whenever I was at home? I wanted to have some quality time with her before I went back to the hospital again.

"Come on, Lily, you've had all that time with your mummy. Don't you want to spend an hour or so with me? Can you remember us making breakfast together, then having a cup of tea in your bedroom with Anna and your fairy tea set? We can do that again if you want."

She turned away from me and began to cry, hiding her face on her mother's shoulder.

"It's not you," Tess said. "She's scared to be in the extension after what happened."

Lily turned my way and said through her sobbing, "You shouldn't go there, Daddy. The bad men with guns might come back and make you go to heaven again."

My stomach roiled, bringing waves of nausea on hearing those words spill from my four-year-old daughter's mouth.

Franco had told me what had happened, but my anger

with him and Tess caused it to slip from my mind. What kind of father did that make me?

"You never have to worry about bad men again, do you hear me? And I'm so very sorry, Lily. I never meant to upset you. Of course you don't have to go back to our home. In fact, I was thinking we could stay at the hotel in London, then we can visit with Jonesy when he feels well enough. Would you like that, my darling?"

Lily nodded and sniffled loudly before reaching for me. I didn't hesitate to take her, though I knew I didn't have the strength to carry her down the stairs. But while I might not have the physical strength, I was determined to provide her with the emotional support she so obviously needed. And if being here brought her fear and mental suffering, then I'd find us a new home. One where she could overcome the psychological demons that Yannis Markos created.

Chapter Sixteen

TESS

When Signor Russo told me my life would be at risk if Franco and I got together, I was reluctant to believe him. I couldn't imagine Roman being that cruel. But hearing Kolya tell me how he wanted me to disappear from his life as if I'd never even existed made me realise that Signor Russo had been right all along. Kolya had accused me of cheating. He said that Barinovs aren't known to forgive and forget, and it was obvious he'd made up his mind about my encounters with Franco. He wouldn't let me get a word in when I tried to tell him we weren't in a relationship—or that I would never have slept with Franco if I'd thought for one minute that my husband was still alive.

Kolya took Lily to get some breakfast, and although I didn't want her out of my sight, I needed to shower and put on clean clothes. I'd had the ones I was wearing on for the past twenty-four hours, and as I was on my period, I needed to check if there were enough tampons left in my bathroom.

Mark, Greg, and Nate were sitting at the kitchen table when I made my way into what had once been my home.

This place had held so many happy memories for me, but now all it brought me was fear and mistrust. My home had been breached once before, and a bullet from an unknown assailant could have easily taken my life. But if Kolya had meant what he said, then my death could be at the hands of someone I knew and cared for, possibly someone I loved.

That realisation hit me hard enough to render me mute, failing to answer the questions from Mark and Greg. They enquired if Kolya had found me, and after noticing my red-rimmed eyes, asked me if I was okay. Nate never said a word, yet the accusing look he gave me spoke a thousand or more. He blamed me for Franco leaving. That much was obvious.

Instead of answering, I nodded while attempting a smile and then made my way to our bedroom—the room where my husband had often declared his love for me in more ways than one.

As I stripped away my clothes and stepped into the shower, I thought back over my life with Kolya. I knew he'd killed two of the men who'd hunted me, and Franco told me about him killing Tariq, so I'd known he was capable of murder. Despite knowing all that, I never once thought he'd turn on me. Yet I saw it so clearly in those cold, ice-blue eyes I'd once thought attractive. The same colour eyes he'd passed on to our daughter.

I couldn't let him pollute her with the same cruel darkness that resided in him and his father. I had to get my daughter away from all things Barinov while I still had breath in my body, which might not be for long if Kolya had meant what he'd said.

Ivan had left with Franco and would be halfway to the airport, but I knew he'd turn back and help me get away if I asked.

I showered and dried as quickly as I could, then sought the tampons from my bathroom cabinet. There were six left in the box, so only five remaining after I put one to use. I kept the rest in the box and added a couple of pads in there, too, hoping it would be enough to hide the burner phone that Signor Russo had given me. If I couldn't get in touch with Ivan, I had my Sicilian friend to fall back on.

After wrapping a dry towel around my body, I picked up the box of tampons and hurried into the bedroom. I was so busy planning in my head what I had to do to get away from Kolya, I hadn't noticed him sitting on a chair by our bed.

"At least you're not pregnant," he said, making me jump. He gestured at the box in my hand.

I backed as far away from him as possible, wishing I'd had the foresight to have locked the bedroom door.

"No, I'm not pregnant," I confirmed.

"Did he use a condom? Or did you allow him to come inside you?"

The first time with Franco had been unexpected, and we hadn't used anything. Despite that, I shook my head and tried hard to keep the lie out of my voice.

"He used a condom."

Kolya took a deep breath, a look of relief on his tired face. "I see. Well, I suppose I should be grateful."

"Where's Lily?" I asked.

"She's with Lainey and Danny, finishing her breakfast. I came back to get her some clean clothes."

I adjusted my towel and sighed. "I doubt anything here will fit her. She's grown so much over these past few months, and I didn't bring many of her clothes from Sicily because they wouldn't be suitable for a British winter. I'll need to buy her some new clothes and have her feet measured for shoes and winter boots."

After placing the box of tampons on top of the small cabin case I'd brought home with me, I opened one of my wardrobes and selected a warm jumper and jeans. Moving over to my drawers, I picked out a pair of knickers and a bra, feeling unnerved by Kolya's unblinking stare. I knew all my clothing would be too big on me, but until I could buy smaller items, they were all I had.

Once I had my clothing for the day in hand, I headed back to the bathroom to put them on.

"Where do you think you are going?" Kolya asked.

"To the bathroom, to get dressed."

"Why? You've never shied away from dressing in front of me before. Perhaps you think only your lover should see you naked now."

This again. Would he listen to me this time?

"Kolya, I've told you before, we aren't lovers. It was something that happened just a couple of times, and it meant nothing to me at all," I told him, although I knew I was wasting my breath. "I've been too messed up and sick with grief to contemplate anything else. I haven't been myself at all, and how could I be, after watching what we all thought was your dead body thrown on a pile with the bodies of Jonesy and Lucas? For God's sake, I killed a man in our daughter's bedroom after he killed Bess, and I shot Yannis in the throat and watched him choke to death on his own blood. I've been in such a mess, and every single day I've had to push myself to act normal for Lily's sake, when all I wanted to do was give up. No matter what you decide to do, I'll always love you, Kolya."

"Then get dressed out here, in front of me."

His face was expressionless, yet his voice held a world of

hurt. Even after hearing he wanted me gone, I still couldn't bear the thought that he was in pain. So I laid my clothes on the bed and dropped the towel. Keeping my eyes on his, I picked up my underwear and put them on.

Kolya never said a word the whole time I was getting dressed. He even watched me rummage in the wardrobe for a belt.

I pulled out a shoebox containing a brand-new pair of sheepskin boots, then sat on the floor beside my cabin case to put them on.

"You and Lily can come with me to London. I need to go back to see Grayson, so while I'm there, you can both go shopping for new clothes, as yours don't fit you either. But I'll be keeping this," he said, holding up my phone. "Just in case lover boy tries to contact you."

What could I say to that? I thought it was a childish move, but I tried not to show him any reaction. He'd just watched me dress and then told me I'd be going shopping for new clothes. For a man I thought wanted to kill me, he seemed to be acting the opposite.

Kolya pushed up from the chair but didn't immediately turn to leave. He opened his mouth as if to say something, then closed it without uttering a single word.

My phone beeped with an incoming message. Glancing down, he announced, "Ivan has arrived at the airport. He says he'll call you later in the week. Too bad you won't be around to pick up."

I won't be around? What the hell was that supposed to mean? Did he mean I won't be near my phone or that I won't be around permanently? As in dead? After all, he did say I was dead to him. Was he telling me I wouldn't get to see the end of the week?

Before I could ask, he powered off my phone and

walked away, leaving me free to retrieve the one from Signor Russo out of my case. I hid it inside the tampon box and put them in my bag, praying I'd get an opportunity to use it. Because of all our high-tech security, I couldn't risk using it here. With all the cameras and hidden microphones, I knew the walls had eyes and ears, so I'd have to ditch my guards and call Russo then.

Opening the narrow drawer I kept my jewellery in, I glanced down at the pretty pieces lying on the black felt lining. Earrings, bracelets, pendants, and rings. Precious metals and gemstones caught the light from the spotlights above. I selected the ones I knew were worth the most and, along with my Rolex and Breitling watch, hid them in the zip pocket inside my bag. I had almost four thousand pounds in notes tucked inside a shoebox that I'd been saving for years. Kolya used to tease me about it, never understanding why I felt the need to do so. I had access to the safe in his office if I ever needed cash, and I could use several cards to buy whatever I needed. But I'd been used to saving and hiding money away—first from my mum so she wouldn't spend it on drugs, and then all the other kids in the children's home. I couldn't seem to break the habit, which was fortunate right now. It meant I had access to enough cash that I wouldn't need to use my bank cards and leave a trail for Kolya to follow.

When Kolya first met me, I'd been a scared but determined runaway, and I'd leave him the same way. Only this time, I'd have my daughter with me, and a lot more cash than I'd had as a teenager escaping from a children's home.

Chapter Seventeen

TESS

Kolya had a few of our guards travel by car to the hotel we used when in London, then had Mark fly the rest of us there an hour later. He'd made sure that the two Russian guards, Dima and Pavel, accompanied us, making me feel more nervous with each passing minute. Dima was one of Roman's bodyguards, and I wasn't sure why he was with Kolya right now.

Lily sat between me and Kolya and chatted away throughout our flight to the capital, telling her father all about our stay in Sicily. It helped pass the time and made me feel a little more at ease. If he or his Russian guards meant to hurt me, they wouldn't do it in front of our daughter.

After a brief pause, Lily stopped talking about Sicily and, tugging on her father's jacket, asked why Uncle Yannis hadn't been in touch.

A wave of nausea left me scrambling for a sick bag in case my stomach rebelled against my efforts to keep it calm.

Kolya glanced my way; the first time I'd noticed him do

so since we'd boarded the helicopter. Instead of answering Lily, I put the sick bag to use and vomited up the mug of tea I'd drunk earlier. The encounters with my husband had diminished what little appetite I'd woken up with, so I'd avoided breakfast and had just a single mug of tea about fifteen minutes before we left, which was a bad idea, as it turns out.

As I threw up, I heard Lily exclaiming I was poorly and that Kolya should help me. A hand patted my knee, but when I looked up, it wasn't Kolya who had come to my aid.

Dima had unbuckled his seat belt and was now crouched in front of me, holding out a plain white handkerchief.

"No, thanks, it's okay; I'm sure I have a tissue," I told him as I scrunched up the top of the bag and began searching through my pockets.

"I insist," he said gruffly, taking my hand and placing the handkerchief inside.

After wiping my mouth, I mumbled, "Thank you, Dima. I'll wash it and get it back to you."

"Keep it. I have many," he replied, then added, "You should drink a little water. Just a sip or two until you feel better. Here, take this."

That was when I noticed Kolya had opened the hidden drinks section. He held up a bottle of still mineral water, but when Dima tried to take it from him to pass to me, Kolya shook his head and said, "You should return to your seat. We will arrive shortly." After removing the top, he handed me the bottle and watched me take a couple of sips.

"We will discuss Lily's question later. I would like to know what you have told her," he remarked.

"I need water too, Daddy. And *I* want a bag in case I'm

sick like Mummy," Lily declared while trying to make a retching sound.

Kolya smiled. "You little faker," he said, tickling her sides until she erupted into fits of giggles.

My vomiting episode had distracted Lily from asking any more questions about Yannis, thank goodness. I had enough to think about without explaining why he wouldn't be around. Unlike Kolya, Yannis certainly wouldn't be coming back from the dead. I'd made sure of that.

Lainey and Danny were already waiting by the helipad on top of the hotel when we landed. They helped me disembark safely, which I was grateful for. I felt dizzy, as well as nauseous, and the world seemed to tilt when I unbuckled the safety strap and stood up from my seat. Whether Kolya noticed my predicament or just didn't care, I really couldn't say. Either way, he never commented. However, once we'd taken the elevator down to our suite in the hotel, Dima placed his hand on my arm to still me and asked, "Did you go without breakfast? If so, you need to eat something before you pass out."

I almost said, *"Finding out my husband wants me dead destroyed my appetite,"* but instead, I replied, "I'll have something before we leave."

Dima nodded and then headed towards the sitting room where Kolya and Lily were.

"How can someone so handsome be so damn scary?" Lainey asked as she watched Dima walk away. Nudging my shoulder, she added, "Don't tell Danny I said that."

"I won't, I promise," I replied. "But you're right: he is handsome, although I've learned the hard way that it's not always those who look scary and menacing that you have to be wary of. Those who commit the worst crimes can often wear a beautiful, friendly mask."

"Yeah, and don't we know it!" she replied with a shake of her head. She was probably thinking of Yannis and Darius, whereas I was picturing my husband and father-in-law.

Kolya left for the hospital with Greg, Dima, and Pavel not long after we'd arrived. Before he left, he promised Lily he'd take her for an ice cream on the King's Road as soon as he returned, and apart from the odd glance, he'd avoided me altogether.

As soon as they were gone, I dialled down to the kitchens and ordered afternoon tea for everyone. It was only mid-morning, but I knew if I could pull off what I had planned, I wouldn't see my guards for a while, or possibly ever again. Although even the thought of that hurt, I had to be realistic about the future. I had little money of my own to hire them back, and I assumed Kolya would take away my access to our bank accounts as soon as he realised that Lily and I were missing—if he hadn't already done so. I had my own bank account with enough to keep us going for up to a year, if necessary, but that wouldn't last long if I had to employ personal protection. I hoped that, somehow, I could return to this life. That Kolya could get past what he saw as my betrayal and infidelity. I hoped...

Although I was anxious about what had to happen, I tried to put it out of my mind for an hour. I wanted to enjoy what little time I had left with the friends who'd guarded us over the past few years. So I tried to enjoy our last hour with them while eating tiny sandwiches, cakes, and scones with jam and fresh cream.

Nate was quiet the whole time, despite everyone trying to bring him into our conversation. Most of it was about how they were all so shocked and thrilled to see Kolya last night, and how they couldn't wait to see Jonesy again. I joined in with them so as not to raise suspicion, wishing more than anything it would be safe for me to see Jonesy before we left.

As soon as we'd finished eating, Mark and Danny went to get the vehicle ready for our shopping trip. Lainey offered to take Lily to the toilet, so I pulled Nate to one side and told him I was sorry that Franco, his good friend and fellow army buddy, had needed to leave.

"You should have walked away. I warned you it was a bad idea, but neither of you would listen. I'm assuming the boss knows all about it by the fact that he can barely look at you," he said.

I closed my eyes and nodded in confirmation.

"You fucked up, Tess," he muttered. Then he moved as far away from me as possible until we took the lift down to the hotel foyer and he had to do his job.

"And don't I know it," I whispered to no one in particular.

Chapter Eighteen

TESS

Mark drove us to my favourite mother-and-child clothing boutique, Bel Bambino, which was situated between a host of designer stores on Sloane Street. I shopped so regularly at Bel Bambino that Kolya set up an account there, and I'd been to quite a few of their evening events. The owners gave valued customers sneak previews of their exclusive new-season designs over champagne and canapes.

For once, traffic through the city seemed to move somewhat freely, having encountered only one set of road works and, thankfully, no protest marches. Mark parked the Range Rover outside the shop next door and waited in the vehicle for us. He risked a parking fine by doing so, but it wasn't as though Kolya couldn't afford it.

Once inside the shop, I was quick to gather several items for Lily to try on—including a coat, earmuffs, T-shirts, leggings, jumpers, and underwear—while Sally, my favourite sales advisor, measured Lily's feet. Heading to the ladies' section, I chose a few pairs of knickers and two white bras before making my way over to Lily.

Lainey, who was beside my chatty daughter the whole time, remarked on how much her feet had grown when I approached. Even in winter, the Mediterranean climate had been wonderful for Lily, and I hoped Signor Russo could hide us away somewhere similar, even if it was only for a short time while I figured out my next steps.

Sally had another lady take the clothes I'd picked out to a fitting room at the back of the shop while Lily and I chose new shoes, trainers, and Wellington boots. Danny went to check out the fitting rooms beforehand, making sure it was safe for me and Lily; Nate remained beside the entry door, monitoring the two other customers who were browsing through the maternity section.

Once Lily had tried on her new shoes and made sure they were a good fit, I asked Sally to take them back to the fitting room for us so she could try them on with the clothes I'd chosen. She did as I asked and led the way to a separate room at the back of the shop, where all five larger-than-average fitting rooms were.

The gentle notes from classical guitars strumming out through discreet speakers accompanied us on our way, yet it did little to settle my nerves. Thankfully, the music seemed much lower in the fitting rooms, enabling me to think more clearly.

Lainey traded places with Danny and stood guard a few metres away, so I closed the door to the fitting room, my hands shaking and stomach churning.

This was it! I had to deceive my friends, and although it didn't sit well with me, it couldn't be avoided.

As quickly as my shaking hands could manage, I undressed Lily and helped her put on some of the new clothes, pulling the price tags off when I knew they fit her. This store never bothered with security tags, so I knew that wouldn't be a problem. To keep Lily busy, I asked her to put on her new shoes by herself, and while she did so, I cracked open the fitting room door and beckoned Lainey over.

Sally noticed what I was doing and asked, "Do you need me to bring other sizes?"

"If you wouldn't mind," I answered. "But I just need a word with Lainey first."

"What's up, Tess? You don't look very well at all," Lainey noted.

"This is so embarrassing, Lainey. I'm on my period, and I've leaked through to my jeans. I haven't got any tampons or pads with me, so would you mind popping to the pharmacy down the road to buy me some? Sally can bring me new undies and trousers while I'm waiting."

"Of course. Any particular brand?" she asked.

"I'm not fussy, as long as the tampons are super and have an applicator."

"No problem. I'll let the guys know I won't be long," she said before waving Danny over.

As soon as Lainey left, I asked Lily to put on the earmuffs and pulled Sally into the fitting room with us, grateful that we were the only customers trying on clothes.

"Do you need help with anything, Mrs Barinov?"

"I need you to help me escape my guards, Sally. If I go back with them, I could be in all sorts of danger. Not from them, but from others who might wish me harm. Is there another way out of here, other than the front door?"

"Yes, of course. We have the fire escape at the back that opens onto a shared courtyard, then there's a gate that leads onto Pavilion Road. But if you think you're in danger, shouldn't you call the police?"

If only it were that easy, I thought as I racked my brain, trying to come up with an explanation as to why it was better to run than to trust the police.

"My experience with the police isn't something I'd ever wish to repeat," I told her. "My only option is to run, but I have someone willing to help me. I just need to shake my protection detail and call them. Can you help me do that?"

Despite looking like she didn't fully believe me, Sally nodded. "Okay, what do you need me to do?"

I'd spotted a navy-blue floral coat with a large matching overnight bag in the ladies' section that I could use instead of the one I was wearing, and I asked if she could bring them without my guards noticing, along with a pair of skinny jeans and a long-sleeved shirt. I told her to charge everything to the account we held at the store, handing her the price tags I'd already removed from Lily's clothes.

"I'll get everything from the stockroom so that they don't see them, and I'll leave the coat by the back door," she whispered as she slipped out of the fitting room.

I took a sneaky look around and spotted Danny standing between the till and the row of fitting rooms. He saw me looking and smiled. God, I hated doing this to him. He'd kept me safe and warm when I'd arrived in London as a teenage runaway, escaping a life-threatening situation, and I knew he'd help me if I asked. But Danny had turned his life around working for Kolya, and I couldn't take that away from him. He deserved the very best in life, and he wouldn't get that with me.

I closed the door to the fitting room and squatted down next to my daughter. After removing her earmuffs, I asked, "Would you like to play a game of hide-and-seek with me against Lainey, Danny, and Nate?"

Lily's eyes grew wide as she smiled and nodded. "Shall we hide in another fitting room?"

"Oh no, I think we can do better than that. We can sneak out of the back door and hide out there."

"Are you sure it's okay to do that, Mummy? We aren't supposed to go anywhere without our guards."

"That's true. But it's okay to do it this time, Lilypot. I'll keep you safe; I promise," I assured her. "When Sally comes back with some new clothes for me, I'll put them on and then we can play. But you need to be super quiet and hide away quickly. Do you think you can do that for me?"

Lily made a zipping motion over her lips and then smiled, her pale blue eyes twinkling with excitement. I gave her a conspiratorial wink and then helped her put on a thick, hooded winter coat.

There was a rustling sound outside the fitting room, then I heard Sally say, "Mrs Barinov?"

I opened the door and brought her inside. She handed me the jeans, shirt, and bag, and then helped me remove the tags. The clothes were a size smaller than I used to wear, but they were still slightly too big, highlighting just how much weight I'd lost.

I popped Lily's earmuffs back on again so she wouldn't hear much of what we were saying.

"Are you sure you don't want me to call the police?" Sally asked while I stuffed my shoulder bag, the underwear I'd selected, and a change of clothes for Lily in the new overnight bag.

"Honestly, Sally, if it were that simple, I'd have done it already. The safest thing for me right now is to take Lily and get out of the country quickly and stealthily, and to make that happen, I need to escape my guards and leave London immediately."

I couldn't tell Sally that as soon as Kolya knew I was gone, he'd have Kevin hack the CCTV around Sloane

Street and beyond to trace me. I wouldn't want to get Kevin into trouble with the law, not that he'd allow anyone to prove anything. Kevin was clever enough to cover his tracks whenever he crossed a legal line. No one of his calibre wants that kind of attention. And, oddly enough, though I knew Kolya might want me dead, I didn't want to get him into trouble. Maybe that's why I didn't see my leaving Kolya as a long-term thing. Despite what Signor Russo said, I still hoped that given time, Kolya could look past what happened with me and Franco. And, yeah, I know how idiotic that sounds. How can someone who wishes you harm in a major way be deserving of your loyalty? Nevertheless, I couldn't bring myself to hurt him or our guards.

"Right, we're ready to leave," I announced. "You said that the courtyard out back leads onto Pavilion Road. Where would be the best place to stay hidden until I could call a cab?"

"There's the doctors' surgery a few doors down, but it's closed for lunch until two, and just across the road, there are the garages and rear entrance to the flats in Hanover House. They're all privately owned, so you need to have a key or be buzzed in by an owner. If you go around the corner onto Hans Place, where the front entrance of Hanover House is, there's a central garden with trees surrounded by even more privately owned flats. Then further on, there's an embassy. If you go the other way, you end up at Harrods. I really don't know where to suggest, other than Harrods or one of the other stores, but it will take you longer to get there, so you've more chance of being seen."

I closed my eyes and sighed. Escaping my guards seemed almost impossible.

Sally touched my arm in support. "I'm sorry I couldn't

be any more help, Mrs Barinov. I'll try to stall them as much as possible to give you more time to run."

"Thank you, Sally, you've been a big help. I'll never forget it," I told her. Handing her the clothes and shoes I hadn't packed away for Lily, I said, "Could you pass these to Danny and have him take them to the till so we can leave?"

"Of course. As soon as he's out of sight, head left, through the swing door and past the doors on your right. You'll end up in a large kitchen/dining/meeting area. The fire door will take you out into the courtyard, where I've left the coat that you wanted. The door's alarmed, so you'll need to disable it by pressing and holding down the button for five seconds. After three beeps, you'll know the alarm is off. We leave the gate to Pavilion Road unlocked during the day, so just lift the latch."

"Thank you so much for helping me, Sally," I whispered as she opened the fitting room door. Sally nodded in acknowledgement, and I watched her walk up to Danny with the armful of clothes.

With the door open just an inch, I could barely see what was happening, but I heard Sally say, "Mrs Barinov asked if you could take these to the till." Then to her colleague, she announced, "I'll just be a few minutes, Rachel. Mrs Barinov has requested the bra measuring service."

Hitching the bag over my shoulder, I opened the door a little wider and saw Sally gesturing madly with her hand behind her back, waving me off towards the rear of the shop. So I placed my finger over Lily's lips, picked her up in my arms, and darted out of the fitting room as quietly as I could, grateful that the classical guitar track coming through the speakers seemed a little louder than before. Or was it just the adrenaline coursing through my veins that made every single step of my escape route seem noisier, heavier, and a thousand times more impactful than they should be?

Thankfully, Sally had left the coat unzipped, so I whispered to Lily to keep quiet and stand by the fire door while I put it on, keeping an eye on where we'd just come from in case we were being followed. Once I'd zipped up the coat, I pulled up my and Lily's hoods, knowing all too well how our copper-coloured curly hair stood out from the crowd. After grabbing my bag, I pressed the alarm button until I heard the three beeps Sally had mentioned, then opened the fire door and picked up Lily again.

"There isn't anywhere fun to hide out here, Lilypot, so how about we go through that gate to see if we can find somewhere better?" I suggested.

Lily looked around and pouted. "There's not even a tree or anything big we can hide behind."

Though I lifted the latch carefully, I still cringed when the tall wooden gate creaked open.

"Mummy!" Lily admonished. "You aren't supposed to make any loud noises when you're playing hide-and-seek, or people will find you. Don't you remember the rules?"

"Sorry, sweetheart," I whispered as I darted down the virtually empty road that ran behind Sloane Street. The tall buildings on either side blocked out a little of the midday winter sunlight, and I felt a few spots of rain on my hands and face.

A suited man on a blue bike rode down a small slipway to the garages and flats of Hanover House, so I took a chance and followed him, turning every few seconds to make sure we weren't being followed. Sadly, the back entrance to the flats wasn't undercover, so anyone approaching the slipway would see us.

The guy in the suit keyed in a code and, after a click, pushed open the door.

"Let me hold that for you so you can wheel your bike in," I said, pushing past him into the foyer.

"Thank you," he replied, barely looking at me or Lily as he wheeled his bike towards a small lift.

I let the door slam shut behind me and breathed a sigh of relief. It was almost too easy, but we still weren't anywhere I would call safe.

The suit guy wheeled his bike into the small, mirrored lift, twisting the handlebars so it would fit. When the doors closed, I considered taking out the burner phone to call Signor Russo, but I knew we couldn't stay where we were; it wasn't far enough away from our guards in Bel Bambino.

"Come on, Lilypot, let's take the stairs," I said as I followed the sign.

Chapter Nineteen

TESS

Now that she was almost five years old, carrying Lily was a lot harder than it used to be, so I was glad it was only one flight up to the main entrance of Hanover House. Its gleaming white marble and glass foyer overlooked the tree-lined communal garden in Hans Place, and the large entryway was warm and brightly lit. So I made sure Lily and I stayed hidden from the outside before lowering my hood.

Standing beside a lush green plant, I placed Lily on one of the four black leather armchairs while I rummaged around in my bag to find the burner phone. Sweat was running down my back, and I was breathing so hard I was afraid I'd have a panic attack.

"Tess, what are you doing here?"

I froze with my hand in my bag, unsure whether to just turn around or grab Lily and run. The woman's voice seemed familiar, though I couldn't quite place it.

Her heels clipped loudly against the marble floor, and seconds later, I felt a hand on my arm. I almost grabbed it so I could take her down, whoever she was, but her next words stopped me.

"I didn't realise you were back in the country. During the holidays, I convinced Evan to make another donation to Sarah's Legacy on behalf of Alderly Gin. He's donating quite a sizeable sum, so Alderly's press office would like to propose a small media event for the handover of the cheque."

I turned around and tried to smile at my old foe Caroline Dawson, or rather, Caroline Alderly. She wore a mid-grey woollen military-style coat and kitten-heeled knee-length black boots. Her long blonde bob was meticulously styled, and as always, her make-up was on point.

I took a deep, calming breath before replying. "Thank you, Caroline. Please tell your husband his generosity is very much appreciated. I'm sure if you speak to Karen, she'll be happy to arrange a media event for the handover."

Caroline nodded but didn't verbally respond. She seemed instead to be studying me carefully. Her scrutiny was unnerving because I knew from her CIA background, she would see far more than most.

"Where are your guards?" she asked as she stepped between me and Lily.

"We're playing hide-and-seek," Lily announced before yawning loudly.

"Is that so?" Caroline flashed me a look that said she didn't believe us.

When neither Lily nor I offered anything else, Caroline said, "Look, Tess, I know we haven't always seen eye to eye, but I'd like to think we've formed a friendship of sorts over the past couple of years, and I'm someone who will always help a friend in need. Right about now, you look as though you might need help getting away from here."

I nodded reluctantly. While I'd rather not accept the help of someone who knew Kolya, right now, I had no other choice.

"I have a cab coming to pick me up in"—she glanced down at her gold Cartier watch—"two minutes, so if you need to get out of here, you can share my cab and I'll take you home with me. Evan won't be back until tonight, which will give me time to speak to one of my old contacts, and I'll arrange—"

"No, that won't be necessary, Caroline, but thank you," I said as politely as I could, although I felt sick inside from what she'd been about to propose. I recalled asking Kolya more about her after Alderly's last donation to Sarah's Legacy. I remembered from a conversation we'd had previously that she was ex-CIA. Kolya had laughed and said, *"There's no such thing as ex-CIA, Tess. Once CIA, always CIA. It's in their blood."* He'd been right, of course. He always was about things like that.

"I could guarantee you and your daughter safe passage to a new life anywhere you want, Tess. All you'd have to do is—"

"Give you inside information about KOLCAT's future deals or my father-in-law's business back in Russia? I don't know anything, Caroline, but even if I did, I'm not a grass. And while I might be ready to leave my family, I would never purposely hurt them. So you can take your offer of help and stick it where the sun doesn't shine. Come on, Lily," I said, holding out my hand. "We need to run as fast as we can up the road before someone comes out to look for us, okay, or we won't win the game."

"Mummy, you said that lady thinks you're a grass. That's silly. You aren't green," she said with a giggle. A hint of nervousness cut out any real mirth. Lily knew this wasn't a game anymore.

"My offer of help doesn't have to come with any conditions or stipulations, Tess. I just wanted to give you options if you needed them." Caroline gestured outside. "Look, the cab has arrived. Do you want to join me or not? I'll make sure we take you anywhere you need to go, and I'll pay for the journey, but you've got to let me know what's happening here because I've never seen you without at least three guards on your tail."

"I ditched them in a shop on Sloane Street about four minutes ago," I told her. "We're both wearing different clothes now, and as far as our guards are aware, we're in the fitting rooms trying on more. We escaped out of the back of the shop and ran down Pavilion Road, coming into this building through the back entrance. I just need to get a taxi to Heathrow Airport so I can leave the country as soon as possible. I have someone who can keep us safe, but unless I can get out of the country, that's never going to happen."

"Sloane Street! That's way too close for comfort." Caroline pinched the bridge of her nose and closed her eyes for a split second. When she opened them, it appeared as though she'd taken on a different persona.

"Right. Here's what's going to happen. Both of you keep your hoods up—your hair is a dead giveaway—and stay here beside this column until I signal for you to come out. When I do, pick up your daughter and make your way down the steps to the cab as quickly as possible; no looking around, just stay focused on getting to the vehicle. Once inside, I want both of you to lie low on the seats until I say so. I'll tell the driver we're getting you away from a domestic abuse situation, so we can't strap the little one in until we're out of the borough. That should stop him from asking any further questions."

I nodded in agreement, then tugged Lily behind the column while Caroline took my bag and made her way down the steps to where a traditional black London taxi cab awaited.

I watched as she scanned the area for any sign of my guards, then spoke to the driver. A few seconds later, she gestured for us to follow her, so I picked up my daughter and put up our hoods. After opening the heavy glass door, I dashed down the steps and jumped into the taxi, lying down with Lily across the back seats. My heart thudded violently in my chest, and even though I'd heard Caroline slide the door closed with a loud clunk, I still held my breath, waiting for someone to stop us from leaving. Numerous visions began running through my head as the taxi pulled away. Of Danny and Lainey panicking in the store when they realised we'd gone; of Nate and Mark following the taxi after seeing us leave Hanover House. The first brought tears to my eyes, the latter caused me to hyperventilate.

"Tess, come on, you're going to be fine. Take a deep breath; that's it. You can do it," Caroline encouraged. She'd been sitting in the pull-down seat across from us but had unbuckled her seat belt and came to sit by my feet.

"What car was your close protection team using today?" she asked. "Can you remember the make, model, colour, and licence plate?"

It took a few moments of steady, deep breathing to answer. Lily protested about being laid across the seat, so I shushed her before answering.

"Range Rover. It's a dark charcoal grey that looks almost black in dull light. I'm not sure about the registration. We don't use private plates for security reasons, but that vehicle was new to our fleet last year, so it will have a recent registration plate. It's only the third time I've been in it."

Why hadn't I taken notice of all this when we exited the Range Rover on Sloane Street? How could I ever think of escaping to safety with Lily when I couldn't even do something as simple as memorising a reg plate?

"Are you sure the airport is the safest place for you?" Caroline asked. "Surely, that will be the first place anyone would look."

"I'm hoping by the time our guards tell Kolya we've gone, it will already be too late for him to find us."

Caroline's eyebrows rose. "Kolya? He's alive?"

"He is." I braced my arm against the door as the taxi turned a corner. I thought Caroline might have already been made aware of it, but maybe Kolya had been wrong about her CIA career. Perhaps she really had left it all behind.

"They found him and Jonesy yesterday. He came home last night, but Jonesy's still in the hospital."

"I see," Caroline said as she took out her phone.

"Who are you contacting, and where are we?" I asked as her fingers deftly typed out a message.

"Just business," she replied before glancing out of the windows and adding, "We've just passed the Victoria and Albert Museum."

"You didn't message Kolya, did you?" I gestured towards her phone with my free hand.

Caroline shook her head. "No. I told you, it's business."

"CIA business?"

Caroline avoided my question by asking one of her own.

"Why do you need to get away from your husband when he's only just returned, seemingly from the dead? I'd have thought you'd welcome him back with open arms. Unless you had something to do with his disappearance?"

My whole body recoiled; I could hardly believe what Caroline was suggesting.

"What? No, of course I didn't. I love my husband, and I can't tell you how happy I was to see him last night."

"So why run away with your daughter?" she queried.

"It's complicated," I replied.

"I don't want to run away, Mummy," Lily said with a sniff. "I want to go for ice cream with Daddy. He promised."

"We can have ice cream at the airport, Lily, and you can choose a toy to take on the plane with us," I told her. It would be the first time that either of us had flown on a commercial flight.

"I don't want to go on a plane without Ivan or Daddy, and I don't want another toy. I just want Anna," Lily declared crossly.

She began struggling to sit up, so I asked, "Where are we now?"

"Hammersmith. Traffic's running freely for once, and I can't see the vehicle you described. Can you think of any others that Kolya's team might have in use?"

"Here in London, there's at least one other seven-seater charcoal-grey Range Rover from last year's fleet, a black Mercedes S550, and a navy-blue Mercedes S600. We have a limo, but I doubt they'd follow us in that."

Caroline looked around again as she rooted through her purse. She glanced behind us one last time before holding out her hand to pull me up.

"As long as you both keep your hoods up, we should be okay," she said with such confidence I could almost believe her.

When I grasped her hand, I felt a thin plastic card press into mine.

"The pin number is twelve twenty-five. Just think of Christmas," she whispered as she pushed my hand towards the front pocket of my new bag. "There's ten thousand dollars on that card. Rule number one: don't leave a trail for anyone to follow. Use that card or cash for any future transactions. Rule number two: when you get to the airport, take the next European flight available, even if it's not to your intended destination. You can always get an outbound flight from wherever you land, but at least you'll be out of London."

I unzipped my pocket and slipped the bank card inside, a hundred questions running through my head as I did so.

I swallowed past the lump in my throat before saying, "Thank you, Caroline, for everything," knowing that I owed her so much more than the amount on the card.

I avoided glancing out of the window as I sat Lily up and put our seat belts on, knowing if I saw a charcoal-grey Range Rover, I would totally freak out.

When I fished out the burner phone from the tampon box, Caroline asked, "Will you tell me who'll be helping you when you get to your destination?"

I shook my head. "You've been complicit enough as it is. I wouldn't want to put you in any danger."

She raised one eyebrow. "Do I look like I'm scared? I can assure you, Tess, despite me being all *lady of the manor* now, I'm not without my resources."

I had no doubt about that, but I didn't want to put Signor Russo's name out there, so I ignored her as I powered up the phone and pulled up the contacts. It took a few tense seconds for the call to connect, but once it did, the phone was answered with a gruff *"Sì?"* after only two rings.

HELEN BRIGHT

"Tell Gianni I need him," I said, remembering the words Signor Russo had me repeat.

The call ended so abruptly that I did nothing but stare at the screen for a few moments, wondering if my faith in Signor Russo had been misplaced. But then the screen lit up and the phone began ringing. The old utilitarian ringtone was a balm to my anxiety-ridden psyche.

"Tess? Where are you? What do you need?"

Hearing Signor Russo's voice brought tears of relief to my eyes.

"I'm in a cab with Lily, driving out of London. We're heading for Heathrow Airport. Can you help us?"

"Bella, no. The airport is too open. How long have you been without your protection detail?"

"Just under fifteen minutes." I tapped on the plastic partition separating us from the driver.

"How long until we get to Heathrow?" I asked.

"About half an hour, maybe forty minutes, depending on traffic. You need to let me know which terminal, love," he replied.

"We're just heading out of the city now, so we'll be arriving at Heathrow within forty minutes or so. We'll fly to either Rome, Naples, or maybe Florence, depending on which flight is leaving first. Will you be able to help me in either of those cities? Or do I need to come to you?" I asked Signor Russo.

"You are in London now? Listen to me, Tess. You need to turn around and make your way to Lorenzo's Italian restaurant in Covent Garden. I can have someone waiting for you there within ten minutes," Signor Russo commanded.

"I can't do that. There's nowhere in London that's safe for me. They'll know we're on the run by now, and believe me, the city and my husband have eyes everywhere. If they saw me entering a property, then whoever was offering me shelter would be in danger. I won't risk anyone else being hurt. I couldn't live with having that on my conscience, as well as everything else."

Caroline tapped a few buttons on her phone before announcing to the driver, "Terminal five."

The taxi driver glanced back at us through the rear-view mirror, then gave her a thumbs-up.

"Tess, I don't like this. Please reconsider heading to Covent Garden. I know I can guarantee your safety there," Signor Russo implored.

He sounded stressed, which wasn't like him at all.

Closing my eyes, I said, "I'm sorry, Gianni. Please believe me when I say that leaving London is the only option that will keep me safe right now."

I hoped that using his first name would show him how serious I was and make him understand that I wouldn't reconsider my decision.

After a short, tense silence, Signor Russo said, *"Call me again with your flight details as soon as you get through security. I'll send someone to meet you, but you must promise to comply with what-ever I tell you when you reach your destination, Tess; otherwise, there is no point in all this. You may as well surrender yourself to your husband and father-in-law if you refuse to heed my orders."*

Though he couldn't see what I was doing, I nodded slowly and whispered, "I promise," before ending the call.

Chapter Twenty

KOLYA

After having yet more blood tests and a thorough physical examination, I could finally visit Jonesy. He was slightly groggy, having just come back from surgery, but the sight of him helped me breathe a little easier, despite the heartache of my wife's betrayal.

For almost four months, the man had been my only companion. The one who'd given me the strength and courage to face the torturous abuse our captors had consistently delivered.

The man who'd kept my sanity in check.

"Boss," he greeted, which pissed me off, as we were more than just employer and employee. I'd had Jonesy use my first name since we'd been abducted, and to have him revert to calling me boss felt fundamentally wrong.

"You don't call me boss anymore," I told him.

"Why? Are you giving me the sack because of the duff arm and hand?" he quipped, his odd nasal tone making the words harder to understand.

Jonesy's left arm was set in a cast from his biceps to his

knuckles; tape and dressings covered his nose and part of his face. Although each of the surgeries had gone well, Jonesy had weeks of recovery ahead of him, something my impatient friend would have a hard time with.

"No matter your health or limitations, Jonesy, you will forever have a job with me. You've always been more than just my guard, but I think you'll agree, we are far beyond employer/employee now."

He shrugged his shoulders. "But what kind of job? If this doesn't heal properly, close protection detail will be out of the question. It would be hard to restrain someone with only one working arm."

"Don't be so defeatist. The surgeon said everything went well," I told him.

Jonesy huffed out a dismissive breath. "I'm not fucking stupid; the break was there for weeks. They can't guarantee I'll have the same range of motion as before."

I dismissed his negativity with a quick flick of my hand. "You've been at the forefront of planning the security detail of my entire family for years; you don't have to be hands-on to do that."

Scowling, Jonesy replied, "I couldn't cope with being stuck behind a computer all day like Kevin. It would drive me mad."

"I didn't say you'd be stuck behind a computer, and to be fair, neither is Kevin. But try not to think about it now. You need time to recuperate and start your physiotherapy. If you need further surgery, so be it. You were fit and healthy before all this, and I have every faith that you'll surpass any target you set yourself. When you feel up to it, I'll book an appointment with the cosmetic dentist Grayson recommended, and we'll visit my tailor on Savile Row."

Jonesy traced his fingers over the dressing across his nose.

"Does it hurt?" I asked.

"It's not so much the pain that's bothering me, but the pressure. My eyes are heavy, and it feels like it's taking over my face."

He was beginning to look quite grim, which is saying something. I'd seen this man thrown back into our makeshift cell after being beaten and tortured, so you'd have thought I would have been used to seeing him battered and bruised.

"They seem to be swelling more as we speak, and they're bruising underneath," I remarked.

"Makes you wonder how vain and fucking nuts these celebs have to be to have this stuff done voluntarily," he said. "I spotted one of those women from that daytime telly programme that Nan watches when I came out of the recovery room. You know the one I'm on about: blonde hair, big tits, laughs like a hyena on crack. Can't remember her name, but she was married to that footballer you had thrown out of your hotel for flashing the waitress. She must only be in her mid-forties, and I overheard her telling the nurse it was her second facelift. Fucking loons, the lot of them."

I burst out laughing, recalling Nan watching the TV show that featured news, celebrity gossip, cooking, baking, and wardrobe advice.

"Hyena on crack, a brutal but apt description," I stated, laughing again as Jonesy tried to smile.

"Oh, shit, that fucking hurts," he grumbled.

"Ah, but just think, Jonesy. Your nose will be straight for the first time in years. How old were you when you broke it?"

"Fifteen the first time. One of my mates nicked a bottle of rum from the back of his mam and dad's Christmas stash. We went down to the old playground near where my grandma Alice lived and got absolutely smashed. Ryan bet he could climb to the top of the dome-shaped climbing frame faster than all of us, so I accepted the bet. I won easily, and when I got to the top, I stood and beat at my chest and yelled like Tarzan. When Ryan tried to stand, he went dizzy and fell into me, sending us tumbling to the ground. I broke my nose and knocked myself senseless on one of the first bars I hit, and Ryan broke a rib. Billy and David went to fetch our families, and I swear all hell broke loose when my auntie Annie arrived and saw the empty bottle of rum. I love that woman to bits, but I thought the devil had possessed her that day. Ryan's dad was six foot three and built like a brick shithouse, but my auntie Annie was a lot scarier than him. After we got back from the hospital, she didn't half let me have it."

"Have you spoken to her?" I asked.

"Spoke to her and my cousin Dylan last night. I persuaded them to wait until after my surgery today to come and see me. James has arranged for rooms at the hotel for them. I hate seeing my auntie Annie cry, and that's all she did on the phone last night; bless her. I bet Tess and Lily were the same."

Looking down at my hands, I admitted, "It was an emotional reunion in all sorts of ways."

When I glanced back up at Jonesy, I could see questions in his eyes, but he didn't need to hear about my problems right now.

Tapping my nose, I prompted, "You said you were fifteen the first time. I wasn't aware you'd broken it more than once."

"Second time was in the army. I'd just been promoted to lance corporal, and it was our second tour of Afghanistan. A private had been shagging the new combat medical technician, Sonia. Nice girl, she was. Shy, but bloody good under pressure. Why she got involved with Nicky *No Balls'* Ball, I'll never know. He was a good-looking fella, I suppose, but he was an arsehole with the ladies. Anyway, he'd been calling her a slag and mouthing off to the lads about everything she'd let him do to her. Sonia got upset and complained about it to our staff sergeant, who gave Nicky No Balls a good bollocking. When he came back, No Balls got right in her face and called her a fucking whinging cunt, so I took him down with a punch under the jaw. I was walking away when the fucker tackled me from behind, and we fought for a bit. If he'd been as brave in combat as he was that day, he could have made a good soldier, but he'd earned his nickname because he froze up on active duty after an explosion. He was a fucking liability. One of those soldiers who looked good on paper but not on the battlefield."

"Did you get in trouble with your superiors for fighting?" I asked.

"Nah, No Balls had it coming; they knew that. And after tending to my broken nose, that pretty little medic showed me just how grateful she was. I tried telling her she didn't need to, but before I knew it, she fisted my cock and pumped like she was going for gold at the Olympics."

Chuckling, I said, "You're a dirty dog, Jonesy."

"Sonia was insatiable, I swear. We were together for three months, and I'd have married her if she'd been up for it. But she wanted career progression and trained to be a nurse. After she qualified, Sonia worked in the field, treating both military and civilian patients in active conflicts. Can't tell you how proud I am of that shy little medic," he said as he closed his eyes.

"I'm sorry, Jonesy. I'm keeping you awake when you should be resting."

"Don't apologise. Chatting with you has kept my mind from wandering back to...somewhere I'm desperate to forget."

I grabbed his uninjured hand and held it tight. "Then it looks like we're each other's therapy, my friend."

After a few more minutes, Jonesy drifted off to sleep. I let go of his hand but didn't leave his bedside. Even the thought of leaving made my chest feel tight, so I closed my eyes and got as comfortable as possible in the reclining chair, hoping that my unfaithful wife wasn't pining for her lover.

Chapter Twenty-One

KOLYA

A hand on my shoulder startled me awake. The physical touch was most unwelcome in my current wary state, and the fact that Dima saw the fear in my eyes was humiliating.

I'd only had around fifteen minutes of sleep, and I could have done with a lot more.

"What is it?" I hissed, keeping my voice low so I didn't wake Jonesy.

"Your wife and daughter are missing," Dima replied. "She escaped her guards while out shopping. Your man Kevin tracked her phone to this hospital. Is she around here somewhere, or do you have it?"

It took a moment for his words to register, but when they did, my stomach sank, and my heart pounded hard against my bony ribs. Despite my exhaustion, I pushed to my feet and grabbed the lapels of his jacket.

"Does it look like she's here?" Shaking my head, I whispered, "I confiscated her phone this morning. It's in the left pocket of my jacket."

Retrieving my jacket from the back of the chair, Dima fished out Tess's phone.

"Can you think of anywhere she could have gone?" he quietly asked. "The shop assistant told your guards that your wife said she was in danger and needed to escape. Is there a reason why she would say that?"

Grabbing my jacket from Dima, I motioned for him to follow me out of Jonesy's room.

Pavel approached us as we entered the corridor. Speaking to us in Russian, he said, "The car will be out front in two minutes. Mikhail and Oleg will remain here to keep watch over Jonesy. The rest of us are at your disposal."

I took out the new phone Kevin gave me, which had been on silent since I'd entered the hospital, and noted I had three missed calls: two from Kevin and one from Nate. I was about to call the latter when the phone vibrated with a call from Kevin.

"Tell me you have their location," I commanded as we walked towards the exit.

"Not yet, boss, but I'm working on it. Danny said that Tess and Lily had been alone in the fitting room barely four minutes before Lainey returned with something Tess had asked her to buy. When she approached the door, Sally, the sales advisor, tried to stall her, which put Lainey on alert. Tess had told Sally she was in danger and needed help to escape. Sally reluctantly informed us that Tess left through the back of the store, which leads onto Pavilion Road. Other than the back of the rest of the shops on Sloane Street, there's a doctors' surgery and the back entrance to the privately owned flats at Hanover House. Danny, Nate, and Lainey ran out and checked all down Pavilion Road. The shops all had locked gates, and the doctors' surgery was closed for lunch. You can only access the back entrance to

Hanover House if you have the key code. So Danny and Lainey ran towards Harrods, and Nate headed around the corner to the front of Hanover House on Hans Place. He's taken a photo of a black taxi cab that has just left the front of Hanover House. I'm in the process of finding out where the cab is headed from the reg plate, but I can only see one passenger from that angle. Looks like a woman with blonde hair, but the photo isn't clear enough to identify her."

"They had four guards with them, Kevin. How could they let them get away after everything that's happened?" I yelled, choking out the last few words, trying hard to keep my emotions at bay.

"Tess sent Lainey out to buy her some tampons from the pharmacy down the road. Lainey let the guys know before she left, so they kept an eye on the fitting room area without hanging outside the door. They'd already done a thorough check, and no one had any idea that Tess wanted to run. Did you?" Kevin queried. "And why would she? She knows how unsafe she and Lily are without their guards, especially right now."

I thought back to this morning when I'd watched Tess get dressed. She came out of the bathroom carrying a box of tampons. Didn't she take them with her? Or was that just a ploy to help her escape her guards?

Unable to hide my anger, I turned away from Dima and Pavel and whispered, "Perhaps she won't be without a guard. Franco left this morning; Tess and Lily were with him last night, and she probably still had her and Lily's passports in her bag. Find out if he boarded his flight or if he'd actually even booked a flight."

Kevin sighed, "Boss, I can assure you, Tess doesn't feel the same for Franco as he does for her."

"I didn't ask for your opinion, Kevin; I gave you an

order. Get back to me when you have an update, and arrange for a helicopter landing slot at Heathrow in"—I glanced at my watch—"forty minutes. I'm heading to the hotel now. Get Mark back there immediately. He can fly my Russian guards there because the rest of my team are fucking incompetent."

There was a brief silence before Kevin's one-word acknowledgement.

"Boss."

Chapter Twenty-Two

KOLYA

Nate, Danny, and Lainey appeared frantic when I entered my suite back at the hotel. Yet no matter the worry and fear on their faces, the anger I felt at Tess's deception negated any traces of empathy I had for her guards. Even the fact that Franco had boarded his plane hadn't eased the gnawing ache of betrayal. Kevin had called the taxi company and confirmed that the cab Nate spotted would be dropping off at Heathrow terminal five shortly. He'd captured the vehicle on CCTV as it left Hammersmith, and from the image, it appeared there was another adult passenger who wore a dark floral coat with their hood up. The coat matched the description of the one that Tess took from Bel Bambino as she fled. Kevin couldn't say for sure if there was a child with them, but we all knew Tess wouldn't go anywhere without Lily. Unfortunately, the taxi company was unwilling to give the name of the passenger who'd booked the cab, or how many passengers they were carrying.

Addressing everyone in the room, I stated, "Your incompetence left my wife and daughter with an opening to escape. Tell me why I shouldn't fire every single one of you?"

"Boss, I—"

I cut Nate off with a sharp glare and a wave of my hand, focusing instead on Danny and Lainey, who'd bristled notably at the word escape.

Lainey narrowed her eyes as she opened her mouth to speak, but Danny stepped forward and cut her off.

"Why would she need to escape? I felt something was off about how she was acting earlier, and you could barely even look at her before leaving. What did you do or say to make her feel that either she or Lily was in danger? That's what she told Sally—that she was in danger. What did you threaten her with, Kolya? After all that she's been through since you were abducted, what would make Tess feel like she had to run?"

Danny had used my name instead of boss, quite unusual for the once anxious ex-soldier who was sleeping rough on the streets of this city before I took him into my employ.

"What are you insinuating, Danny? I can assure you that the only people who put my wife and daughter at risk are the ones who didn't do their jobs today. I didn't fuck up Tess and Lily's safety; you and the rest of her guards did that epically. And that's something I cannot forgive. So, Danny, Lainey, I'm terminating your employment with immediate effect. Gather whatever personal effects you have here and leave. Kevin will box up any belongings you have at Oxford and send them to a forwarding address."

"What? You can't just fire us?" Lainey bellowed incredulously. "Tess wasn't abducted; she escaped. She could have done that no matter who was guarding her if she had enough reason and will to do it."

Marching up to me, she pointed in my face and asked, "Why did you have her phone? You must have had an idea that this could happen if you took away her means of communication. What else did you take, huh? What the hell happened between you and Tess this morning that would frighten her enough that she'd go to such extreme lengths to get away from you?"

Lainey folded her arms across her chest while she waited for me to answer. She cut quite an intimidating figure, and I was tempted to keep her in my close protection detail going forward. But I had to set an example somewhere, and when Tess and Lily returned, I would make sure their guards were nothing more than men or women I employed—not the close friends she's made of them in the past. Danny and Lainey were very special to Tess. All her guards were, but the two angry, bewildered people in front of me had shown that they would ally themselves with my wife no matter why she left. And when Tess returned, I would ensure she was as isolated as possible.

"I suggest you leave now of your own accord before I have you thrown out," I said as I turned away dismissively, though not before noticing Danny's shaking head.

Beckoning Nate, I commanded, "Follow me."

"Wait, boss, Kolya, fuck!" Danny said as he barged after us. "Tell me you have eyes on her. Mark said he was flying your Russian crew to Heathrow. Is that where she's headed?"

"Tess is no longer your concern, Danny. She obviously didn't give a fuck about you, Nate, Mark, or Lainey when she decided to put not only her life, but also the life of our four-year-old daughter in danger. Now, if you do as I ask and leave immediately, I'll ensure that you and Lainey have excellent references to help you find further employment, but if you continue to hang around and badger me for information I just don't have, you'll both get nothing."

I left Danny standing there with his mouth agape as I turned on my heel and walked the short distance to my office.

Feeling emotionally and physically drained from my dash from the hospital and the encounter with Lainey and Danny, I sat in my chair with my elbows resting on my desk, my head in my hands. I didn't invite Nate to sit across from me because that would make him more comfortable. I wanted him to be wary of the threat I posed to not just his job, but also his relationship. After all, his partner ran my technical security detail from an office in my home, and Nate had lived there with him for years. I doubted Kevin would give up on the healthy, seven-figure salary I paid him.

"Close the door," I said before raising my head and locking eyes with Nate.

After doing as I asked, he turned back towards me, his arms by his side, his posture stiff and unyielding as if standing at attention. "Boss, I'm sorry. If I had any idea that—"

"Is she planning on meeting up with Franco?" I asked as calmly as I could.

"Tess never said anything to any of us about leaving. And before you ask, Franco never mentioned it, either. He wouldn't allow her to do something as crazy as this, even if he hadn't given up on the possibility of a relationship with her. He values her safety above all else. But you know that already. It's why you kept him on, isn't it? Franco would die for Tess without a second of hesitation."

Raising my brows, I echoed, "The possibility of a relationship with her? He actually thought I'd let her go one day? I wouldn't have guessed he was delusional, but then again, I never thought the bastard would betray me so thoroughly."

Nate's right hand clenched to form a fist, his jaw tensing as he fought hard not to defend his friend and fellow soldier. Feeling so weak and compromised, it was I who suddenly became wary.

This wasn't going as planned, so I decided to change tactics.

"Take a seat, Nate," I ordered, gesturing at the chair in front of him.

Spinning in my chair, I took the bottle of whisky and two glasses from the cabinet behind me and poured us both a healthy measure. At first, Nate seemed reluctant to take the glass from me, but then he grabbed the liquid olive branch and tossed it back gratefully. I could manage no more than a tiny sip before the ulcers in my mouth from malnutrition began to burn like fucking hell. My eyes watered as I fought hard not to reach for the bottle of water Nate offered me.

After about thirty seconds, the alcohol numbed the pain from the ulcers enough that I almost thought the burn was worth it… Almost.

"I think maybe you should leave the whisky for a while, boss," Nate said with a sympathetic smile. "It's gonna take time for you to do a lot of the things you usually take for granted, but you'll get there. You and Jonesy. The main thing is you're back, and Riass and his whole regime are fucked."

I nodded in agreement, then took a deep breath before asking, "How long was I gone before they started sleeping together, Nate? How long did it take for my wife to get over me?"

He shook his head, about to deny the validity of my

questions, so I followed them up with, "Tess admitted she'd slept with him, so you're not betraying secrets here. I just... I need to know."

He kept his eyes on mine, letting me see the truth in his words.

"She's not over you, boss. Tess feels too much for those she loves to let it die. I honestly don't know if there was anything between them, but I know she stayed in his room after her panic attack back in Sicily. She had a cup of steaming hot chocolate in her hand when it happened, and some scalded her legs when she dropped it. When we'd finally gotten her to calm down, we carried her into Franco's room so we could doctor the burns. I didn't want to leave her with him, but I was on the shift to watch over the villa's security. She was still pretty shaken, and I told her it could influence her decision. I said she should either come with me or go back to bed, and I thought she'd leave with me, but then Franco came back into the room and had a few words with her. She stayed, but I don't think her head was in the right place, not after what had just happened to her. Franco's one of the best friends I've ever had, but I was angry with him that night. He should have taken Tess back to her room, but...."

"But instead, he took advantage of her vulnerability," I said.

"No...well...I don't know. It wasn't just Tess who was vulnerable. I honestly don't know how Franco and James survived that attack at the airport. And seeing Tess suffering because of it ate him up inside." Nate sighed before adding, "She was so fucking brave and determined that day, just as she was during the attack at home. But fighting to save everyone—taking the life of two men, one of whom was known to her—has left her struggling to cope with everyday life. Tess couldn't sleep more than a few hours without waking the whole villa up with terrifying screams. It took her a while to come out of the nightmares. She'd be clammy with a cold sweat, and she'd shake and throw up. She was losing weight fast and became anaemic. Your wife needed help, boss, yet we couldn't trust anyone but George with what had happened or where we were. After KOLCAT had the cyber and physical attack, we didn't think it was safe to bring him out there with us, especially after his mom died, so Tess had to suffer through what I know is PTSD without the right psychological help."

Nate wiped his hand across the lower half of his face and glanced down at the carpeted floor.

"I wasn't very nice to her when we left here earlier," he admitted. "I argued with Kevin most of last night, and I was hurt that my buddy had left for good without saying goodbye. I told Tess she'd fucked up, and I didn't offer her comfort when I could see that she was upset by whatever had happened between you."

"Don't beat yourself up about it, Nate. Tess has to learn that her actions have consequences," I said firmly, despite my insides churning with worry. It seemed like Tess wasn't in the right frame of mind to be trusted with anything, never mind the safety of our daughter, and I said a silent prayer that sending my men to the airport wouldn't be in vain.

"I'll apologise to her as soon as she returns," Nate vowed. "Tell her how sorry I am for treating her like it was all her fault."

"No, Nate. Apologising would only be rewarding her behaviour. What she has done today is stupid and reckless beyond belief, and if you want to stay on as her guard, you will do as I say and give Tess the cold shoulder unless her safety dictates otherwise. I'll get George to evaluate her as soon as possible so that he can provide whatever psychological or medical approach necessary for her recovery. You know how Tess feels about counselling—she will do whatever she can to avoid it, and for her, the ability to confide in you might negate the need to share her feelings with a professional."

Nate appeared shocked by my request. "I can't just ignore her, boss. That would devastate her."

"That was an order, Nate, not a request," I declared. "Need I remind you who is in charge here? I can terminate your employment as easily as I did Danny and Lainey's, so if you want to hang on to your job, you will do as I ask and keep an emotional distance from my wife. I'll assign Pavel, Oleg, and Mikhail to watch over Tess and Lily, and I will ask them to report on your behaviour."

I could tell that Nate was having a hard time holding his tongue, but he was smart enough not to push the matter further.

Giving him an out, I said, "Make sure that Lainey and Danny have left the hotel. I don't want them here when Tess and Lily get back."

Nate sighed and shook his head as he eased up out of the chair. When he got to the door, he turned around and said, "You need to watch the video footage of the attack. Maybe then you'll understand how fragile your wife is right now." Then he left my office without looking back.

Chapter Twenty-Three

TESS

I gathered Lily in my arms and, after thanking Caroline and the taxi driver, ran into the airport as quickly as possible.

Having only ever waited in luxurious VIP lounges to fly on KOLCAT's private aircraft, I naively hadn't expected the departure area at terminal five to be so…overwhelming.

Stressed-out parents with one or two pushchairs, excitable kids, and too many suitcases struggled to negotiate their way through crowds of holidaymakers while harried businesspeople clutching laptop bags studied the various screens showing flight times and departure gates.

To say it was busy would be an understatement. It seemed as though every check-in desk had a queue of at least thirty to fifty people waiting. It was the same with the British Airways desk, and I was currently the second in a growing line of would-be passengers waiting to buy tickets. There was a flight to Rome leaving in fifty minutes, and I desperately wanted us to be on it.

"Mummy, I need a wee," Lily said as I set her on her feet.

"Give me five minutes, and I'll take you to the toilet," I assured her while praying to whatever god that was listening for the guy in front of us to complete his transaction and bugger off.

When he finally walked away, I stood in front of the desk and waited for a pretty dark-skinned woman in a BA uniform to finish her task. I noted from her badge that her name was Shona.

"Can I help you?" she asked as she looked at me and frowned. I realised that Lily and I still had our hoods up, so I pushed mine back and said, "I'd like to buy two tickets for your next flight to Rome."

While tapping away at her computer, Shona asked, "Have you any luggage to check in?"

"Mummy, I need a wee now, not in five minutes," Lily whined while dancing from one foot to the other.

Ignoring Lily, I placed our passports on the counter and said, "No, just hand luggage."

"In that case, we have a flight leaving in forty minutes, but you'll have to hurry through security because the gate will close in less than twenty."

"Perfect," I said with a sigh of relief.

I unzipped our coats and wiped my clammy hands on my jeans while she took our details. My back was damp with cold sweat, and I tried hard to keep focused and gain control of my rapid breathing. The last thing I needed was a panic attack in the middle of a busy airport.

I glanced about at the hordes of people bustling in and around the terminal, hoping beyond hope that I didn't see the familiar faces of any of our guards. My stomach was in knots and would most likely remain that way until we were in the air.

"Are you okay, Mrs Barinov?" Shona asked as she handed me our passports and tickets.

Placing our travel documents in the front of my bag, I zipped it up and grabbed my daughter's hand. Lily tugged on it and mouthed something I couldn't understand, so I crouched low enough for her to whisper in my ear.

"Mummy, I need a poo now as well as a wee. That's because you made me wait," Lily grumbled while kicking her foot against the British Airways logo in front of the desk.

"Don't worry, Lilypot. We're all done now," I assured her.

After kissing Lily's cheek, I stood up and answered Shona while adjusting my bag.

"I'm fine, thanks, but my daughter needs the loo. Could you direct me to the nearest toilets?"

"Of course, there are three blocks of toilets before security and two after. The first block is just before the shops on your left."

"Thank you," I said as Lily and I moved away from the desk and headed through the airport.

While I knew getting through security was a priority, I didn't want Lily to have an accident, so we dashed inside the nearest toilets.

Luckily, there weren't any queues for those, and within a few minutes, we were on our way again.

Barely a minute later, a hand grasped my shoulder, and a deep voice with a strong Russian accent scaled my fate when he said, "Mrs Barinov, we are here to escort you and your daughter back to your husband. I advise that you come with us quietly and not make a scene."

Before I could react, Dima stepped in front of us with

two men flanking him. After saying hello to Lily, he picked
her up and strode swiftly through the airport.

The hand gripping my shoulder loosened, yet what else
could I do but follow?

Chapter Twenty-Four

TESS

Lily had fallen asleep during the short helicopter flight back to the hotel, which I was grateful for. It meant she hadn't seen the steady stream of tears I cried as I held her small, warm hand in mine.

When we landed, Dima went to carry Lily into the lift down to our suite, but I wouldn't let him. Despite feeling physically and emotionally exhausted, I wanted to hold her in my arms while I still had the chance.

Dima stayed by my side until we came face-to-face with Kolya in the sitting room and gave me a look I couldn't quite determine before he left.

Kolya came towards us and ran his fingers down Lily's flushed cheek. "How long has she been asleep," he asked. His voice sounded croaky as if his throat was dry.

"Five minutes," I told him with an equally croaky voice courtesy of my tears.

"Put her to bed and come back out here. You and I need to get a few things straight," he stated.

"No chance, Kolya. I know what will happen once you separate us."

Kolya seemed confused, but then he shook his head and gestured towards the sofa. "At least lay her down and take your coat off; you look as if you're about to collapse."

I wasn't the only one. The sweatshirt and jeans he wore seemed three sizes too big for him, and it appeared he might fall if he didn't sit soon. It hurt to see Kolya looking so ill and weak, even though I knew he wished me harm. Still, I did as he asked, wrestling Lily out of her coat as gently as possible and then laying her down with a cushion under her head.

After placing my bag on the floor beside her, I took off my coat and draped it over the arm of the sofa before sitting beside Lily's feet. As soon as my backside touched the cushion, Kolya grabbed my bag and emptied the contents onto the floor. The tickets, passports, money, and phone came tumbling out, closely followed by my old bag stuffed with the new clothes from Bel Bambino and the jewellery I'd taken from home. Thankfully, he didn't open the small outer pocket where I'd hidden the card that Caroline gave me.

Furious, I demanded, "What the hell are you doing?"

Kolya made himself comfortable on the carpeted floor and completely ignored me.

Pushing my old bag to the side, he ignored the money and picked up the burner phone and tickets. "I could ask you the same thing. Let's see where you were planning to go, shall we?"

After pocketing our passports, he quickly scanned the tickets before crushing them in his fist and tossing them in the bin.

Cocking his head to one side, he asked, "Was Franco

supposed to meet you in Rome, or were you flying to the States from there?"

Franco? Is that why he'd thought I'd escaped?

"What are you talking about? I wasn't meeting Franco; I just wanted to get away."

Kolya picked up the burner phone and noted the outgoing and incoming calls between me and Signor Russo. I wished I'd taken the time to put a lock on it. Not that it would have mattered; Kevin would have cleared that obstacle in no time.

"There's only one number on this phone. Was Franco so confident in his ability to keep and protect you that he didn't think you'd need anyone else?" he asked as his finger hovered over the call button.

"It doesn't matter how many times I tell you I don't want Franco and that I wasn't going to meet him. You've already made up your mind. Once again, you get to be judge, jury, and…" I hesitated for a second or two before I was able to say, "…executioner."

Because that's exactly what he would be. Kolya might not do the deed himself, but my death would come from his or Roman's order.

"No doubt Franco will still be in the air, but let's see if he has an answerphone message for you."

I shook my head. No good could come of this. I didn't want to get Signor Russo in any trouble, but I knew there was nothing I could do to stop Kolya from calling that number.

Signor Russo answered immediately. *"Tess, where are you now? Are you safe?"*

The shock on Kolya's face when he heard Signor Russo's gruff accented voice almost made me smile.

"Who the hell is this?" he demanded.

Signor Russo was silent for a moment before asking. *"Where is Tess Barinov?"*

Kolya glared at me. "My wife is here; now it's your turn to answer *me*. Who the hell are you, and how do you know my wife?"

"Let me speak to Tess, and then I'll answer your question."

Kolya shook his head, his cheeks flushed red with anger over Signor Russo's demand, but curiosity got the better of him, so he put the call on hands-free and pushed the phone nearer.

In as clear a voice as I could manage, I said, "Signor Russo, I'm so sorry. I wasn't able to make the flight out to see you after all."

I didn't want to get him into trouble for trying to help me, and I hoped he'd understand that and go along with it.

"These things happen, mia cara, do not worry. Just give me an address, and I will send someone to collect you and your daughter immediately."

Kolya wore a *What the fuck?* expression. As if he couldn't believe his presence was being dismissed so easily and by someone so powerful. He obviously knew who Signor Russo was.

"That won't be necessary, Signor Russo. My wife has decided to stay at home where she belongs. Please accept my gratitude for keeping my family safe while I was...missing. If there is ever anything I can do for you, please let me know."

"Mr Barinov, I'm glad you and your guard are home safe. Your wife was becoming ill with grief over your death. She would have done anything to have you back again. But while she was staying in my villa, we had a conversation about trust and safety, and I offered my protection if she ever thought that she and your daughter might come to harm. I gave Tess the phone you are using to call me and told her to get

in touch if she felt someone in her circle was about to turn on her. Your wife is a remarkable young woman, Mr Barinov. She is smart, loyal, loving, and fiercely protective, and she is certainly not a liar. So when I received a call from her asking for my protection, you can bet your Russian ass I took that seriously."

Kolya glared first at me, then at the phone, before locking eyes with mine.

"I can assure you, Signor Russo, that my wife and daughter's safety is, and always has been my top priority. My father speaks highly of you, and as I've said, you have my gratitude for providing a safe haven for my family while I was missing. I am well aware of how remarkable my wife is; I don't need anyone to tell me that. But I am also aware that the past few months and the trauma she's endured have taken their toll on her mental health, and she perhaps sees danger when it is simply not there. I'm told her sleep was suffering, and I can see she's lost quite a bit of weight. I have someone ready to sit down and discuss everything with Tess, which will get her on the road to recovery. Once she's feeling better, Tess and I will visit so I can thank you in person for all you have done for my family."

"That's quite a speech, Mr Barinov, but no matter the sincerity in it, I'd still like to hear from your wife," Signor Russo said. The man was officially my hero, and his authoritative tone and give-no-fucks attitude was all I needed to hear. But despite how powerful his organisation was, I seriously doubted they'd be a match for Roman and Kolya together. So it was up to me to step in and protect him.

"My husband is right, Signor Russo. I'm second-guessing everything that's happening around me right now, and I feel so drained. I need to take some time to get fit and well again, and I'm thinking of doing that at Glengarran.

It's so peaceful there, and I couldn't think of a better place to rest."

Rest in peace; that's what people wish for the dead. And if I were given a choice where I could meet my end, I'd choose Glengarran.

"I remember you and Lily telling me about it," Signor Russo said. He chuckled before adding, *"Perhaps she will find her loch monster, or you could buy her the puppy she asked for."*

My eyes filled with tears at the memory and the fondness in his voice. I knew this was probably the last time I got to speak to him, and I wanted him to know how much I valued his friendship.

Biting back a sob, I said, "Thank you for everything, Gianni. I will never forget all that you did for me and my daughter. Your friendship and willingness to help mean the world to me, and despite things not quite working out, I hope you can rest easy knowing your debt is settled."

Kolya frowned, trying to figure out what I was talking about, but I couldn't tell him that Russo was only helping to honour a debt he thought he owed Franco.

"Mia cara, this might have started as a debt, but we have since become friends, and if you ask my wife, she'd say famiglia. As such, I expect you to keep in touch and update me on your health. I hope to hear from you and your daughter next week. Sofia will be with us, so Lily can chat with her about her loch. Maybe when you are feeling better, we can come and visit the place."

Swallowing back my tears, I answered, "I hope so."

Before Kolya could end the call, Signor Russo said, *"Mr Barinov, I want you to understand that expecting to hear from your wife and daughter was not a suggestion. I will call this number a week from today, and I will require your wife to be around to answer."*

Chapter Twenty-Five

KOLYA

I stared down at the phone before picking it up and taking it off hands-free. I had to use the armchair to push myself up from the floor, and even though Tess seemed wary of me, she got up from the sofa and held out her hand to help me. I pushed it away, hating that she saw me so weak and in need of assistance. It was irrational, I know, but I was angry about what that Sicilian bastard had been insinuating, and I wanted to speak to him privately.

Covering the phone so that Russo couldn't hear, I said, "I'll be five minutes. Don't think about running again. I have every exit guarded." Then I walked to my office with as much dignity as my dragging feet would allow.

Once there, I held the phone up to my ear and stated, "The phone's not on hands-free anymore; I am alone in my office. My wife will speak with you sometime next week, but not because you demand it. I can read between the lines, Signor Russo, and I don't like the picture you are painting of me. My wife's health and safety have always been a priority, and that will never change. She doesn't need you or anyone else to keep her safe. Now, I appreciate that you were looking out for Tess, but if she knew what you were insinuating back there, she might try to flee again."

I sat back in my chair and closed my eyes, hating what I was about to bring up.

"By now, news channels will be headlining stories about my rescue, *and* my captor's demise, so my family and I are at risk from any supporters affiliated with him and his fellow terrorists. My guard and I survived our abduction and captivity, although we suffered greatly. You see, the bastards wanted something from me, and they thought that by torturing me—and more so my guard—I would break and give them what they needed to activate the weapon they stole. If they captured my wife and daughter, they would suffer far greater than Jonesy and I did. Or maybe they would kill them and flaunt their deaths for all to see? So, tell me that *you* understand something now, Signor Russo. Scaring my wife into leaving me will do her more harm than good. And don't ever think you can dictate what should or should not happen within my family."

Signor Russo's gruff voice was silent, and at first, I thought he'd hung up, but then he cleared his throat and responded with, *"I will call next week as planned, Mr Barinov, and if I find out she has come to any harm, you'll wish you'd never been rescued."* Then he hung up the call.

I threw the phone at the wall, my anger so strong it was almost palpable. It rebounded off the wall and landed at my feet with not a mark on it. Not that I expected it to shatter. It was an old-style Nokia handset; they were as tough as fucking steel.

I'd just been threatened by an old Mafia don. Me, the youngest son of the deadliest pakhan in Moscow!

The old bastard had balls, I'd give him that, but if push

came to shove, I doubt he'd follow through with any threat. Despite their longstanding friendship, my father wouldn't allow that. Not that I needed him to fight in my corner. I own a fucking arms dealership; Russo would have to be certifiable to take me on.

After all the shit I'd just gone through, I wouldn't have to be pushed too hard to retaliate.

My gut churned with the need for revenge. Yes, I knew that Riass and Bashir were suffering at the hands of my father and his men, but it wasn't enough for me. I needed to be the one delivering their endless torture and pain. I wanted to watch them struggling to take their last breath as I pissed all over their dying bodies. They needed to feel as humiliated as Jonesy and I felt every single day since they abducted us.

There was one more person who needed to suffer a torturous death, and that was Darius Anagnos. Lucas was killed because of him. Jonesy and I lived through fucking hell because that traitorous bastard conspired with Yannis fucking Markos. How many pieces of silver did it take for the Greek Judas I'd employed to sell me out?

Thinking of Darius fuelled my ever-present rage, and I was tempted to pour myself a large glass of whisky; then I remembered the burning pain in my mouth from earlier and knew I'd be a fool to put myself through that again.

I needed to get rid of some of this rage before I faced my wife or I'd end up taking it out on her. Not that she didn't deserve some of it. Her actions today were plain fucking stupid, and she needed to realise that.

George was coming over later, and he'd be visiting with Jonesy when he felt up to it. But I needed to speak to someone immediately, or I swear my head would explode. Ivan had gone fuck knows where, and I didn't want to bother my son while he was over in the States dealing with the questions about my rescue and the supposed deaths of two of the CIA's ten most wanted terrorists.

Picking up the phone Kevin had given me, I began scrolling through the limited contacts until I found my brother's name. The phone rang a few times before he picked it up. In a wary voice, he asked me to state my name.

"Yuri, it's me."

"Kolya, how are you feeling? My God, I know we spoke after your rescue yesterday, but… Fuck, brother! You don't know how good it feels to hear your voice again. I'll be over to see you once we've dealt with these two squealing cunts."

"So, you're making them suffer?" I questioned, although I already knew the answer.

"Kolya, I'm sitting here with my fists wrapped in ice, all because fucking Riass was a hard-faced bastard who refused to part with information about any possible sleeper cells or wannabe martyrs. We need to eliminate anyone who could come after you or your family. Father is giving him a lesson in dentistry as we speak. If that doesn't work, he will remove his eyes and castrate him."

The image his last words created made me smile.

"Yuri, do you ever wonder if our father missed his calling? Perhaps he could have been a surgeon or a dentist?"

"Ah, but they generally insist on anaesthesia before removing part of someone's anatomy. Roman Barinov has no patience for that."

Smiling, I admitted, "That is true."

"It didn't take much for Bashir to sing like a canary. We've eliminated two bases in the UK from the information he gave us. I doubt he will give us much more, but we're keeping him alive to see if we can make him scream any louder. My men are taking bets on how long they'll last."

"Do me a favour, Yuri. Piss on them both before you kill them."

Yuri was silent for a few seconds. He knew why I would request that.

After clearing his throat, Yuri replied, *"It will be done."*

After ending the call, I contemplated what I should do about Tess. Part of me wanted to keep her here and get her the help everyone said she needed, but another part of me couldn't even bear to see her face.

Despite finding out she wasn't running to Franco, my fractured mind still had images of them together. The fact that she planned on leaving me when I needed her support now more than ever made me want... I don't know what I wanted. All I knew was she'd broken my heart, and I shouldn't be the only one to feel that pain.

I held on to the desk as I pushed up from my chair, lights flashing behind my eyes with the effort it took to stand upright. I was too fucking tired to deal with Tess rationally.

My stomach growled painfully, so I picked up my phone and ordered a variety of food to be brought up to the suite. The nutritional meal replacement drinks the hospital prescribed had an unpleasant aftertaste, and I'd abandoned the last one I had after just two sips. I had other flavours to try, but I certainly wouldn't be having the so-called *strawberry milkshake* again. Right now, I could only eat small portions without my stomach protesting violently, but my guards didn't have that problem. Lucky bastards.

I was told that Tess and Lily had afternoon tea before they left, but I hoped they'd sit down and eat with me before I sent them away. Because that's what I needed to do for my own sanity. I couldn't be around my wife and wasn't fit enough to run about after a four-year-old. I couldn't take them back to Oxford after Lily's reaction this morning, so I would do as Tess suggested and send them to Glengarran.

But I'd ensure they'd have only one familiar face accompanying them.

With what little energy I could summon, I made my way to the sitting room. Tess still sat on the sofa beside our daughter, her chin resting on her knees, her arms wrapped tightly around her shins. She appeared nervous, and so she should be.

After making myself comfortable on a chair, I informed her, "I've ordered food for everyone, and I expect you to eat with me."

Tess glanced my way, the skin around her amber eyes still red and puffy from crying.

"Is that your version of the last supper, then?"

Confused, I asked, "What are you talking about?"

She rolled her eyes. "I'm not dumb, Kolya; I know you plan to kill me. So how long have I got left? I want to make as many memories as possible with Lily while I have the chance."

What the fuck? Was she out of her mind? How on earth had she come to that conclusion? The same deplorable conclusion that Russo was hinting at.

I stared at her, half expecting her to take the words back, but she left them hanging there for me to digest. Tess was serious.

A tidal wave of shock and disbelief surged through me. Despite the betrayal I felt at her sleeping with Franco, I still loved Tess with all of my broken heart.

How could she think I would do something so heinous as taking a mother from her child? Me! A man who watched his eleven-year-old son grieve the beloved mother he lost in a riding accident, all while having to deal with my own grief. I'd told her how terrible it was to watch him cry, day in, day out, knowing nothing I could do would take away his pain.

Tess and I built a life together. I shared that experience with her so she would know me better, so she could understand my driving, obsessive need to keep my family safe. But it seemed she didn't know me at all.

The shock and disbelief morphed into something much darker. Something that slithered through my veins like pure evil. Tess would pay for what she said—for thinking so little of me and the love we'd shared.

Shaking my head, I replied as calmly as I could manage, "You seem to know everything, Tess. You tell me."

Chapter Twenty-Six

TESS

Frost so thick you could almost mistake it for snow had covered the ground at Glengarran, and my breath fogged in the chilly morning air. Lily pretended she was a fire-breathing dragon as we strolled along the edge of the loch and onto the small wooden jetty. We'd been here for three days, and I still hadn't acclimatised to the bitterly cold high-land temperatures.

Lily wanted to go out in the rowing boat that was tied to the edge of the jetty and pulled a face when I refused. If we went out in the boat, we'd have to take a guard, and that was the last thing I wanted to do.

Nate wasn't talking to me, and neither were the Russian guards Kolya had assigned us.

Kolya had fired Danny and Lainey the day I escaped, although he insisted the blame lay squarely at my feet. I wasn't so sure about that. Nate and Mark were with me that day, and they still had their jobs.

Mark flew us here via helicopter from the airport at

231

Inverness before heading straight back to the KOLCAT jet. He'd spoken to me and seemed friendly enough, but I could tell he was disappointed in me. He could join the queue. I was disappointed in myself too because, if I'd made Lily hang on a bit longer, we'd have been through security and would have been safely on our way to Rome.

Kolya still had my phone, so I couldn't even call Danny and Lainey to apologise and ask how they were. I hoped they didn't hate me for lying to them that day. I should have confided in them and let them know what I was planning to do.

I'd thought that not involving Danny and Lainey would protect them, which makes me a complete idiot and a terrible friend.

They'd been so much more than guards to me, and I swore I'd come back and haunt Kolya for taking away their livelihoods. Especially Danny's. He'd come so far after living on the streets of London with little Bess, and I didn't want to be the cause of yet more trauma for him.

"Come on, Mummy, let's look for fish," Lily said as she pulled me further onto the jetty. Frost made the wood slippery underfoot, and as there were no railings, I cautioned Lily from stepping too near the edge.

"But we can't see under the water from here," she whined.

"Too bad, Lilypot. It's way too cold to go tumbling into the loch."

"Can you remember when Ivan and Jonesy were on the boat, and it tipped over?" she asked. "That was so funny, especially when Jonesy came out and pushed Dave in for laughing at them. Dave wasn't happy about that at all, was he, Mummy? And he called Jonesy a naughty word."

"No, he wasn't happy," I agreed, smiling as I recalled

the memory from last August, wishing more than anything that I could turn back time.

I glanced over at Nate, who stood barely five feet away. If he'd heard what Lily said, he hadn't acknowledged it. His face remained the same as it was since he'd bumped into me at the hotel before we left: cold and almost expressionless, impervious to all but Lily's laughter. When he did react, his short-lived smile never reached his eyes. I had a theory about that. I think he knew that Kolya was going to have me killed, and he felt sorry for Lily. Shame he wasn't sorry enough to help us get away.

As we headed back inside, I wondered whether Kolya had asked Nate to do the deed, and if *that* was why he was creating a distance between us. I suppose it would make it easier for him to pull the trigger—if that was how Kolya planned on doing it. I hoped it was. A bullet to the back of the head would mean I had a quick death without any suffering. I just hoped they'd do it without telling me what was happening, so I had no time to feel afraid.

Would I have a funeral? Or would he do what he did with Farid Ali and burn my body until there was nothing left? He could list me as a missing person, say I'd been abducted and act as the grieving husband. I didn't really care about any of that as long as he threw my ashes into the loch as we did with Sarah's. I'd left a note for Ivan, asking him to ensure I shared the same final resting place as my beloved foster sister.

Although Ivan was Kolya's cousin, he was also my best friend, and I trusted him like a brother. I hoped more than anything that I'd get to tell him goodbye in person.

Since arriving at Glengarran, I'd made sure I was never without Lily. I knew they wouldn't kill me in front of her, so I had more chance of staying alive if I had her with me at all times. This puzzled Mrs Braeburn and John, the old gamekeeper. They often took Lily to the kitchen with them to bake and tell stories about the castle and the loch, filling her belly and imagination simultaneously. They had no clue what was on the cards for me, and I didn't want to put their lives at risk by asking for help. So, whenever they took Lily, I went along with her instead of working or having a quiet moment to myself.

The work situation worried me. I'd been banned from using the landline, and as Kolya had my mobile phone, I hadn't any way to contact Karen, Amina, or anyone else from Sarah's Legacy. I wanted to put a plan into action in case Kolya pulled the funding. He might keep it on for a while to make him look good with the press, but we needed to find more funding for the charity, just in case.

Karen had been checking in on Jean while I was in Sicily, and I hoped she'd continue to do so when I… when I couldn't.

I wished I'd had the chance to visit Nan and Jack before coming here. I wanted them to have a place in Lily's life. We'd missed them so much while in Sicily, and I knew that, no matter what Kolya wanted, Nan would tell her about me even if no one else would.

I had nothing to do all day but look after Lily, which I wasn't complaining about. I wanted Lily to remember me when I was gone, so I was trying my best to create some good memories with her.

I'd started writing letters for her to open on her birthdays. While she slept, I sat in the chair beside her bed and wrote everything I wished I could tell her as she grew older, but it was a heartbreaking task. The first one wasn't so bad because it was only five weeks until her fifth birthday. In that letter, I apologised for not being there and said I hoped she enjoyed her day, then I reminded her of all the fun things we'd done in Sicily. But for every subsequent birthday, the letters were so much harder to write. I wouldn't know what she'd been learning at school or what new achievements or milestones she'd reached. I wouldn't be there when she lost her first tooth and was excited about the tooth fairy's visit. I'd never get to see her ride her bike without training wheels or watch her learn to skate, and as the years rolled on, I wouldn't be able to help with her homework or discuss periods and having boyfriends.

Kolya would rob his daughter of a mother's love and guidance. And yet, no matter how hard I tried, I still couldn't hate him.

Maybe my brain wasn't firing on all cylinders, or I was too bloody sick and twisted after becoming a killer myself; who knows? I tried to rationalise it in my head, telling myself that the Kolya Barinov I loved was still missing—because the man who returned certainly wasn't him. But I knew in my heart that wasn't the case. It *was* the same Kolya, he was just showing me a side he kept hidden while we were together. Oh, I knew he was a killer; he'd murdered three men to protect me. But I was his innocent young saviour then. The virgin wife he could mould and shape into a woman he could be proud of.

Sleeping with Franco changed all that.

I wondered what Franco was doing now. Was he spending time with his sister and her family? Did he plan on staying in the States, or was he considering working for Signor Russo? Would he feel guilty for leaving when he found out about my death?

My mind was overflowing with questions that would probably never get answered. No wonder I was finding it hard to concentrate on even the simplest of tasks. Like unzipping our coats and removing the rest of our outer-wear, trying to remember what Mrs Braeburn said we were having for lunch today. Not that I had an appetite. Waiting to be killed was an efficient way to lose weight, although I certainly wouldn't recommend it.

Chapter Twenty-Seven

KOLYA

I thought all my worries were over when Jonesy and I were rescued, but that couldn't have been further from the truth. First, I found out that my best friend, Yannis Markos, had sold me out to the terrorists, then my wife, who'd been fucking her bodyguard, tried to run away with our daughter. Darius, the traitorous guard who'd colluded with both Yannis and the terrorists, had disappeared into thin fucking air, and then my son...well, he needed a lot more than a father's love.

I needed a plan, a way to move forward with my life and accept the changes in it. If only my mind and body would cooperate...

Being stuck in the hospital for two nights hadn't been part of said plan, but despite my protestations, I felt much better for it.

Having IV fluids and nutritionally balanced, portion-controlled meals certainly helped, but staying in the same room as Jonesy improved my mental and physical health more than anything a doctor could order. And Jonesy felt the same.

When we discussed it with George, he told us it was understandable we'd feel that way. We had nothing but each other in the most atrocious circumstances and must have felt tremendous separation anxiety when one of us was taken away to suffer abuse and torture. Whenever we were brought back to our cell after they tried to break us, it eased the fearful anxiety that we experienced. We helped each other survive the shit our captors put us through, but trying to get back to our normal, everyday lives after living in Riass's hell was never going to be easy. So it was no wonder we became anxious whenever we were apart.

George said the separation anxiety, which was also linked with our survival, would eventually pass, and there were various coping mechanisms he could recommend. He could also prescribe medication, but neither Jonesy nor I wanted to go down that route if we could help it.

The morning after I sent Tess and Lily to Glengarran, I paid a visit to Mrs Khatri, the cosmetic dentist whom Grayson recommended. However, Mrs Khatri was unwilling to do the work needed to replace my tooth until my iron levels had risen. Call it vanity or insecurity…I just didn't want to be seen with a fucking missing tooth. When I voiced my displeasure and told the dentist I'd go elsewhere, she said that was up to me, but anyone who was willing to work on me while I was in such poor physical condition was nothing but a charlatan. She offered to give me a temporary denture plate to clip onto my other teeth until my anaemia had resolved, and I reluctantly accepted.

While she was taking a mould of the inside of my mouth, I began to experience dizziness. I didn't say anything to the dentist, wanting to get the whole process over and done with so she could crack on with making the plate. But when it was time to leave, I got up out of the chair and collapsed in a dead faint.

I was out for less than a minute, but I had my whole team panicking. Thankfully, Mrs Khatri caught me before my head hit the side of the chair and gave me immediate assistance when I roused. Within an hour, I was in a bed beside Jonesy with a cannula in my arm and Grayson giving me hell for being a stubborn bastard who refused to listen to his doctor.

Dima called my father, who called James, who flew back to London immediately and gave me the same spiel as Grayson. But quite honestly, he looked almost as bad as I did. When I asked him what was wrong, he said he'd not been sleeping, so I sent him back to the hotel and told him to get some rest. But when he came to visit me the next day, he didn't look much better, and as he handed me one of those vile, meal-replacement drinks, I noticed his hands were shaking.

I didn't want to ask what was wrong because I knew he'd lie to me and tell me he was fine, so I waited until later that afternoon and called Tanner, one of his close protection team. Tanner had been guarding James since he was a teenager, and I knew he'd tell me if I had any need to worry.

Tanner informed me that James had started drinking after I'd been abducted, and he thought he might also be doing drugs, although he couldn't say for sure. Tanner said that he and Carl had tried to get James to admit he had a problem, but he insisted he was fine and had threatened to fire them if they continued to harass him about it.

Tanner and Carl had planned on having a conversation with me about my son's recent behaviour and their suspicions, but they thought I needed more time to recover before dealing with the inevitable kickback from James. Tanner also said that he'd kept James's recent problems from Tess because he knew she'd want to help, but apparently, James's behaviour toward Tess while in Sicily had been poor, and after what had happened on Christmas Day, James had kept his distance.

When I asked what had happened on Christmas Day, Tanner couldn't say because James had come back into the room. Instead, he told me to ask Kevin or Yuri. If Kevin hadn't been on his way to the hospital to visit us, I would have picked up my phone and called my brother, but I also wanted to hear it from someone who wasn't family. Thinking me too weak to deal with my adult son, Yuri might have tried to help James himself. I didn't want that to happen. I needed to be involved every step of the way so I could put to bed the fear of losing my son to addiction once and for all.

Chapter Twenty-Eight

KOLYA

Kevin and Rashid entered our room and did the usual sweep for bugs before setting up one of our wheeled, over-bed tables between our beds. Kevin took out a laptop while Rashid set up an anti-listening device against the window after informing our nurse that we weren't to be disturbed for the next two hours.

James had been reluctant to let me watch videos of the day mercenaries invaded my home until I was out of the hospital and had several sessions with George. However, I was an impatient man, and I knew that my son's ability to make rational decisions about anything remotely distressing might be compromised. There was also the video Riass sent, but the thought of watching it filled my soul with dread.

Jonesy and I were the only ones who hadn't watched all the footage until today. Kevin had ensured that everyone in my team, including the guards my father sent over from Moscow, saw what went down when they tried to attack my family. They had to be ready in case anyone tried to hit us again.

"I know that Nan's been checking in with you since you got back, so you don't need me to reassure you that she's fine," Kevin said as he got ready to press play.

"She's coming to visit tomorrow," I told him. "She and Jack are staying at the hotel for a few days."

Jonesy nodded. "She's baking me an apple pie. I can't tell you how much I've missed that woman's smile. We talked about her a lot, especially on the rougher days; knowing we had people like Nan waiting for us at home helped us keep fighting to stay alive."

"What about me?" Rashid asked as he handed Jonesy a bar of chocolate.

Jonesy looked puzzled. "What do you mean?"

"Did you talk about me a lot? I bet you missed *my* smile. Go on, admit it."

"Why would I talk about you? And no one can see your smile behind that fucking rug you call a beard."

Rashid glanced at Kevin and me. "He's just jealous because he can't grow one."

"I grew a beard last year, but I shaved it off because I couldn't stand the feel of it," Jonesy reminded us.

Laughing, Rashid replied, "You call that a beard? I've seen more hair on a porn star's fanny."

Kevin and I agreed.

Jonesy shrugged his shoulders. "Well, at least I won't have pervy Pete giving me the eye."

"He phoned me when he heard you'd been abducted," Rashid said. "He and a few others we served with wanted to put a team together and go looking for you. Then someone leaked the video Riass sent, and everyone thought you were dead."

"Who's pervy Pete, and why is he pervy?" Kevin asked.

"He was one of the tank crew. Welsh, like me, a good-looking fella who could charm his way into any woman's bed if he wanted, but Pete had a very particular fetish."

Intrigued, Kevin prompted, "Go on."

"Pete liked his women hairy," Jonesy said. "And I'm not just talking about hairy fannies."

"He liked them to have hairy legs, armpits, back, a bit of a tash," Rashid added.

"We used to give him hell for it, but he'd laugh it off. He liked what he liked, and that was that."

Rashid nodded. "I thought he'd have married Melinda by now. They've been engaged for ten years."

"Is she hairy?" I asked.

"Like Chewbacca on steroids," Jonesy replied. "But she's a smashing woman. Heart of gold."

Rashid agreed.

When Kevin and I had finally stopped laughing, he leaned forward and pressed play on the first video.

"The first images are from rooftop camera two," Kevin said as we watched a large black military-style helicopter descend onto the helipad. "We were expecting Yannis's arrival, but as soon as the camera picked it up and I saw the size of it, I knew it wasn't him. I called Tess and flipped the switch to activate the lockdown process while Dave, Carl, and Tanner grabbed our weapons, but someone on that big fucking bird had your phone and overrode my lockdown command."

As soon as it landed, eight armed men dressed head to toe in black, including balaclavas, hit the ground running, heading straight for the extension.

"This is from poolside camera one as it landed. Nan was covering the plants with frost-proof material. Lily had wanted to go with her, but Tess made her tidy her room and help put the laundry away," Kevin told us. "And thank

God she did, or Lily could have been caught in the crossfire."

Kevin turned up the sound so we could hear as well as see what was happening.

Nan turned to look at the beast of a helicopter and frowned, standing there staring at it for a few seconds before reality hit. Then she dropped the material she was holding and tried to run back to the extension, but she slipped on the material and landed hard on her left side. She cried out in what must have been agonising pain, and the sound twisted my gut—but watching two armed men approach her did far worse.

"Fucking hell, Kev, I know we're not watching this live, but I want to shout at her to get up and run," Jonesy said. I was in full agreement.

"Her hip had been playing up for months, but it must have broken on impact, and I'm surprised she didn't break her shoulder, too," Kevin said.

I watched as one of the gunmen aimed his rifle at Nan before lowering it and moving away; the other knelt beside her and held out his hand.

"He wanted to help her," I said.

Kevin nodded. "We think that was Darius. We didn't know it at the time, but they had specific targets. While we were waiting for the ambulance to arrive, Nan insisted that one of them wanted to help her. Tess said she didn't think Lily had been a target either, but you'll see all that later."

The camera switched again to show Carl and Tanner running out of the kitchen door wearing Kevlar vests. They opened fire on two of the gunmen before taking cover behind our poolside shower wall. The other gunmen kept firing at their cover as they moved towards my home. Bullets from AR-15s took chunks out of the tiled wall and decorative planters as Carl and Tanner yelled for Nan to stay down. One of them shot the man beside Nan in the arm, and his weapon hit the ground. More shots were fired at Carl and Tanner, and others hit my kitchen windows. The man beside Nan picked up his rifle in his other hand and pulled the trigger, spraying bullets all around the outside of the extension.

"This is a fucking shit show," Jonesy observed. "Those men can't have been military trained. There's no coordination; they aren't using good cover to advance forward, and I know you said they had specific targets, but they were firing at everything, so anyone could have been caught in the crossfire."

Tanner caught a bullet in his leg, but he and Carl kept firing back.

The camera zoomed in on the kitchen door as Dave stepped out and immediately took down two of the shooters —one in the chest and the other in the head.

"Go on, Dave, give 'em fucking h—"

Jonesy's rallying words died in his mouth as we gasped in horror when a bullet skimmed the side of Dave's head and took off the top of his ear. He hit the door hard and slid down to the floor.

"Jesus Christ," I whispered. "He's lucky to be alive."

I'd seen Dave back at home, so I knew he was fine. The plastic surgeon had done a superb job at reconstructing his ear, and the scarring at the side of his head was minimal.

Two of the gunmen stepped over Dave and entered my home.

"Definitely not ex-military. They would have popped him again to make sure he was dead," Jonesy concluded.

Kevin agreed, adding, "That's what Nate said."

The man that Dave had shot in the chest must have

been wearing a vest because he got up and headed towards the kitchen door. Before he could make it, Carl shot him in the back of the head.

I owed so much to the men who defended my family and home, and though I'd prepared for a situation like this, I never actually thought it would happen. But then again, I never thought that someone would have the balls to kidnap me, so I'd have to rethink the way my family and I lived our lives from now on.

Our guards had been injured and tortured, and one had lost his life. This could never happen again. Roman Barinov was a name that most evil men feared, yet it hadn't been enough to prevent all this shit from taking place. Perhaps I would need to make Kolya Barinov a name that people feared more than any reigning Bratva king.

Kevin got up and selected a new file. "These are the camera feeds from inside the property from the kitchen to the bedrooms."

Kevin crouched behind the upturned kitchen table with his rifle at the ready. I knew the table was thick enough to provide a solid cover. He shot the lead gunman in the chest and pelvis, but the guy kept firing as he went down— spraying bullets haphazardly around the kitchen. The second gunman narrowly missed Kevin as he made his way through the kitchen, and to make matters worse, yet another gunman shot up everything in the room, raining shards of glass and crockery everywhere, destroying every piece of furniture in his path. Despite the danger, Kevin finished off the first shooter before spinning around and killing the third with one shot, but the second gunman had already passed through into the hallway, veering off towards James's room. When he found that empty, he went to Lily's bedroom door.

Kevin got up and closed the video, bringing up another before turning to face me.

"You did well, Kevin," I assured him, though my voice was filled with irrational fear. I'd seen Lily, Tess, and James and knew they were unharmed. Nevertheless, I felt anxious about what was to come.

"Not well enough," Kevin replied.

"I beg to differ," Jonesy said. "You only had the table as cover against three armed men, but you still took down two of them."

Kevin shook his head and then turned back to his laptop. "This video begins when Tess first hears the helicopter. She went to the window so Lily could wave at Yannis when he landed. The call she took was from me, telling her to take cover and that I couldn't get the shutters to come down."

The video transported us into Lily's bedroom. Tess laid that damn doll that looked like Lily on the bed before moving towards the windows. She had Lily in her arms and struggled to take out her phone. We couldn't hear what Kevin said to her, but she replied, "Kevin, what's...?"

Tess stared at the scene unfolding outside, her mouth hanging open in shock. We watched as her expression changed into one of resolve, and she sank into a crouch below the window. Danny's dog, Bess, was wagging her tail beside her. She no doubt thought that Tess was playing a game.

"Mummy, I'm scared. Those people have guns," Lily cried.

Tess kissed Lily's forehead and tried to soothe our daughter's fear. "Shh, it's okay. They won't come near you. I'll keep you safe, I promise. But I need you to do something for me, Lily. It's a bit like hide-and-seek. I'm going to lay you down inside one of your big drawers and put some pillows beside you, so if someone opens the drawer, they won't see you. And I need you to be really quiet and still for me, sweetheart. You can't make a noise until you hear someone you know calling your name, okay?"

My brave little girl nodded and pressed her lips together.

Tess shuffled away from the window and stood beside the drawers holding our hidden weapons stash. She opened one of the larger drawers underneath, threw its contents on the floor, and then laid our daughter inside.

Tess wedged a pillow and a throw cushion in the front of the drawer to protect Lily. Next, she pulled a Kevlar vest from under the bed and double-layered it behind the drawer front for good measure.

"Remember, Lily, keep quiet and still, even if you hear gunshots." Tess did something to her phone and passed it to our daughter before adding, "If you don't hear anyone for a long time after the gunshots end—longer than it takes to sing the fairy song in your head twenty times, then you can call Lainey and Danny and tell them where you are, okay?"

Lily must have nodded because Tess whispered, "I love you lots, Lilypot," as she closed the drawer.

Sounds of gunfire and someone crying out made Tess pause for a moment.

"Come on, Tess, you can do this," Jonesy said in encouragement.

I, however, became mute, unable to speak as I stared at my wife's pale face. I willed her to move and grab herself a Kevlar vest, but she must have forgotten about it. We'd be having words about that when I saw her.

She was shaking so hard it took two attempts on the fingerprint scanner for the drawer containing the hidden weapons to open, but once it did, Tess took no time at all loading the full magazine clip into the rifle. After pocketing another full clip, she dropped to the floor, army-crawling away from the drawers to crouch between Lily's desk and toy box. From that position, she was a few feet from the back of the door, so she had a clear shot at whoever opened it. It was also far enough away from the drawers that they'd escape the bullets if they opened fire on her.

The sound of gunfire hitting glass, furniture, and walls in the kitchen could be heard clearly in Lily's room, and Danny's dog barked loudly. Tess pulled Bess to her side and tried to soothe her, telling her she was a good girl when she finally stopped barking.

After wiping her shaking hands on her jeans, Tess held up the rifle, her finger poised and ready over the trigger.

Bess growled as the door handle lowered. "Shh," Tess whispered, though she kept the rifle still as she stared down its sights.

A tall figure dressed head to toe in black moved cautiously into the bedroom, and with their eyes focused on Lily's bed, lowered their weapon.

"We assume he thought the doll was Lily," Kevin said. But neither Jonesy nor I could speak until the gunman began backing out of the room.

"I think—"

Before I could finish speaking, Bess ran out from beside Tess and leapt towards the gunman with a loud growl.

It took a split second for him to raise his rifle and shoot.

"No," Tess screamed before opening fire, shooting him repeatedly as she held the rifle higher. His body jumped and recoiled as each bullet hit, but my brave wife didn't stop shooting until she put a bullet between his eyes. When his lifeless body hit the wall and slumped to the floor, she finally lowered her weapon.

Tess shook her head before glancing down at Bess. When she saw the gruesome sight below, she let out a pained cry and sank to her knees beside her. Bess was missing the top of her head—blood and shattered skull fragments lay all around her. Tess reached out and touched her back leg, whispering how sorry she was and that she'd look after Danny for her. My eyes filled with tears, and I swallowed hard to clear the lump in my throat.

A noise out in the hallway had Tess raising her rifle again. The sound of gunfire had ceased, but my wife wasn't taking any chances.

"Tess, are you okay in there?" Franco shouted. Tess scrambled to her feet without letting go of her weapon.

"Franco, is it safe?" Tess asked.

"It's safe, honey. I'll come get you," he replied.

"TESS!"

"TESS!"

James and Ivan's voices were frantic with worry and fear.

Franco stepped over the gunman's body and, after stowing his Beretta in the back of his jeans, held up his hands in a placating manner. "It's just us, Tess. You can put down the rifle. You're safe now."

Ivan and James followed Franco into the room and stared at Tess's hands. She was still holding the rifle.

"Tess, where's Lily?" James questioned, though he, too, held up his hands.

Ivan glanced around the room and spotted Bess. "Oh, no, what did they do to you, little girl?" he choked as he dropped to his knees beside her.

"She tried to protect me, Ivan, and he killed her, so I kept on shooting until I knew he wouldn't get up again,"

Tess told him as she lowered her weapon. Then she stepped into his open arms.

"You did well, *milaya moya*. You kept Lily safe, yes?" he asked.

"I hid her in a drawer," she told him.

"I'll get her," James said, taking a few steps towards them. Before he could get there, Franco and Ivan yelled, "NO!"

"We need to move this fucker first and cover Bess up," Franco said. "And it'd be best to put a blanket over Lily's head while we carry her through to our quarters. She shouldn't have to see her home like this."

As I watched Ivan drag the duvet from Lily's bed and place it carefully over Bess, I said, "Stop the video, Kevin. I've seen enough."

Chapter Twenty-Nine

KOLYA

"I'm so proud of Tess," Jonesy said as he stared at the now blank screen of Kevin's laptop. "Apart from forgetting to put on the Kevlar vest, she did everything she should have. All that training we did with her paid off. She wasn't letting that fucker anywhere near Lily."

Kevin shook his head and then glanced across at me. "Tess shouldn't have had to do it. I should have removed your phone's ability to override the security system, but it never even entered my mind to do so. You set the password and changed it regularly, and I knew you'd never give it away."

"Fucking Darius is to blame for that, Kev, not you," Rashid stated.

"He must have watched me key it into my phone," I growled.

"When did you change it?" Jonesy asked.

I thought back to when I'd changed the password for the security system app on my phone. No matter where I am or what I'm doing, I change all my passwords on the fifteenth of every month, always have done. Without my diary, I couldn't be sure who was guarding me on the fifteenth, but it was highly probable that Darius had been with me.

"I changed it on the fifteenth of October, and I can't recall whether he was with me, but it doesn't matter either way. Darius is a dead man walking."

"Too fucking right!" Jonesy agreed.

"How was Tess immediately after the attack?" I asked.

Watching her hide our daughter and witnessing her shaking hands as she took out the rifle was bad enough, but seeing that split second of horror on her face when the gunman shot Bess—the moment she knew she had to kill him—was something I will never forget. Yes, she was horrified, but she was also brave and determined. My wife would have given her life to save our daughter. Hearing Tess tell little Bess how sorry she was and that she'd look after Danny for her, all while stroking the little dog's leg, had brought tears to my eyes.

I'd sacked Danny and Lainey the day my wife tried to escape. The man had lost his job and home because I acted impulsively and vented my anger at the people Tess valued the most. But he must have been mourning the loss of his four-legged companion, the brave little terrier who'd tried to protect my family. She'd been with him when he was sleeping rough and helped him survive on the streets of this unforgiving city.

I was such a bastard, and I hoped they'd accept my apology and take their jobs back.

Kevin took a drink of water before he carried on speaking. "Tess was obviously upset, especially when we took her to Nan. She'd heard her cry out and thought she was dead. After giving Nan a shot of morphine, we carried her to the hallway in the manor to wait for the ambulance. She was in excruciating pain, but we had to move Nan from where she'd fallen. The extension was a mess, inside and out, and we didn't want anyone seeing the bodies of the men who'd attacked us."

"Poor Nan. She must have been so scared," Jonesy said.

"More so for Tess, Lily and the rest of us than herself," Kevin replied. "Nan asked us to bring Tess and Lily before the ambulance came; she needed to see for herself that they were okay."

"The woman has a heart so big that even a cunt like Darius couldn't hurt her," Rashid said.

"When Nan and Jack left in the Ambulance, Tess went into the kitchen where we were treating the injured. She spoke to everyone, reassuring them that they'd receive the best medical care. Ivan flew them to this hospital, and when Lily fell asleep, we all sat around the table and discussed the attack and what should happen next. Tess had to put Yannis in his place over a few things; he'd landed as the ambulance was due to arrive and was annoying the hell out of us."

"He'd come to check if his mercenaries had killed my son and cousin," I surmised. Just saying the words filled me with as much anger as it did dread, and my gut churned.

Everyone nodded in agreement.

"Tess said she wanted to go to Moscow to stay with your father, but James vetoed the idea."

"Why?" I asked. "If Tess and Lily had gone to Moscow, they would have been protected.

"James said that once Roman had them in Moscow, he'd never let them leave, and to be honest, boss, all of us agreed. I mean, you preferred to keep them away from your father as much as possible."

"This was different, though. Someone had come into my home intent on killing members of my family. The best course of action would have been for Tess, Lily, and James to spend time in Moscow until all threats were eradicated." I couldn't understand why they'd failed to see that.

My head throbbed as distress, anger, and frustration clouded my mind.

"Yannis said Tess and Lily could stay with him on Athilos, and James thought that was for the best," Kevin informed us.

"Did he now?" I grumbled.

"Tess said she'd rather stay on the yacht than with Yannis, but while they were there, a storm blew in, and the sea was too rough for them to remain. So, Tess, Lily and a handful of guards went to the villa. When the storm passed, Tess, Lily, Ivan and Franco walked down to see Adrianna. She had some photos of Lily from your last visit. While they were there, Adrianna mentioned she had some of you from when you used to visit before you met Tess. Apparently, she'd been secretly taking photographs of Yannis for years. She used to position herself by the rocks and snap photos of him and his guests. While going through the files, Tess learned from Adrianna that Yannis had met with Darius since you'd been abducted, and there were photographs to prove it. On a hunch, Franco searched through more files and discovered photos of Yannis with the assassin who took Tess down instead of you."

Jonesy swore. "What a sick, twisted bastard that fucker was. He tried to off you yet still carried on as if he was your friend for years. How cold and dead inside do you have to be to do something like that?"

"Well, he's certainly cold and dead now; Tess saw to that," Rashid replied. "Carl and Tanner said she didn't even hesitate. Ivan was carrying her onto the plane because she refused to leave James and Franco. She had Danny's gun in her bag, and with one shot, she took Yannis out for good, which created an opening for Carl to eliminate his guards."

"I wish I'd been there to see it," Jonesy said.

Rashid smirked. "Carl said that the bullet hit Yannis in the throat, so it would have taken a few seconds before he croaked it. I'd have loved to have seen the look on his face when he knew he was going to die."

"He deserved far worse than that," I declared. "I would have enjoyed making him suffer."

"Wouldn't we all?" Kevin said as he went to put the laptop in his bag.

Jonesy grabbed his arm. "Don't put it away yet, Kev. I want to see the video that Riass sent."

Kevin frowned. "Are you sure? I thought you might want to give it a while. Watching the attack was rough, but..."

"You were underneath Lucas," Rashid added. "We could see that he was dead, and to everyone who watched it, it looked like you two were, especially when you didn't move when they kicked your bodies."

Jonesy stared at Rashid. "You said that so we'd know to prepare ourselves for it, didn't you?"

"Forewarned is forearmed and all that," Rashid replied as he tapped Jonesy's shoulder.

Their close friendship and easy banter made me feel slightly envious. It also made me realise how stupid I'd been to write off Yannis's behaviour. I should have recognised it for what it was: a sign of a narcissistic psychopath who'd do anything to gain more wealth and power, even kill their best friend and his family.

I never had any close friends when I was growing up. Being the son of the deadliest pakhan in Russia made other parents wary, and most would discourage their children from associating with my brothers and me. In many respects, we were isolated from the outside world, and the few friends we had were sons of the men who worked for my father. That was probably why I valued the friendships I made while at uni, and why I often overlooked Yannis's unreasonable behaviour.

Kevin opened his laptop again and found the video that, despite my curiosity, I was sorely tempted to avoid.

"If it gets too much for either of you, just say the word, and I'll stop the video," Kevin said before pressing play.

Chapter Thirty

KOLYA

The video recording was so short, but its impact on Jonesy and I was seismic.

Seeing Lucas's dead body displayed on top of the pile as if it were a trophy was something that we'd never forget. Jonesy was underneath him, and I lay on the muddy ground underneath Jonesy. We'd been beaten badly, yet I could remember little of it. We'd obviously been drugged because there was no way we wouldn't have reacted to the kicking we received just seconds before the video ended. There was blood on our shirts, and we were as still as the dead, so I could understand why everyone thought that Jonesy and I had been killed.

Kevin gave us a translation of all the verbal shit Riass had spouted throughout the video and told us they'd initially thought that Darius had been burning on the large fire.

With my eyes fixed on Jonesy, I stated, "When we find Darius, we'll make him wish he *had* been burning on that fire."

Jonesy agreed. "I want him to suffer everything we went through before we kill him, then I'll etch Lucas's name on a bullet and shoot him in the gut. We can throw ourselves a party while we watch him die a slow and painful death."

"I hope you're inviting me to that party," Rashid said.

"And me," Kevin added. "But James told your father that *he* wanted to be the one to kill Darius, and Roman agreed to honour his wish."

"That won't be happening. I will not allow the taint of murder to darken my son's soul. No matter how deserving of death the person might be, killing them can harm your conscience irreparably. Besides, I don't believe James to be mentally capable of such an act," I said while glancing between Kevin and Rashid.

I could have kept the matter of James's alcohol and possible drug abuse between the family, but in my absence, I knew these men would have seen enough of his troubling behaviour to form their own opinion, and I trusted them to give it to me straight.

I'd discussed the matter extensively with Jonesy and knew I would need to make some tough decisions—ones that James may not thank me for.

"Kevin, I need you to tell me what happened on Christmas Day. What did my son do to upset Tess and Lily?"

When Kevin finished telling us about James's drunken rant—where he'd basically told his four-year-old sister that God was so cruel that he'd take her mother away, just like he'd done with me—I realised my son would need more help than I'd anticipated.

James adored Lily, and normally he would never do or say anything that would hurt her, but it was becoming increasingly clear that he was fighting a corruptive demon called addiction. However, it didn't stop me from being angry with him. Thinking of the fear and upset he caused my daughter made me grateful that he wasn't here; I'd have probably lashed out at him if he were, and as a parent, that didn't sit well with me.

Kevin went on to tell us how distant James had become toward Tess the longer I was missing, and he told us what James had said to her before he left them in Sicily.

"Sounds to me like James was trying to use alcohol to mask how low he was feeling," Rashid observed. "But who can blame him? He thought you'd been killed by terrorists, and he watched your body being kicked around like it was nothing."

Kevin nodded. "He worried that you'd been tortured before they killed you, and when he saw what had happened when the mercenaries attacked, it was like something inside him snapped. He felt guilty that he hadn't been there to protect Lily and Tess, and he was angry with me because I'd phoned Tess first instead of him. But Tess and Lily were my priority because they were in the house, and I didn't call James until we were all fully armed, which was only around forty seconds after I called Tess. By the time they'd unlocked the door to the range and made their way to us, it was almost over."

"You did the right thing, Kev," Jonesy assured him. "Arming yourselves was the priority. It could have been a very different outcome if you'd wasted even ten seconds on a phone call."

"We were only carrying handguns because the fucking press had taken to flying drones over the estate. There was a photo of Andy and Jack carrying rifles on the front page of one of the Sunday papers with the headline 'Family Fear ISIS Attack on UK Soil,' with a subheading that read, 'The family of murdered arms dealer Kolya Barinov are under armed guard due to ongoing threat from Islamic State terrorist cells in the UK'. They'd written the usual spiel that a source close to the family said...blah fucking blah, but it was enough to set alarm bells ringing throughout the security services. Luckily, you couldn't see the *type* of rifles Andy and Jack were carrying, or they'd have been up shit creek without a paddle. That fucking paper caused us a lot of headaches. James had to speak with someone from Thames Valley Police, counterterrorism, and the home secretary because of that particular headline. They wanted to know what intelligence we'd received and if we thought it was a credible threat."

"Fucking vipers," Jonesy muttered.

"Honestly, boss, James had it rough in those first few weeks," Kevin said. "On the day we found out you'd been ambushed and supposedly killed, he had to endure meetings with officials in the States to assure them that the stolen missile couldn't be used against the US and its allies. He also had the same shit to deal with from the UK government. Lily was pulled out of school and brought home immediately, but Tess was working at Sarah's Legacy in Sheffield, so it took longer to get her back to Oxford. They were pulling into the airport when James rang and told them to turn around and head to the motorway, and we were all scared to fucking death that something would happen to them on the way home. We got the video from Riass before they arrived, and Tess knew as soon as she walked in and saw our faces that the worst had already happened. Because of the missile theft and staff deaths in Turkey, we felt it was safer to avoid all airports for the time being. James couldn't be sure if the KOLCAT jet had been compromised, so he made alternative arrangements and arrived back in the UK around four the next morning."

Rashid added, "I flew out to Turkey that evening and started making enquiries. Your father sent Dima out to meet me, and James demanded updates on our progress every four hours. We travelled all over the middle east for weeks, but every time we thought we had a lead on Riass's whereabouts, we'd hit a brick wall."

"Roman said he didn't believe you'd been killed because the video wasn't anything like the others Riass had posted. He favoured public executions, and we couldn't see any bullet wounds on anyone but Lucas. Whenever we received what we thought was credible intel, Tess and James hoped and prayed that it would lead us to you, and it was hard for us to watch their despair when it all came to nothing. That's why, after the attack in Oxford, Tess asked Roman not to tell her about any more leads. After killing that gunman in Lily's bedroom, she knew she wasn't mentally able to deal with the constant disappointments. He agreed and said he'd not say any more unless he could deliver you in person, which is exactly what he did, although I didn't believe it was the best thing for Tess," Kevin admitted.

"James was managing both KOLCAT US and UK, as well as poring over every little detail about your ambush, the attack in Oxford, and the ongoing search for you. He was running himself into the ground, and we all tried to warn him. Eventually, your brother convinced him to fly to Greece to see Tess and Lily, and that's when all the shit went down with Yannis. I think that's what tipped James over the edge because Nate said he'd been drinking heavily since he arrived in Sicily."

I found all the information overwhelming. Hearing and seeing how my family suffered because of Yannis, Darius, and fucking Riass spawned a myriad of emotions that tumbled like heavy rocks through my already weakened psyche.

I was Kolya Barinov, a billionaire businessman, engineering genius and owner of a world-renowned company, yet I felt like a complete failure. My name, status, and business achievements meant nothing if the people I loved were suffering. I knew I'd bear mental scars from my ambush and captivity, and I accepted it. But it appeared my wife and son had wounds that were just as deep.

I hadn't realised I was crying until Jonesy came to sit on my bed and said, "Hey, come on, Kolya. We'll get him sorted out, don't worry. James is strong like his dad. He'll overcome whatever shit he's going through because we won't let him fall. Most of us have known him since he was a kid, so he's like family to us. Once you get him to acknowledge he has a problem, George can get him into rehab or some treatment programme. Same with Tess; you know she needs help. They might not want to admit it, but they'll give in eventually. Neither are good liars. Can you remember when Carl had his favourite Playboy mags go missing and kept accusing Tanner? Whenever James came out of his room, he looked as guilty as hell, and within three days, he'd confessed and tried handing them back."

Rashid chuckled. "I remember that. Carl said he wouldn't take them back because he thought some of the pages would be stuck together. When Lucas coughed and said, "Wank fest" under his breath, everyone started laughing. James went bright red and ran back into his bedroom. He wouldn't come out for the rest of the day, poor kid."

The memory made me smile. Although he'd received a telling-off for taking something that didn't belong to him, the event gave him an opportunity to ask some awkward and embarrassing questions about the changes his teenage body was going through. He knew the basics about sex, but my poor son had begun to think the number of erections he'd been experiencing meant there was something physically wrong with him.

We'd already decided that Tess would be the one to have 'the talk' with Lily when she was old enough because the thought of my daughter asking questions about sex filled me with dread.

Crying in front of these men made me feel both embarrassed and ashamed, so I wiped my eyes and took a deep breath before saying, "I'm sorry; I don't know what came over me. Watching the videos and hearing what's been happening was a lot for me to deal with."

I'm not sure what I expected to see in their expressions. They were all tough, no-nonsense ex-soldiers with that typical British stiff upper lip, but they looked at me with concern and empathy. Rashid's eyes were red-rimmed, and Kevin had tears running down his cheeks. Meanwhile, Jonesy—the man who'd kept my spirit intact for the past few months—clasped my forearm in support and said, "Don't forget the pact we made in that hellhole, Kolya. We don't ever apologise for crying. Doesn't matter that we've been rescued; it still stands. We've got this, mate, trust me."

No one moved or spoke for at least thirty seconds, and the only sound in the room was the faint ticking of the clock above the door.

"Don't know about you lot, but the lack of fucking tea is making my eyes water. Anyone fancy a cuppa?" Rashid asked, breaking the silence and lightening the mood in one go.

Chapter Thirty-One

KOLYA

Grayson came in with a nurse as we were drinking our tea and told us we could go home, although Jonesy would need to come back for several appointments with orthopaedics and physiotherapy.

Before he left, I spoke to Grayson about James and asked for his advice. Kevin opened the laptop again and brought George into the conversation via video call, and between us, we came up with a plan.

Jonesy called his aunt on the way to the hotel and told her he was leaving the hospital. Luckily, she was still in Lassiter's, so she and his cousin would wait for him to arrive. He wasn't looking forward to telling her he wouldn't be going home with them, but neither of us felt comfortable without the other, so Jonesy decided he'd stay at Glengarran with me.

As we arrived back at Lassiter's, I received a call from the dentist to say that my denture plate would be ready tomorrow. Greta, my PA—whom James had retained—had organised appointments for Jonesy and me with my tailor, and prior to us leaving for Glengarran, a hairdresser from the salon downstairs was coming to give us both a trim.

Before James arrived, I placed a call to Peter Cramer of Cramer's Jewellery here in London. I'd purchased my and Tess's wedding rings from his family-owned shop on Bond Street, and I asked if he had anything similar in stock. They'd stolen mine when I was first captured, and my hand felt bare without it. The ring was a symbol of my and Tess's love and commitment, which is something we needed to work on after everything that had happened. I hoped that seeing a wedding band on the third finger of my left hand would show Tess that no matter what her fears were, I could still be the devoted husband she knew before we were so cruelly separated.

Although I was still angry and upset with her for sleeping with Franco, I knew she was under a great deal of stress at the time. She'd tried to tell me it meant nothing, but I'd been unwilling to listen, and it had certainly meant something to me.

I confided in Jonesy about it, and he was certain that Tess would never have looked at Franco that way if I'd still been around. I didn't tell him about Signor Russo, or that Tess had thought I wanted her dead. It was still too much for me to think about and angered me more than her affair with Franco. I hope it hadn't taken her long to get over that notion. She'd travelled safely with Lily to Inverness in a luxury jet before being flown by helicopter to Glengarran. I'd made sure they'd had a meal before she'd left, but all Tess did was push the food around her plate. She had protection in the form of armed guards and could roam the property and grounds at her leisure, so she should know by now that her health and well-being were important to me.

I told my staff that Tess wasn't to be informed about my

hospital stay. She would have wanted to fly back to London to see me, and I needed time to come to terms with what she'd done. Jealousy was an emotion that was hard to control, and I wasn't sure if I felt strong enough to deal with it when I was feeling so weak.

I hadn't miraculously gotten over her betrayal during the past three days, but I could think about it rationally now, especially since seeing those videos and hearing more about Tess's strength, determination, and bravery in those terrifying situations. Tess would fight to the death for those she loves, and I hoped she'd fight just as hard for our marriage.

Greta had arranged for clothing to be sent to the hotel for Jonesy and me, and when I entered my bedroom, I found a selection of warm, casual clothing draped across the bed. I'd sent her my and Jonesy's measurements, which had horrified yet didn't surprise me, and as always, Greta had excelled in her brief. The clothes were three sizes smaller than I'd worn before my capture, yet they were all to my taste, and even the jeans seemed softer than regular denim. The cotton long-sleeved T-shirts and soft cashmere jumpers sat delicately against the bruised and broken areas of my sore skin. Most of the cuts and scrapes had scabbed over, but some were still quite tender and would catch me off guard if I moved or even lay a certain way. I was still suffering pain from Riass and Bashir's beatings, which pissed me the fuck off, and I wished more than anything that my father had kept them alive so that Jonesy and I could deliver them as much agonising torture as they had given us.

My father called to inform me of their demise as I was getting ready to leave the hospital, and at the time, I felt relief in knowing they were gone, but that soon changed after our brief journey to my hotel in Mayfair. Even lounging in the buttery soft leather chairs in the sitting room felt uncomfortable.

"George is on his way up," Kevin informed me with a yawn. "Sorry, boss, I was up late sorting out the new app for the internal cameras at Glengarran. I'm not sure why we can't get the sound and video feed to run in sync. I'll have another go at it when I get back to Oxford."

"Send me the details as soon as it's ready," I told him.

"Will do," he said while looking at me in a way I couldn't decipher.

"What is it, Kevin?" I asked wearily.

"I'm worried about Tess. She seems wary of her guards, even Nate. I can't ask him why because we aren't speaking, but unless she and Lily are going to bed, she won't go anywhere in the house without Mrs Braeburn or old John, and she'll only go outside if one of the estate staff is around. Tess is glued to Lily's side constantly, and she's starting to look ill again—like she did in Sicily when she wasn't sleeping."

"I'm heading up there tomorrow, Kevin, so I'll find out what's going on with her then."

"Aren't you going to call her?" he asked.

I shrugged my shoulders. "There's no point. Tess wouldn't tell me what was troubling her. You know what she's like."

"Tess has changed, boss. When you were captured, her world spun out of control, and she had to learn a new way of coping. The only time she hid her feelings was when she tried to convince us that her nightmares were getting better. But I could tell she was lying even over our video calls. Tess was desperate to get to Glengarran, but it wasn't possible while Riass was still a credible threat. Now she's there, she seems… I don't know. She's just not right, that's all. Maybe if she had her phone and could speak to—"

I banged my fist on the lamp table and yelled, "No! She cannot have her phone back until I know she can be trusted."

"Trusted to do what exactly? She's hardly going to try to escape with Lily from the Scottish Highlands. Everyone's been calling me to ask how she is and—"

"Who?" I demanded.

"What?"

"Who has been calling her, Kevin?"

"Karen and Amina, Nan, Jack, and Jean's nurse. They were all wondering why her phone was switched off."

"Is Jean ok?" I asked with sickening trepidation. Why the fuck had I not contacted her? Tess would never forgive me if something happened to Jean while she was unreachable.

Kevin nodded. "There's been no change over the past couple of weeks, but her nurse had seen the news about you being found and wanted to say how relieved she was. Tess was in contact either by phone or email every day, but she hadn't responded to a video call request. Tess never misses those, so Jean's care team was getting worried."

"I'm sorry, Kevin. I left her phone here, and I never even thought about it while I was in the hospital."

I wasn't exactly telling the truth. The phone was here and was probably out of charge by now, but I had thought about it. Often, in fact. I can't remember how many times I'd imagined Franco calling her phone and wondering what was wrong when she didn't pick up. I hadn't checked it yet because I wanted to deal with James first, but I assumed he'd try to get in touch. You don't walk away from being in love that easily, especially when the woman you loved was Tess. I knew that only too well.

Before Kevin could question me further, I heard the door to my suite open, and George entered the room.

"No, don't get up on my behalf, Kolya," George said as he put his briefcase on the sofa and took off his jacket.

Turning to Kevin, I asked, "Would you mind ordering us tea and coffee and a few sandwiches to be sent up from the kitchens? Ask them to deliver a selection of desserts, too. I need to keep up my calorie intake, and I doubt I'll want to eat much after speaking with James. Check with Dima to see what everyone wants before you put the order in."

Kevin took out his phone before heading out into the hallway.

"Is James on his way?" George enquired.

"Greta said he's been held up due to a conference call from the States starting later than scheduled. He'll be here within the next thirty minutes," I informed him.

"I have a list of places I feel might be appropriate, but James must be willing to accept the help you're offering."

He had to be. As his father, I would fight until my dying breath to get him fit and healthy. I just hadn't expected I'd need to fight *him*.

Chapter Thirty-Two

KOLYA

Despite wearing clothing that fit me for the first time since my rescue *and* having a full set of teeth thanks to my new denture plate, I still felt like shit. I almost called off my visit to Cramer's to collect the new ring, especially after having been snapped by the press after coming out of the dentist. They were like vultures—each flash from their cameras picking at my bones and eating away at my confidence.

It wasn't my only reason for having second thoughts about the ring. Hearing some of the vile comments about Tess from my raging son last night had left me with thoughts that my fractured mind shouldn't have been entertaining. Deep down, I knew they were bullshit barbs meant to hurt and blame everyone else for his addiction and weakness, but those barbs had certainly hit their mark where my marriage was concerned. Although I tried my best to ignore them, they'd kept me up most of last night, so I was too fucking tired to deal with the world today.

To say James was angry about my intervention would be an understatement of epic proportions, and it took hours of

271

argumentative conversations and, yes, tears and pleading from both of us to finally get him to open up about his addiction and recent behaviour. What shocked me more than anything was that his drinking and drug-taking had started almost a year before I was abducted.

He was used to having drinks after work with colleagues from KOLCAT, but he'd avoid drinking during the day, even when meeting with officials and potential clients. That all changed when he began a clandestine affair with the wife of Daniel Trent, the US Secretary of Defence. They would meet two afternoons and one evening a week at the hotel James owned in Washington, where in my son's words, they'd "Drink, fuck, and get high enough to drown out the wrongness of their affair." The woman had been the one to introduce James to cocaine, and pretty soon, he found it hard to live without the increased pleasure, energy, and self-confidence it gave him.

James had fallen in love and believed her when she said she'd leave her husband. Carrie Trent was twenty years older than my son and had two teenage children, but James hadn't cared about any of that. She had him looking at property in Washington that they could move into, something close to the school her children attended.

He said she broke off the affair without warning and wouldn't give an explanation as to why. James was worried about her and confided in his friend Brad, who also works for KOLKAT US. He told him all about the affair and asked for his advice on the matter. James was shocked to find out that Carrie had propositioned Brad at a fundraising event six weeks beforehand while she was still seeing him. Brad hadn't taken her up on it, so she'd focused her attention on another man around his age while her husband was busy.

Both shocked and incensed, James left work so he wouldn't take his hurt and anger out on any of his staff. He spent the rest of the afternoon taking cocaine and drinking vodka, trying to forget that he'd been played like a fool. He made himself ill and almost ended up in the hospital. Carl and Tanner had threatened to call me if he pulled a stunt like that again, and he promised them he wouldn't. But he couldn't let Carrie's betrayal go and decided on a little payback.

James contacted a private detective and had them follow Carrie. Four weeks later, he had a report and photographs detailing the cougar's affair with her latest toyboy, which he sent to her husband anonymously.

He wasn't sure what he expected to happen, although he said he needed Carrie to hurt the way he'd been hurting. But nothing changed at all for the Trent family. The private detective confirmed that, although Carrie had behaved herself for a few weeks, she was back to screwing men almost half her age, as was her husband, apparently. No wonder he hadn't given a fuck about what she was doing.

He met with Daniel Trent the day that I was taken captive. After seeing the video that Riass sent, he believed I was dead, yet he still had to brave meetings with several officials in the US to assure them that the weapon Riass had stolen was no threat to America and its allies. He said he couldn't have gotten through that day without a few lines of coke and had carried on using it until he ended up in Sicily with Tess and Lily. He replaced the drug with alcohol during his stay, but the excessive amount he imbibed made him feel angry and argumentative, especially towards Tess.

James hated the fact that he'd put Tess and Lily in danger by agreeing with Yannis that they should stay on the island with him. He'd argued with the betraying bastard as

Tess and Lily were about to land that day in Kefalonia and said he knew that Yannis and his men would attack them. James admitted that he wanted to be the one to kill him, but instead, he'd ended up under Franco on the runway, and my brave wife had saved his life by killing Yannis herself.

He couldn't get his head around why he was so conflicted about Yannis's death, but George had assured him that it was okay to grieve the man he thought he knew while hating the despicable person he'd become. James said that he felt as though he'd been living a lie for years and concluded he'd been played once again by someone who was supposed to care.

James appeared to have felt belittled by Tess, although it wasn't because of anything she'd done to him personally. He seemed jealous of my father's love and respect for Tess and said everyone worried about how she was coping while expecting him to carry on as normal.

He said that her nightmares had scared the shit out of him, and he'd felt guilty that she'd had to shoulder the burden of killing Yannis, as well as the gunman who attacked our home.

During one of his angry rants, James expressed that he didn't like the fact that my brother had spent most of his nights at the villa sleeping beside my wife. He said that Yuri seemed far too close to Tess, and he'd often caught him kissing and cuddling up to her throughout the day. The fact that Yuri and I looked so alike made it seem as though she'd replaced me for him, and he'd been angry with them both, although he hadn't expressed it until Christmas Day.

Instead of having a go at Tess and Yuri, he'd upset Lily after Lainey said prayers before they ate. Hearing Tess and his sister cry because of something he'd said destroyed James.

Even though it wasn't common knowledge, James knew that Yuri was gay, but after seeing how he was with Tess, he'd begun to question my brother's sexuality.

I told him not to be ridiculous. But his words had sown seeds of doubt and resentment I simply couldn't shake, and I was determined to have it out with my brother before I left for Glengarran.

James had thrown a few accusations my way too. He said I always prioritised work over family, and if I'd been around more when his mother was alive, she might still be here today. He accused me of not loving her as much as I do my 'current wife' and said that my family had never treated Catherine as well as they do Tess. I told him he was wrong and that I loved them equally, but he knew it was a lie.

What I feel for Tess goes beyond love.

It's both light and dark, obsessive and possessive, and had I died at the hands of Riass, it would have transcended with me into the afterlife and remained until we were reunited in heaven or hell.

James was also right when he said that my family hadn't treated Catherine as well as they do Tess. Don't get me wrong, the woman bore me a son, so my father loved and respected her. But Catherine rarely visited Moscow with me, and when she did, she never seemed comfortable around them unless she was flirting with Yuri, which was a lost cause, as we know. Or was it?

My family adored Tess from the moment she saved my life after taking a bullet with my name on it. But that grateful adoration turned to love when they finally met her in person. My father calls Tess his daughter and has often declared that she was born to be a Barinov. He's right. She was always meant to be mine. My wife. My heart. My soulmate.

James refused to go to a rehab clinic. Still, he agreed for George to set him up with a programme consisting of whatever medical intervention was necessary during the dependency withdrawal process, paired with daily counselling sessions. George thought that considering what had happened during the attack at our home in Oxford, it would be better for James to stay somewhere that wouldn't trigger traumatic memories. It was also the place where we'd grieved for his mother, who died after falling from her horse on the grounds of the estate.

It was decided that James would stay in our suite at the hotel with a nurse and a counsellor specialising in addiction. Dave and Greg would replace Carl and Tanner as his guards until he was well enough to face the outside world, which George advised could take anywhere between four to eight weeks.

Grayson came by with a nurse and, after examining James, drew a few samples of his blood to have analysed at the hospital. He'd asked James to write down what he'd taken in the last twenty-four hours, and when I saw what he'd written, I felt physically sick. He'd done lines of coke from breakfast until well into the evening, and he couldn't recall how much vodka he drank throughout the day. He said it wasn't as much as he usually has because he'd had a design proposal to go over before his conference call today. He was under the impression that the 30mg of temazepam he took nightly for his insomnia didn't count because it was a prescription drug from a doctor in the States.

Grayson was furious. He said that any doctor who'd recommend such a high amount every night should be struck off. He offered to call in on James every evening before he left for home. I told Grayson I'd ensure he had a deluxe room and board if he wanted to stay in the hotel during the week, and he agreed it would make things a lot easier for him.

I was relieved beyond measure knowing that James was finally getting the help he needed, yet I was angry with myself for not noticing that something was going on with him. Spending time with my children should have been my priority, but as always, I'd let work get in the way of family. That would have to end.

"Boss, we can't park any closer," Andy said as he pulled up three doors away from Cramer's. "We can wait until the delivery van moves, or Carl, Tanner, and Dima can escort you in from here.

Bond Street was busy today despite it being cold with intermittent rain and sleet. The sky was heavy with dull grey clouds, and you'd be forgiven for thinking it was much later than midday.

The well-lit, tastefully decorated shop windows all screamed luxury and expense. Each item on the racks of clothing being wheeled from the delivery van into the shop next door to Cramer's would probably cost the average person an entire month's wage.

Turning towards the men guarding me today, I declared, "I want to be in and out as quickly as possible. Andy, drop us off here but take the van's parking spot as soon as it leaves. Let me know if you see any more photographers hanging around. I don't want my pitiful image being tomorrow's front-page news."

Chapter Thirty-Three

TESS

"I hope you're going to eat some of this," Mrs Braeburn said as she handed me another potato.

We were having chicken and mushroom pie this afternoon, and I'd volunteered to peel the accompanying vegetables.

"I'll try," I told her, and I truly meant it. Mrs Braeburn's pies were so tasty and filling, and her pastry-making skills were second to none. However, I wouldn't admit that to Nan.

"You're wasting away, lass," Old John commented as he looked up from the book he was reading to Lily.

"Dinnae worry, John. A good slice of pie will put some meat on her bones," Mrs Braeburn quipped as she crimped the edges of a large pie. She'd made three of them, enough to feed a small army. Father Creahan was calling in this afternoon, and she never let him leave without a hearty meal.

The kitchen at Glengarran was an eighteen by twenty-foot fusion of period features, painted wooden cabinetry and modern stainless steel. A thick oak table that comfortably seated twelve people dominated the space from where Mrs Braeburn ruled the centuries-old roost. The old Aga oven still threw out enough heat to keep the large room cosy, and there were four leather armchairs positioned strategically around it. It's where I'd been spending most of my time during this visit.

Old John nodded towards my belly. "You're not, ya know... in the family way, are ya?"

Mrs Braeburn gasped in horror. "What is wrong with ya, man? Ya dinnae ask a lassie that."

Unperturbed, Old John replied, "Well, the lass is off her scran, and she's more peely-wally than is healthy if ya ask me. She had to put her wedding ring on her necklace after losing it in the bowl of tatties, which should tell ya there's something amiss."

"John Campbell, you'll mind ya manners in ma kitchen, or you'll be oot in the dreich."

Holding up a peeled potato, I asked, "Can someone please translate that conversation? You completely lost me at peely-wally."

"He pointed out that you're off your food and looking paler than usual," Mrs Braeburn replied.

"Ah, so that's what peely-wally means."

Lily giggled. "That sounds *really* funny. Peely-wally, peely-wally."

"And what about dreich?" I asked. "You said, 'Oot in the dreich'."

She nodded towards the long kitchen window. "See what the weather's like right now—grey sky, drizzly and damp? That's dreich, and if he doesnae behave himself, he'll be eating his pie from the wee bird table oot there."

Mrs Braeburn shook her head in Old John's direction before carrying on with her task.

Margaret Ellen Braeburn had spent most of her sixty-seven years at Glengarran, beginning her working life as a maid for the old Laird and his family when she was fifteen. Eventually, her work ethic and commitment to the Glengarran Estate earned her the position of housekeeper, and I couldn't imagine anyone more suited to the role.

Although she had a slender frame and stood at barely five foot five inches tall, Mrs Braeburn was as strong as an ox, and her well-practised death stare had left our burly Russian guards in no doubt whatsoever of who was in charge here.

Oh yes, our housekeeper took the stern look to a whole other level. Yet, when she smiled, her baby-blue eyes and perpetually rosy cheeks changed her features completely. She always wore her pure white, shoulder-length hair up in a bun during the day, but whenever she attended any social gatherings, Mrs Braeburn preferred wearing it down in stylish loose waves.

Our relationship had been rocky in the beginning. Suspicious by nature, Mrs Braeburn thought I was yet another young gold-digger who'd seduced and married an older man. That changed when we'd scattered Sarah's ashes in the loch, and she'd learned more about my background from Jean, with whom she'd become fast friends.

She toned down her accent in front of Kolya and our Russian guards, but she was decidedly more Scottish around me.

"Are you still going to teach me how to knit, Mrs Braeburn?" Lily asked.

"Of course I am, Lily. I've ordered a set of short,

chunky knitting needles just for you. That reminds me, John, did ya happen to notice if the wool shop was open this morning?"

A loud ringing from the phone on the kitchen wall interrupted his reply.

I wasn't allowed to answer the phone, which Mrs Braeburn was seriously unhappy about. She couldn't understand why I was living under so many restrictions when I was supposed to be—in her words—the lady of the house.

After wiping her hands on her apron, she picked up the cordless phone and said in her well-practised posh voice, "Glengarran Estate, Mrs Braeburn speaking. How may I help you?"

Within seconds, her face broke into a beaming smile. "Kevin, hello. Tell me you're paying us a visit. Your man is here, and he's as miserable as the weather."

"I heard that," Nate yelled from the hallway. He was helping Jim, one of the estate workers, with the new internal security cameras. No matter how often they tried to fix them, no one could get them to work. It was driving Kevin mad, but Mrs Braeburn always dismissed his concerns. It made me wonder whether she was sabotaging the cameras on purpose. And why shouldn't she? Glengarran was her home, as well as her place of work. I could understand that she felt spied upon. It was an invasion of her privacy, no matter the reason for it.

Mrs Braeburn smiled at whatever Kevin had said and then passed me the phone. Before my hand made contact, it was intercepted by Artyom, one of the new Russian guards.

After gruffly asking Kevin what he wanted to speak to me about, he paused for a moment, then his pale face turned a vibrant shade of pink.

"Here," he said as he pushed the phone towards me. He pointed towards the utility room without making eye contact.

I was so grateful for the chance to speak to Kevin that I didn't question his odd behaviour, although I was curious as to why I'd finally been allowed to talk to someone.

After closing the heavy utility room door behind me, I said, "Hi, Kevin. I can't tell you how happy I am to hear from you, but I'm surprised they've let me have the phone."

"I don't think he wanted to relay the questions I'd just asked him in public," Kevin replied before he burst out laughing.

"Why? What did you say?"

"I said that the boss has requested I pack some personal items for you, and I told him to ask you what sex toys and lube you wanted me to add."

"Oh my God, Kevin, I can't believe you did that," I said through an unladylike snort of laughter. "No wonder he was so embarrassed."

"Serves the nosy fucker right. Not giving you access to the phone is ridiculous," he grumbled.

I sat myself down on the step stool and leaned back against the washing machine.

"They're following Kolya's orders, Kevin, so don't go blaming them for all this."

"Oh, believe me, I know who's to blame, and I told him I don't agree with what he's doing."

Despite knowing what else Kolya had planned for me, I couldn't help asking, "How's he doing, Kevin? And how is Jonesy? I wished I'd seen him before I came here."

"You can't let on that I told you this, but Kolya collapsed when he was at the dentist and was rushed to the hospital. They put him in with Jonesy, and he spent three days in there recuperating. It's where he should have been from the start," Kevin insisted.

"Kolya's always been stubborn," I replied with a sigh.

My stomach sank to my feet when Kevin said they'd rushed him to the hospital. I should have been beside my husband, looking after him in his hour of need, but obviously, I was no one to him now. Soon enough, I'd be nothing more than a memory.

At least I'd get to say goodbye to Kevin.

"I love you, Kevin. I just wanted you to know that. You've been such a great friend to me over the years, and I want to thank you for all you've done to keep Lily and me safe. I know what happened with Franco reflects badly on me, but I hope you can look past that and remember all the good times we had. All the fun and laughter."

"I love you too, Tess, but that sounded like a goodbye, so now I'm worried. Tell me you don't plan on running again, sweetheart; the Scottish Highlands aren't somewhere you want to be roaming at this time of year."

I closed my teary eyes and shook my head, grateful that Kevin couldn't see me.

"I'm not running," I whispered. "So please don't worry about me. I just wanted you to know how much you mean to me, that's all. Could you tell Danny and Lainey that, too, and Nan and Jack? I'm so sorry that Danny and Lainey lost their jobs. I truly didn't think that Kolya would take it out on them. When you get the chance, take whatever jewellery I have left at Oxford and send it to Danny, please. Tell him to sell it and put the money towards somewhere to live. I never want him to struggle again, Kevin."

"I swear you have nothing to worry about where Danny is concerned, Tess. You can call and speak to him and Lainey once you get your phone back. They're both so worried about you. They wanted to head straight to Glengarran when they heard you were there. I told them to wait because I think the boss will be in touch with them soon. Karen

and Amina have also been blowing up my phone. They've never been out of contact with you for this long unless you've been on holiday, so they've been worried. Karen said that Jean had asked for her hair permed, so the mobile hairdresser's going to do it on Friday. Nan and Jack are flying up to Glengarran next week, so you'll see them soon enough."

Would I, though? Would Kolya let me live long enough for Nan and Jack to see me one last time?

Of course, I couldn't ask Kevin that, and it was obvious that Kolya hadn't made him aware of his plans for me. I had no doubt that if he knew, Kevin would try to rescue me, but that wouldn't go down well for him when Kolya found out.

No matter how much I wanted to live, I couldn't put those I loved in danger.

"How's my other half?" Kevin asked. *"Mrs Braeburn said he's as miserable as the weather."*

"He certainly looks it, but he hasn't spoken to me since before I tried to leave, so I couldn't say for sure," I admitted.

Kevin was so quiet that I thought we'd become disconnected. Then, in a chilling voice, he queried, *"So you're telling me that Nate has been ignoring you?"*

"Well, yeah, pretty much. I think he blames me for Franco leaving. He did warn us, Kevin, but we ignored him, so I can't blame him for being angry. And I'm sure that Kolya gave him hell when I tried to leave, so he's probably upset about that, too."

"That's no fucking excuse, Tess. He's your friend, as well as your guard. You don't give your friends the cold shoulder when they need you the most. You're isolated enough already. I swear I didn't know he was acting like such a dick. We haven't spoken properly since he left Oxford with you, but don't worry, I'll be on the phone with him as soon as you hang up."

"Leave it, Kevin. I don't want to cause another argument between you two. I can't bear the fact that you're not speaking to each other. You need to get over whatever it was that caused the argument and make it right. You're in love, so stop hurting each other. Believe me, life is way too short to live with nothing but heartache."

Chapter Thirty-Four

TESS

Father Creahan sat in the wingback armchair closest to the roaring fire, his cheeks and nose glowing a rosy red. The priest had celebrated his sixtieth birthday while we were in Sicily, although with his weathered skin and pure white hair, he looked a little older. I made myself comfortable on the matching oxblood leather Chesterfield sofa, trying to think of a way to broach a subject that had entered my mind while writing those future letters to Lily.

If I couldn't be with my daughter throughout her life, then I needed to be with her in heaven. But the fact remained that I'd killed two men, so I'd broken one of the ten commandments. Twice! Add in the fact that I'd slept with Franco while my husband was still alive, and you have another one. "Thou shalt not commit adultery." Although, technically, I don't think the higher-ups should count that one. But if they did, my chances of getting through those pearly gates would be zero.

I wanted to know if God would be lenient with me. I

mean, I shot those men to save my family, not because I was some serial-killing nut job.

Earlier, Father Creahan had everyone around the dinner table thanking God for Kolya's and Jonesy's safe return, and he prayed that Lucas be granted a place with Him in heaven.

Lucas was an ex-soldier, so it was likely that he'd killed someone—either directly or indirectly. I'd never been in the military, yet I'd taken on a soldier's role when I'd shot and killed Yannis and the mercenary. So maybe I could go to heaven after all.

Mustering up excuses why I'd had to forsake religious and moral rules could be considered darkly comical when you consider the family I married into, but that's where my mind had taken me. As I've said before, my husband thinks the commandments are merely suggestions, not rules. If my death weren't so imminent, maybe I could do the same. But it was, so…I can't.

I needed to know I'd see my daughter again, or I would never rest in peace.

Mrs Braeburn had taken Lily up to her room so she could put on her pyjamas. She'd spilt both gravy and custard on her baby-pink jumper and had even got it in her hair. Mrs Braeburn insisted I allow her to take care of Lily while I entertained our visiting priest in the grand sitting room, and I allowed it this time. I wasn't worried about someone killing me off with a priest present. Even our new Russian guards joined in with the prayers before eating with us.

"You look as though you've got the weight of the world on your shoulders, Tess. What's troubling you?" the good father asked as he sipped on the merlot I'd poured him.

Father Creahan and I were alone in the toasty warm

sitting room. Still, I glanced at the door before speaking, making sure it remained closed. The curtains were open, and the fast-approaching wintery darkness sent an uneasy sense of foreboding scuttling down my spine.

"I wanted to thank you for mentioning Lucas in your prayers. People seem to have forgotten that only two men came back last week. Lucas was a loyal and honourable man who deserved to live a long and full life. Did you know he served his country before coming to work for Kolya?" I asked.

"Yes, they showed a photograph of him in his army uniform on the news after that video was posted online. Such an awful thing for his family to have seen. I honestly didn't think any of them would have survived."

I nodded my weary head in agreement before asking, "Father, do you honestly believe that God allows soldiers into heaven if they've killed someone in the line of duty? After all, "Thou shalt not Kill" is one of the ten commandments."

Father Creahan seemed taken aback by my question, and he paused for a moment before answering.

"As I understand it, everyone in the military must swear to God almighty to serve and protect their Queen and country. Their vow of protection means defending the vulnerable both here and in foreign lands beset by conflict and tyranny. Obviously, they understand that can often mean using deadly force, but it is a rare soldier indeed who will make light of taking a life in the line of duty."

Trying to clarify what he'd just said, I asked, "So what you are saying is, because they killed to protect others, their slate is wiped clean upon their death?"

Father Creahan smiled. "I don't think it's that simple, Tess. Most soldiers carry the weight of their actions for many years after they leave the military. No matter how honourable or necessary, or however many lives they saved, their memories are often their own form of purgatory."

"And don't I know it!" I stated under my breath.

"I'm sorry, did you say something?" he asked as he glanced towards the window.

The unmistakable sound of a helicopter reached me seconds before the sitting room was filled with light.

"Would this be your husband?" Father Creahan asked.

I failed to answer, rendered mute in abject fear. The last time I'd felt this way on seeing a helicopter land was when my home in Oxford was attacked by mercenaries. I was as scared right now as I was back then, though I knew who the passenger was this time.

It was Kolya!

My husband had come to reap my soul.

Chapter Thirty-Five

TESS

"Tess, what's wrong? You're shaking."

Taking a much-needed breath, I focused on the priest kneeling before me, my clammy hands clasped between his rough palms.

"I have to get to Lily," I whispered, pushing unsteadily to my feet. With my daughter beside me, I'd be safe. But she was currently upstairs with Mrs Braeburn, and I wasn't sure how long I'd zoned out for. I hadn't even been aware that Father Creahan had left his chair.

I stumbled towards the door, each breath I took seeming harder to summon than the one before. For a split second, I considered blocking the doorway with furniture and unlocking the room's hidden weapon stash, but a deep voice with a melodic Welsh accent had me dashing out into the hallway, fear be damned.

"Jonesy," I cried as I launched myself at the man who never failed to put a smile on my face.

"Oomph," he grunted as I propelled him into the newel post at the bottom of the stairs.

"Oh, God, I'm so sorry, Jonesy," I said when I noticed the cast on his left arm. The extensive bruising under his eyes and the tape across his nose made it appear as though he'd gone ten rounds with a heavyweight boxer. Our poor guard must have suffered terribly at the hands of those despicable men, and I hoped that Roman had returned that hurt a million times over.

Jonesy slung his good arm around me and pressed his lips to my forehead.

"You don't know how good it feels to see you, love," he exclaimed in a croaky voice.

"I'm sorry I didn't visit you in the hospital. I wanted to, but…"

"You were here keeping your daughter safe, as you've been doing all along. I'm so proud of you, Tess. When I saw the video footage of—"

Father Creahan cleared his throat, and I felt Jonesy's torso stiffen before he kissed my forehead again.

"It's good to see you, Jonesy. God saw fit to answer all our prayers and send you home. It…feels as though I'm witnessing one of His miracles!" the teary-eyed priest exclaimed.

He wasn't wrong. It was a miracle that Kolya and Jonesy had survived their ordeal.

Jonesy let go of me and shook Father Creahan's hand. "Thank you, Father, your prayers were much appreciated. You'll have to excuse me, though. It's been a long day, and I think I could sleep standing up."

"Of course. And there's no better place than Glengarran to rest and recover from your ordeal. I'll come by again later in the week, and if you'd like to talk to someone, be it a spiritual discussion or not, feel free to give me a call."

"Thank you, Father," Jonesy replied before glancing

back at me. A look of concern crossed his bruised face, sending a cold shiver down my spine.

Did he know what Kolya had planned for me?

"Kolya!" Father Creahan exclaimed. My stomach churned as I glanced behind Jonesy and spotted my husband and Dima heading through the arched doorway, their eyes fixed on me.

"Good evening, Father. I trust—"

A turbulent wave of nausea hit me from out of nowhere, and I couldn't escape to the downstairs bathroom fast enough to avoid the sudden unexpected reappearance of Mrs Braeburn's chicken and mushroom pie.

Chapter Thirty-Six

KOLYA

"Do you like my picture, Daddy?" Lily asked as she waved her latest masterpiece in front of me. My darling daughter had drawn her very own loch monster, or so she had proclaimed. As a sketch, I was impressed, yet once she dug out her crayons, it lost some of its charm. It now resembled something Stephen King fans would have been proud of, although I couldn't tell her that.

"I love it! You're so artistic, Lily. You must have been practising a lot while I was away."

She nodded her pretty little head and smiled proudly.

"Santa brought me some paints and felt tips for Christmas, and Signor Russo showed me and Ivan the best place to sit to paint the orchards—*that's where there are lots of trees with fruit on them,*" she added.

Her mention of the Sicilian don had me glancing across from my seat at the large oak dining table to the open stone fireplace, where Tess sat cross-legged in front of the roaring fire. Signor Russo would be calling to check on my wife in a couple of days, and the very idea of it made my temper flare.

It was something that added to the very long list of things that had pissed me off since my return, and at the very top of that list was the woman I married. Or, to be precise, the things she had done.

It would be so much easier if my love and concern for her had diminished, yet frustratingly, that wasn't the case at all. I loved and admired her more than ever, but I could tell those feelings weren't reciprocated. When I arrived here this evening, she took one look at me and threw up in the hallway, sparking concern from everyone around her.

Mrs Braeburn had fussed over the both of us when she emerged moments later with my daughter. She sent Tess upstairs to get cleaned up and to change into her pyjamas, saying she'd heat up some chicken broth for her later. After giving me an unexpected hug, the normally so reserved housekeeper informed me that my wife had hardly been eating since her arrival and said she was becoming increasingly concerned about her.

In the five days since I last saw her, Tess must have dropped at least seven pounds in weight. Her pink fleece pyjamas hung so loosely that she had to keep pulling the bottoms up, and there were darker shadows under her pretty amber eyes. She had barely spoken two words to me since my arrival, and it galled me to know that she had more concern for Jonesy, who was sound asleep upstairs, than she had for me.

I deserved the same attention and concern. More so, even. But it seemed as though she had given up on me, on us. She'd even removed her wedding ring, and after all the trouble I went to earlier, seeing her ring finger bare had felt like a knife to the heart. I was currently wearing a plain temporary wedding band until the replica of my original ring was delivered. As a symbol of my commitment, I had Tess's name and the date of our marriage engraved on the inside, fool that I am. The way I felt right now, I could rip it off my finger and sling it into the fire.

After passing some brighter crayons and another sheet of paper to Lily, I prompted, "I think you should draw another loch monster so that yours has a friend."

Lily shook her head. "It doesn't need one because I'm its friend."

"Then perhaps you should draw something else that a loch monster might need."

She tapped an orange crayon against her chin and pursed her lips as she pondered my suggestion.

"I know… I could draw an underwater house so it can go there when it's too tired to swim."

"That's an excellent idea. Every loch monster needs a home to rest in after swimming around all day. I'll go and sit with Mummy, and you can surprise her with it when you've finished."

My daughter's beaming smile made my breath hitch. I thought I'd never see that again. I'd spent every day thinking that my life would end brutally at the hands of Riass or that torturing bastard Bashir in a hellhole far away from my wife and children. I would picture their smiles and recall the sound of their laughter, but the longer I remained in captivity, the more it hurt to do so.

I finished off what little remained of the creamy hot chocolate Mrs Braeburn had made and placed a noisy kiss on Lily's cheek. She giggled and kissed me back, nuzzling my nose while mumbling, "Eskimo kisses, Daddy."

My heart swelled with love, dampening down some of

the ever-present anger and frustration that had dominated my day.

The heat from the fire warmed my aching limbs as I crossed the room to Tess. She continued staring into the flames, refusing to acknowledge my presence. If I weren't still feeling so weak, I'd have sat on the rug beside her, but I worried that once I got down there, it wouldn't be so easy to get back up again.

With my hand on the mantlepiece for support, I turned to my wife and asked, "How are you feeling now?"

Tess shrugged her shoulders.

"Are you ill? Do you need to see a doctor?"

She turned her head towards me slowly. "Bit of a pointless exercise, don't you think?"

If not for the look of utter defeat in her eyes, I would have said her face was emotionless.

"Why would seeing a doctor be a pointless exercise? Unless it was just the sight of me that repulsed you?" I waited for her denial—wanted her to tell me not to be ridiculous.

There was no denial, only a slight shrug of her shoulders before she stared once more at the flames.

I was right. She had given up on us.

My wife had always fought for what or whom she believed in, and I couldn't understand why she wouldn't fight for our marriage. She genuinely seemed happy to see me on my return, but that changed the day that Franco left.

Thinking about that fucking prick had my anger flaring higher than the flames before me. I didn't want to picture them together, yet it was impossible not to. It belonged in the past, along with the memories of my captivity and the knowledge that my friend had wanted me and my son dead. But it took so little for everything to surge to the forefront of my mind and control my emotions, cancelling out my good intentions of how tonight should progress.

Instead of offering Tess an olive branch, I now wanted her to hurt as much as she'd hurt me. I needed her to suffer through the feeling of not being loved enough to forsake all others.

Taking a deep breath, I began with, "I should have listened to everyone when they warned me against marrying you. They told me I wasn't thinking straight after my attempted assassination. It's something I thought a lot about during my time in captivity, and I realised they were right. Several times I thought I was at death's door, and though I wanted to live so I could see my children again, the thought of being reunited in heaven with Catherine warmed my heart. She was and is the love of my life. It's why I'm wearing the ring she gave me on my wedding day..."

I made a show of twirling the brand-new ring around my finger, but apart from a quick glance, Tess showed no emotive reaction.

"Oliver queried my feelings for you. He suggested I felt guilty because you'd been hurt while saving my life and that my love for you was tied in with that. After all, we had nothing at all in common, and you could never be my equal. Just a troubled young woman with more courage than sense. We should have divorced when you were eighteen and could live independently, but you ended up pregnant, so I was tied to you then."

Again, Tess showed no reaction to my harsh words, which made me want to yell in frustration. Why wouldn't she call me out on my lies? My wife wasn't stupid. She knew the depth of my feelings for her.

I gripped the mantlepiece harder. Trying to conceal the pain and frustration.

After swallowing down the lump in my throat, I continued to spew even more hurtful lies, watching carefully for any form of reaction.

"Because of my experience with Catherine, I thought that having a child with a woman meant something, but that's not the case at all. Love doesn't factor into it. It's just basic biology and something I could have had with any number of women."

In a movement so fast it was almost a blur, Tess leapt to her feet and pointed a finger in my face.

"Don't you fucking dare make our daughter feel any less than what she is… a child born out of the love and devotion of parents who adore her. I will not have Lily feeling the way I felt when I was growing up. I am not—how did you phrase it? '…any number of women.' I am your wife. Someone you professed to love day in, day out until Riass got his hands on you. If you want to tell her that you truly didn't feel that way and she's just 'basic biology,' then go ahead. Make someone else you're supposed to love feel like shit. But if you do, I swear to fucking God I'll come back and haunt you, Kolya."

Though she barely raised her voice, the impact of her words thundered through my head. I glanced across at Lily, who'd turned in her chair to face us; her latest drawing clutched tightly in her hand. Had she heard any of what I'd been saying?

The abrupt swell of suffocating shame almost brought me to my knees. Tess must have noticed because she dragged a high-backed chair from the table and made me sit.

"I'm sorry," I whispered. "I didn't mean any of it."

Tess looked at me with nothing but disdain. "Then why say it?"

"To provoke you into an argument. I wanted to hear you tell me I was talking total bollocks like you used to whenever you disagreed with something I'd say. I thought you'd fight for us, even if the one you were fighting was me."

"What good would that do me, Kolya?" Tess shook her head before adding, "Besides, when you hurt the ones you love, you also hurt yourself, and I'm in enough pain already, so I think I'll pass."

Tess left me pondering what she'd just said as she walked over to Lily, peering over her shoulders at her latest artistic creation.

"Wow, they're brilliant pictures, Lilipot; I love the colours you've used. Shall we take them upstairs and put them on the wall in your bedroom? Once we've done that and brushed our teeth, we can climb into bed and read the new fairy story on your iPad."

"Can we read two stories instead, Mummy? Because I'm *really* not tired," Lily insisted.

Tess pretended to think about it for a few seconds, then replied, "Fine, you can have two stories, but only if you give your daddy a quick kiss and come upstairs with me without complaining."

I pecked Lily on her cheeks several times, telling her I loved her between each noisy kiss. I wanted to go with them so I could lie on Lily's bed, listening to the fairy stories her mother read while imagining our family was as perfect as it had been, but I knew Tess would refuse me. And who could blame her after my behaviour tonight?

I needed to get my head together and control my anger, or it could be me who destroys what I value the most. Thankfully, I had someone arriving tomorrow who could help me with that, and hopefully, he could speak to Tess, too.

Before she closed the door behind her, I shouted, "George will be arriving tomorrow morning, Tess. I'll arrange for you to have a session with him after lunch."

I half expected her to say no, to tell me she didn't need George's help, but in a raspy voice, she croaked, "I look forward to it."

Chapter Thirty-Seven

KOLYA

After pouring myself a whisky, I retired to the sitting room and made myself comfortable in a chair by the fireside. The smouldering embers from a charred piece of wood emitted enough ambient light to forgo the table lamp.

I knew I shouldn't be drinking, but with so much going on in my head, I hadn't the willpower to abstain.

I was ashamed of my behaviour, and I only hoped that my intelligent little girl hadn't believed or understood a word of what I'd said to her mother. Frustratingly, none of the crap I'd spouted had any impact on my wife—until my words unwittingly involved Lily. Only then did she show me a hint of her fiery temper. Yet, that fire came in defence of our daughter, not our marriage. I played her words over in my head, and the last few hit me like a freight train. *"...I swear to fucking God I'll come back and haunt you, Kolya."*

Despite my sending her and Lily to a place she loved and with extra guards for protection, Tess still believed I wanted her dead. No wonder she thought that seeing a doctor would be pointless. Tess thought she was going to die soon.

I needed to see her at once to put that ridiculous notion to bed, but I didn't want Lily overhearing anything her mother said about me wanting her gone. My poor daughter had been through enough already.

Once Lily was asleep, I'd go to her room and ask Tess to join me for an open and honest discussion. She needed to know how wrong she was, and I needed to apologise. Again.

How had my life become such a fucking shitshow? My family was falling to pieces in front of me.

Though it's not an excuse, being so worried about my son hadn't helped matters tonight.

I returned to the hotel yesterday to find James in a foul mood, wanting to back out of his rehab agreement. A little over twenty-four hours without drugs or alcohol had him swearing at everyone, refusing to eat, and kicking furniture around the penthouse suite. We got into an argument when I told him I'd use whatever means necessary to force him to get clean. In answer, James put his fist through an expensive wall canvas, busting his knuckles on the wall behind it.

Two guards had to restrain him while the nurse tended to the broken skin on his hand, and while she did so, I threatened to have him taken to a strict, no-frills facility my father had recommended in Moscow. I was lying, of course; my father had suggested no such thing. Roman Barinov would be furious if he knew about my son's addictions. He'd consider it a weakness, although he'd rain holy hell down on the woman who'd introduced him to cocaine—something I could get on board with.

Picking up the new phone Kevin had given me, I scrolled through the limited contacts and pressed the green button.

"Kolya, how are you feeling today?" Yuri sounded as tired as I felt, but then, being the second in command of the Barinov Bratva kept him busier than most. Despite his involvement in the Russian Mafia, in which men often become cold and unfeeling, my brother is someone who understands the complexities of the human mind, especially when trauma and emotions are involved. So I knew I could speak freely.

"Physically, much better, but mentally, I'm fucked!"

"That's understandable, Kolya. I'd be more worried if you hadn't been affected by your time with Riass. To sail through that would make you inhuman, nothing more than a shell of a man. You are allowed to struggle, brother. Take whatever help and time you need to reclaim your life and your various roles within it. Everyone will understand."

I placed my whisky glass on the lamp table and rubbed my weary eyes. "Everything's changed, though, Yuri. I want the life I left behind, not the one I'm dealing with now."

"What do you mean? Talk to me, brother; tell me what's troubling you. Father said you'd asked him to give you and Tess time to reconnect before he started bombarding you all with phone calls. Are you two having problems?"

After letting out a heavy, troubled sigh, I told Yuri everything that had happened since my return, including Tess's affair and how she'd attempted to leave me. I spared no detail, even though there was plenty I wanted to hide. Then I took a leaf from my wife's book and stared into the fire while I waited for Yuri to process everything. Watching ash fall from the charred edges of the wood and disappear into the grate kept my eyes from closing. Unburdening all my worries on Yuri had me on the brink of exhaustion.

I expected Yuri to sympathise with me over Tess, so his angry words surprised me.

"How in God's fucking name could you allow Tess to believe you wanted her dead? She's your wife, Kolya! The mother of your daughter.

She saved both your life AND James and Lily's lives when faced with men sent to harm them. Tess deserves to feel safe after all she's been through," he yelled furiously.

"I know, I just… I was so angry with her, Yuri. I told her before we married about what James and I went through after Catherine died; how hard it was to see my eleven-year-old child grieving the loss of his mother. Tess should have known I'd do anything to avoid seeing that again. She should have known I'd never harm her," I defended.

Yuri ignored me and added, *"And I can't believe you told her that Catherine was and is the love of your life. How could you even stand to hurt my sister-in-law that way? Did Riass replace your heart with a swinging fucking brick?"*

I shook my head as I fought for words to explain myself.

"You're acting like I'm the only one at fault here, Yuri. Tess slept with Franco and tried to flee with my daughter."

"Your fucking guard took advantage of a grieving young widow with PTSD. Despite how much the man was in love with her, the bastard knew better than to make a move on Tess while she was so vulnerable. But, Kolya, it wouldn't matter if she'd fucked every single one of your guards while you were presumed dead; she's still your wife and Lily's mother. Tess is to be protected at all costs, and if you can't do it because of your unnecessary need for revenge, then I will do it for you."

A tsunami of pent-up fury swept over me, drowning out all reason. He might be my brother, but Yuri just crossed a major fucking line.

"I bet you'd love that, wouldn't you? Taking care of my wife. James said you were always kissing and cuddling her. Tell me, Yuri, did you enjoy being in bed with her?"

"What are you insinuating, Kolya? That I wanted to sleep beside her? Do you think I got a thrill out of waking her up when she was in the throes of a horrifying nightmare? Or when I had to put my hand

over her mouth so that her terrifying screams wouldn't wake your daughter? Perhaps Tess shaking so violently that the bed moved did it for me, or when she scrambled to the bathroom to throw up?"

The images Yuri's words conjured had blasted through my fury, but he wasn't finished yet.

"She was struggling, Kolya, and everyone was worried about her. So, yes, I cuddled her. And I often kissed her on the cheek or forehead. You might have spent most of your life in England, brother, but you're still Russian. You know we kiss and hug when we greet people, and we openly show affection when with family. Tess is my sister-in-law, and I adore her. The fact that James had a problem with it says more about him than it does about me and your wife."

I nodded in agreement, although he obviously couldn't see me. Yuri didn't deserve any of the anger directed at him tonight. He was a good, selfless man and a loving, supportive brother—a better man than I could ever be.

Tears of shame pooled in my eyes, distorting my vision. After dabbing them with the sleeves of my jumper, I picked up my glass and gulped down my whisky, the familiar burn no longer as painful.

Yuri sighed before admitting, *"James said some awful things to Lily at Christmas. He was obviously struggling with your loss and everything else that had happened. I knew he was drinking heavily, but I had no idea about the drugs. If I had known, I would have got him some help."*

"I know you would, Yuri. I'm sorry I let what he said about you and Tess get to me. It's no excuse, but since my return, I've had nothing but drama and heartache, and I feel so overwhelmed. I want to share the burden of my son's addiction with my wife, but understandably, there's an emotional void that I know I've contributed to," I sobbed, unable to stop the tears from falling.

"When I arrived home that first night, Tess held me so

tightly, as if she was scared I'd disappear again. I'd give anything for her to do that now. Yet, I can't control my anger when I'm around her. The things I said to her tonight...all ridiculous lies that were meant to provoke a reaction. It was childish and so fucking wrong."

I cried like a baby, my shoulders convulsing with each gulping sob.

"Let it all go, brother. Every painful experience or emotion you've felt since that bastard terrorist got his hands on you. Keeping it locked away inside gives him power, despite his death. Don't allow the spectre of him and his fucking sidekick any space in your head. If you do, you can kiss goodbye to any meaningful relationships with those you love. It would be like giving him access to your family, which is something we cannot allow."

Yuri was right, as always, but after all those months suffering at the hands of those evil fuckers, neither Jonesy nor I would find it easy.

Thinking about Jonesy made my gut clench as a sliver of panic rushed through me. Despite knowing he was safe and well in bed, out for the count after taking strong painkillers and a sleeping pill, I had an overwhelming need to check on him.

"I need to be with Jonesy," I said out loud. "Being beside him gives me a sense of peace in this chaotic world of mine. I feel vulnerable without him."

"It's a good job I know where that's coming from, Kolya, or I could be forgiven for thinking I wasn't the only gay Barinov," Yuri said with a chuckle.

Laughing through my tears, I replied, "He's not my type."

"Kolya, the man is tall, good-looking, has a wicked sense of humour and can sing like a professional. What's not to like about the

Welshman who saved my brother's sanity?" he questioned with a hint of humour in his voice.

"You're barking up the wrong tree, brother. Jonesy is as straight as they come, and he's hung up on one of Tess's work colleagues—an ex-police officer named Karen."

"Ahh, that's too bad. Make sure the next guard you hire is single, gay, handsome enough for a Barinov, and looking for a long-distance relationship with a Russian that most men fear."

I hated the fact that my brother was in this position. Homosexuality is a taboo subject within the Bratva, and my father would not welcome a gay son with open arms. Yuri knows he can speak freely in front of me about pursuing a relationship with someone of the same sex. I want nothing more than to see my brother find someone who makes him happy.

"Kolya, about James," Yuri began determinedly. *"What are we going to do about the woman who led him on before stamping all over his feelings and introducing him to drugs? Although I know he's an adult and is responsible for his own choices, we cannot let her get away with what she did to him."*

"I agree. James already tried outing her to her husband, who is the US secretary of defence, but it seems he turned a blind eye so he could continue having sexual liaisons with gay men. Their whole fucking marriage and public appearance are based on lies. You know what kind of pull the higher-ups have with the American press. They get them to hide stories in exchange for guaranteed exclusives."

"Fuck the press, Kolya. Give me a few weeks, and I'll do what we Russians do best. I'll gather enough fucking evidence to drown them both in a sea of undeniable social media stories that can be viewed worldwide. I know of a group that, for the right price, will organise a propaganda campaign that will squeeze the fuck out of Daniel Trent and his wife's protective bubble until it bursts in a shower of public

humiliation. No one messes with our family without suffering the consequences."

I sat forward in my chair, listening intently while Yuri orchestrated the demise of Carrie and Daniel Trent's place within the US political arena.

In my current mental state, the thought of inflicting this type of revenge on the fucked-up couple gave me an almost hedonistic high, which lifted my spirits enough to focus on making it up to my wife.

"Tell me how much you need to make all that happen as soon as possible, Yuri. I look forward to seeing the look of devastation on their faces when Trent is forced to announce his resignation."

"I'll get onto it immediately. But for now, as your older brother, I'm ordering you to rest. You'll feel much better after a solid eight hours of sleep."

"I will, but there's something important I need to do first," I told him, thinking about how I needed to apologise to my wife.

"Of course, brother. Kiss your Welshman goodnight from me, too," he chuckled.

"Fuck off, Yuri."

Chapter Thirty-Eight

TESS

After setting the alarm on Lily's iPad for an hour and fifteen minutes, I tucked it under the quilt and slipped my arm around her. With only a single bed in her room here at Glengarran, there wasn't much space for me to sleep comfortably. Not that it mattered. I spent most nights dozing in the chair by her bed after writing out the letters for her future birthdays. I'd also written clear instructions for Ivan, knowing he would do his best to ensure she received them.

God, I missed him. Lily had asked me every day if he was on his way home, and she couldn't understand why he hadn't taken us on holiday with him. Ivan was someone we couldn't live without, and we loved him dearly.

Lily slept peacefully beside me, her little hands resting under her right cheek. My daughter was the most beautiful little girl in the world, and I was so proud to be her mother. I prayed that Kolya would allow me more time with her before he...

A floorboard creaked outside her bedroom door, and my

eyes flew to the handle. In the dim light from the bedside lamp, I watched as it turned, closing my eyes as the door began to open. I listened carefully while feigning sleep, hearing someone breathing heavily, as if climbing the stairs had exhausted them.

Whoever it was approached Lily's side of the bed, and after standing still for a moment, I heard them gently kiss her cheek. It had to be Kolya. None of the guards would come into the bedroom while she was sleeping unless there was an emergency.

I tried to keep breathing as evenly as possible, maintaining the façade of sleep, but it wasn't easy while so many dark and deadly scenarios ran through my mind.

What if he was here to drag me away from our daughter so that he could end my life tonight?

My heart thundered in my chest as he made his way around to my side of the bed, and it took everything I had not to jump up and lock myself in the bathroom.

He ran his hand down my arm, and then...he kissed me. His lips caressed my cheek as his warm whisky breath whispered against my skin.

"I love you, Tess, and I would rather die than see you hurt. What I feel for you borders on obsession, and no one could ever compare. You mean everything to me, my darling, always have and always will."

Kolya moved away from the bed and paused momentarily before turning off the lamp.

Safe in the darkness, I opened my eyes ever so slightly and watched him walk towards the door, closing them again when light from the landing filtered into the room as he left.

Chapter Thirty-Nine

KOLYA

Even though Glengarran had the most up-to-date central heating system that local authority planners and Historic Environment Scotland would allow, waking up there on a cold winter's morning was a shock to the system, especially after losing so much weight.

After closing Lily's bedroom door last night, I'd checked on Jonesy before heading off to bed. It was the first time since our marriage that I hadn't slept beside my wife in the old Scottish castle. We always came here together, and I hoped that Tess would be sleeping next to me again by tomorrow.

Despite everything that had happened last night, I slept surprisingly well, and for the first time since my return, I had the energy to shower and dress without taking a break. Wanting to keep the air of positivity about my day, I hesitated before checking my wife's phone. If Franco *had* tried to contact her, it would change my mood entirely, and I didn't want him to spoil what had started out as a good day for me.

Thankfully, there were no messages from Franco, but there were several from Ivan and at least a dozen from Karen and Amina. I'd already informed Jean's caregivers that Tess was having issues with her phone, and they'd promised to contact me if there was an emergency.

Ivan tried calling Tess late last night and left a message saying he'd spoken to Yuri and was worried about her. After that, he'd sent a message saying that he'd booked an early flight home and should land at Heathrow at three this afternoon. There was another message demanding she check in with him as soon as possible.

Ivan had also messaged me for the first time since he left, telling me he was on his way home and would speak to Kevin to arrange transport from Heathrow. Despite knowing that Kevin would have it all in hand, I messaged Ivan to let him know we were at Glengarran, so he should rest up at the hotel in one of the guard's rooms before making his way here, filling him in on what was happening with James at the penthouse suite so he wouldn't disturb his rehab.

I hoped Ivan would pay heed to my message. If he came here immediately, my wife and daughter would be thrilled, and as per usual, he'd end up with all their attention. I wanted them to myself for a little longer, so I could work on making us a family again.

Tess's phone bleeped, indicating that the battery was low again. I'd charged it up when I got out of the hospital, but I'd spent so many hours listening to the playlists she'd made after I'd gone missing that there was little power left.

I searched through the bedside drawer and pulled out a spare charger before plugging it in. I'd give it back to her this afternoon after her session with George; otherwise, she'd spend whatever spare time we had this morning checking in with work, and it was already gone eleven.

After pocketing my phone, I glanced in the mirror before heading downstairs. The difference in my appearance was remarkable. Barely a week since my return, the deep hollows under my cheekbones had begun filling out, and my eyes were no longer sunken. In short, I no longer looked like a walking corpse, yet I had a long way to go before I resembled the man I was before we were captured.

I fucking hated the feel of the temporary denture plate, but it was better than seeing myself with a missing tooth.

Nate and Artyom were standing in the hallway with one of the new security cameras in their hands when I passed. They barely glanced my way when I wished them good morning, offering little but a murmured "boss" in return.

Hearing the deep, rolling timbre of Jonesy's voice as he sang along to "Green, Green Grass of Home" on the radio had me passing by the dining room and pausing in the kitchen doorway. Tess and Lily sat at the long kitchen table with Mark while Jonesy leant back against the countertop beside Mrs Braeburn, who passed him a mug of tea.

The radio presenter announced that "Wild World" by Cat Stevens was coming up next, and Mrs Braeburn almost squealed in delight, which was most unlike her.

"Oh, please sing that one for me, Jonesy. I can remember queuing up with my sister to buy that record when it first came out," she said.

Jonesy did as she asked while Tess, Lily, and Mark looked on in amazement as the housekeeper closed her eyes and swayed from side to side along with the music.

At the beginning of the second verse, Jonesy's eyes switched to Tess, and he sang the rest of the song to her. The words hit me deep in the chest, gripping my heart in a hold so tight I could barely breathe. He sang that he never wanted to see her sad, to take care if she wanted to leave—warning her to beware of all the bad out there.

Fuck that. No matter how good the song was, there was no way I could allow those lyrics to put ideas into my wife's head. Tess leaving was out of the question. I would do anything to keep her with me, even if she hated my guts. A life without her would be no life at all.

I stormed into the kitchen, my upbeat mood flying straight out of the window, until my daughter yelled, "Daddy," before pushing her chair away from the table and running up to greet me. Although it took some effort, I managed to pick her up and hold her while she showered me with kisses.

"I wanted to wake you up, but Mummy and Jonesy said you needed your rest. Jonesy was waiting outside your bedroom door, but when he saw Mummy and me, he followed us downstairs."

Jonesy shrugged but appeared uncomfortable. "I just wanted to check you were okay. You know how it is..."

I nodded in understanding, my anger dissipating. I understood all too well. That irrational, clawing fear that the worst would happen when we were separated was why I'd checked on him last night.

Mrs Braeburn placed a mug of tea on the table and pulled out the chair beside Tess.

"Good morning, sir. Take a seat by your wife, and I'll whip up a hearty Scottish breakfast for you. Will you be eating here or in the dining room? I'm afraid everyone's already had theirs, although someone could use another for all she ate of the last one."

The unusually chipper housekeeper glanced at my scowling wife before heading to the large refrigerator.

"The butcher made a delivery earlier this morning, and he added plenty of tasty Lorne and extra thick smoked bacon. The eggs are fresh from our own hens, and both Mark and Jonesy had double yokes in theirs."

"I'll eat in here today if you don't mind," I replied, glancing at my wife as I spoke. Lily scrambled down and took off after Mrs Braeburn, no doubt checking if she had any goodies for her.

I felt Tess tense as soon as I sat beside her, and she stared down at her clenched fists apprehensively.

Was it anger or fear that made her so on edge? Anger, I could deal with, but fear…

Wanting to reassure her that she had nothing to worry about, I touched her forearm and whispered, "Relax, my darling. You have nothing to fear from me."

Tess shook off my hand as if it burned and pushed from the table so quickly that her chair fell over.

"Come on, Lily, let's see if Old John has found that book for you," she said as she rounded the table and headed for our daughter.

"Tess, wait, I—" Before I could finish, Dima placed a hand on my shoulder and said, "There's something you need to see."

Chapter Forty

KOLYA

I grabbed my mug of hot tea and glanced at my wife as I rose from the chair. She never looked back at me even once, which was as humiliating as it was disheartening because everyone in the kitchen noticed.

Mark pushed back his chair. "I'll follow her, boss. You go with Dima."

"Send Pavel and Oleg out instead," I ordered. "You need to fly to Inverness to collect George. Kevin has his flight details."

"On it," Mark replied before downing the last of whatever was in his cup.

Dima pulled out his phone and spoke to Pavel as he headed out into the hallway.

"I won't be long, Mrs Braeburn. Please, keep my breakfast warm and put the kettle back on. This could be one of those days that requires a tremendous amount of caffeine."

Jonesy followed me into the hallway, where Dima beckoned us towards my study. Nate and Artyom were already there waiting.

"What's this about?" I asked as Jonesy closed the door behind us.

Dima swiped through his phone and then placed it face-up on my desk. Kevin's voice came through the speaker loud and clear. "Boss, I've had Dima look at the security system to see if he could shed some light on the problems we've been having, and I think we've found the cause."

I glanced across at my guards and asked, "What did you discover? Is it faulty?"

Nate and Artyom appeared uncomfortable, and even Dima hesitated to speak.

"The system itself is fine... when it's not being tampered with," Kevin replied cautiously.

It took a few seconds for what Kevin had said to sink in, but when it did, I realised why everyone was hesitant to speak.

No one wanted to blame Mrs Braeburn—the woman who'd provided my men with hearty meals and enough hot drinks to stave off the icy cold of this chilly Scottish winter.

"Oh shit!" Jonesy said. "I wouldn't want to be the one who has to tackle her about it."

"But it might not even be her," Nate suggested defensively. "Some of the estate staff have access to the property."

Dima shook his head. "You do the woman a disservice if you think she does not monitor everyone and everything that happens around here. Mrs Braeburn runs...how do you say it? A tight ship."

I was in complete agreement with my Russian guard. "If Mrs Braeburn didn't tamper with the cameras, someone must have done so at her behest. Either way, we cannot let this go."

"You can't sack her, boss. This is her home, her life, her everything," Nate stressed.

Glaring at him, I replied, "I can do whatever I like, Nate. I may allow everyone to speak freely in my presence, but I make the decisions here. The cameras are part of a range of security measures that need to be implemented to keep my family safe. However, I'm not an ogre. I understand Mrs Braeburn's commitment to Glengarran, and I know I'd be a fool to let her go."

"I have a suggestion," Dima said. "But I need to know whether she has signed a legal agreement of trust."

"You mean a confidentiality agreement," Jonesy volunteered.

Dima nodded. "Yes, exactly, a confidentiality agreement. If she has, then I think you should show her the recent video evidence of why the cameras are necessary."

"Fuck! Do you think that's wise?" queried Jonesy.

Wise? No, but it would get the point across, I thought

"Kevin, send me all the videos of the bastards who attacked my home. I agree with Dima. Mrs Braeburn should see for herself why we insist on such extreme security and personal protection within and around the property. Maybe then she'll stop sabotaging the cameras."

Chapter Forty-One

KOLYA

As tasty as every morsel of food on my plate had been, I still couldn't eat it all. I explained to Mrs Braeburn about Jonesy and I having to increase our portion sizes incrementally after being starved so often during our captivity. Jonesy mentioned that he'd already told her this, yet she chose to ignore him. According to Mrs Braeburn, the doctors in London didn't know what they were talking about, and she would ensure that by the time we left Glengarran, we'd be as fit and healthy as we'd been on our previous visit.

I pushed my plate to the side and placed my hand on her arm before she got up to take care of it.

Jonesy turned my open laptop toward me and nodded, indicating that each video had been successfully downloaded.

"Mrs Braeburn, I wanted to ask you something, and I want you to be honest with me," I began, then added, "I know that Kevin informed you that my home in Oxford came under attack about a month after I was captured."

"He did, and I was so worried about Tess and Lily.

319

They'd been through so much already, and the last thing they needed was not to feel safe in their own home. Thank the Lord that your guards were enough to scare them off," she said while tapping her forehead, chest, and each shoulder to make the sign of the cross.

"Yes, well, I'm afraid that Kevin was protecting you from the true horror of what happened that day, and perhaps that's why you felt that the cameras you tampered with weren't necessary."

Mrs Braeburn's face paled, yet she looked me in the eyes when she folded her arms across her chest defensively.

"There are security cameras, warning systems and lighting covering almost the entire estate. Anyone who was mad enough to approach the castle would be picked up long before they got to the door. There's no need for cameras in here," she declared.

"I truly hope you are right, Mrs Braeburn. However, my team felt it necessary to have them installed just in case, and you had no right to render them useless."

"I didn't break them," she countered. "I just removed some of the wirings, so they'll be easy enough to fix should you insist on having them."

"Oh, I insist, Mrs Braeburn, and you're about to find out why. But first, I want you to cast your mind back to the confidentiality agreement you signed when I agreed to keep you on as housekeeper. I trust you remember it and the oath you swore to keep whatever you saw here during your employment to yourself?"

"Of course, I'm what the young ones call *old school*. In all my years as a housekeeper here at Glengarran, I have never disclosed anything that would be considered personal about the families who've resided here."

"I don't think you fully comprehend why I command

the utmost discretion from every member of my staff, Mrs Braeburn, but hopefully, what you are about to see will set you on the right path. It will also show you why you should never interfere with those cameras again."

For security reasons, Kevin insisted the videos were sent on an encrypted file, so after typing in the password, I turned the laptop towards the unsuspecting housekeeper and pressed play.

Chapter Forty-Two

KOLYA

Jonesy handed the sobbing housekeeper another tissue, looking as uncomfortable as I felt. Mrs Braeburn had tears in her eyes from the moment she saw Nan fall and break her hip and almost lost her mind when Dave was hit. But watching my wife hide our frightened daughter away before arming herself in preparation for an attack broke something inside the proud Scottish woman. She cried out when little Bess was killed and was right there with Tess when she filled the mercenary with bullets.

I closed my laptop and set it aside, awaiting questions I didn't want to answer, but what I got instead surprised me.

"Have one of your guards teach me how to load one of those guns they used. I'm as good with a shotgun as any man on this estate, so it won't take me long to learn how to load a semi-automatic rifle. No one will harm your wife and wee Lily while I'm around. I know every single hiding place within these walls, and trust me, I'd pick them off one by one as soon as they stepped through the door. They wouldn't get the chance to destroy this place because they'd be on their way to hell with a bullet in their skull."

"God, Mrs Braeburn, I didn't know you were this scary," Jonesy declared.

Scowling at him, she replied, "You shouldn't take the Lord's name in vain. Anyway, what's scary about a woman wanting to protect the people and the home she cares for? It's in our nature."

Jonesy laughed. "So, you're saying it's because of the female disposition that you'd send them to hell with a bullet in their skull?"

"Well, I doubt they'd get into heaven if they tried to shoot people," she quipped.

Despite being upset after watching the videos again, I couldn't help but smile at the astonishing woman beside me. Our courageous, astute housekeeper was growing on me by the second, and I wanted to understand her reasons for sabotaging the cameras.

"Mrs Braeburn...be honest with me about why you didn't want security cameras running inside Glengarran."

She dabbed her eyes with a tissue before replying, "I don't like the feeling of being watched. Not that I do anything wrong, you understand. As you know, I have my own sitting room, bathroom, and a small kitchenette next to my bedroom down the way," she said, pointing towards the back of the property. "But I rarely use it because most of the time I'm in here. I have the fire going while I attend to all the Glengarran estate business, so it's easier and warmer to cook and eat while I'm here. Old John comes in and spends a few hours warming his bones by the fire, and when the rest of the staff start and end their day, they often stop by for a cuppa. It's more than just a kitchen; it's the heart of the home for me."

It was obvious that she was being truthful, but one look into her pretty blue eyes told me there was more to what she'd just said.

"It must get lonely here when you're by yourself, especially in the winter months," I acknowledged.

Mrs Braeburn frowned, and I thought she was about to dismiss my words, but then her features softened as she nodded in agreement.

"The old laird rarely left Glengarran after his wife died, so if anyone wanted to see him, they had to come here. Someone was always stopping by, so I'd cater to him and his visitors and prepare whatever he needed for the day. But it's different now. You and the family only visit four or five times a year, so I spend the rest of the time ensuring the estate runs smoothly. And I must admit, I do get lonely. Perhaps it would be different if my husband were still alive, but sadly, that's not the case."

"I'm sorry for your loss," Jonesy said, rubbing her shoulder in support.

"Dinnae worry about me, Jonesy; he's been gone almost fifteen years now."

Mrs Braeburn shrugged her shoulders, but the odd slip in her accent revealed her vulnerability.

"How about I do you a deal?" I said, breaking into her moment of melancholy. "We'll switch off the cameras in the kitchen whenever we aren't in residence. Then you can spend as much time as you like here without feeling you're being watched."

"I would appreciate that," she said. Then she hesitated a moment before adding, "We also play poker in the dining room on Thursday evenings. It's just the estate staff and Father Creahan, and we don't play for money, so we aren't doing anything wrong."

Trying hard not to smile, I clasped my hands together and rested my thumbs against my lips, while the woman I thought was so pious defended her right to use my dining room as a gambling den.

"We used to play in there with the old laird, so it's become a tradition. I inherited his chips and other paraphernalia. We light the fires in both the sitting and dining rooms on alternate days from autumn until late spring to help stave off the dampness. As you know, despite them having central heating, those rooms always seem so cold. Having a fire burning is more cost-effective, but it seems a shame to waste the heat, so we play poker in the dining room by lamplight to give it a bit of atmosphere."

Taking a deep breath to hide my laughter, I said, "Well, I can't say I'm not upset, Mrs Braeburn. I mean, I've owned Glengarran for years, and you've never once invited me and Jonesy to your poker games."

Jonesy tutted and shook his head. "I don't know about you. Kolya, but I'm feeling particularly unloved right now."

Mrs Braeburn glanced between me and Jonesy, her mouth opening and closing as if she was unsure what to say. Then she smiled mischievously.

"You're always welcome to join us, although I have to warn you, I've been playing for years, so be prepared to lose."

"Did you hear that, Jonesy? I believe our brave little housekeeper just issued a challenge."

"I did indeed. Although, I think it's only fair that we bring Ivan, Nate, and George in on this. You know how they love playing poker."

"The more, the merrier," Mrs Braeburn stated.

My phone beeped, alerting me to an incoming message.

"Speaking of George... Mark just informed me they are

on their way. I'll let him know he's invited to *poker Thursdays*, and if you're lucky, he might tell you why they call him *The Shark*."

Mrs Braeburn shrugged her shoulders and, with an air of confidence, replied, "I can assure you, I won't be the one needing a bigger boat."

Chapter Forty-Three

KOLYA

My daughter's laughter was as clear as a bell as she, her mother and Old John passed by the kitchen window.

The outer door to the mudroom squeaked as it opened, and we heard Old John say, "Remind me to oil those hinges, wee Lily, or Mrs Braeburn will have ma guts for garters."

"I don't know what that means," Lily said.

"It means she won't be very happy with him, and she'll probably tell him off," Tess informed her before adding. "Wellies off before you go into the kitchen, Lilypot, or Mrs Braeburn will give *you* a telling-off, too."

Lily mumbled something before declaring, "Oh, no, my socks have come off inside my wellies."

"Oh, my goodness! Have your wellies eaten your socks? Didn't you feed them before you put them on?" the old gamekeeper questioned, which made my daughter howl with laughter.

"He's so good with Lily," Jonesy remarked as we waited for them to enter the kitchen.

"Aye, and she's good for him, too," Mrs Braeburn said

as she picked up my breakfast plate. "Well, I'd better put the kettle on. Would you two gentlemen like another cuppa?"

Neither of us refused, handing our cups over as the kitchen door opened and Lily darted inside.

"Daddy, look what I've got. It's a book about Glengarran. Old John's going to read it to me, and if I'm good, he'll play the bad pipes for me tomorrow."

"Bagpipes, Lily; b, a, g. Bag!" Tess corrected. Her cheeks had a healthy pink hue, courtesy of the chilly breeze blowing through the Highlands.

Pavel and Oleg followed my wife inside and waited patiently until Mrs Braeburn handed them a hot cup of tea.

The housekeeper was in her element, and I could see what she meant about the kitchen being the heart of Glengarran. Despite the castle's stunning formal rooms, the kitchen felt much more homely. It reminded me of how we all gathered in our kitchen back in Oxford before my world fell apart.

Though I could understand why Tess and Lily no longer felt comfortable there, I selfishly wanted them to overcome their fears so we could return home and be happy again. I missed Nan more than ever, and it hurt to know she wouldn't be looking after us again.

Nan had made it plain when she visited me in the hospital that she needed to retire, and Jack was fully on board with her decision. After seeing what happened to her when our home was attacked, I could understand why Jack would want to keep her out of harm's way, but they weren't even interested in keeping their cottage on the estate.

I looked up to find Mrs Braeburn hugging my wife, who wore a look of utter confusion.

"No wonder you've been off your scran, lassie. You've been through sheer hell."

Tess glanced my way, her eyebrows raised in question. I gave her a swift nod, letting her know I'd trusted our housekeeper enough to spill some of her secrets. However, Tess didn't appear too happy about it, although I shouldn't be surprised. Nothing I did seemed to make my wife happy lately.

"George will be here shortly," I informed her. "I need to have a quick chat with him before you have your session."

"Okay," she replied before switching her attention to our daughter, who was examining the cast on Jonesy's arm with great interest.

I bit back my frustration at the ease with which Tess dismissed me. If I were to make any progress with her, I needed to appear calm and act with restraint, which seemed a tall fucking order right now.

My phone rang with a call from Kevin. I couldn't hear what he was saying due to all the noise in the kitchen, so I moved into the hallway and headed towards my study.

"What's up, Kevin?"

"Boss, the cameras are up and running. I've just had Dima go into each room and speak so I could check the sound, and everything was coming through loud and clear. Put me on speaker and pull up the app on your phone. I need to ensure you have access to them before I sign off for lunch.

I did as he asked, and as we checked through the cameras in each room via my handset, the sound of rotor blades thrummed through the speakers.

"Sorry about that, Kevin. It looks like there's a window open in the dining room," I said as I turned to watch Mark land the helicopter.

"At least we know it's working, boss. Right, I'm going to

grab some lunch. Give my regards to George, and I hope Tess has a productive first session with him."

As I said goodbye to Kevin, an idea as immoral as it was unethical began forming in the back of my mind. Due to this morning's discovery and subsequent fix, I now had audio and visual access to each of the downstairs rooms at Glengarran, and this afternoon, Tess would be in one of those rooms discussing all her worries and fears with George.

Watching her first and possibly only therapy session would cross a big fucking line, but then, so had my wife's affair with Franco, and if I could forgive her that, then she couldn't complain about the invasion of privacy. George, however, would have more than enough to say, so it would be for the best if neither of them found out.

Before leaving my study, I grabbed my in-ear headphones from my desk drawer and stuffed them inside my laptop bag. Dima opened the front door for George just as I entered the hallway, so I shook his hand and asked if he had a pleasant journey.

"It wasn't bad at all, Kolya," he replied as he put down his suitcase and shrugged off his heavy winter coat. Being a regular visitor at Glengarran, he'd come prepared for the wintery weather.

"How was James when you left?" I asked as he followed me into the sitting room.

George strolled towards the roaring fire and knelt to warm his hands.

"He's struggling, but that's to be expected at this stage. Cold sweats and tremors, irritability, insomnia and exhaustion. His body is going through a tough but necessary detox. James had the option of having a steady, medicated withdrawal or going cold turkey. He went with the latter, and as he has medical professionals on hand, Grayson and I approved. His appetite has increased, likely due to the cocaine withdrawal, but he's also nauseous from the lack of alcohol. There will be rough days ahead, but you should be proud of him, Kolya. I know I am."

"I've tried not to think about it, but it's damn near impossible. Worrying about James has only added to the list of shit my mind has to process, and I'm failing miserably. Poor Tess bore the brunt of it last night, and it's the last thing she needs. I've tried to apologise, but she won't hear me out."

"Kevin showed me the videos of the attack on your home, and, of course, Nan and the guards who stayed in the UK continued their sessions with me. Your wife must have been traumatised enough before she..." George paused momentarily and removed his wire-framed glasses before adding, "James gave me permission to discuss his treatment and therapy sessions with you, and during every session since his return from Sicily, he's mentioned the day that Yannis was killed. I know that Tess shot him, and I can't begin to comprehend how that act has impacted her mental health."

I shook my head; even mentioning that bastard's name brought me so much emotional turmoil.

"Every single fuckup in my life over the past six years has been down to him. If I could burn every fucking memory of Yannis Markos from my and my family's minds, I would do it in a heartbeat," I raged.

I ran my hands through my hair and tugged on the short strands.

"I get so fucking angry, George, and unfortunately, Tess has become my target. She did something while I was gone —something I'm trying not to let ruin our marriage."

George glanced my way as he stood, arching his back as if it pained him.

"Is this a conversation between friends or patient and therapist?" he asked.

I debated my answer. I could get Mrs Braeburn to bring George some lunch and monopolise his day with my fucked up emotional baggage, or I could go with my amoral plan of listening in as my wife spills the secrets of her turmoil and betrayal.

The latter won, confirming that I was obviously sick in the head; otherwise, why would I choose to endure such torture?

Chapter Forty-Four

TESS

"Would you like another cuppa, George?" I asked, pointing to his half-empty cup.

"No, thank you, Tess. I still have half a cup left." George replied before taking a sip.

"Perhaps a biscuit, then? If you wait here, I'll nip to the kitchen and bring some," I said, jumping up from my spot on the sofa.

"Tess, I don't want tea or biscuits, and you don't need to check on Lily. I'm here for you. This is your session, so just sit here and try to relax. Stop worrying about everyone else and concentrate on yourself for a change."

That was easier said than done. During this visit, the only time I'd been separated from Lily at Glengarran was when I was speaking to Father Creahan. Kolya wasn't here then, and Mrs Braeburn had reassured me she'd bring her back to me as soon as Father Creahan left. No matter how many times Kolya said he wouldn't hurt me, I still couldn't trust him.

Before heading upstairs, Kolya slipped his laptop into

the bag I bought him for his birthday. He said he'd catch up with the work that James left unfinished and then try to get some sleep. I thought James would have returned to the UK when his father was taken to the hospital, but he must have remained in the States. I found that quite upsetting. Kolya should have had at least one family member with him during his stay.

Lily was in the kitchen with Mrs Braeburn and Old John. Pavel and Jonesy had volunteered to watch over my chatty daughter, while Nate expressed an interest in having a go at playing the old gamekeeper's bagpipes. Old John and Mrs Braeburn laughed so hard they almost cried, which Nate took as a challenge. He had such a competitive nature, but I knew he'd fail at this one.

Mrs Braeburn had announced that she and Lily would bake some scones before she taught her how to knit. My daughter was thrilled, and it took me back to a time when Jean had tried to teach Sarah and me to crochet. Sarah was so much better than me, yet neither of us had managed to make anything.

I was desperate to see my foster mother, and I cursed Kolya for taking my phone so I couldn't video call her.

"Tess," George prompted. "Tell me everything that happened after I last saw you in Oxford."

I laughed, but there was no humour in it.

"If you want to know everything, then you'll need something stronger than tea," I declared before heading to the drinks cabinet.

"I already know some of it, Tess. As you're already aware, Kevin showed me the videos from when your home was attacked, and I know that you shot Yannis."

My hands started shaking when he mentioned Yannis,

causing me to spill the whisky I was pouring onto the fancy silver tray.

"Shit! I need to get a cloth. Mrs Braeburn will go mad if I don't wipe it up."

George grabbed my arm before I could set off for the kitchen. Then he nudged me away from the drinks tray and dabbed the spilt whisky with some tissues.

"Problem solved," he said as he tossed the tissues into the bin. Then he handed me a glass of the twenty-year-old Scotch before he poured one for himself.

George gestured toward the sofa. "Take a seat, Tess, and let's get started. I know you're uncomfortable, and I wouldn't normally push, but you said you needed this when you were in Sicily, and I doubt that's changed. You've known me for almost six years, and you allow me to spoil your precious daughter, which shows how much you trust me."

I laughed again as I took my seat. "I trusted someone else with my daughter, and I ended up killing him."

George took a quick swallow of his whisky and frowned. "I'm going to ask you a question now, and I want you to think long and hard about your answer. Did you ever have any doubts about Yannis before the day you discovered his betrayal?"

He sat back in his chair and made himself comfortable while he awaited my answer. Since the last time I saw him in person, George's hair had turned more white than grey, which suited his light skin tone and kind blue eyes. Eyes that seemed to see inside my mind and search through all my secrets. I wish it were that simple. Saying them out loud was proving such a hard task.

I shook my head and admitted, "There were things about him that I didn't like. I'm sure Kolya has complained to you about the arguments Yannis and I had over the years. He would often say things that bugged me. Snide comments about Kolya not being around or things we did as a family that he disapproved of. He could often come across as a bit of a misogynist, yet he would always apologise and convince me I had him all wrong, and then he'd say the sweetest things. But he was always so good with Lily. Of course, now we know why and what he thought about me."

"What do you mean?" George asked.

"Before I shot him, he told James that Lily was the golden child, just like James had been before he became an adult. You see, Kolya and Yannis had a deal. As his godfather, if anything should happen to Kolya, Yannis would look after his son and have a say in how KOLCAT was run until James was twenty-one. Kolya couldn't risk it falling into his father's hands. I mean, could you imagine how panicked governments around the globe would be if the Russian Mafia gained control of KOLCAT? But then Kolya married me, and we had Lily, which meant we would also be beneficiaries."

George nodded, so I assumed he already knew about this from Kolya. We heard the familiar sound of rotor blades and turned to watch the helicopter rise.

When it was all but a speck in the dull grey sky, I took a sip of my whisky and added, "Ivan and Nan—the godparents I chose—would be the ones who'd care for Lily if anything happened to Kolya and me; I made sure of that. But because Kolya insisted that Yannis also be her godfather, the latter assumed he'd have the same rights to Lily, her inheritance, and KOLCAT as he did when James was a child. Kolya never corrected him because he knew Yannis would kick up a fuss. He said it was because Yannis didn't have any children of his own and thought of James and Lily as his substitute kids."

"I see. How did you feel about him not coming clean with Yannis?" he asked.

"I thought he should tell Yannis straight, but as always, he didn't want to risk him throwing a strop. Kolya would always excuse his behaviour and say something like, 'It's just Yannis being Yannis,' but even he started to get fed up with it."

George removed his glasses and placed them on the side table beside his whisky. "You mentioned that you now know what Yannis thought about you," he said. "What did you mean by that?"

I smiled as I replied, "I remember what James told me word for word. He'd asked him what his plans were for Lily and me, and Yannis replied, *'Tess being a grieving billionaire widow makes up for the fact she's nothing more than a common, foul-mouthed little bitch. Marrying her would have been the means to a very wealthy end for me.'* As I told James, Yannis realised too late that this common, foul-mouthed little bitch has a good aim, and I'll fight to the death if someone comes after my family."

"I think that's a normal response from someone facing the same threats you had, Tess," George concurred. "But looking back at the actual moment, how do you feel about his death now?"

"I'm glad he's dead, but I wish I hadn't been the one to kill him. My nightmares seem to stem from that. Do you know how he died?" I questioned.

"I know that you shot him," George replied.

After taking a deep, calming breath, I went over what had happened before we got to the airport in Kefalonia. George listened intently, nodding here and there without interruption. But when it came to describing what happened when I got to the plane, I hesitated, knocking back the rest of my whisky with one quick swallow.

"Shots rang out, but Mark, who was covering me, wouldn't let me stop to take a look. I was terrified, yet I was more concerned about James and Franco as they were behind us. I stumbled when climbing the steps, and Mark fell on top of me. He'd been shot in the arm, but the Kevlar vest took the other bullets. Ivan came thundering down the steps and lifted Mark off me. Carl helped him into the plane, and Ivan tried to get me to follow, but I couldn't leave James and Franco. Yannis and three of his men were hiding behind a service vehicle about four metres from the nose of the plane, and by this point, James was lying on the tarmac with Franco coving him. There was no way that Franco could get a shot in from that angle, and when I heard him cry out in pain, I knew I had to do something. Carl pushed past me and Ivan and leapt over the last few steps, opening fire on the service vehicle. I still refused to move, so Ivan grabbed me by the vest and threw me over his right shoulder. I had Danny's gun in my bag, and in the few seconds it took to get to the top of the steps, I had Yannis in my sights. I aimed for his head, but with Ivan jostling me, it hit him in the throat. Yannis clutched his neck, but there was nothing he could do. He glanced up at me as his hands fell to his sides, and then he collapsed. Dead. I watched the man who I thought had killed my husband drown in his own blood, and instead of feeling relief, it both sickened and upset me. No matter how much therapy you could offer, I don't think I'll ever come to terms with that."

I paused for a moment, trying to push the image of Yannis's dying moments out of my mind before I carried on speaking.

"When Yannis was hit, his guards stopped to check on him, which Tanner said was a rookie mistake, but it gave Carl an opening so he could get in there and take one out. Roman's men got the other two when they made a run for it. Then it was over, apart from the clean-up, which I had no part of. Although two of our guards had been shot, no one in our party lost their lives. Killing Yannis and his men saved James and Franco and protected everyone else on that plane. Bullets were flying everywhere, George; that's how deranged Yannis had become. All that gunfire near an aircraft that was almost full of fuel...."

I shook my head, not wanting to say the words out loud, and thankfully, George didn't finish off my sentence.

Chapter Forty-Five

TESS

"You mentioned you'd been having nightmares. Tell me about them," George demanded before throwing another log on the fire.

So I did. I told him about how Yannis's dead body often became Kolya's and how my nightmares evolved over the weeks we were away. He leaned forward in his chair; his interest teamed with nods of understanding about my feelings and experiences. George asked if having someone sleep beside me helped, and I told him, in all honesty, that the only real benefit was that my bed buddies could wake me before my terrifying screams woke my daughter.

George pursed his lips and then glanced at his watch.

"We've been chatting for almost forty minutes, and you've talked about Yannis's betrayal and death and how he features in your nightmares, yet you've not mentioned the attack on your home, and specifically, the armed man who came into Lily's bedroom and shot little Bess. The man you killed while protecting your daughter. How has that affected you, Tess? Does what happened that day feature in your nightmares? I saw the video, and your fierceness and courage were remarkable in what must have been terrifying circumstances. But those circumstances have passed, and you're safe here at Glengarran, where you can finally relax."

Anger bubbled inside me, spewing words out of my mouth like lava from Mamma Etna.

"Safe? I was safer on the day you're referring to than I am here. At least I had people looking out for me and the means to defend myself. And to answer your question, killing that mercenary in Lily's bedroom doesn't affect me in the slightest. He invaded my home, armed and ready to murder people I love, and he shot Bess, who was only trying to protect me. It was either me or him that day, and it sure as fucking hell wouldn't be me. He was a nobody, a figure in black carrying a deadly weapon to a place where my daughter used to sleep. He deserved to die the same as that Greek wanker did. And because of them, I probably won't get to see my daughter again in heaven. They turned me into a cold-blooded killer, George, and no matter how I've tried to spin it, I am *not* a soldier and certainly don't repent. I will never seek forgiveness for keeping my daughter alive and well."

I pushed up from the chair and began pacing the room, trying to shake off the rage and utter frustration at feeling so bloody helpless.

A minute or two passed before George asked, "Why don't you feel safe here, Tess? I know your husband wouldn't let you and Lily come here without adequate protection from an unknown threat, especially after everything that's happened."

I huffed out a laugh. "Ah, but that's just it, George. I know my enemy this time. I married him when I was seventeen years old in the church on the hill," I said, pointing out of the window.

George studied me carefully, waiting for me to elaborate, yet I was unsure if that was in his best interests. If I told him and something happened to me, he might start questioning Kolya, and I doubt that would go down well with my husband.

"Why do you feel unsafe and that Kolya is your enemy?"

I stopped pacing and faced him, wondering whether to divulge the reason for my all-consuming misery. George was paid plenty for his services and ability to keep secrets, so I doubted he'd go against Kolya, his walking-talking means to a wealthy retirement.

"While we were in Sicily, I had sex with Franco. Twice." I waited to see condemnation in George's eyes, but there was no judgement, just a nod and a gesture for me to sit.

After sinking onto the sofa, I opened up about the event that exposed my unhealthy sleep regime.

"The first time it happened was after an argument when Franco called me into his room and revealed he'd been filming me at night. I was furious, not only about the invasion of privacy but because he'd exposed my lies."

"Your lies?" George queried.

After a huge sigh, I began telling him about my conversation with Signor Russo regarding the night that Franco's father was killed, the FBI's sleep deprivation tactics, and their positive effect on Russo's nightmares. Then I told him how I'd adapted that to prevent my terrifying episodes.

"Everyone believed I was listening to guided meditation from a sleep guru, but instead, I set my phone to go off every fifty minutes. That way, I wouldn't get the chance to get into a deep enough sleep for my nightmares to take over.

It worked, but after about a month, I was looking and feeling like shit."

"I can imagine."

"Actually, you don't have to imagine, George," I said. But rather than elaborate and tell him I was doing it now, I continued with my story.

"Franco had suspected I wasn't being entirely honest with them about why I was no longer waking the villa up with blood-curdling screams, so he set up the cameras and filmed me over a few nights. I was furious and gave him hell for it, threatened him with the sack and everything. Franco had locked the door earlier, and he wouldn't give me the key, no matter how much I demanded or what I threatened to do. Then he did something he'd done once before when I'd been emotionally overwhelmed. Franco asked me to fight him."

George frowned. "He wanted you to fight him? Physically?"

"He did it just before Sarah's funeral when I was ready to give up the idea of getting up to speak during the service. He goaded me into sparring with him until I was angry enough to find the strength to take him down. He wanted to show me I'd got enough fight to overcome whatever life threw at me, and he gave me a coping strategy for the day."

"Which was?"

"A bloody painful nip, that's what he gave me. Franco nipped me hard enough to bruise. But you know what, George? It worked. That sharp bite of pain kept me focused and helped me do and say everything I wanted before we said goodbye to Sarah, and I'll be forever grateful to Franco for that."

George smiled, and I returned that smile; my mind wandering back to the day I stood there giving a big *fuck you*

343

to detectives Dickhead and Twatface before telling everyone my plans for Sarah's Legacy.

"So, getting back to your argument with Franco in Sicily," George prompted.

"I refused to fight him, so he picked me up and threw me on the bed, pinning me down. I tried throwing him off, but I was tired and weak and couldn't summon the strength to move him. He said that depriving myself of much-needed sleep wasn't acceptable to him, and he proposed we start my training sessions again. He thought the physical exercise would help tire me out and give me the fight I needed to face each day. And I did need it, George. In my heart, I felt I'd died alongside Kolya in Estonia. I wasn't sure I could go on without him anymore, even for Lily, which made me feel like the worst mother in the universe.

"But I knew what Franco was trying to do because, as I've said, he did it for me before Sarah's funeral. I thanked him, but I told him it wasn't an easy fix this time. I had years of grief ahead of me. Franco said the same still applied, and I should find something to help me get from one day to the next. But it had to be something that allowed me to feel, not bottle everything up. He said that keeping my hurt and demons locked away would keep me static, and I couldn't move into a new day if I were broken. He was being so sweet and understanding about what I was going through while encouraging me to find a way to live my life again, and, I don't know, it just happened. We had sex right there in his room, and it made me feel alive, but immediately afterwards, I felt so guilty. I ran back to my room and jumped in the shower, trying to wash away the guilt and shame while hoping that Kolya couldn't somehow see what I had done. Then I crawled into bed and slept for hours without having a nightmare."

George nodded once again. He seemed to do a lot of that. He'd said very little in all the time we'd been here.

"How was your relationship with Franco after you had sex?"

"Nothing changed at all other than starting fitness training again. I wasn't interested in a relationship with him, and even though Franco had admitted that he was in love with me, he didn't try to pursue anything. But then again, we'd both been warned against it."

"By who?"

"Signor Russo caught the aftermath of another argument between Franco and me—one where Franco had admitted he was in love with me. It wasn't the first time he told me; he said it in a roundabout way when we were planning to leave Yannis's island. Apparently, Kolya had known how he felt yet chose to keep him around, which I think was just plain fucking cruel, something I've since come to associate with my husband."

George raised an eyebrow but didn't question what I'd said.

"Signor Russo had words with Franco, and then later, while we were walking through the orchards, he told me that Roman wouldn't allow me to have a relationship with anyone."

"Did he say why?"

"He said Roman Barinov wouldn't let anyone outside the family raise Lily. He mentioned Yuri, suggesting that Roman would eventually want me to marry him so I'd keep the Barinov name, and more or less said that I'd be in grave danger if anyone found out I was involved with someone. Signor Russo told me that I couldn't trust anyone, not even Nate, so the man knew what he was talking about in that respect. Nate has had fuck-all to do with me since Franco left.

"Anyway, because Franco's father had given his life to save Signor Russo, he claimed he owed Franco a debt, and Franco said the only thing he needed was my and Lily's safety. So, later, Signor Russo sent me a burner phone with only one number programmed, telling me to keep it charged. He said if I ever thought that people in my circle —guards, friends, and family—were about to turn on me, I had to call the number and say, 'Tell Gianni I need him'."

"Did you believe what Signor Russo said about people in your circle turning on you? Tess, the guards here would protect you with their lives."

"I didn't believe him at first. I mean, I realised Nate wasn't happy when he knew what would happen between me and Franco. It was after I'd come downstairs one night to get a hot drink. We'd been out shopping in Catania and experienced a minor earthquake. A shopkeeper pointed out that Mount Etna was spewing fire, which freaked everyone out, especially Lily. I was fine until after we went to bed, but I thought a hot drink would settle me, so I went downstairs, spoke to Nate, and then went into the kitchen. I started thinking about Kolya and became so angry with him. I felt like I'd not been enough for him because he'd often been away during our last year together. I was so overwhelmed with emotion that I had a panic attack, and as I was carrying the hot chocolate, I scolded my legs. Franco and Nate came running in to help me and carried me through to Franco's room so they could put cream on the burns. Nate didn't want to leave me there and tried to tell both of us it was a bad idea. But Franco had become my rock, and I needed him to make me feel wanted and alive. The strange thing is, even though I thought that sex would help, it made me feel like the worst person in the world."

"Because you were vulnerable after just getting over a panic attack?" George suggested.

"No, it was because every moment I was with Franco, I compared him to Kolya. There were intimate things he wanted to do that I refused because I felt they belonged to my husband, so we just had sex. I closed my eyes and imagined I was with Kolya, that it was he who held me and made me feel like I was enough. I mean, what kind of woman does that, George? I had a wonderful man who loved me and my daughter and wanted to take care of us forever, and all I could do was think about the husband who prioritised work over his family. But then, why wouldn't he? Catherine was the love of his life; he made that clear last night."

"Kolya said that?"

"That and plenty more. Believe me; I know where I stand. But then, he'd already told me I was dead to him the day he found out about me and Franco. He said he wanted me to disappear so that he'd never have to hear my voice again. Then he confiscated my phone. That's when I knew I had to leave, so I grabbed the phone Signor Russo gave me, along with some money and jewellery, and then planned our escape. Lily and I were in Heathrow Airport when they caught us."

George got up and came to sit beside me.

"Kolya adores you, Tess. I know that for certain, and he's desperate to make things right. People often say and do things they regret when they are suffering from emotional and physical trauma, and you must realise that Kolya went through hell during his captivity."

"Don't you think I know that, George? I've lived the

effects of that hell every single day since he returned. I can tell you first-hand how traumatic it is to think that someone is going to kill you. And believe me, when that someone is your husband, it fucks with your mind as well as your heart."

"Tess, I'm sure that—"

"When they brought me back from Heathrow, I asked Kolya how long I'd got left, and do you know what he said?"

George shook his head, his eyes full of sorrow.

"He said, 'You seem to know everything, Tess. You tell me.' He did it to fuck with my head…as if admitting he was going to end me wasn't punishment enough. I don't even know if I'll live to see my daughter's birthday, George. And yet, I hate knowing how much he suffered and seeing him so weak."

I laughed, yet it was devoid of humour. "I must be some sort of masochist because I still love the man who wants me dead."

The laughter morphed into sobs that wracked my whole body. George put his hand on my arm, trying to comfort me, but I pushed it away and went to sit in front of the fire, rocking back and forth. I felt caged—as if trapped in an all-consuming darkness where my only salvation was the light and heat from the hypnotic flames as they leapt and danced before my tear-filled eyes.

I'm not sure how long I sat there, rocking and crying in utter despair, but it was enough time for the flames to have subsided. All that was left were glowing embers on the log George had thrown on earlier. The sleeves of my jumper were damp from my tears, and I grabbed a couple of tissues to blow my nose. I probably looked as bad as I felt, but I didn't have it in me to care.

"Tess," George ventured hesitantly. "How long is it since you've had a full night of uninterrupted sleep?"

I threw the tissues on the fire and watched them burn before turning to face him.

Shrugging my shoulders, I admitted, "Months, probably. I honestly don't know."

"Are you still waking up every fifty minutes?"

Turning back towards the fire, I replied, "I set the alarm on Lily's iPad. I don't usually sleep during the first fifty minutes. It's like I'm waiting for the alarm to go off, you know…like when you know you have to sleep because you need to be up early for work the next morning. But after that first alarm, it gets easier. I suppose I'm in a routine now."

"An unhealthy routine that we need to break before we do anything else," he said.

"No point trying to get healthy if you're going to die, George."

"Stop that, Tess. You are *not* going to die. Kolya doesn't want to hurt you, no matter what he said. And don't worry; I'll be here to keep an eye on you. I think you both have a lot of healing to do before you can move on from everything that's happened. Counselling will help, but we need to get you physically healthy too. Sleep deprivation can often be a factor in depression, as well as other major illnesses. While I don't agree with Franco filming you without your consent, I understand why he did it. You are making yourself physically and mentally ill with what you are doing, Tess, even though I understand your reasons for doing it. I also think that setting the alarm to dictate how much you sleep gives you an element of control in a life where you've had nothing but chaos. But there's another way to do that: you can take a short course of medication to help build a healthier sleep pattern. You said you took some sleeping pills in Sicily, but I can give you a much stronger dose. And I'll be sleeping down the hall, so I'll be around to check on you. What do you say, Tess? I'm giving you the power to decide whether to make a positive, healthy change. Will you take it?"

What could I do? I knew I wouldn't be able to carry on as I was because being so bloody tired and weak was crippling, and I needed to make every second that I spent with my daughter count.

"Okay, I'll agree to a short course of sleeping pills, but I'll need someone on standby in case I end up having nightmares again."

"I'll sort something out, Tess, don't worry. I brought a few pills with me, and I'll write you a prescription for the rest. You might feel drowsy twenty-four-seven when you first start taking them, but that should subside within a few days. And—"

George was interrupted by the sound of the helicopter coming in to land, and I wandered over to the window to see who Mark had brought back with him.

When the tall, tattooed man stepped out of the helicopter, I almost collapsed with relief.

Ivan noticed me at the window and waved as a grin lit up his handsome, tanned face.

Chapter Forty-Six

TESS

I ran into the hallway like the devil was at my heels, launching myself at the only man I trusted. Ivan tossed his suitcase by the door and caught me in his arms, hugging me tightly. I told him how much I'd missed him and that I didn't think I'd ever see him again.

"Do not worry, *milaya moya*. You will not get rid of me that easily."

Ivan lowered me to my feet and gripped my shoulders, looking me up and down with a critical eye.

"Tess, you look like shit! You've lost weight and look exhausted. Don't tell me you're waking yourself up again."

"I'm sorry, Ivan. I know I promised not to do it again, but things have become difficult and—"

"Kolya, how are you feeling?" Ivan said as he glanced over my shoulder. I leaned into his side as I turned to look.

Kolya was halfway down the stairs, his face ashen. His pale blue eyes stared straight at me as he approached. I stepped away from Ivan, almost bumping into George in my haste. Kolya brought his fingers to his ears, removing a

351

set of wireless headphones before greeting his cousin with a hug.

"I'm feeling better every day, and I'm glad you're back. I tried calling you several times, but your phone was off. Tell me, cousin, have you been working with Yuri? I know he contacted you after he and I spoke last night. Has he had you searching for Darius?"

Kolya's tone seemed almost accusatory, yet Ivan didn't bite.

"Everyone is on the lookout for that fucking prick," he said before exclaiming, "George! It's so good to see you again. How is your wife?"

George shook Ivan's hand and replied, "She's fine, thanks for asking. I must say, you look rather well. I don't think I've ever seen you looking quite so tanned."

"Neither have I," Kolya agreed. He cocked his head to the right and squinted. "Where did you go, Ivan?"

"IVAN!" Just as I had done, Lily dashed out of the kitchen and launched herself at our gentle giant.

"I've missed you so much, Lilypot," he said while raining kisses all over her face.

"Then don't go on holiday without me and Mummy ever again," Lily replied.

Ivan tapped her on the nose. "Your daddy missed you, so you and your mummy needed to stay with him."

"But we didn't stay with him. We came to Glengarran, and Daddy stayed in London with Jonesy. They got here last night, but Daddy hasn't even taken me out in the boat to look for my loch monster." Lily rolled her eyes before asking in the babyish voice that got her whatever she wanted, "Will you take me, Ivan?"

"I'll take you tomorrow if it isn't raining, but only if you're good."

"I'll be good, Ivan, I promise."

Jonesy stood in the kitchen doorway and grinned. "I might tag along if you do all the rowing."

"Jonesy!" Ivan lowered Lily to her feet and strode towards Jonesy with a beaming smile. He pulled him into his arms for a hug, rocking them from side to side as he declared, "It will be an honour to row for you, my Welsh friend. Seeing you standing there smiling after what you must have been through is nothing short of a miracle, and I've thanked God daily for sparing you and Kolya."

Mrs Braeburn ushered Ivan into the kitchen with a promise of tea and scones. Lily was hot on his heels, chattering away about how nice they were because she'd helped make them. I went to follow them, but George placed his hand on my arm to stop me. Handing me a small square envelope," he said, "Take two of these about thirty minutes before you go to bed; they should start to work fairly quickly. As I said earlier, some people feel drowsy even during the day, so take it easy and rest if necessary. Also, don't drink alcohol while taking them. The drop you had earlier was minimal, so you should be fine, but I'd prefer it if you had a good meal and plenty of water to be on the safe side. Avoid caffeine during the evening, and try to reduce the amount you have throughout the day. I know you're a tea fiend, Tess, but this medication is much more effective if you avoid stimulants. If all goes well tonight, I'll write you a prescription during our session tomorrow afternoon."

Aware that Kolya was standing just three feet away listening to all this, I said, "Thank you, George. I'll ask Ivan if he'll stop with me and Lily tonight in case I have a nightmare. He stayed with us in Sicily, so he knows the drill."

"You should sleep beside me where you belong, Tess,"

Kolya insisted. "I can wake you up if you have a nightmare."

Seeing Ivan had given me courage…or possibly frazzled my brain cells because I replied, "Kolya, right now, *you* are my fucking nightmare," before turning to leave.

"Tess, please, you need to listen to me. I—"

"Kolya," George interrupted, his tone harsh. "May I have a word?"

Chapter Forty-Seven

TESS

George wasn't exaggerating when he said it would take around thirty minutes for the sleeping pills to work. I was exhausted. Every part of my body felt so heavy that it was hard to adjust my position on the chair by Lily's bed. Thankfully, she was fast asleep, having had such a busy day that her eyes closed long before Ivan reached the end of her story.

His mattress lay on the floor beside Lily's bed, but the man himself had left to get a shower. I didn't have the chance to talk to him about what had been going on between Kolya and me because Lily refused to leave his side, and he'd spent most of his time in the kitchen eating whatever Mrs Braeburn put in front of him.

I wanted to have a conversation about what I needed to happen in the event of my death, but I could hardly keep my eyes open. Clutching the folder containing letters I'd written for each of Lily's birthdays, I closed my eyes for a few seconds and...

"Hey, sleepyhead, let's get you tucked up in bed," Ivan whispered as he cradled me in his arms. I must have fallen asleep because I hadn't even heard him come in.

"No, not yet. I need to talk to you about the letters in case...." I yawned and rubbed my eyes before realising I was empty-handed.

"Ivan, where are my letters?"

"Letters? I put the folder you were holding on the dresser."

"I need you to give them to Lily on her birthdays," I told him while trying hard to keep him in focus. God, those pills were strong.

"Why can't you give them to her?" Ivan asked as he lay me on the mattress and pulled up the quilt. He tucked a wayward curl behind my ear before kissing me on the forehead.

"Because I might be dead."

Ivan stilled, his face mere inches from mine.

"What are you talking about, Tess? You aren't going to die."

"I need to be prepared in case Kolya has me killed. He knows about me and Franco, Ivan. Signor Russo warned me what would happen, but he said it would be Roman I'd need to be wary of, not my husband. Kolya told me I was dead to him, and he wanted me to disappear so he doesn't have to hear my voice again. When I asked him how long I had left, he wouldn't tell me. So, please, Ivan, promise me you'll give Lily the letters on her birthdays and..." I yawned again, almost losing my train of thought.

In a gruff voice, Ivan prompted, "And?"

"Don't let her forget me, Ivan. Remind her about all the fun we had together, and make sure she knows that even though I've gone, I'll always love her."

"Listen to me, Tess. No one will hurt you while I'm around, not even Kolya, and you'll...."

Though I tried so hard to stay awake, Ivan's voice faded to nothing as sleep pulled me under.

Chapter Forty-Eight

KOLYA

Jonesy, Dima, and I were sitting around the desk in my office, trying to sort out our security schedule for the next four weeks. I hoped we'd be getting back to normal by then so that Tess and I could pick up our regular working routines. Lily's schooling was a different matter. It seemed highly unlikely we'd end up back in Oxford, so maybe it was time to consider a private tutor.

I had Kevin on a video call, filling in the digital planner as we spoke. We could have left it until tomorrow morning, but I wanted to take my mind off the accusatory conversation that George and I had after his session with Tess.

"When will Danny and Lainey be back?" Jonesy asked.

"They'll be arriving the day after tomorrow. It's Lainey's birthday today, so they flew to the States to spend it with her family."

"I wasn't sure Lainey would work for you again after the way you dismissed them. I knew Danny would want to be with Tess, but Lainey has a strong, stubborn streak, and I thought she'd tell you to fuck off."

I recalled our conversation, or rather, my pitiful attempt at grovelling, and I couldn't help but smile. Although the tough-as-nails guard hadn't sworn at me, I could feel her fury down the phone line.

"She told me, in no uncertain terms, the only reason they'd even consider coming back was because they cared about Tess and Lily, and we left it at that."

Dima tapped his pen against the planner I'd printed out. "So, we have Danny and Lainey for Tess and Lily, along with Pavel, Ivan, and Nate. I will be guarding you, as will Mark and Artyom. Rashid, Dave, Andy and Greg will be with James, and Steve, Oleg, Mikhail, Carl, and Tanner will stay with Kevin in Oxford."

"Well, actually," Kevin cut in. "I wouldn't mind spending some time with Nate. He and I have barely seen each other since everyone left Greece."

I tapped my chin while scanning Dima's planner. "Okay, so we'll swap Carl and Tanner over to Tess and Lily and send Nate and Pavel to Oxford."

Dima made the corrections and handed the planner to me so I could confirm it.

"That looks okay. Kevin, send everyone a digital copy and arrange transport for those who need it."

"Will do. And, Boss, when Danny—"

Kevin was interrupted when the door to my office flew open and slammed against the wall.

Ivan stalked towards my desk and threw an A4-sized folder at me.

"Ivan, what the—?"

Without a word of warning, his fist flew towards my face, connecting with my jaw. The force of his unexpected punch threw me back enough to send my chair toppling over, and I landed unceremoniously on the floor, seeing nothing but stars.

"Ivan, what the fuck are you doing?" Jonesy yelled before crying out, "DIMA, NO!"

When my eyes could finally focus, I saw that Dima had the barrel of his gun pressed against Ivan's temple.

"Dima, lower your fucking weapon," I commanded, then winced because my mouth and jaw ached so badly that my words came out garbled. And was that... "Shit! You've snapped my fucking dental plate."

"I ought to snap your fucking neck, you coward," Ivan spat. "How could you do that to her, Kolya?"

"Ivan, calm the fuck down," Jonesy said as he grabbed his arm.

Dima lowered his gun. "Take his advice, Ivan. I don't want to hurt you, but you've just attacked Roman Barinov's son. Despite you being family, he could still have you punished."

Ivan shook his head. "I don't care who his father is. He deserves a world of hurt for letting his wife believe he'd kill her."

"What?"

"Jesus, Kolya."

"No!"

Dima, Jonesy, and Kevin—who was still on the video call—stared at me with equal amounts of shock and disbelief.

"Is this true?" Dima asked. "Is that why she tried to run away with your daughter?"

I shook my head in denial, which was a bad idea because my mouth and jaw were throbbing enough already.

"She took my words out of context because of what that Sicilian Mafioso told her. Tess should have known I wouldn't hurt her," I reasoned while using the fallen chair to push myself upright.

"But you didn't correct her, did you, when she asked how long she had left?" Ivan growled. He grabbed the folder off the desk and threw it at me again.

"Your wife has been writing letters that I'm supposed to give to Lily on her birthdays... The birthdays she thought she wouldn't be alive to see. Go ahead and read them, Kolya. Read about all the things a mother wishes to tell her only child as she grows. Notice the blurred ink from your wife's tears when her words become more heartfelt. How could you allow her to suffer such pain?"

Dima and Jonesy swore, the latter asking, "Why, Kolya? You love Tess. Why did you let her think—"

"Because while I struggled to stay alive, she sought comfort in another man's bed. Her lack of loyalty could have ruined our marriage, Jonesy, just like Yannis's deception has ruined me."

Ivan leaned towards me menacingly. "Tess hasn't ruined your marriage, Kolya; you've done that all by yourself. If anything, it is you that ruined her. Tess saved your life, and how did you repay her? Not by encouraging her to continue her studies and gain a satisfying career; no, you coerced that beautiful seventeen-year-old into marriage and knocked her up so she'd be tied to you and your dangerous world forever. You brought that fucking Greek bastard into her life—a man she argued with regularly, yet you still kept him around—and you tried to change her to suit your and your first wife's upper-class circle of friends and lifestyle instead of celebrating her individuality. But worst of all, being married to you has turned her into a killer, and her mind cannot cope with that. You should be doing everything you can to show her how precious she is to you, but instead, you have her wondering which day will be her last."

I closed my eyes so I couldn't see Jonesy and Dima's expressions because every word of what Ivan said was true.

"I'm sorry for what I said that led her to believe I wanted her dead. I was angry with her and lashed out with words meant to hurt, but I didn't mean any of it, and it upset me to learn that Tess thought I could do such a thing. James was devasted when his mother died, and it was so fucking hard seeing him cry all the time. I told Tess all about it, and I thought she understood how soul-destroying it was. I couldn't understand how she thought I'd force Lily to experience the same loss as my son. So when she asked how long she had left, I played along to hurt her."

Opening my eyes, I chanced a look at Jonesy. He stared at me in disbelief, as if he didn't know me at all. That hurt more than my aching jaw.

"I've tried to reassure Tess that she's safe, but she won't hear me out. Your Sicilian saviour Russo put the idea in her head. He even gave her a burner phone to call if she felt she was in danger. Tess contacted him the day she escaped with Lily, and he said he'd come for her if she needed him. So I'm battling fears put there by him, as well as my own hurtful statements."

Leaning against the desk, I admitted, "I love my wife more than anything, but I won't deny that I'm hurt by what happened between her and Franco. I'm trying to put things right, I swear, but I'm damaged goods, Ivan. My mind, my body, every bit of me is fucked. It feels as though everyone expects me to carry on as if nothing has happened—like once I've eaten a few good meals and fattened up a bit, I'll be fine. But I won't because, despite being here surrounded by guards and people I love, I'm constantly on edge. The only time I feel settled is when I'm with Jonesy and can see he's alive and well. I'm angry and frustrated, and it would be better if Tess and Lily weren't anywhere near me right now, but I need them, Ivan. I need their love to help me heal what Riass broke."

Ivan sighed, his expression morphing into one of understanding.

"I promised Lily I'd take her out on the boat in the morning. That will give you and Tess time alone to talk. Use it wisely, Kolya, because if you can't keep your anger at bay, I will take Tess and Lily away until you gain control of the demons Riass left behind."

The anger he mentioned roared to life when he said he'd take my wife and daughter away.

"I'll excuse your behaviour here tonight; you were upset after hearing what Tess had to say and from reading those letters, but don't for a moment think I'd allow you to take her away. Tess is my wife, and she belongs by my side for better or for worse, and I'll—"

"Don't try to threaten me, Kolya. You know that if you hurt me, the wife you propose to love would never forgive you. Neither would your daughter, son, and brother. You are my family, but so is Tess. You have the money and the power in your relationship, while your wife has only what you allow, which is why she felt she had no choice but to accept her fate when she believed you wanted her dead. Tess thought she had nothing and no one to help, but she was mistaken. Tess will always have me. I won't allow anyone or anything to destroy her. I will see her rise from the ashes of this fucked up life you created like the phoenix she was born to be, and she'll burn brighter than ever."

I burst out laughing, a loud, maniacal laugh that had Jonesy and Dima eyeing me with concern.

"Ivan, if you think I have all the power in my and Tess's relationship, you are a fool who has never been in love. That woman has had power over me from the moment my eyes gazed into hers as we rushed her to the hospital, and when I fell in love with her, it multiplied exponentially. It continues to grow every single fucking day, like a dangerous obsession that's consuming whatever Riass left of my sanity. If Tess doesn't forgive me, my life will be over because I can't live without her." I placed my right hand over my heart and added, "It beats for her, Ivan, and if she leaves me, it will cease."

"Then show her that, Kolya. Tell her how much she means to you. But don't expect to be forgiven so easily, if ever. What you had her believing is something she will never forget, so you will have to ensure that the rest of her life is filled with love and happiness. Whatever Tess asks of you, grant it without question. Treat her like a goddess and worship her daily because she's worth it, Kolya. Women like Tess are one in a million."

"Ivan is right," Dima stated. "And if I had known why he attacked you, I would have let him beat you bloody. I remember how she was that morning when we left Oxford. She threw up during our flight to London, and I thought it was because she hadn't eaten. She looked so scared when we caught her at the airport. If I had known why she wanted to escape, I would have put her on a plane instead of escorting her back to you."

Kevin's voice echoed through the speakers. "I didn't realise you had scruples, Dima."

Shrugging his shoulders, Dima replied, "I have honour, is that not the same?"

"Right, I think we're done here," Jonesy declared. "Kevin, send the updated security plans out when they're done. Ivan, I suggest you get a good night's sleep if you're taking Lily out tomorrow. If she's as lively as she was today, you'll need it. Dima, you've said your piece, so let's forget about what happened here tonight and move on. If you feel you can't do that, say the word and Kolya will replace you."

Dima shook his head. "I'm good."

With a dismissive wave, Jonesy said, "Great, well, everyone fuck off to bed then."

Gesturing to my upended chair, he added, "I think you and me need to sit down and discuss what's been happening with a glass of Glengarran's finest, Kolya, because I certainly fucking need it after hearing all that!"

Chapter Forty-Nine

TESS

My bladder told me it was a good time to get up, but the rest of me vehemently disputed that idea. I rolled over and reached out for Lily, but all I found was an empty bed. Cranking my eyes open, I quickly realised I was alone on the mattress Ivan had brought in the night before. Sunlight streamed in above the top of the pink velvet curtains, yet it hadn't done much to raise the temperature in the old Scottish castle.

If Ivan hadn't been at Glengarran, I would have been running around panicking while trying to find Lily, but I knew my big Russian protector would be watching out for the both of us. Besides, I didn't have the energy to run around anywhere today.

To say I was lethargic was an understatement. George had told me the pills he gave me could make me drowsy twenty-four-seven, but this was ridiculous. I hardly had enough energy to stand, never mind get to the toilet, and I worried I'd actually wet myself. Thankfully, I was able to make it in time, and after splashing my face with water and brushing my teeth, I began to feel more *with it*. However, getting dressed proved difficult, and putting my socks on especially so, with at least three attempts going awry on my right foot.

Going downstairs was somewhat disorientating. I had to sit after just three steps because I felt like each one was rising up to meet me, and it was so bloody cold that I really didn't want to hang around. Dima noticed me sitting there and offered to help. My first instinct was to say no and get the hell away from the man who used to be Roman Barinov's head guard, but Dima's hazel eyes were filled with genuine kindness and concern, so I linked my arm through his and accepted his steady support as he escorted me downstairs and into the kitchen. Once there, he pulled out a chair for me to sit on and told Mrs Braeburn to make sure I had plenty to drink and a good breakfast.

"You look half asleep," Mark said before biting into a slice of toast. "Are you still having nightmares?"

I shook my head. "George gave me some sleeping pills. I did as he told me and took them forty minutes before I went to bed, but it feels like I took them an hour ago. I'm proper knackered, Mark."

Crouching down beside me, Dima said, "Take it easy today. No climbing the stairs without help, and make sure to fill your belly. It will give you energy and make you feel better. Your husband wants to speak to you, but he can wait until after you've had your breakfast."

Before I could make up an excuse to avoid speaking to Kolya, Dima quietly insisted, "Do not be afraid, Tess. No one wishes you harm, least of all your husband. If I had known what was in here that made you so scared," he said, tapping my temple, "I would have kept you safe until Kolya got his head out of his ass. He loves you, *zhar-ptitsa*. But even though he is home, part of him is still suffering at the hands of those terrorists." Dima tapped my temple again, indicating which part of Kolya he meant.

I wasn't sure what he wanted me to say to all that, but he seemed to be waiting for some kind of acknowledgement, so I nodded before asking, "Dima, what does *zharptitsa* mean?"

He cupped my cheek and smiled. "It means firebird. Ivan said he'd see you rise like the phoenix you were born to be. You already have the flames," he added, tugging on one of my copper-coloured curls.

"When did he say that?" I asked.

Dima grinned as he got up to leave. "It was after he flattened your husband with a punch to the jaw."

"He what? Why did he do that? Is Kolya all right?" I questioned while imagining how hard the impact of one of Ivan's punches would be.

The handsome Russian guard shrugged his shoulders. "He had it coming, and you can see for yourself how bruised he is when you finish your breakfast."

Mrs Braeburn set a cup of tea in front of me. "Dinnae worry about wee Lily. Ivan made sure she was wrapped up warm before he took her out on the boat with Old John. He'll undoubtedly fill her head with imaginary tales about her loch monster."

"Are you not a believer, then?" Mark asked.

"Pfft, there's nae goes on around Glengarran that I dinnae know aboot, and I've lived here for most of my life. If there were anything to see, I'd have spotted it years ago. Besides, the only people allowed to live on the estate are the owners and their employees, so if something were in the loch, it would have to earn its keep or find itself another home."

"Ooh, that was harsh, Mrs B," Mark said while trying to hide his smile.

"Well, this estate won't run by itself; we all have to pitch in," she replied, placing two fried eggs on toast in front of me.

"Ivan ate all the bacon and sausage, so I've put an order in with the butcher for more. He'll drop it off in an hour or so when he brings our regular delivery. Ivan asked for roast beef with all the trimmings and an apple pie for dessert. The poor man was starving this morning when he sat down to breakfast."

Mark got up and placed his cup in the dishwasher. "You should double your order, Mrs B. Ivan looked stressed to me, and you know what that means."

After swallowing the toast I was chewing, I turned to Mrs Braeburn and added, "I agree. Ivan has an emotional eating problem, so if he's stressed or upset about something, we should double up on the food orders; otherwise, the rest of us will go hungry."

Mrs Braeburn wisely did as I suggested and doubled our food orders for the next two weeks. It didn't take long for me to finish my breakfast, and she remarked that it was the first time I'd cleared my plate since I'd arrived. But instead of it giving me energy, I felt more exhausted than ever, and I couldn't shake the cold chill. Dima had said that Kolya wanted to speak to me, but I needed to clear my head and feel more alert before that happened.

"I think I'll go for a walk," I announced. "The fresh air will wake me up a bit, and I can wave at Lily and her crew."

"I'll let Nate know," Mark said as he pulled out his phone. "He's guarding you today. Pavel's already out there watching those numpties on the loch. Rather him than me. Honestly, Tess, I'm finding it hard to cope with the weather after being in Sicily. It's below freezing today, so I'm surprised they've not come back inside."

"I know what you mean; I've felt cold since waking up. But I wondered if it was a side effect of the sleeping pills."

"They probably won't be helping, but I think it's more about the weather. There's snow on the hills above Glengarran, and the whole estate is covered in thick frost," Mark replied as I made my way to the mud room.

Away from the warmth of the kitchen, I realised how right he'd been. Even my thick cable knit jumper and long-sleeved T-shirt couldn't protect me from the wintery chill.

After slipping my feet into my sheepskin boots, I put on my down-filled puffer jacket and pulled the fleecy gloves with mini heat pads out of my pockets, grateful for their almost instant warmth.

"Do you want to take a hot drink out with you?" Mrs Braeburn asked. I hadn't heard her come into the mud room and was startled.

"Crikey, I didn't hear you come in. It's like you're in stealth mode," I joked.

"Either put your hood up or wear a hat, lass. You lose plenty of heat from your head no matter how much hair you have," she stated.

I lifted my hood and then opened the door.

"Bloody hell! It's like being in the Arctic Circle," I remarked when the frosty air hit my face.

"Here, put this on over your jacket," she said, slipping a long wax-cotton coat over my shoulders. "It will keep your legs warm."

The body and sleeves of Kolya's old coat were too long, but I appreciated the extra warmth once it was zipped up.

"I'm only heading to the edge of the loch to wave them

in, so I won't be long," I said before stepping outside and closing the door.

I hadn't gone more than fifteen feet before I slipped on the icy path and almost ended up flat on my arse. Out of the corner of my eye, I saw Pavel snickering at my mishap before his attention turned to the rowing boat tearing across the loch.

After huffing out a disgruntled breath, which was as thick as fog in the frosty air, I carried on walking. The biting wind stung my nose and cheeks, and when I glanced up at the thick grey clouds gathering to the east, I thought snow might be on its way.

The closer I got to the water's edge, I could hear my daughter's wild, uninhibited laughter, and Old John shouting words of encouragement to Ivan as he rowed. I waved at them, but they didn't seem to notice. I cleared my throat and shouted "LILY" in as loud a voice as I could manage, yet there was still no response. They were too busy laughing and enjoying themselves to hear anything from the shoreline, so I headed for the jetty, hoping I could be heard from there.

When I stepped onto the frost-covered wood, I almost slipped again, so I carefully manoeuvred to the middle of the jetty using Ivan's scuffed footprints from earlier.

"Tess, come away from the edge," Nate yelled. Glancing behind me, I watched him gingerly making his way down the stone patio steps. I decided to give him the same treatment he'd been giving me and just ignored him.

After using my teeth to tug off my right glove, I placed my index finger and thumb under my tongue and whistled loudly. Everyone on the rowing boat looked my way and waved. Ivan began rowing back to the jetty, and Lily bellowed, "Love you, Mummy. Love you, Daddy."

The hairs on the back of my neck raised as a cold chill I couldn't blame on the weather raced down my spine. I spun around and saw Kolya walking along the path from the mud room. I knew he wouldn't do anything sinister with Ivan and Lily around, but that didn't stop my heart from thumping harder and faster. I remembered when it used to do that with desire for my husband, not fear, and wished more than anything that I had access to a DeLorean with a built-in time machine.

Despite the freezing temperature, beads of sweat ran down my back, and as I turned to see how far away the boat was, black spots appeared in my vision.

I closed my eyes and took a few deep breaths. This wasn't the time to have a panic attack; Lily would be upset, and Ivan would be furious with Kolya if he saw me lose it.

After a few more deep breaths, I opened my eyes and focused on the spectacular highland scenery beyond the loch. No wonder artists flocked to paint the Scottish glens. The winter sun shone on snow-capped hills, and there was still so much greenery despite the less-than-favourable temperatures.

The little boat would be here in less than thirty seconds at the rate Ivan was going, so I strolled to the edge of the jetty to greet them.

Just as I got there, my right foot hit an icy patch of wood, and though I tried so hard to steady myself, I skidded straight over the slippery edge.

Chapter Fifty

TESS

The shock of hitting the ice-cold water was quickly replaced by fear when I realised I could barely move my arms. All the extra layers, including the two heavy winter coats, must have quadrupled in weight when saturated by water, and I rapidly sank to the bottom of the loch. I wasn't sure how deep it was, but when I looked up, I saw very little sunlight penetrating the surface. I held my breath and managed to unzip the oversized wax-cotton coat, but getting out of it was a struggle; my water-logged puffer jacket underneath resisted the separation. I unzipped the jacket and tried to shrug them both off this time, but it was getting harder to hold my breath, and the intense cold had seemingly numbed my brain as well as my limbs. I thrashed around, fighting to get rid of the cumbersome outerwear anchoring me to the bottom of my dark, wet prison, but then I...

Water filled my mouth and nose, and though I tried hard not to, I...

Lily... I needed to get to Lily. My lungs burned, despite

the temperature of the water that filled them, and I knew I was drowning.

A strange warmth infused my whole body, banishing the cold, and all I wanted to do was sleep…but…

Something tugged at me, pulling me up through the water, yet I sank back to the bottom of the loch seconds later, my body feeling lighter somehow.

A sudden bright glare caused my eyes to open wide, and to my heart's joy, my beautiful foster sister appeared a few metres away from me, surrounded by glimmering white light. Sarah had been dead for almost six years, so I knew my time on Earth was coming to an end. The thought of not being with Lily, Ivan, and even Kolya broke my heart, but I had no more fight left in me. Sarah beckoned me towards her with a radiant smile, and as I neared, she opened her arms.

Before I could take those last few steps, my mother appeared in front of me, but she wasn't smiling like Sarah. No, my mum was angry with me, and it looked like she wanted to lash out, which made no sense at all.

Despite all her failings, of which there were many, my mum had never raised a hand to me in anger. In fact, the only time I'd known her do anything violent was when she stabbed the man who tried to kill me.

I took a step closer, but she pushed me away forcefully, and it felt as though something was pulling at my hair. She came at me again, pointing towards the surface, and with another hard tug on my hair I….

Chapter Fifty-One

KOLYA

Dima and I strode into the kitchen expecting to see Tess and Mark, but only Mrs Braeburn remained.

"I thought Tess was having breakfast," I stated.

"She was still feeling sleepy, so she's gone for a quick walk to liven up a bit and clear her head. Nate wasn't far behind her, and Mark's filling the log baskets for each downstairs fire. We need to keep them going today because they've forecast snow for later this afternoon."

"Lily will enjoy that," I remarked while heading to the mud room. I didn't want to venture out in the cold but I was determined to speak to my wife. With my head still throbbing from all the whisky Jonesy and I drank last night, the glare from the sun on the frosty ground was the last thing I needed to see. My jaw was swollen and bruised, and I couldn't believe Ivan had broken my dental plate after all the trouble I had gone through to get it. Jonesy and I tried fixing it with superglue last night, but now the damn thing was rubbing on my gum, and I had to take it out to eat breakfast.

Dima and I grabbed our warmest coats while Mrs Braeburn informed us that she'd given Tess my old one to wear on top of her jacket. "I bet she looks like I do in this," I grumbled.

While my weight loss probably wasn't as noticeable in my thick winter coat, I certainly felt the difference when we opened the door. There was too much room in both the arms and body, and I hoped Tess would agree to speak to me back in my study or the sitting room in front of the roaring fire rather than outside.

We spotted Nate making his way towards Tess, who was standing in the middle of the jetty. Lily waved and shouted something as the icy wind whistled through the trees, so I couldn't hear what she said.

I tried to keep up with Dima as we headed towards the jetty, but I didn't have the energy. Breathing in the cold air didn't help, and I had to adjust my scarf around the lower half of my face for protection.

Dima's phone made a series of beeps. He tapped the screen and pulled up a live video feed.

"There's a car on the way up the drive," he said. "It's the priest. Were you expecting him?"

Groaning, I replied, "No, and I could do without his interference today. Do me a favour, Dima; tell Mrs Braeburn to keep him occupied for an hour or so. The woman loves to feed him, so it won't be a hardship."

Dima beckoned for Pavel to replace him before pocketing his phone and heading back towards the mud room.

Tess turned around and spotted me, and I hoped she would either stay where she was or walk towards me, but of course, my obstinate wife turned away, dismissing me as if I wasn't important. Although, who could blame her after what I'd done?

The boat appeared to be heading back to shore. I couldn't imagine how cold they must have been out there on the loch. At least the castle and trees inland protected us from the biting wind.

I quickened my pace when I noticed Tess moving towards the edge of the jetty, and when I looked, Nate had—

A shrill yelp followed by a heavy splash had me glancing towards the now-empty jetty.

"Tess!" Nate yelled as he and I sped towards the long wooden structure, removing our coats as we ran. Nate slipped and fell flat on his ass but scrambled back up and dove into the loch.

Pavel and I reached the edge almost simultaneously, but he pulled me back as I tossed my too-big coat behind me.

Handing me his phone, he yelled, "No, you need to call for help. The water is too cold, so they will need assistance. We must remain here to pull them out."

With shaking hands, I dialled 999, gave the address and explained what was happening. Anxiety caused me to stammer and repeat myself several times as I begged them for help. A minute had passed, and there was no sign of Tess *or* Nate.

I heard Lily crying, with Ivan and Old John yelling something at the top of their lungs, but my mind couldn't interpret what they were saying.

"*Blyat!* I'm going in. Stay here," Pavel said as he kicked off his boots.

Just as I was about to ignore Pavel and dive in, Nate emerged with what I first assumed was Tess, but Pavel cried out. "*Ty cheblyad?* That's just her coat."

Nate let go and dove back down just as Ivan manoeuvred the boat to the side of the jetty, securing it with rope before shoving my screaming daughter into my arms. Then without pause, Ivan dove straight into the loch, closely followed by Pavel.

I held my hysterical daughter tightly, desperately wanting to say something to ease her fears. But anxiety gripped my tongue as well as my heart, and I was unable to reassure her that everything would be okay.

Footsteps thundered onto the jetty as more people joined us, but I couldn't take my eyes off the water below.

"This is taking too long. She's been down there for almost two minutes. I need to go in and find her," I cried, pushing Lily behind me, but Jonesy yanked me from the edge.

"You are in no fit state to go in there, Kolya, and you know it," he cautioned. "They need to concentrate on saving Tess, not you."

Grabbing his sweatshirt, I begged, "If we lose her, Jonesy, swear to me you'll put me down. I refuse to live in a world without Tess."

Before he could answer, Mark yelled, "Ivan's got her, boss."

Nate and Pavel emerged after Ivan, the latter thrusting my unconscious wife towards Mark and Dima, who dragged her onto the jetty and checked for a pulse. Her eyes were closed, and her lips were a frightening shade of blue.

"Fuck! She's not breathing," Mark yelled.

I fell to my knees beside her pale, still form and cried out like a wounded animal as Dima and Mark started CPR.

Dima did thirty chest compressions, and then Mark gave her two breaths, and I could do nothing more than pray as Tess remained unresponsive. On and on this went, my prayers to God turning into threats as the bottom fell out of my world and my daughter sobbed hysterically.

"Take her to Mrs Braeburn," Jonesy commanded in a croaky voice. Lily screamed for her mother as she was carried away from the jetty, but I couldn't take my eyes off my wife's lifeless body.

Dima and Ivan spat out words in Russian, swearing and begging for Tess to breathe.

"How long?" Mark yelled after another two rescue breaths.

"A minute and a half," Jonesy declared as Dima resumed the chest compressions.

Droplets of ice-cold water flew over me as Ivan pounded his fists on the jetty and wailed, "Don't you dare fucking leave me, Tess."

I took her left hand in mine and burst into tears. I didn't want to leave this world after fighting so hard to live, but if Tess didn't survive, I couldn't either, not even for my son and daughter.

"I love you, Tess; please come back to me. I am nothing without you. Please don't leave us. Lily needs you. Please, Tess. Please!"

As Mark prepared to deliver two more breaths, a gurgling sound had Dima rolling Tess onto her side. Water gushed from her mouth as she struggled to take a breath, coughing uncontrollably while spewing out frothy pink fluid. I pushed Mark out of the way and lay beside her while she emptied her lungs, uncaring of whatever else came up with it. She was alive, and that's all that mattered to me.

I swore as Ivan pulled me away from Tess and picked her up.

"Put her upper body over your shoulder and carry her to the sitting room," Dima commanded. "We need to remove her wet clothes and get her warm immediately. And have Oleg and Mrs Braeburn bring down as many blankets as they can gather."

I scrambled to my feet and followed Ivan up to the front door as quickly as possible, adrenaline making my earlier lack of energy a thing of the past.

Keeping up with Ivan had me gasping for breath, and I had to take a moment before helping him and Mark undress my shivering wife in front of the sitting room fire.

"I love you, Tess," I told her while unbuttoning her jeans and tugging them and her underwear down her legs. Her socks came off with her sheepskin boots, and I tossed everything behind me, uncaring for what they ruined as they landed with a splat. Tess didn't answer or acknowledge me, and though her eyes were open, her lack of focus was worrying. I rubbed her legs, trying my best to create heat where there seemed nothing but ice.

"Ivan, you, Nate and Pavel need to strip down too. We have enough to deal with without you all getting hypothermia," Jonesy said.

Ivan ignored him as he and Mark finished undressing Tess, and I noticed the wedding ring I thought she'd discarded threaded through a chain resting between her breasts.

I'd never even asked her about it, assuming she'd given up on our marriage, but considering how much weight she'd lost, I realised it might not have fit her anymore.

Yet another misconception about the woman I was supposed to cherish.

"Ivan, listen to Jonesy and do as he says," Dima insisted. "You won't help Tess if you stay as you are."

Ivan stood, backing away a few steps before stripping completely bare. I heard a loud gasp as Mrs Braeburns tearful eyes landed on my naked cousin's cock. Averting her gaze, she hurried towards my wife and sobbed as she began covering her in thick woollen blankets.

"I hadn't realised you'd already called 999. They said the helicopter was ten minutes out," she informed us. "Lily's in the kitchen with John, Artyom and Father Creahan."

"Thank you, Mrs Braeburn. Could you pack Tess a bag for the hospital?" I asked.

"And bring some clothes and shoes down for me," Ivan added.

"Of course. I'll just…." She kissed Tess on the forehead before getting up to leave, her shoulders heaving as she sobbed her way to the door.

"Kolya, why don't we strip down and lay either side of her? Our body heat combined with the blankets and fire will help her get warmer," Jonesy suggested.

"Body heat, of course; I just didn't think."

Jonesy and I stripped to our boxers as quickly as possible and slid beside my freezing-cold wife under the blankets. The room went quiet as we did so, the sight of our starved, battered bodies silencing our guards.

Oleg came in with more blankets and a duvet, and pretty soon, the heat became stifling, yet Tess remained cold and mute. I'd seen a few programs on TV where people who had drowned were brought back to life, and they'd spoken with their rescue team, yet Tess hadn't uttered a word. I braced myself on one arm and gazed into her eyes, checking whether her pupils were fixed and dilated.

"Look at me, Tess. Please. Tell me you're okay."

It took several heart-stopping seconds for her eyes to lock with mine. Her mouth opened as if to speak, but she began to cough, so I rolled her onto her side facing me.

Tears dripped down her cheeks, and I kissed them away, telling her how sorry I was and how much I loved her.

"Don't cry, my darling. You're going to be okay. Everyone you love is here with us, and—"

Tess shook her head, her wet curls falling across her face.

Ivan sank to his knees beside me. "I'm here with you, Tess, and Lily's in the kitchen with Old John. Tell us what you need, and I'll get it for you."

Tess grabbed Ivan's hand, and in a croaky voice, she asked, "Where's my mum?"

Chapter Fifty-Two

KOLYA

Almost six years ago, I sat by the bed of a young, copper-haired beauty, wondering what role she would play in my life. But that was in a private hospital in London after someone had attempted to assassinate me. Now here I was in Raigmore Hospital in Inverness, gazing at that same copper-haired beauty, wondering if she could find it in her heart to forgive me.

Pale and thin with shadows under her eyes, it was like looking at the seventeen-year-old runaway who'd taken a bullet meant for me. But Tess would be twenty-four this year, and she'd lived a life of luxury since I'd made her mine. She should be fit, healthy and happy instead of lying here recovering after almost losing her life. Again.

Her first words after being brought back from death were, "Where's my mum? Tess's mother was a junkie prostitute who'd committed suicide ten years ago after killing a man who was beating her daughter. Tess rarely had anything good to say about the woman, so asking for her mother above our daughter, me, or Ivan was worrying.

Lily had come to see her mother before she was transported to the air ambulance, and Tess had reassured our daughter that she was okay and would be home soon. Lily didn't seem convinced and clung to her mother like a little monkey, fighting and screaming when she was prised away. A heartbreaking scene for all who witnessed it.

George had arrived back from his trip to Glengarran village as we left, and the look he gave me spoke a thousand words. I'd assured him yesterday that Tess would come to no harm from me, and the minute he'd left the estate to run a few errands, she almost died. So I wasn't looking forward to that conversation.

It had taken almost two minutes to bring Tess back to life after she'd drowned, and I desperately hoped she hadn't suffered any brain damage while starved of oxygen. The doctor seemed to think she was okay, but he said that only time would tell regarding any adverse effects.

After getting her core temperature under control, they hooked her up to a heart monitor, and six hours later, she was currently receiving IV fluids and antibiotics to prevent an infection in her lungs. I wasn't comfortable letting her stay in an NHS hospital, but it was too risky to move her right now.

I had to insist on a private room for security reasons, and the staff weren't too happy with the guards stationed along the corridor. However, after a conversation with the chief executive, they bent over backwards for us.

I'm sure my bank account being three hundred grand lighter had nothing at all to do with it.

Even though Tess was sleeping, she didn't appear relaxed. Was she about to experience one of the nightmares I'd heard about? The doctor said she needed to rest, but I would not allow her to endure another terrifying ordeal. I'd failed to protect her once today; I wouldn't fail her again.

Picking up her cannula-free hand, I kissed each of her fingers individually before pressing it against my cheek. I watched her eyelids flutter, then open as she took in her surroundings. She glanced across at me warily and tried to tug her hand away, but I wouldn't let go.

"Why, Kolya?" she asked.

I frowned at her, confused.

"Why didn't you let me drown?"

I shook my head, unable to believe she could ask such a thing.

"I tried to tell you so many times that you'd got it all wrong. I never wanted you dead; how could you think such a terrible thing? I know that someone put the idea in your head when you were vulnerable, and me lashing out after hearing about Franco didn't help, but can you imagine how you would have reacted if I'd asked you how long I'd had left?" I questioned.

Looking me dead in the eye, she answered, "I would have told you that you'd got me all wrong and spent however long it took to reassure you of that fact."

After swallowing the lump in my throat, I whispered, "I'm sorry. I was jealous and so fucking angry with the world, and you took the brunt of it. I wish I could tell you that I'll never hurt you again, but until I get past what happened with Riass, Bashir, Darius, and that fucking bastard Yannis, I can't guarantee it. I should let you go, send you and Lily far away from me, but I need you, Tess. I need your love, fire, strength and no-nonsense attitude to help me banish my demons. Tell me you'll forgive me, Tess. Please."

Tess shook her head. "I don't know, Kolya. I'm not the same woman you left behind when you flew to Estonia. The fire and strength you speak of, I don't know where that went, and I can't blame it all on what's happened since Riass took you. The life we live, the time we've lost because you travel so often with KOLCAT, and the constant need for security...it's just too much. I can't live like that anymore. I want an uncomplicated, easy existence, Kolya. I want peace."

Deciding to point out the obvious, I replied, "Tess, even if you left me, you would still need security for Lily, so you'll always have that in your life."

"But it would be *my* life, Kolya: my home, my rules, my friends. Since being with you, I've ridden piggyback on the life you lived with your deceased ex-wife. We socialise with Catherine's friends, live next door to the house you shared, and stay in one of the hotels her father used to own whenever we go to London, Paris or Berlin. Even your business bears part of her name. I've lived in the shadow of 'the love of your life' for nearly six years, and I deserve better than that."

Fuck, Tess was right in some of what she'd said, but not about how I feel about her.

"I told you I didn't mean what I said, Tess. I never loved Catherine the way I love you. You are everything to me, and I wouldn't survive if I lost you. What I said to you was cruel and unnecessary. And you are right; you deserve better than the life we've been living. But we can change some of that. We can live somewhere else, wherever you choose. You don't have to see any of Catherine's friends ever again. I'll cut down on work and hand the travelling over to management. We'll still need security, but—"

"How long do you think that will last?" Tess sighed. "You're a man who likes to be in control, Kolya. I'd give it two months, maybe three; then you'd be off again, putting yourself and the family in danger. Chasing success that you don't need because Christ knows you've had enough to last a lifetime. Lily needs a father who will put her first. Someone who is present, not jetting off abroad and risking their life for money they don't need. If you can't give us that, then we're done. I want better for her…and for me."

Tess withdrew her hand from mine and tried to push herself up the bed.

"Let me help you," I insisted, though my heart was breaking.

"I think it's best if I sit up. I need to cough, but my chest really hurts."

I pressed the button for the nurse and passed her a small grey cardboard bowl. "The doctor said if you need to cough, do it into here so he can check what's coming up."

Tess grabbed the bowl as I used what little strength I had to help her into a better position.

"Mark and Dima performed CPR on you for almost two minutes, so you're bound to feel pain from all the chest compressions they administered. The doctor has you on fifteen-minute obs, you have a heart and blood pressure monitor, and we're directly behind the nurses' station. There will be someone beside you every minute of the day until you can come back to Glengarran, so if you need anything, just ask."

Tess coughed into the bowl but nothing came up. I wasn't sure whether that was a good or bad sign, so I decided to ask the doctor when he came by.

A nurse bustled into the room and switched off the buzzer. "Good evening, Mrs Barinov. My name is Cheryl, and I'll be looking after you until the nine o'clock changeover. How are you feeling?"

"Rough," Tess replied as she coughed again.

"My wife is in pain," I stated. "Is there anything you can give her that will help?"

The nurse checked Tess's chart. "You've been written up for IV fluids, antibiotics, and paracetamol. You only have a little of the antibiotic left, so I'll switch it over to paracetamol once it's empty. In the meantime, let's check your obs."

Nurse Cheryl had an Australian accent and a smile that instantly put me at ease.

Tess coughed again before asking, "Can I have a drink of water, please? My mouth is dry and my throat feels raw."

"I'm sorry, Mrs Barinov, it's IV fluids only until the doctor says differently. It's the coughing, you understand. We can't risk you taking any more water into your lungs."

Ivan glanced around the open door and asked, "Is it okay to come in now?"

"Ivan!" Tess exclaimed. "I didn't know you were here."

"Where else would I be?" he said as he strode into the room. In his thick black sweatshirt, indigo jeans and black biker-style boots, my tattooed behemoth cousin cut a rather imposing—if somewhat menacing—figure.

Cheryl turned to face him. "I've already told you. She's only allowed one visitor at a time."

"That's fine," he said. "Kolya can wait in the hallway while I sit with Tess."

"I don't think so," I protested.

Tess grabbed my hand. "Please, Kolya, let me have ten minutes with Ivan. Go and grab a coffee or something. You look like you need this bed more than me."

"If you insist," I grumbled. "But I'll be outside the door if you need me."

I shot Ivan an irritated glare before kissing Tess's cheek.

The fact that she didn't flinch gave me hope that all was not lost between us.

Chapter Fifty-Three

TESS

Ivan placed both hands on my cheeks and pressed his lips against my forehead.

"I thought I'd lost you," he whispered. "I hadn't realised how deep that part of the loch was, and it was so dark down there, Tess, but I wasn't coming up without you."

The nurse wrote something on the chart at the bottom of my bed and said she'd be back in ten minutes. When the door closed behind her, I said to Ivan, "So it was you who fished me out of the loch?"

Ivan nodded. "Nate thought he had you, but it turned out to be your coat, so he went back down for you. Pavel and I dove in after him, and I have thanked God repeatedly for leading me to you. I grabbed you by the back of your jumper and your hair, then hauled you to the surface."

I closed my eyes and smiled. "I saw Sarah while I was down there. She was surrounded by the brightest light I've ever seen. I've heard stories about that sort of thing before —you know, about people on the brink of death seeing a bright light—but I can't say I truly believed them. Yet seeing

Sarah changed all that. I knew it meant I was dying, but it was comforting to know that she'd come for me and I wouldn't be alone when it happened. But, before I could reach her, my mum appeared in front of me. She looked so angry with me, Ivan, and I couldn't figure out why because she'd never been angry with me in her life. But I get it now. She shoved me so hard it threw me back, and at the same time, I felt a tug on my hair. She pointed towards the surface, and that's when you must have got a better hold of me. My mum came to help me, Ivan. You both did."

Ivan stared at me, his brows furrowed as he took in everything I'd said. "You never made a sound, and I knew you weren't just unconscious, yet I refused to believe it was too late. Dima and Mark began CPR, but it took forever to get you breathing. Fuck, I think I aged thirty years in those two minutes."

"Well, you don't look any older," I joked before bursting into a short coughing fit. When I finally stopped, I added, "Thank you for saving me. I'm sorry I scared you, and I hope you, Nate and Pavel haven't suffered any ill effects from being in the loch in such ice-cold temperatures."

After making himself comfortable on the edge of my bed, he said, "Pavel and I are fine, but Nate had some trouble when he went back down after realising he'd got your coat." Ivan patted his chest. "He took in some water, and he couldn't get warm. The doctor is keeping him here for observation for a few hours, but if all is well, they said he could go home with antibiotics later."

"Oh God, poor Nate. Tell him thank you from me, and Pavel too. Nate hasn't been speaking to me since I attempted to leave Kolya, but I'm so grateful that he tried to save me."

Ivan huffed. "Nate's feeling guilty about that, and if he

weren't in the hospital, I would give him hell for it. He broke down and cried before Mark flew us here and kept saying he was sorry. He said Kolya had told him to give you the cold shoulder and keep an emotional distance from you. Your husband thought you would be less likely to share your feelings with George if you confided in Nate. But I think what he did was cruel, and I felt like punching him again when I heard."

I clasped Ivan's hand and smiled. "Even though he probably deserved it, I don't want you fighting with your cousin. He looks bad enough without adding any more bruises."

With his eyes closed, Ivan replied. "He does look bad, Tess. It's been over a week since they were rescued, yet when he stripped down to warm you up there were still so many cuts, scrapes and colourful bruises. And he's so thin, Tess. His ribs, pelvis and collarbone stuck out so much that I almost cried for the second time today. I knew they would have suffered, but seeing the evidence of that was startling. No wonder he's acting out of character."

"Kolya didn't get undressed the night they brought him home after being rescued," I told him. "But everyone could see he'd been starved and beaten. I can't imagine what he and Jonesy went through, and after suffering all that abuse, he found out about Franco and me the morning after he came home. I could tell he wasn't ready to deal with it, but when he confronted me, I couldn't lie to him."

Ivan lowered his voice. "While Mark and Dima were giving you CPR, I thought about getting you and Lily away from Kolya as soon as you were well enough. And if that's something you want, I will make it happen. Tess, I promise. But you have to be sure it's the right decision because once you leave, there's no coming back. Not while Roman is still alive."

I could tell Ivan was serious about what he'd just said, but something in his deep blue eyes made me pause. Ivan was hiding something from me. He'd had the same look back in Sicily the morning we left. And why mention Roman?

Chapter Fifty-Four

TESS

I grabbed hold of his big hands and whispered, "What are you hiding, Ivan? You know you can trust me—just as I know that whatever happens, I can trust you."

Ivan glanced at the door before turning back to me. "This goes no further, Tess. If word of what I'm about to tell you reaches Roman, then all the heartache and sacrifice over the past few years will have been for nothing."

I nodded and tried not to cough, my worry for Ivan growing by the second.

"Aleksei and Talia are alive, Tess, and they have a beautiful son named Simeon. He's fourteen months old, and I was supposed to attend his first birthday party, but after what happened with Kolya, it wasn't safe for me to leave. He became ill the night before we left Sicily, and I flew out to see him the morning after Kolya returned. They live in a well-guarded compound in Antigua, and only Yuri and I knew their whereabouts...until now."

I stared at Ivan in complete shock. How was this possible? Aleksei and Talia's light aircraft had gone down off the coast of Monaco almost two years ago.

As if reading my mind, Ivan explained, "The accident was staged. I met with them in Monaco, took their luggage, and chartered a boat to the exact location they planned to parachute out of the Cessna. They each wore a waterproof GPS tracker in case the jumps didn't go as planned, but everything went smoothly. Their guards saw them take off, and others were waiting at their destination, but as you know, they never made it. I swear my heart was in my mouth as I waited for their parachutes to open. Talia was ten weeks into her pregnancy by then, and I was so worried for her and the baby, but they were both fine. In fact, Talia was laughing when I pulled her onto the boat. Aleksei landed a little further on, and as soon as I picked him up, I took them to a pre-arranged destination where they had new passports and papers waiting, along with a lift to a private airstrip near Marseille. Yuri had a pilot ready to transport them to Madrid, where they caught a flight to Antigua. They've been there ever since, and I visit as often as possible."

"So all those holidays you took last year weren't fishing trips around the Bahamas," I said. Ivan shook his head.

"As you know, after Aleksei and Talia were declared lost at sea, their assets were shared between Kolya, Yuri and me. Of course, Yuri and I had already ensured that Aleksei and Talia had access to an offshore account in their new names, so there was no rush to deposit the rest of their money. I transferred a little more on every visit and set up an account in Simeon's name when he was born. As you rightly guessed, Yuri is his biological father, so I send him photos and give him regular updates, but he is Aleksei and Talia's son. Yuri's only stipulation when he agreed to be their donor was if Talia became pregnant, she and Aleksei would raise their child as far away from the Barinov Bratva as possible, and Aleksei readily accepted."

I could hardly believe what he was telling me. Tali and Leksi were alive and well and had a son... What the actual fuck? Kolya and I cried for them. My husband hired a team of divers to search for their bodies.

Ivan carried on speaking, trying to justify why he and Yuri had orchestrated the couple's escape.

"Roman's behaviour towards Talia could be classed as mentally abusive in the months before they left. He blamed her for being unable to conceive, even though it was Aleksei who was infertile. What you saw and heard when we visited was nothing compared to what else had been happening, and Aleksei had started to fear for Talia's life. But he knew his father wouldn't let them leave, so their exit had to be believable, something neither Roman nor the authorities could question."

"So you staged a plane crash," I stated. Ivan nodded, then closed his eyes.

"I wanted to tell you and Kolya," he said. "I knew Kolya would take his brother's side and help however he could. But Yuri and Aleksei wouldn't allow it. They said that Kolya had never been able to lie to his father, which I know to be true. But it meant I had to lie to both of you. A lie of omission and one that made me feel so uncomfortable, especially when I saw how hard Kolya was grieving. However, Yuri and Aleksei were insistent, and my only hope was that they'd change their minds when Simeon was born. I wanted him to know Lily; wanted her to delight in the fact she had a cousin. You would love him, Tess. With his dark hair and pale blue eyes, he looks like a miniature version of Yuri, Aleksei and Kolya, even at this young age. He says mamma and dadda and had begun to call me Vanvan before I left. So if you truly wish to leave Kolya, you wouldn't be without family, Tess. You and Lily could make a new life with Aleksei, Talia and Simeon."

Ivan's expression showed he wasn't keen on Lily and I leaving Kolya or him, but I appreciated that he gave me the option. I still wasn't happy about being kept in the dark about Aleksei and Talia, more so for Kolya than myself. Kolya had been utterly distraught to learn of their supposed death, and he would be hurt when he found out that they hadn't trusted him with the truth. That kind of deception, especially from a family member, wouldn't be easy to forget. Kolya deserved better than that, and I wouldn't deprive him of his daughter. Even when I tried to run, I didn't want it to be permanent. I'd held out hope that creating distance between us would give Kolya time to come to terms with what had happened between Franco and me.

"Call me crazy, Ivan, but I'm not ready to leave my family, especially you. Kolya said he's sorry and has asked for my forgiveness, but I don't want to feel rushed into making decisions about our future. Other than the bank accounts I share with him, financially, I have nothing of my own, and he could cut me off if he thought I wanted to leave him." I shrugged my shoulders and winced at the ache around my sore ribs.

"I can support you," Ivan stated. "My grandfather left me and my cousins with more money than we could ever spend, and as you know, I own several successful businesses. What's mine is yours, Tess. Always. But you do have assets. You have the Princess Annis, and I'm sure Kolya said you'd get Glengarran if you ever divorced."

Thinking about the yacht left me feeling sick to my stomach. Kolya had bought it from Yannis for my twenty-first birthday for ninety-five million euros; who knows how much the price had depreciated since then.

Knowing for a fact I would never set foot onboard the luxury yacht again, I asked, "How do I go about selling the Princess Annis? It not only belonged to Yannis, but Roman's men flew his body back there after I killed him. I want it gone as soon as possible, even if it means dropping the price for a quick sale. We'll have to remove all the hidden weapons, and the staff should be given a hefty redundancy package."

Ivan placed a finger against my lips. "Leave it with me, Tess. I might know someone who will buy it, and in the meantime, I will provide for you financially."

Tracing the rose tattoo on his left arm, I thought about the plan I'd started to make before I found out Kolya was still alive.

"I want to buy a house somewhere in Yorkshire, so I can spend more time with Jean and get to the Sheffield office of Sarah's Legacy without travelling for hours," I told him. "Will you come and live with us? It will need to be somewhere big enough to house a few close protection guards for Lily. Once I get my phone back, I'll ask Danny and Lainey if they'd consider working for me, and I'll probably need to hire two more to work on a rota basis."

Ivan smiled. "You won't need your phone for that. Danny and Lainey will be at Glengarran tomorrow."

"What? How come? I thought Kolya had dismissed them after I ran away with Lily."

"He did, but Jonesy said Kolya knew he'd made a mistake as soon as they left. Lainey made him eat humble pie before she agreed to come back." Ivan rubbed his belly. "I could eat a pie right now. One of Nan's apple and raspberry pies with custard or ice cream."

As if on cue, Ivan's stomach rumbled loudly.

"When did you last eat?" I asked.

Ivan appeared sheepish. "I raided the machine in A&E while we waited for the doctor to come and speak to us, but you know I don't count a dozen bags of crisps and chocolate bars as real food; I mean, who does? So, you could say the last meal I ate was breakfast, which was hours ago," he whined.

Ivan's twisted logic around food and snacks made me laugh out loud, which suddenly became a coughing fit that caused Ivan to buzz for the nurse. Before she came in, I told Ivan to go back to Glengarran so he could keep an eye on Lily. She'd been so upset when the paramedics transported me to the air ambulance, and no one had been able to settle her.

Nurse Cheryl strode into the room with an exhausted-looking Kolya hot on her heels. Ivan told them about my coughing fit and refused to leave until she'd reassured him that I wasn't about to take a turn for the worse.

Chapter Fifty-Five

TESS

After taking note of my obs, Nurse Cheryl walked me to the bathroom with my IV stand so I could pee. Then she helped me get settled back in bed before switching out my antibiotics for paracetamol. Kolya seemed put out that I hadn't let him assist me, but he didn't look like he could hold my weight if I fell.

Once the nurse left, I turned to Kolya and said, "You look like you should be in this bed."

With one brow raised, he smiled cheekily and asked, "Is that an invitation?"

I huffed out a breath. "In your dreams, buster."

"Always," he said, his eyes never leaving mine as he picked up my hand and kissed each finger.

"You used to do that a lot when we first got together," I remarked.

"Did you like it?" he asked.

"Yes," I answered honestly. "Why did you stop?"

Kolya shrugged his shoulders. "Why kiss each finger when I could kiss your lips, your neck, your breasts, the inside of your thighs and your—"

I held up my hand in interruption. "Yeah, yeah, I catch your drift."

Kolya sighed. "There were a lot of things I should have been doing to keep you happy; I realise that now."

I waited for him to say something else, but he just shook his head.

A light buzzing broke the silence. Kolya took out his phone and pressed the green button to receive an incoming video call from Jonesy.

"I have someone here who wants to speak to her mummy and daddy before she gets ready for bed," he said before passing the phone to Lily.

"Mummy," Lily yelled. "Are you staying in the hospital? Jonesy said you're a lot better now, so why can't you come home?"

"I am a lot better now, Lily, but the doctor wants me to have some more medicine before he lets me leave. Your daddy's staying here to look after me, so I'll be back with you soon. I want you to be a good girl for Jonesy, Ivan, and Mrs Braeburn, so don't argue with any of them about brushing your teeth before you go to bed.

Lily rolled her eyes and insisted, "I'm always a good girl, Mummy. Everyone says so."

I began to cough, so I passed the phone to Kolya.

"Hello, my darling, have you missed us?" he asked.

Lily nodded. "Daddy, are you and Dima and Nate going to stay with Mummy all night?"

"Yes, Lilypot, we'll be here. Why? Will you miss us?"

Lily became quiet for a moment before asking, "Have you got a gun?"

Kolya glanced at me as if to say, *What the fuck?*, before

turning back to our daughter. "Why would I need a gun, Lily?"

"So you can protect her. Mummy had a gun so she could protect me when the bad men came, and then everyone else carried a gun in case they came back."

Kolya's breath hitched, and for a split second, I thought he was going to cry, but he cleared his throat and said, "Lily, my darling, I swear that the bad men will never, ever come back. You do not need to worry about them anymore."

Lily shook her head. "But it's not just the bad men, Daddy. What if the angels take her to heaven like they did you, Jonesy and Lucas? And Aunt Tali and Uncle Leksi. They kept you for *ages*, and they only let you and Jonesy come home. I don't want them to take Mummy, even for a day. So if they come for her, tell them to bugger off; if they don't, you'll just have to shoot them."

Neither of us said anything for a moment, nor did Jonesy or whoever was with him.

Lily broke the silence by demanding, "You have to promise me, Daddy."

"I promise," he mumbled before pulling himself together and declaring, "Bugger off is swearing, Lily, and you know you shouldn't swear."

"Why not? Jonesy says it all the time?"

"I DO NOT say it ALL the time," he insisted.

"No, but you say fu—"

"That's more than enough from you—you little tell-tale," Jonesy said as he tugged on her ponytail. "Now, say goodnight to your mummy and daddy before you get ready for bed. Ivan will be here soon, and he won't be happy if you haven't got your pyjamas on."

Lily blew us a kiss and said, "Night-night, Mummy, night-night, Daddy. I love you."

"Love you lots, Lilypot," Kolya and I replied before closing the call.

Kolya pushed up from his chair and walked over to the window. He let out a heavy sigh before saying. "You were right, Tess. This is no way to live. The guards are necessary; they come with being the billionaire son of a Bratva king, but the business I run, the weapons that evil men like Riass want to steal? I don't need that tainting the lives of my family.

"Because of Yannis and KOLCAT, you had to kill two men, one of whom is haunting your dreams like a nocturnal fucking poltergeist. Because of Yannis and KOLCAT, my son is going through a rehab programme for his drug and alcohol addictions. And now, to top it all off, my poor innocent daughter is so traumatised after everything that has happened, she just demanded I shoot angels."

Kolya sank to his knees and covered his face with his hands, his chin resting on his chest. Instinct had me grabbing my IV stand and climbing out of bed to get to him.

When I reached him, he glanced up at me and insisted, "You shouldn't be out of bed. I don't deserve comfort or compassion from you. Not after the things I've said and done."

"Probably not. But you have it anyway, Kolya. So take what you need."

With his head on my belly and arms around my waist, Kolya cried until he ran out of tears.

Chapter Fifty-Six

KOLYA

Fifteen days later

George underlined something in his notebook before asking, "Do you feel these group therapy sessions are helping?"

Sitting on the sofa between me and Jonesy, Tess replied, "Yes, absolutely." She was holding hands with us, something she did automatically whenever Jonesy or I spoke about something distressing.

Tess had been released from the hospital within three days but returned four days later for a follow-up. It was now fifteen days since she almost lost her life, and though she still had a cough, it seemed much better today. The doctor prescribed another course of antibiotics to be on the safe side, but other than that, my wife showed no ill effects from her near-death experience.

At first, we either had individual or joint sessions with George, but a couple of days ago, he suggested that the three of us sit down together to discuss whatever we felt was holding us back. I think it was mainly for my and Jonesy's benefit to explain the complexities of our separation anxiety.

I refused to leave the hospital until I brought Tess home, which meant Jonesy joined us from day two. When we explained the cause behind our irrational need to check on and spend time with each other, Tess burst into tears, making Jonesy and I feel awful. She'd been through enough already, and neither of us wanted to add to her worries. So, after a short conversation outside her hospital room, Jonesy and I decided it was best if he headed back to Oxford, which turned out to be a terrible idea.

After three days, I was a complete mess, and Jonesy fared no better. Even though we video-called regularly, it wasn't the same as him physically being there. I needed to see him eat, move around without pain, and listen to him breathing while he slept. Adding all that to the worry I felt about my wife's health—as well as our marriage—caused an unwelcome setback in my recovery.

I lost my appetite and found it hard to sleep, pacing around all night and checking that everyone was okay. I scared Ivan half to death when he woke up to find me hovering over him and Tess to check they were still breathing.

Yes, he was still sleeping beside Tess, and as much as I hated it, I couldn't very well complain. I wasn't mentally fit enough to chase away her demons.

As soon as Jonesy returned, so did my appetite, and after we both promised George that we'd take his advice before doing what we thought was best, I began to feel optimistic about the future. The fact that Tess and I were spending time together with our daughter only added to that positivity, and overall, the atmosphere at Glengarran was much lighter.

Neither Jonesy nor I wanted to burden Tess with the atrocities committed against us during our captivity, but George said that she *needed* to know in order to understand and help us move forward in our relationship. The fact that she was even considering our relationship had me persuading Jonesy to involve my wife in our therapy sessions.

Tess was doing much better than everyone expected. The fact that she'd suffered the terrifying experience of drowning hadn't caused any issues mentally. Well, not yet, anyway. Instead, my wife found comfort in seeing both her foster sister *and* her mother during her near-death experience, although it was the latter who'd struck a chord with her psyche. Tess seemed convinced that her mother's ghost had pushed her towards Ivan, saving her life for the second time.

Being a sceptic, I wasn't sure what to make of her underwater visions, but George didn't seem concerned, and I would never again question something that made her happy.

She often stood by the shore gazing at the loch, and when I joined her yesterday, I asked what she was thinking about. Tess smiled serenely and replied, "Life, love, and making the most of second chances."

The old Kolya Barinov—the successful, confident man I was when I left for Estonia—would have immediately assumed she was talking about our marriage. I would have instantly taken charge, organised my staff and whisked her away to a private island where we'd spend endless hours making love. But all I did was hold her hand and hope... hope that the woman I loved chose to honour her vows and remain by my side until my dying breath.

Chapter Fifty-Seven

TESS

Lily's fifth birthday party was a spectacular success, and I hadn't felt as happy as I did when she blew out her candles for as long as I can remember.

Apart from Jean and Roman, all the adults my daughter and I adored had attended on the day, and Signor Russo called so that little Sofia could wish Lily *buon compleanno* all the way from Sicily. He'd been calling regularly since he found out I almost drowned, not fully trusting that Kolya had my best interests at heart, despite my husband's reassurances. Kolya had invited Signor Russo and his family to Glengarran to see for himself that I was safe and loved, and my Sicilian friend promised he would take him up on that offer when the weather improved.

What made Lily's birthday even more special was that she had a dozen children around her age attending her party.

We'd been invited to the local mayor's Ruby Wedding Anniversary party in the village hall a fortnight before Lily turned five. Kolya had been friends with Thomas Murray since he purchased Glengarran, and he allowed him to use the golf course whenever he wanted.

Thomas and Sheila Murray had three children, nine grandchildren, and at least a dozen nephews and nieces. Every single one of them attended with their families, so there were plenty of people joining them. The party was held at the same place they celebrated their wedding day forty years before.

The village hall was a surprisingly large venue with a bar that did exceptionally well during the event, which lasted almost eight hours. Several of Glengarran's estate workers and nearly all the local shopkeepers attended. Although Dima and Kevin called it a nightmare in terms of personal security, we all had a fantastic time, including our guards.

Despite not knowing many attendees, we were all made to feel welcome; I hadn't laughed or danced or drank as much in years, and I was able to thank the locals who'd sent me get-well-soon cards and flowers when I was in the hospital. Lily made so many new friends that day, and after speaking with their parents, Kolya and I had them come to Glengarran for play dates.

Every invitation we sent out for Lily's birthday party was accepted, and Glengarran had been filled with the joyful sound of children's laughter almost all day. Malcolm McCleary from the post office performed magic tricks, and Susan Donaldson, who ran the village playgroup, was in charge of the party games and face painting. Susan had five-year-old identical twins whom Lily was fascinated with, and ever since they met, she'd been telling everyone how unfair it was that she didn't have a twin.

When we finally got her to bed, our daughter demanded a baby sister for her sixth birthday. Kolya smiled and told her she might end up with a baby brother instead. Lily pulled a face and said we'd have to send him back if he was like Jodie Cray's brother because, and I quote, "He's too rough, hates my dolls, and won't play pretend tea parties." Little Joshua Cray had been more interested in Ivan and his tattoos. A few children thought Ivan was a giant, prompting Old John to tell them stories from Scottish folklore.

Hearing Kolya talk about Lily having a baby brother or sister resurrected feelings and memories I'd tucked away in the dark recesses of my mind.

Kolya and I were trying for a baby before he was captured, but that seemed like another lifetime ago. I hadn't wanted Lily to be an only child like me, and I desperately wanted to be a mother again. But a lot had happened since then, and Kolya had no right to tell Lily she might get a baby brother without first discussing it with me.

While we were on friendly terms now, we weren't exactly a couple. Though Kolya knew I was entertaining the idea of us moving forward in our relationship, we still had a long way to go before I'd consider us together. Building trust would take time, and our situation was more than complicated. Neither of us were the same people we were when we made plans to have another child. We needed to get to know each other again. Needed to heal from the mental wounds we suffered both during and after our separation. We needed to forgive.

As soon as Lily fell asleep, I jumped to my feet and hurried towards the door. We'd closed it behind us when we brought Lily up to bed because of the noise from downstairs. While the children's party might be over, the adults were still celebrating, and I was sure I heard Nan and Jack singing "I Got You Babe."

I felt Kolya at my back as I was turning the handle.

"Don't run," he whispered. "I know why you're trying to escape, but you have to know I'd never pressure you for another child if it's not something you want anymore. Besides, I don't know if I could get you pregnant after what happened."

"I don't want to talk about it," I insisted as I opened the door.

Kolya grabbed my hand. "Can't we be alone for a few minutes? We've been so busy today that we haven't had time to sit down and chat."

George had set us a task last week. He said that Kolya and I should spend ten minutes alone every day to talk about whatever was on our minds. It wasn't as easy as you might think with a household as full and as busy as ours. It made me realise how often that had been the case with us before everything went south. It was hard to admit that some days, the only time we'd been alone was when we went to bed.

Chapter Fifty-Eight

TESS

Despite wanting to go downstairs to spend more time with Nan and Jack, I let Kolya tug me along to what had been our bedroom. I hadn't been in the room since Kolya came to Glengarran, and I paused in the doorway of what I considered Kolya's domain now.

Kolya sat on the bed and tapped the quilt next to him.

"Close the door and come and sit beside me, Tess. You've been running around all day, so it won't hurt to have five minutes rest."

Being alone in what used to be our bedroom felt so different than in the sitting room or on a stroll around the grounds. My lightweight jumper and jeans suddenly felt too warm, and my hands were clammy. Nevertheless, I was committed to following all the rules George had set out for us, so I crossed to the bed and sat beside Kolya.

"Seeing Lily playing so well with all those children made my day," he said. "Being around adults for all this time has made her incredibly bright and quick-witted, but she needs to mix with other children, or I fear she'll struggle when we finally get her into another school."

I nodded in agreement. "I'm so glad we went to Thomas and Sheila's anniversary party. She met so many lovely little girls and boys there, and thankfully, their parents weren't put off by our need for guards and, you know," I said, tilting my thumb in his direction, "what happened to you, Jonesy and Lucas. I've been worried that schools might not accept her if they think she could put them in the path of someone like Riass."

I felt Kolya flinch when I mentioned his name, so I put my arm around him and said, "I'm sorry. I didn't mean to—"

"No, don't apologise, Tess," Kolya interrupted. "I've been thinking the exact same thing. I threw an obscene amount of money at the school back in Oxford to have Lily's close protection detail in attendance, but that was before I was kidnapped. It was all over the news, and Riass's video went viral. Headteachers are bound to be wary about accepting Lily. Even when I find a buyer for KOLCAT, we'll have the shadow of what happened hanging over us for years."

I jumped up from the bed and turned to face him. "You're selling KOLCAT?" I questioned. "Why?"

Kolya shrugged his shoulders. "It's time. I'm not the man I was, Tess. My confidence is at an all-time low, and I doubt I'll be able to concentrate enough to develop anything new this year. KOLCAT has commitments we need to honour, so it will take a year or two before we can hand over the reins to whoever buys it. I'll speak to James about it tomorrow, and if he agrees, I'll set the wheels in motion."

"Are you sure about this, Kolya? I mean, you love the

designing and creating aspect of the business. You're always so enthusiastic whenever one of your ideas comes to fruition."

Kolya frowned. "After what you said in the hospital, I thought you'd be happy about it."

I shook my head, but he was right: it *would* make me happy. Yet this was his business, a successful enterprise he'd built from scratch. Was this really what he wanted?

Apart from sitting together and holding hands or the occasional hug during our therapy sessions, I'd been avoiding physical contact with Kolya, but I was so shocked by what he'd just told me that I stepped between his knees and rested my hands on his shoulders.

"This is a major decision, Kolya. Are you sure you shouldn't take some time before you announce it? Maybe wait until you're feeling more like yourself again."

Placing his hands on my hips, he tugged me against him. Looking up at me, he said, "What I did at KOLCAT —designing, manufacturing, and selling the weapons... it was too much. I see that now. You were right when you said I like to be in control. The people I have working beside me at KOLCAT are all extremely gifted individuals who don't need me to oversee their work. Yes, I'm heavily involved in the design process, but from a manufacturing standpoint, they don't need me there at all. And as we know, brokering deals for weapons and defence systems is a hazardous business—one that's not conducive to being a happily married father of two who wants to keep his family safe."

His ice-blue eyes never left mine; his expression so serious, so determined, left me in no doubt that this was something he'd thought a lot about. And yet, he'd failed to mention it, despite our daily chats.

"Why didn't you tell me you were considering this, Kolya?" I asked. "You never even hinted about it."

"I'm sorry, Tess. It's been on my mind since I was rescued, and I've been trying to figure out a partial return for both me *and* James. God knows my son could use some time away from it. Even the video calls I've held with my team feel off somehow. At first, they were all stepping on eggshells around me, frightened to say the wrong thing, but now it feels as though I'm an outsider intruding on their time and their perfectly run company," he admitted glumly.

"And that's something you should be proud of, Kolya. A good boss and a great working environment can create exceptional employees. Didn't you once tell me that?" I said with a smile.

He returned my smile and pulled me onto his lap. "Yes, I remember. It was the week after you opened the Sheffield branch of Sarah's Legacy—your first Monday morning meeting that you were so scared to lead, yet everyone said you did a brilliant job. I was so proud of you that day. You came home full of confidence and excitement about the future, and you couldn't wait to get me into bed after you'd accosted me in the shower. You were insatiable."

I huffed out a laugh, "That's not how I recall it. If I remember correctly, you kissed me in the kitchen in front of everyone before carrying me off to bed. I was embarrassed to face everyone the next morning."

I don't know how it happened, but somehow my hands had ended up in Kolya's hair, and our faces were so close that our lips were almost touching. The alarm bells that used to ring in my head whenever I thought he'd kiss me were strangely silent, and rather than dread the intimacy, I found I welcomed it—craved it, even. Yet Kolya stayed completely still.

His breath was warm against my lips, and I opened mine in readiness, but again, he didn't make a move. My heart was racing, my chest rising and falling with each deep breath. If he didn't kiss me soon, I'd—

Kolya's kiss was so soft and gentle that his lips barely touched mine. He gazed at me with such love, such longing; I felt my heart and soul cry out with joy and acceptance. This was us, how we were meant to be.

I kissed him back with a passion that would leave him with no doubt about how I was feeling, and he groaned loudly, twisting us around so I lay on the duvet with him on top of me. His lips never left mine, but his hands were everywhere. My cheeks, my neck, then my chest—cupping my breasts and thumbing my nipples—creating low moans from deep within my throat.

I rocked my hips, grinding myself against his growing erection. I'd missed this, missed him, my Kolya.

He suddenly stopped, staring down at me in wonder. "Oh, I've…oh, thank God. I…" Kolya gasped and then rolled off me as he burst out laughing.

I propped myself up on my elbow and gazed down at him, utterly confused, but all that did was make him laugh harder. Within seconds, I was laughing along with him. I couldn't help it. Kolya's laugh was infectious, always had been.

He grasped his erection through his jeans and, with a loud guffaw, declared, "It's not dead; it fucking works."

Chuckling, I asked, "What on earth are you on about, Kolya?"

After unbuttoning and unzipping his jeans, he pulled down his boxers and said, "I'm sorry, Tess, but I've got to see this."

His erection sprang free, and with it came another howl

of uncontrollable laughter. I stared at his thick, hard cock, wondering what he found so funny about it. It looked exactly the same to me.

"Erm, Kolya, would you mind sharing the joke?" I asked before glancing down at his groin again.

"It's no joke, my love. Look," he said, wrapping three fingers and a thumb around the base of his cock and waving it at me.

Frowning down at the impressive appendage, I asked, "Why? It looks the same it always does when it's hard."

Kolya wiped tears of mirth from his eyes and said, "Exactly. I was worried I wouldn't be able to get an erection. Jonesy said he got a semi when the nurse gave him a bed bath, but my cock hasn't shown any sign of life since we were captured. No early morning salute, no twitching in the shower, nothing. I thought..." His expression turned serious for a moment as he admitted. "I thought it might be down to the beatings they gave us. They kicked me so hard I thought my ball sack had burst. I was in complete agony and could only pee in dribs and drabs."

The anger I felt whenever he or Jonesy talked about the torture and beatings they endured was overwhelming. I wanted to comfort them *and* seek revenge against the terrorists who had stolen our happiness. But Riass and Bashir were dead, so there was no vengeance to seek. I could, however, offer comfort. It would normally be in the form of holding hands or, when pushed, a hug. But as I glanced down at Kolya's rapidly deflating erection, another type of comfort sprang to mind.

I slid down the bed until I was eye level with his cock.

"What are you doing, Tess?" Kolya asked rhetorically. It was obvious he knew because his cock began pulsing back to life before my tongue ran the length of his semi-hard shaft.

I ignored his stupid question and took him in my mouth, feeling him grow as I tightened my lips around his girth.

Kolya stroked the hair back from my face and groaned as he watched me give him pleasure. "Oh, fuck, Tess, I," whatever Kolya was about to say was swallowed up by his throaty groans until he gasped and tugged on my hair.

"Enough," he panted, his ice-blue eyes glazing with lust. I released his cock with a loud pop and crawled up the bed towards him.

"I want to be between your legs when I come inside you," he said.

Kolya's hands shook as he undid my jeans, pulling them and my knickers down my legs until I kicked them off. I reached for his jumper, but he stilled my hands and shook his head.

He stroked his fingers across my belly and down, brushing them over my clit with a featherlight touch.

"Kolya, please. I'm already wet. I don't need any fore-play, I—"

He cut off my words with a kiss that had me whimpering with need. Ignoring my pleas, he slid two fingers inside me, stroking my G-spot like the expert he was before bringing his fingers back to my clit. His touch was intimately familiar and oh-so effective, and I smiled through our kiss because, again, this was us. Me and him. Him and me. Together, like we'd never been apart.

I shoved his hand away from my sex and demanded. "Get inside me. Now!"

He positioned his cock against my entrance, and we both gasped as he pushed inside.

"I love you," he whispered while kissing along my jaw

and down my throat. "My wife, my life, my Tess. Mine for always."

"Always," I agreed as we made love for the first time in almost six months. It was desperate and beautiful, and though we hit that orgasmic high together, it was over far too soon.

Chapter Fifty-Nine

TESS

After a quick clean-up, Kolya and I dressed and left the bedroom. Before we reached the top of the stairs, he pushed me against the wall and kissed me senseless. So senseless that I didn't hear Ivan walking up the stairs until he said, "I assume I'll be back in my own bedroom tonight?"

Kolya stopped kissing me and, without looking at his cousin, replied, "You assumed correctly."

"Wait," I said. "Lily's fast asleep, so you can't move your mattress tonight. Kolya and I can sleep in Lily's room, and you can have our bed. Our guests have taken up all the other bedrooms."

Ivan nodded, then frowned. "If you've been doing what I think you've been doing, then you better change your sheets."

Blushing, I mumbled, "We'll change them."

Ivan gave a quick nod but didn't turn to leave.

"Is there something you need?" Kolya asked.

"Yes," Ivan replied. "Tess, can you speak to Mrs Brae-burn and find out what I've done to upset her? She can't seem to look me in the eyes lately and always makes a hasty retreat whenever we're alone. I was going to ask her myself, but she and Nan have had too much of the sloe gin that Jack made, and they're currently debating whether Paul Newman was more handsome than Elvis Presley in his heyday."

"I vote Paul Newman," Kolya said.

I shook my head. "I watched King Creole with Jean, and I thought Elvis was the best-looking man I'd ever seen, and his voice was amazing."

"But Cool Hand Luke is one the greatest films ever made," Ivan argued. "Paul Newman was a handsome man and a brilliant actor."

I held up my hands. "Guys, I'm not getting into this right now. There's cake waiting for me in the kitchen and—"

"No, there isn't," Ivan grumbled. "James, Tanner and Yuri finished off what was left, and Jonesy ate all the sausage rolls."

Kolya sighed and shook his head. "Ivan, you haven't stopped eating all day. Is there something that's bothering you?"

Ivan's eyes flashed to mine. He and Yuri were going to tell Kolya about Aleksei, Talia and their little boy tomorrow, and Ivan was worrying about how he would take it.

"Come on, big guy," I said as I looped my arm through his. "I'll speak to Mrs Braeburn while I make you a sandwich."

Kolya followed us down the stairs, and as luck would have it, Mrs Braeburn was on her way to the kitchen. I followed her in there and closed the door behind us.

"I'm aboot tae put the kettle on if ya fancy a cuppa. A dinnae ken how I've ended up as tipsy as this. I've only had three o' Jack's sloe gins. Noo, gi' me a bottle o' whisky, and I'll drink anyone under the table."

"You proved that at Thomas and Sheila's party," I reminded her.

Mrs Braeburn smiled. "Aye, it was a grand do."

"Sit yourself down, Mrs B, and I'll make the tea," I told her.

Jack's homemade sloe gin must have been potent because her Scottish accent was stronger than ever, and she was starting to sway, so I decided to make her a sandwich, too.

Taking a loaf out of the breadbin, I asked, "Has Ivan done something to upset you?"

She turned to face me and shook her head. "Ivan was brought up wi' good manners and a healthy respect for women. He wouldnae dream o' upsettin' me."

"He said you're avoiding eye contact and making a hasty retreat if it looks like you'll be alone with him."

Mrs Braeburn blushed. "Aye, weel, ya can assure the man I'm nae upset wi' him. It's just..."

Somehow, her blush became even redder, spreading over her face and down her neck before she admitted. "I saw him. All o' him. The day ya fell intae the loch and nearly... They brought ya in tae the sittin' room in front o' the fire, and we fetched tooels and blankets for ya."

"Tooels?" I questioned, trying to decipher her words.

"To dry yerself wi'," she said before shaking her head and saying, "Towels."

With a smile, I said, "I'm sorry, Mrs B. I hate to ask, but could you tone down your accent a little? This Yorkshire lass is struggling to understand you."

Mrs Braeburn rolled her eyes before she carried on speaking, so it was safe to say she was more than tipsy.

"Ivan, Nate and Pavel stripped oota their wet clothes and grabbed a few tooels and blankets. They were naked and shivering when I walked in, and as ya ken, when a man's feelin' the cold, their willies retreat, if ya get ma meanin'," she said while raising her eyebrows.

I nodded, not trusting myself to speak in case I burst out laughing. I knew without a doubt that if it weren't for the alcohol, Mrs Braeburn wouldn't be telling me this.

She shook her head before adding, "Ivan's an exception tae that rule, I can tell ya. I swear, Tess, it was as long as ma rollin' pin. And when he stepped forward to grab a tooel, the damn thing was swingin'. I couldnae take my eyes off it. I cannae imagine how big it would get when he...."

She raised her brows and put a hand over her mouth to stifle a giggle.

I burst out laughing, and Mrs Braeburn soon joined in. I couldn't believe this was the same starchily prim woman who ran Glengarran.

After wiping tears of laughter from her eyes, she said, "I've taken tae prayin'."

"About Ivan's willy?"

Oh God, I thought. *Where was she going with this?*

Mrs Braeburn frowned. "Ya shouldnae pray aboot willies. Nae lass. I prayed for the woman he marries because I couldnae imagine takin' that thing up—"

Slapping my hands over my ears, I said, "Nope, I do *not* want to hear anyone talking about having sex with the man I consider my brother. Besides, I've been sleeping beside him on and off for weeks. Ivan loves to cuddle in his sleep, so I've often woken up with him spooning me. Having felt what sometimes happens to men in their sleep, I think your imagination might have got the better of you."

Although probably not by much, I must admit. Ivan was six foot eight. He was hardly going to be small.

The man himself strolled into the kitchen. "Tess, I'm starving. Did you make that sandwich you promised?"

Gesturing at the loaf, I said. "I'm doing it now, but I got sidetracked when I asked Mrs Braeburn if you'd done something to upset her. You'll be pleased to know you haven't, and our lovely housekeeper has been praying for you."

Ivan walked over to Mrs Braeburn and kissed her on the cheek. "Thank you," he said. "It never hurts to have God on our side. And now that I know you're not upset with me, perhaps I can persuade you to bring out your rolling pin and make me another meat pie."

I collapsed in fits of laughter as Mrs Braeburn's face turned so red she almost glowed.

Epilogue

KOLYA

Four months later

"What do you think, my darling?" I asked my awestruck wife as we pulled up in front of a property she and Ivan had spotted online.

Caldon Hall was an impressive three-story eighteenth-century manor house set on fifty acres of land in South Yorkshire.

"It's beautiful!" Tess exclaimed while pulling out the brochure the estate agents had sent. "Can you believe something this big was only sixteen million?"

I raised a brow but said nothing while Tess and Ivan discussed which rooms they hoped to turn into offices. If the property was for sale in the south of England, you could add another ten million to that price.

Money was no object to me, Tess knew that, but my wife had insisted that she and my cousin buy our next home. It caused an argument that threatened to derail the progress we'd made in our marriage, so I backed down and let her have her way.

Tess had sold the yacht I bought her for her twenty-first birthday and was using the proceeds to buy a home in South Yorkshire, so she could visit Jean more often and be nearer to the Sheffield office of Sarah's Legacy. Caldon Hall was located on the outskirts of Penistone, near Barnsley, so it was a short drive to both locations. There was also a private school nearby that was willing to take Lily, which was a bonus.

Lily wanted to stay at the primary school at Glengarran. She'd been attending the small village school for the past three months and had made several friends. But travelling to and from the Scottish Highlands was time-consuming, even with the use of private jets and helicopters, and Tess wanted to devote as much time as possible to her foster mother before dementia stole her away for good.

I was also looking forward to cutting back *my* travelling time. James and I had several buyers interested in KOLCAT, but after weeks of serious vetting, we knew that only one of them would be acceptable to the British, German, and American governments. It was essential to keep those governments happy. We had offices, manufacturing, and storage facilities in those countries, and we still had ongoing contracts with the British and American military.

I wasn't sure whether James would be happy about selling KOLCAT, but my son was keen to have a fresh start in life and, with Ivan's help, was considering making an offer on an aviation company. He'd been clean for almost five months, and I couldn't be prouder of my brave, determined son.

I still wasn't sure what I would do after we sold KOLCAT.

Tess, Jonesy and I still had regular sessions with George, so it was better not to rush into finding a new challenge until I'd dealt with the mental fallout my captors had left behind. Jonesy and I felt a burning need for vengeance I feared would never be extinguished until we found Darius. He'd been in the wind since Adrianna spotted him on the island Yannis had owned, but we *would* find him, of that I was certain.

Killers rarely disappear for good, and in the case of Roman Barinov's sons—who'd delivered death to their enemies on more than one occasion—that had been proven twice over. James and I couldn't believe it when Yuri and Ivan told us that Aleksei and Talia were alive. Not only that, but they also had a son. I was an uncle to a child I'd never even met. I was hurt and angry that they'd kept me in the dark, more so with Yuri than with Ivan, who hadn't wanted to deceive me.

James and I wanted to fly out to see Aleksei immediately, but Yuri said it could put him in danger if anyone in the Bratva discovered whom we were visiting. We had to be content with a video call, which wasn't nearly enough. We also couldn't involve Lily in case she told her grandfather, so visiting as a family was out of the question.

I made it clear to all concerned that they should inform my father as soon as possible, which hadn't gone down well with Yuri and Aleksei. I knew he'd be angry and that there would be repercussions, but they were out of their minds if they thought the great Roman Barinov wouldn't eventually find out. After all, he'd found me, and I was being hidden away by terrorists.

Feeling somewhat guilty, I took out my phone and messaged my father, asking how he was doing and letting him know we were looking at the house that Tess had been telling him about.

Ivan got out of the front passenger seat of our Range Rover when the doors opened on our lead and tail cars. Seconds later, Nate came around to open Tess's door.

"You okay?" he asked as he helped her out of the vehicle. "You look a little pale."

Tess glanced up at him and smiled. "I'm good. It's just so warm today, and I didn't sleep well last night."

She was telling the truth, but there was another reason why Tess was looking a little pale.

I slid my arms around her and rubbed her upper back. "Let me know if you feel sick or need to rest. Mrs Braeburn packed us enough food to last the day, and there's plenty of water in the cooler."

"I'm fine," she insisted. Nodding towards the steps of the property, Tess announced, "It looks as though the estate agent is already here. I bet she's parked in the stable block. It said online they were using it as a garage."

Flanked by Dima, Pavel, and several other guards, we approached the columned portico. The smiling estate agent, Mary Sorrel, stood before the large Georgian door and held out her hand to greet us.

"Good morning, Mr and Mrs Barinov, Mr Volkov," she said as she shook hands with me, Tess, and Ivan. "It's great to meet you in person after all our online and phone correspondence. My assistant is waiting for us in the main dining room with refreshments. As you know, it's the only room with furniture. I doubt many properties could fit in a dining table as long as that one," she said with a smile. "We could head over there now before I show you around, or if you prefer, we can call in later. My partner, Marcus Raines, whom you've been corresponding with online, will be here shortly to show you around the grounds and the cottages you passed as you came up the driveway. They need serious

427

structural repair, but as they're not listed buildings, you can do whatever you want with them, subject to planning, of course."

Ivan turned to my wife and asked, "What would you prefer to do, Tess? Do you feel up to taking a tour around the place?"

Eyes wide and sparkling with excitement, she replied, "I feel a lot better now, but I'd be taking the tour even if you had to carry me around."

Sunlight streamed through the tall windows in the spacious hallway, highlighting the beautiful coppery curls tumbling down her back. I tugged on one, and she spun around and smiled.

"I'm already picturing a tall Christmas tree over there by the stairs," she said. "What do you think, Kolya?"

Overwhelmed with emotion, I pulled her into my arms and kissed her softly. "I think it would be perfect, my darling."

Jonesy and I had been tortured and beaten on Christmas Day last year. We wouldn't have known what day it was if Riass hadn't informed us.

Tess, Lily, and James had been in Sicily, suffering through their first Christmas without me. Everyone tried to make my daughter as happy as possible, but according to those who were present, it had been a disaster.

Tess and I vowed to make this Christmas special no matter where we spent it. As long as we were together, nothing else mattered.

TESS

Caldon Hall was stunning. During our tour around the property, I'd been so overwhelmed by the classical architecture and simple yet beautiful decorating that I had tears running down my cheeks. As always, Kolya and Ivan had fussed over me like I was something delicate that needed protecting from anything and everything, and they insisted I rest instead of taking a tour of the grounds.

When I'd watched them drive away with Dima and Jonesy in the old Land Rover Defender, I was glad I'd stayed behind. Going off-road with dodgy suspension wasn't my idea of fun, especially while pregnant.

I was barely eight weeks along, and the morning sickness, which often lasted all day, was making me feel so lethargic. If napping was an Olympic sport, I could win a gold medal for England.

Nate came over to sit beside me at the ridiculously long dining table, several photographs from the estate agent in hand. "It's much bigger than it looks from the outside, especially the aerial view," he said, placing the photographs in front of me. Then he took out his phone, sending Kevin videos of what would likely be their apartment.

Nate was trying so hard to bring our relationship back to where it was before we came back from Sicily. He deeply regretted how he'd treated me after I tried to escape and told me how hard it was to see me suffering and not offer a shoulder to cry on. And yes, I knew that Kolya had told him to keep an emotional distance from me, but it hurt to know he'd accepted his orders. I would have told Kolya to fuck off and to stick the job up his arse, but Nate had gone along with it. I'm not saying it was easy for him; after all, his other half ran Kolya's technical security, so it would have made their relationship difficult. My husband had a lot to answer for, but he was hardly in the right frame of mind after being rescued and finding out about me and Franco. Nate didn't have that excuse, and although I'd forgiven him, I certainly wouldn't forget. Still, the man dove into icy waters to save my life, risking his own in turn, so I decided to let bygones be bygones and accepted his friendship and sincere apologies.

Caldon Hall formed a perfect square with a large open courtyard in the centre. The previous owners had begun converting the property into twenty-four impressively sized apartments and had obtained planning permission for a swimming pool in the courtyard. Ivan and I had chosen the south and west wings for ourselves and planned on creating several two-bedroomed apartments for each of our guards through the entirety of the east wing. We'd keep the stunning front staircase, dining room, sitting room and library as they were because they were much too pretty to change.

James wanted to convert the stable block instead of living with us or in one of the apartments. He was still unsure what he wanted to do with our old home back in Oxford, but he'd spent very little time there since he'd undergone treatment for his addictions. James had his rehab programme at the hotel in Mayfair, and although the helipad was a bonus, he and his father no longer used Lassiter's as their base while working in the capital. He and Kolya had rented a six-bedroomed house they were looking to buy in Belgravia, and my husband had lined up a viewing for a neighbouring property next week.

Belgravia was a beautiful area of London, but it couldn't compare to the view from Caldon Hall.

Once the building work was completed on the four cottages, I would gift one to Danny and Lainey. I wanted to make sure that the man I befriended while sleeping on the streets of London would always have a home.

Ivan and I had discussed ways to bribe Nan and Jack to move up here with us, and I hoped my pregnancy would seal the deal.

Nan and Mrs Braeburn had agreed to spend some time here training a new housekeeper, and Jack would help select various estate workers to manage all fifty acres of Caldon's land and forestry.

Everything was going so well in our lives, but Kolya and I still had our dark days. Even though my nightmares were now few and far between, they hadn't disappeared completely. I doubt they ever would.

Despite his claims to the contrary, Kolya and I were still a work in progress. But as George pointed out, a marriage only fails when either one or both partners stop trying, and neither Kolya nor I would ever do that.

Therapy was helping, as was the love and support we received from everyone around us. Despite living in Scotland instead of Oxford, some days were so happy and normal that it was almost as if Yannis had never even existed. But he had existed, plotting and planning our demise for the chance to claim Kolya's wealth. Hiring hitmen, mercenaries, and terrorists to torture and kill, breaking our hearts and destroying our lives until I stole his with a single shot. And yet, we all still live in the shadow of his machinations.

Betrayal and deceit of that magnitude can change the way we live, think, act, and trust. It isn't something that can disappear with a click of the fingers; it takes time, hard work, and a willingness to move on, knowing that whatever revenge you dealt them would never be enough to erase the loss, pain, and mental suffering.

Kolya and Jonesy will never move on unless Darius is caught and dealt with. They've come a long way since they were first rescued, both mentally and physically, but they still bear the scars. Killing Darius won't be a mental cure-all; they know that, but they think his death will be one less obstacle in their path.

The unmistakable sound of the old Land Rover dragged me away from thoughts of the bastards I now refer to as Greek tragedies one and two.

"Sounds like they're back," Nate stated as he slipped his phone into his pocket and pushed up from the chair.

"That didn't take long," I replied, pointing out the obvious.

Nate smirked. "Did you honestly think Kolya and Ivan would allow you out of their sight for longer than twenty minutes—especially while you're pregnant?"

I spun around in the chair to face him and whispered, "How did you know?"

"You look like you did when you were pregnant with Lily, and you've been sick so often that it's obviously not a tummy bug."

"It's hit me hard this time," I admitted. "I'm only about eight weeks pregnant, and I'm hoping it will ease once I hit my second trimester. Ivan knows, but we're going to wait until James comes back from Germany to tell everyone else."

"Don't worry; your secret's safe with me," whispered Nate as Kolya and Ivan strolled into the impressive dining room.

"Well?" I questioned.

Kolya sat beside me and pulled out his phone, showing me the photos he'd taken.

"As Mrs Sorrel pointed out, the cottages need serious

structural repair, but all four of them are a decent size, and the stable block should be easy enough to convert. I'll arrange for an architect to draw up some plans if you're going to put in an offer."

Ivan placed a hand on my shoulder. "I think we should buy it, Tess. I have a good feel for the place, and I bet Jean would love the views."

I looked out of the window and nodded. "We could bring her here when she's having one of her good days. I'll speak to her carers about it."

Focusing on the estate agent, Ivan declared, "Considering the amount we'll need to spend on the cottages and various other repairs and renovations, I think the asking price is too high; therefore, we are only prepared to offer fifteen million. If your client agrees, I'll get our solicitor to sort out the legalities and have the money in their account by the end of the week."

Mary Sorrel grabbed her phone and a sheet of paper from the dining table and made the call.

"I'm so nervous," I whispered as Kolya clasped my hand in his.

"Buying a property is a big deal, Tess. It's normal to feel nervous."

"Even though Ivan and I are going halves, it's still a lot of money," I stated.

"Well, I did offer to buy it for you, but you wouldn't let me," he replied grumpily.

I smiled and squeezed his fingers. "I know, but I needed to do this, Kolya."

His expression told me he still didn't agree. Yet even though I would only own half of Caldon Hall, I felt it gave me some much-needed autonomy.

"Besides," I added, "you're paying for the renovations."

It was the one concession Ivan and I had made after Kolya had sulked for almost two full days.

Mary Sorrel ended her call and took a deep breath. "They're willing to drop the price by half a million, but that's as low as they'll go."

Glancing between Ivan and Kolya, I asked, "What do you think?"

Kolya shook his head. "This is down to you and Ivan, Tess. What does your heart tell you?"

"My heart says yes," I replied.

"And what about your head?"

I grabbed Ivan's hand and declared, "It says fuck it, let's do this."

Nate and Pavel put their hands over their mouths to hide their chuckles, but their eyes said it all.

Grinning, Ivan declared, "Mrs Sorrel, call your client and tell them we accept."

She did as he asked before walking around the table to congratulate us and shake our hands. A minute or so later, her assistant and Marcus Raines entered the dining room with a bottle of champagne and several glasses.

Being pregnant, I couldn't have any alcohol, so Kolya had a quick sip and then pressed his lips to mine.

"Champagne kisses," he said.

"I can't think of a better way to celebrate," I replied.

Tucking my hair behind my ear, he whispered, "I can."

Kolya smiled wickedly and helped me up from the chair.

"My wife and I would like to view the library again. Alone," he added before our guards could follow us.

Nate, Pavel, and Dima smirked but said nothing as Kolya led me out of the dining room towards the empty library. Once inside, he closed the door behind us and pressed me against the wall.

With his finger under my chin, he tipped my head back so he could gaze into my eyes. The love in his was clear, as was the lust, and I licked my lips in anticipation of his kiss, but after one tiny peck, he knelt down on one knee.

I expected him to hike up my dress and put his mouth between my legs, but instead, he pulled a small black velvet box out of his trouser pocket and cleared his throat.

"Tess, this is a new start for us. A new home, a new way of life, a new baby," he said, placing a kiss on my lower belly. "I bought this ring as a symbol of my eternal love and commitment to our marriage. My darling wife, you'll always be mine no matter what you decide, but I would be honoured if you'd consider renewing our vows in front of our family and friends. Our wedding was rushed, and because I wasn't honest about my feelings, you were left disappointed, hurt, and confused. Feelings you experienced in triplicate after I was rescued, along with a fear no wife should ever endure. I never want you to feel that way again, so let me prove that I'm worthy of all the love and support you've shown me over the years. Share your hopes and dreams with me, and let me be yours for always."

My eyes filled with tears, and there was a lump in my throat, but I croaked out, "Yes, Kolya, I'll marry you again. Yes to all of it."

He slipped the emerald and diamond eternity ring on my finger before standing up and kissing me.

I closed my eyes and surrendered to the passion between us. I thought I had my happily-ever-after when I was pregnant with Lily, but I still had a lot of growing up to do then.

I'm older now and so much wiser, and despite the years he has on me and his considerable wealth, I finally feel that

Kolya and I are equals. Not just a vulnerable young runaway and her Russian, but a wife who's been to hell and back and lived to tell the tale. A mother, a friend, and a sister to a man she'd just bought a property with. I was also the managing director of a charity that helps vulnerable young people build a life they can be proud of.

"I love you, Tess," Kolya whispered as he placed his hand over where our baby was growing. "I want to make love to you right here, right now, but we need to visit Jean and then head to the airport if we're to make it back to Glengarran before Lily goes to bed."

He was right: we had so much to do today.

I opened the heavy library door and reached for his hand. The diamonds in my new eternity ring caught the light from the windows in the front entryway, creating a spectrum of colours on the chalk-white walls. When he raised my left hand and kissed each of my fingers, those colours seemed to dance.

"I love it here," I told him, twirling around on the black and white tiled floor so I could take it all in.

"I can tell," he said. "You haven't stopped smiling since we arrived."

"That's because I'm happy. I feel relaxed and content here, and despite not having any furniture, it already feels like home."

Kolya smiled, his pale blue eyes twinkling. "My darling, wherever you are is home to me. But I agree with Ivan: Caldon Hall has a good feel to it, and it will be a wonderful place to raise our children."

Thinking back to my childhood home—a two up, two down in Doncaster with mould on the walls and hardly any furniture—I remembered being hungry, cold and scared, worrying about my mum and panicking in the dark because the electricity token would run out and we'd have no money to replace it. I recalled the warmth, love and kindness I'd experienced as a foster child with Jean and Sarah and the confusion and despair when we were taken to the children's home.

My Cinderella tale came with guns and a Russian fairy godfather. Yet I'd come a long way since then—since I risked my life to save the man in front of me. A man I fell head over heels in love with and continue to love through good times and bad.

My once upon a time and my always and forever.

More by Helen Bright

He let her go once. He won't make that mistake again.

After tragedy forces Julia back to her hometown, she takes a job at
Night Movers, unaware her new boss is anything but ordinary.
Can she embrace love that lasts forever?

Turn the page for a free preview…

Bitten and Bound: Chapter One

ALEX

I, Alexander Staithes, one of the most powerful Born Immortal vampires in Europe, was nervous.

I was trying to appear calm and collected; apparently, I wasn't pulling it off.

"Alex, what on earth is wrong with you this evening? You haven't stopped pacing since you walked in."

"Nothing's wrong, Maggie," I replied hastily. "I have a lot of work to do tonight, that's all."

"I could interview Julia on my own if you're busy. I mean, it's not as though we don't know her, or her background," Maggie said with a knowing smirk.

Maggie Saunders had been my employee and friend for over thirty years. The cunning yet adorable human could read me better than anyone, and it appeared she was trying to push me into admitting why I wanted to sit in on this interview so badly.

Julia Layton was the daughter of another employee, George Browne. I co-owned the import/export company,

Night Movers International, along with my brother, Josh, and good friend Nik. Both George and Maggie had joined the company within two years of each other, having been school friends before that. In fact, many of our human employees were friends of mine. It's what I liked most about the company we'd worked so hard to build. It made it easier to trust who knew I was a vampire without the need for mind control to erase the knowledge.

Both George Browne and Maggie Saunders were among the few in this company who knew we were vampires, and which visitors were vampires too.

I first noticed Julia—who was then Julia Browne—when she accompanied her father to one of the company's Christmas parties. Night Movers always held parties for our employees because it encouraged the friendly, almost familial atmosphere that kept the company performing well. It also helped the humans and vampires to mingle and find common ground.

Julia held onto her father's arm as they chatted with other partygoers, and I was struck by her innocence and beauty. I hadn't seen her since she was an awkward four-teen-year-old with a permanent ponytail and braces, and though I spoke with George regularly about his family, I hadn't expected Julia to have blossomed into the beautiful young woman before me.

Julia stood as tall as her father in the high heels she wore, which put her around five-foot-seven barefoot. She was quite curvy, with a defined hourglass figure and long, chestnut brown hair that tumbled around her shoulders in waves.

I went over to talk to George and ask where his wife was that evening. He told me she was caring for a sick friend, so

George had brought Julia, who was then only eighteen years old, instead. George explained she was going away to university that year, so he was glad to be spending time with her while he could. Armed with this information, I began a conversation with her about the university course she had chosen and her career options.

Julia was quite shy and seemed a little nervous, her blue-eyed gaze never holding mine for very long. So I bid her farewell for the time being and told her I'd come back over for a dance later.

I couldn't wait until later came. I felt like I'd do anything to hold her, even for a short while.

Nikolas and Joshua, both vampires and co-founders of my company, came over to quiz me about what had kept me occupied for the last half hour, but they quickly noticed Julia for themselves. Nik went in for a hug from Julia, which annoyed me to the point that I saw red. I mean literally saw red when my eyes changed, forming a red ring around the irises as my temper rose. I quickly looked away before Julia could see, but Josh noticed and placed a hand on my arm before enquiring if I was okay.

"Julia, my lovely, you have grown into a beautiful young lady. I think it's about time we ran away and got married so you can make an honest man out of me," Nik announced in a booming voice, which had infuriated me further, and I could feel my fangs about to descend.

Julia giggled and replied, "Mr Harding, no one could ever make an honest man out of you."

Nik smiled, looking over at a table across the room for a second before he gazed back at Julia. "Oh, you have me pegged, sweet Julia. So alas, it will never be." He bowed low in front of her, saying goodbye with dramatic flair.

I regained my composure when Nik left and went with Joshua to sit at a table nearby.

"What was that all about?" Josh asked. "Alex, you never normally react like that in front of people."

"I'm not sure," I replied. "Perhaps I'm just a little tired."

"Did you feed before the party, Alex? Maybe it would be best to nip out and grab a bag of blood before it happens again."

"No, I'll be fine, Josh, I promise. I just need a bit of peace and quiet for a while," I told him.

"So you wouldn't mind if I went and asked George's daughter for a dance, then?" Josh asked with a hint of humour in his voice.

I couldn't help the growl that seemed to come from my throat, and Joshua burst out laughing.

"Oh, Alex, don't you think she's a little young?"

I looked away, embarrassed at the situation I found myself in. I knew he was right, of course. She was young and needed to experience life before I could even think of her being in my world. Although it didn't mean I couldn't hold her for a short while, I thought, as I walked over to her and claimed my dance.

I knew when I held her in my arms that I wanted her there always. She looked up at me and shivered with what I believed was desire.

Did she feel the same things I was feeling?

As we slow danced to the Elvis Presley song, "Can't Help Falling in Love," I knew something powerful was happening. The way she felt as she moved with me to the music, how soft her hair felt against my cheek, the perfume she wore and her own natural scent that captured my senses. It was a potent combination that was almost too powerful to resist.

Before I did something I regretted, when the song ended, I walked her back to her father. I thanked her for the dance and wished her all the very best at university.

I thought I saw disappointment in her eyes when I said goodbye, but I had to leave the room. Josh followed, concerned about me and my premature departure.

"Alex, wait, what happened in there?"

"I'm not sure. I just have this feeling about Julia... A knowing," I explained. "I feel like she belongs to me, Josh. And I know I've only danced and spoken with her, but I already want more."

"How much more?" Josh asked warily.

"I want everything," I replied.

I decided it would be best to let Julia live her life a little before I sought her out again. I wanted her to complete her studies and return to Barrowfield a confident grown woman, ready to accept what I was.

A year later, Julia announced her engagement to Gavin Layton, and genuine pain pierced my heart.

I had lived nearly a thousand years and, at the time, thought that was long enough. With the help of my work friends and my sister, I kept myself plodding on through everyday life as much as I could without revealing the true depth of my anguish.

Nik and Josh knew what was wrong and tried to help in any way they could. Nik's Russian friend Sergei offered to kill Gavin Layton so that Julia was free again, but I declined hastily. Despite wishing he didn't exist, I wasn't about to start killing humans to achieve that.

I watched her many times without her knowledge over the last fourteen years. She seemed to be happy, and though I loved to see her beautiful smile, I always wished it was me who'd put it there.

Then, in a car accident earlier this year, Julia was seriously injured and lost her unborn baby. George contacted me immediately because of the healing properties of my blood, wanting me to help his daughter recover from her injuries.

I was there when they brought her around after the emergency surgery to fix her hip and deliver her stillborn daughter. I gave her only a small amount of my healing blood because I didn't want to arouse suspicion from the hospital staff.

Julia was desperate to see her daughter, even though she knew she was dead. It had been hours since they had delivered her, so none of the staff thought it was good for her to see the baby. As well as being cold, the infant would have the waxy pallor that death brings.

Using mind control, I got the staff to bring Julia her daughter, giving her better images than what she was seeing. During this most devastating time, her husband was asleep on another floor of the hospital, so he couldn't interfere with my actions. Although, to be honest, my only thoughts were of comforting Julia; I wouldn't have allowed him near, anyway.

I visited Julia several times over the past few months, offering her friendship and support in her hour of need. It was also a way to give her small amounts of my blood to speed up the healing process.

The strain of what happened was too much for her marriage to bear, and they ended up separating. I was glad she was now free of the man who had kept us apart for so many years, but I knew this was just another kick to the already fragile shell she'd erected around herself.

I needed a way to keep her close and take care of her like I should have done all those years ago. The job I was about to offer her could do just that.

Bitten and Bound: Chapter Two

JULIA

"Don't be nervous, love. Maggie says this interview is just a formality, and the job is already yours if you want it."

My dad had been saying that for the last five days, ever since Maggie, our old family friend, had decided to go from full to part-time. She wanted to help her daughter out with childcare when she went back to work after her maternity leave.

Both my dad and Maggie had worked for the import/export company Night Movers International for over thirty years and were well-respected employees.

It was refreshing to see a company keeping its main hub here in Yorkshire. It was good for the area, providing a number of jobs and also funding for local charities and various community projects.

I found myself in the position of job seeker for the first time in almost fourteen years. Apart from the part-time sales advisor role I held in a clothing store during my time at university, I'd never needed to interview before.

I'd met Gavin, my soon-to-be ex-husband, in my first

HELEN BRIGHT

year at uni. We were both doing a degree in business management and had many of the same classes together. He was effortlessly gorgeous, with wavy dark-brown hair and striking hazel eyes. He took me out to a comedy club on our first date, and for the first time since I'd left home, I had fun without missing my parents. I fell in love with him instantly. It was hard not to, and we were engaged within a year.

We married as soon as we finished uni, and after our honeymoon, we went to work for his father's transport company just outside Birmingham.

Our life together seemed perfect for many years. We built up the business, holidayed all over the world, bought a beautiful home and had a busy social life.

We started trying for a baby six years ago. For the first year, we didn't worry too much when I didn't become pregnant. I was coming off the pill and understood it could take a while for its effects to leave my system. When it didn't happen after two years, we began to worry.

Our doctor referred us for fertility tests in our third year of being unsuccessful. Both of us were healthy, and after several tests, they could find no reason why either of us couldn't be parents. So their advice to us was, *"keep taking the prenatal vitamins, keep fit and healthy, and try not to get stressed."* Hello?! Not getting pregnant was the only thing stressing me out.

By this time, most of our circle of friends had children, and we found it hard to remain positive. We argued more and more, both of us finding faults with each other that were seemingly never there before. Then, sixteen months ago, when it seemed like I was never going to conceive, I became pregnant.

We were thrilled, and Mum, Dad and Gavin's parents

448

were ecstatic. To be honest, the pregnancy helped repair the almost cavernous cracks that had appeared in our marriage from both sides, and once again, Gavin became an attentive, loving husband.

It was during a shopping trip two weeks before my due date that my life was ripped apart, and my heart was shattered.

A young man, not even two days out of prison, had stolen a car and was being chased by police when he lost control of the vehicle and drove into the front passenger side door of our car, straight into me.

Gavin and I spun off the road and ended up down an embankment.

We both lost consciousness immediately after the impact, but according to the police officers who were following the car, we were both only out for about five minutes. The driver of the stolen car wasn't wearing a seatbelt and was thrown from his vehicle. He died at the scene.

Gavin regained consciousness first, and to this day, I will never forget the screaming panic and utter devastation in his voice when I finally became aware of our situation.

At first, I didn't think of the baby because of the agonising pain in my hip. I knew it was broken, as was my arm. But Gavin was touching my very pregnant tummy, asking if we were both okay, and I knew then that my darling baby would never get to sleep in the new crib we'd just bought.

A fire crew was on the scene within five minutes, but it took them over an hour to free us both.

My labour pains started when I was placed on the stretcher. The air ambulance arrived, and I was flown to our nearest hospital, so it didn't take long to get there. They quickly scanned my tummy in A&E, but as I already knew instinctively, there was no heartbeat to detect.

Due to all my other injuries, despite my strong contractions, they had to deliver our baby via C-section.

My beautiful daughter came into the world but never took a breath.

My hip had to have extensive surgery, and they set my arm in a cast. Due to the amount of blood I'd lost during surgery, I didn't wake up until the early hours of the morning. My parents were there and quickly explained that Gavin was okay, but because of his broken ribs and concussion, he was on another ward.

Also in the room was Alex Staithes, my dad's boss, although I didn't question his presence at the time.

Apart from being a bit groggy and having a slightly metallic taste in my mouth, physically, I didn't feel as bad as I thought I would. The pain from my hip seemed to lessen within seconds, and I marvelled at the effectiveness of the pain medication they must have given me.

When I found my voice, the first thing I asked for was to see my baby. That set my mum off crying, and my dad said he didn't think it was a good idea.

Mum told me that Gavin had held her after she was delivered, but that was over eight hours ago. I knew what she was saying, even without the words. My baby was cold, dead and too long passed to give me any peace.

Rage and unfathomable grief consumed me. I wanted to climb out of bed and throw people out of my way so I could get to her. I knew this was the maternal instinct to gather and protect kicking in, and although I would never get to take care of my child, I was still her mother, and I needed to feel the bond with her—if only for a short while.

Screams tore from my throat, and tears came seconds

later. I remember Alex standing up and telling the nursing staff forcefully that my daughter needed to be brought to me. Not thirty minutes later, wrapped in a pink hospital blanket, she was placed in my arms.

It was hard to hold her at first because of the cast on one arm and the IV in the other, but I was so relieved to finally have her in my arms, and I was determined to cuddle my beautiful baby girl.

I named her Megan, after my late grandmother. She passed away two years ago, and it comforted me to know she was waiting in heaven to take care of my daughter until I could get there, which I hoped would be very soon.

I sobbed uncontrollably into the dark hair peeking out from her pink hat, and the nurse moved to take her away from me. I tried to turn away to stop her, and then I noticed Alex stand and walk over to us.

I thought he, too, was going to try to take her, but he didn't. I remember him lifting my chin, moving the hair out of my eyes, and wiping my tears away with his thumb. Alex stared into my despairing soul with his beautiful grey eyes and began talking to me. He said Megan was such a pretty baby, and she had my hair colour, which I noticed was true. He also remarked how smooth and pink her skin was and how she felt warm to the touch, which seemed strange as I hadn't thought that earlier. But I could see that I'd been wrong, and it appeared as though Megan was only sleeping.

He kept on speaking, telling me that although she wouldn't be here with me physically, I would always feel her presence. Alex said Megan knew that I loved her, and she loved me too, more than words could ever say. He said she wanted me to live a long and happy life and to remember always that I am her mother.

I looked down at my baby and began telling her about

everything we'd planned for her. I spoke about her family, who loved her so very much, and with tears in my eyes, I told her she'd stay in our hearts forever.

About an hour after I first held her, my beautiful baby Megan was taken away, and at Alex's suggestion, I fell into a deep and restful sleep.

Gavin came to see me the following day, and we cried in each other's arms for the child that would never be part of our future. He'd been cleared to go home, but he'd broken two ribs, and his neck was hurting quite badly. Even sitting still in a chair at my bedside was awkward for him. After an hour, I sent him home to rest.

Over the next four days, with the help of our parents, we arranged Megan's funeral.

———

Six weeks later, I was still undergoing physiotherapy for my hip, neck, and shoulders. The crash had caused severe whiplash, which hadn't become apparent until three days after the accident.

The doctors said I wasn't improving as quickly as they would like, but they thought my emotional and mental state was a factor.

Gavin and I couldn't be in the same room without bickering, so I went to stay with my parents. They lived in a bungalow, which was a big help when moving around with my sore hip.

While I was there feeling sorry for myself one evening, Alex came by. It was the first time I remember seeing him since the accident. I was speechless when I opened the door and saw him standing there. Mum was out, and my first thought was of my dad, but Alex must have sensed this or noticed the panicked expression on my face. He quickly reassured me that my dad was fine and that he'd actually stopped by to see me. I invited him in and offered him tea or coffee, which he declined for water. He waited for me to take a seat on the sofa before he came to sit beside me.

Alex is an extremely handsome man with dark blond hair and stunning grey eyes that have always captivated me. I found it hard to look away from him. He also never seemed to age, like most men, which is utterly unfair to us women.

I remember dancing with him at a Christmas party years ago and totally crushing on him. But obviously, he hadn't been interested in me because he'd left the party early. Probably to meet up with some gorgeous, sophisti-cated woman—unlike the nervous eighteen-year-old I had been.

I left my memories in the past and thanked him for coming to see me at the hospital, apologising for all the upset he must have experienced. I told Alex I didn't think I could have managed without all the support he'd given me that night.

I didn't know why he'd been there at the hospital, but I told him I appreciated his thoughtfulness and assistance.

Alex explained that he'd been in a meeting in the area and met my dad at the hospital to offer his support to our family. He said he considered my father a good friend, which meant he saw all the family that way too.

I remember thinking, and not for the first time, how great this man was. He was running a multimillion-pound business yet made time to come and see me. Alex Staithes was a kind, genuine man who was a great boss to all his employees. He was just too good to be true.

We talked about his business, my slow recovery, and the

problems I was having with my marriage. Honestly, it was a relief to talk about that with someone. Most of my friends were also Gavin's, and I didn't feel I could open up to them.

Alex agreed that time apart would probably do Gavin and me some good, and he offered to be there if I ever needed to talk. It was refreshing to have a man actually listen for a change, and I couldn't help but wonder what it would be like to be in a relationship with this sweet guy.

While thinking about how nice it would be to have his arms around me, I fell fast asleep on the sofa beside him.

For the first time in months, I didn't have a nightmare. Instead, I dreamed I was dancing again with Alex, not as an eighteen-year-old, but as the woman I had become.

It wasn't until I stepped over the bathtub into the shower the following day that I realised I no longer felt any pain in my hip, arm, or neck. Also, my very pronounced limp had completely disappeared. Even the scar had healed to a faint silvery line. I didn't question the reason why; I was just glad to move around without physical pain. And for the first time in weeks, I felt happy to be alive.

Despite how much better I felt, I decided to stay with my parents for another week. Alex came to see me again several times before I left for home, and his presence by my side felt right. Like we could be more than just friends. Although, I never presumed he'd want to be anything other than friends with me. I mean, let's face it, my husband didn't even want to be in the same room as me, never mind someone as wonderful as Alex.

When I eventually went home, I found the situation with Gavin was the same as before, and around five months after our daughter's funeral, we separated. Gavin and I are still friends, but our divorce is in progress.

Although we let our lawyers handle most of our divorce,

my father-in-law bought my share of the house Gavin and I owned. He also gave me a pretty good bonus in my severance pay as a thank-you for putting so much time and effort into the Layton family business, which I'd helped grow into the successful company it was today.

It seems strange not to be as close to Gavin's family, and as I'm now back living with my parents again, I'm no longer near the friends Gavin and I shared.

So, after fifteen years of living away, I returned to South Yorkshire. Starting my life all over again means getting a new job and a place of my own, and that's why this evening, I'm all smartened up in a skirt-suit and blouse for an interview at Night Movers International.

Grab your copy...
vinci-books.com/bittenandbound